Michael Christie received an MFA from the University of British Columbia, and is a former professional skateboarder. His story collection *The Beggar's Garden*, which was a finalist for a number of major Canadian prizes, won the City of Vancouver Book Award. He lives with his family on Galiano Island, British Columbia. *If I Fall, If I Die* is his debut novel.

Visit his website at: michaelchristie.net

IF I FALL, IF I DIE

Will has never been to the outside, at least not since he can remember. And he has certainly never got to know anyone other than his mother, a fiercely loving yet wildly eccentric agoraphobe who drowns in panic at the thought of opening the front door. Soon the confines of Will's world close in on him. Despite his mother's protests, he ventures outside, clad in a protective helmet, and braces himself for danger. He eventually meets and befriends Jonah, a quiet boy who introduces him to skateboarding, and finds his fears fading and his body hardening with each new bump, scrape and fall. But life quickly gets complicated when a local boy goes missing, and Will and Jonah embark upon an extraordinary adventure . . .

MICHAEL CHRISTIE

IF I FALL, IF I DIE

Complete and Unabridged

CHARNWOOD
Leicester

First published in Great Britain in 2015 by
William Heinemann
London

First Charnwood Edition
published 2016
by arrangement with
William Heinemann
A Penguin Random House Company
London

A catalogue record for this book is available
from the British Library.

ISBN 978–1–4448–2993–8

Published by
F. A. Thorpe (Publishing)
Anstey, Leicestershire

Set by Words & Graphics Ltd.
Anstey, Leicestershire
Printed and bound in Great Britain by
T. J. International Ltd., Padstow, Cornwall

This book is printed on acid-free paper

For my mother

Fair seed-time had my soul, and I grew up
Fostered alike by beauty and by fear
— WILLIAM WORDSWORTH, *The Prelude*

I lived on dread — [she wrote]
To those who know
The stimulus there is
In danger — other impetus
Is numb — and vitalless —
— EMILY DICKINSON, '770'

The
Inside
Out

1

The boy stepped Outside, and he did not die.

He was not riddled with arrows, his hair did not spring into flame, and his breath did not crush his lungs like spent grocery bags. His eyeballs did not sizzle in their sockets, and his heart's pistons did not seize. No barbarian lopped his head into a blood-soggy wicker basket, and no glinting ninja stars were zinged into his throat.

Actually, incredibly: nothing happened — no immolation, no blood-bath, no spontaneous asphyxiation, no tide of shivery terror crashing upon the shore of his heart — not even a trace of his mother's Black Lagoon in his breath.

Somehow Will was calm.

The day's bronzy light, shredded by a copse of birch, tossed a billion luminous knife blades onto the front lawn. And he dared to continue down the walk — where he'd watched hundreds of deliverymen stride to their house bearing fresh food for them to eat and new clothes for them to wear — with the paving stones granular and toilet-bowl cool under his naked feet. Venturing out into the unreal arena of his front yard for the first time in his memory, he discovered only early summer crispness in the air — this Outside air — its breeze slaloming through the jagged wisps of his cut-off shorts, in and out of the straps of his Helmet. Will had felt this same air sweep through the window in New York on those rare occasions he opened it, despite how it worried his mother, but something was sapped when it came through. He'd never immersed himself this way, not since his memory got impressionistic and gauzy as if it had been transcribed by a stenographer in full Black Lagoon.

Will was Outside because he'd heard an odd bang while painting a six-foot masterpiece his mother had commissioned for London, a composition she twice in passing compared to Mark Rothko, who was a genius painter, just like him. At first he'd thought another bird had struck the big picture window in Cairo. Will once watched a bluejay — he'd identified it with the bird book he used as a drawing reference — palsying there in the ochre dirt beneath the glass, its neck canted grimly as though trying to watch an upside-down film. Blood rimmed its eyes and its beak was shattered like an egg ready to be peeled. It had thought it would go for a nice flitter through Cairo, over the burnt-orange velour loveseat, through the high, bright cavern of the hallway where Will's masterpieces were hung, past dim London with its ravine of bookshelves and credenza display of his sculptures, over the staircase with its twin railings she'd installed on either side (for safety), and pick off some food scraps around the slow cooker in Paris. Had its mother never warned it about glass? Will had wondered, sitting there fogging the window until the creature finally stilled and Will startled himself with a sob, both of pity, and of thankfulness for their safety

4

Inside. Nothing ever died in their house — except for bugs, lightbulbs, and batteries. Outside, however, was another story.

Though his mother feared pets, other creatures had more successfully entered their home. He'd found trickles of ants in the basement, mouse turds peppering the pantry, and crews of flies sprinting across the windows. Rogue moths snuck through the door when Will opened it for deliverymen, their wings powdery and fragrant like the makeup that sat unused on his mother's long teak dresser in San Francisco. He'd cup the moths in his hands, feel their desperate clatter between his palms, then cast them through the only unscreened window in Venice.

Sometimes people had come. Once the furnace was repaired by an ancient man who smelled of pastrami and wood smoke. And for a time the paperboy would leave his strange, grubby shoes by the front door and play LEGO with Will on the carpet in Cairo. At first it was thrilling, until Will noticed the older boy's proclivity for breathing exclusively through his too-small nose and building only uninspired bunkerish structures, mixing colors together like an architectural test pattern. After a few weeks, Will stopped answering the door when he knocked, telling his mother that he didn't need friends because he was an artistic genius. 'Don't toot your own horn,' she'd said, smiling.

Of course he'd considered going Outside thousands of times — as he'd considered executing a standing double backflip or walking around with his feet magnetized to the ceiling or chainsawing a trapdoor in the floor — but had never dared. Even when he lobbed their garbage bags as far to the curb as he could manage from the front foyer, or watched shirtless neighborhood boys plow their BMXs through the meaty summer heat, he'd never been sufficiently tempted. Mailmen over the years had asked why he and his mother were always home, and Will often replied, 'Why are you a mailman?' with one raised eyebrow, which usually shut them up.

The real reason was that he was her protector. Her guardian. From herself. From it: the Black Lagoon. It wasn't like he was trapped. The doors were not locked. She made no rules, issued no commandments, decreed no penalties, and exacted no punishments. Staying Inside was something he'd invented, intuited, for her sake, to keep her from falling so deep she'd tremble and explode and weep all her tears and go dry and insubstantial as the dandelion fluff that occasionally coasted Inside like tiny satellites. He'd always known that if fear took her for good, he'd be left treading water forever in the ocean of life with nothing to buoy him.

But birds usually made a different sound against the window, more sickening and soft, like a strike from those plush drumsticks used in marching bands, not the sharper bang he'd heard. In a gust of curiosity, Will had set down the fan brush he was using to texture a block of mustardy-green acrylic paint, then removed his smock and slipped out the front door as easily as entering a long-neglected wing of their house.

6

He hadn't actually expected catastrophe, or a bloodbath, but with little to compare to, hadn't ruled them out either. Wordlessly she'd taught him that the Outside was built of danger, of slicing edges and crushing weights, of piercing needle-points and pummeling drop-offs, of an unrelenting potential for suffocation, electrocution, mayhem, and harm. So today a generous portion of him was left mutely astonished that, so far anyway, the Outside was nearly pleasant.

Thrilling himself with his own daring, Will moved now from the concrete out into the grass, grotesquely alive beneath his feet — a carpet made of salad that he half-expected to grip his toes and hold him fast. Luckily, his Helmet would safeguard him if he tripped or a branch dropped lethally from above. After some painfully prickly searching in the cedar bushes, he found it, the source of the bang: a husk of charred matter that resembled a tiny exploded wasp nest, smoking faintly like the humidifier his mother put in his room in the winter. The dirt was blackened around it, the air charred and sulfurous, and it occurred to Will this was some kind of bomb.

Now he glimpsed a figure dart around the side of the house, boy-shaped, something heavy looped over his shoulders, and Will wondered if he'd been hurt somehow by the explosion. Will followed him around the corner, passing the strange dryer vent fuming with the startling Inside smell of fabric softener and warmed clothes, *their* clothes, and had just rounded the rear of his house when he toppled, a nuclear drill of pain boring between his temples, a master-piece film of neon spindles whirling through his eyelids. Some diminished part of his mind registered a demonic shrieking, and he realized then that the noise was being squeezed from his own lungs. Desperately, he shaped the sound into an anguished plea for his mother but knew she couldn't hear him with her Relaxation Headphones on. Amid the murk of agony he gathered the sense that something had struck his forehead and fallen to his feet. He tore open his eyelids. A purple crystal. The sun dazzled it before Will's vision was again welded shut, this time a stickiness there. Still moaning, he bent, felt for it in the grass, and closed his hand around the rock.

'You'll be fine,' a nearby voice said.

Will attempted to again pry open his eyes, but a stinging honey had sealed them. He stumbled forward with his hands lifted in the Outside air, baffled, sobbing, afraid to wipe his face for fear he'd make his mortal wound worse.

'Here,' the voice said, and Will sensed fabric against his face. He took it and pawed at his gluey eyes, prying them open to find a delivery boy, tucked behind the aluminum shed that Will had never entered. The boy had a green garden hose coiled around his shoulder and was about Will's height and age, with stringy bangs that licked at eyes flitting everywhere except upon Will. His brown skin was the tint of the milky tea his mother often drank in her reading chair, balancing the cup precariously on the wooden arm — her most dangerous habit. In his hand

8

was a target slingshot, the kind with thick rubber straps and a brace running up your forearm, a forbidden item that Will had ogled in catalogues for as long as he could remember.

'I didn't even pull it back halfway, so you'll live,' the delivery boy said smiling, the sudden warmth of his face momentarily soothing the ache of Will's probable skull fracture, which he could already feel opening like a pistachio.

'You really think I'm going to live? Like, for sure?' said Will, woozy with blood loss and imminent death. 'I've never heard anyone say that before . . . ' Will pulled the boy's shirt away for a moment, and more blood licked his eyes.

'For a while, anyway,' the boy said, shrugging. 'But sorry, I thought you were someone else.'

'Who? The person who set that little bomb out front?' Will said, secretly wondering if the Black Lagoon could possibly be after this boy as well.

'Yeah,' the delivery boy said. 'Among others.' He unshouldered the garden hose and dropped it to his feet. Will now saw that his smooth chest was festooned with a solar system of a hundred milky scars.

'Oh, are you hurt too?' Will said. 'Did the bomb get you when you were delivering our new hose?'

'I'm fine,' the boy said casually before scrambling over to peek around the corner of the house like a soldier in a firefight.

Will followed him closely to examine his injuries. 'Then how did you get those scars? Did the Outside do that to you?' The delivery boy turned and regarded Will as if he were speaking some cryptographic language, and Will wondered whether the infinite Outside air had tarnished his words somehow.

'What's your name, kid?' the boy said, returning behind the shed, keeping his eyes fixed to the tree line near the creek behind Will's house.

'Will. What's yours?'

He paused, and Will was about to ask if he was okay again. 'My name is Will too,' the boy said.

'Really?' Will said, tickled by the coincidence. 'Are you hiding from someone, Will? Do you have your own Inside you can go to? If not, you can hide here. We could eat some of my mother's bread and look at my masterpieces.'

'You live here?' the boy said, puzzled, tipping his head back toward Will's house. 'I thought this place was empty.'

Will tried not to think about his house. How disturbing it looked from the Outside, how shabby and finite. 'Just me and my mother,' he said. 'But this is my first time in the backyard,' he added. 'I used to be afraid of going Outside, but now I'm mostly not.'

'That's great, Will,' the delivery boy said. 'Really great. But you *do* need to be careful out here. It can be dangerous. You should probably play it safe and go back inside and not tell anyone you saw me? Like your mom or anything?'

'Oh, I'm definitely not telling my mom about this,' said Will, pointing at his forehead. 'I only came out because I heard that bang out front.' It was then he realized that the garden hose at the boy's feet was old and worn. 'But you weren't delivering that hose, were you?' Will whispered conspiratorially, approaching him to lean in close. 'That was already ours, right?'

'Anyway, it was good talking to you,' the boy said in a businesslike voice, jamming his slingshot into his shoelace belt and striding out into the backyard, exposing a lithe back just as baroquely scarred as his front. 'I'd better get — '

' — It's okay, you can have it!' Will interrupted, too afraid to follow him out into all that grass, astonished by how bravely he swam through the ocean of the Outside. 'The guy who does our garden usually brings his own anyway. I'll just order another one.'

'That's real good of you, Will,' the boy said, returning to tentatively pick up the hose. His eyes drifted up to Will's Helmet. 'Too bad I didn't aim a little higher,' he said with an odd smirk. 'But you can keep my shirt. And maybe I'll see you around.'

'Does this mean we're friends?' Will called out as the boy paused near the back hedge and glanced over his shoulder. Will could see his belly undulate evenly as he breathed.

'Whatever, sure,' he said.

'But someone is still trying to catch you, right?' Will said. 'Aren't you scared?'

The boy cocked his head. 'You were serious when you said this was your first time outside, weren't you?'

Will nodded.

'You know what?' the boy said, smiling again. 'I was wrong when I said you should go back

11

inside. There's nothing to be scared of out here.' Will realized then that this boy's brave, bright face was a light he wanted to shine upon him forever. 'Look, I bet your head has already stopped bleeding.'

Will pulled the shirt away and saw it was chocolate brown.

'See?' the boy said. 'Nothing can really hurt you, Will.' Then he vanished into the ferocious-looking woods.

2

When Will returned Inside, the air in Cairo was thick as cream and stunk of couch crevasse. He gagged and ran to Venice, where he blotted his forehead with gauze to find that the actual cut was tiny: a single pit, like a one rolled on a die. Luckily, it hadn't swelled and was high enough to cover with his bangs if he wore his Helmet tipped forward, which he did, both to protect his wound and to conceal it.

He hid the blood-blackened shirt — featuring a skeletal sorcerer wielding an electric guitar — down in Toronto, then returned upstairs to draw a cup of water from the sink in Paris. Slurping, he forced himself to sit, fighting to slow his breathing, while watching steam belch from the lid of the slow cooker — the only culinary appliance his mother could abide other than the breadmaker, because it couldn't scald them, and it rendered food sufficiently mushy to eliminate the always present danger of choking. If ever Will stopped chewing while at the table, even if only pausing before flooding his mouth with milk, she'd leap up and start whacking his chest with her forearm.

By the big chrome clock he knew she'd be just starting Side B of her Relaxation Tapes. She'd been doing them daily in San Francisco for a month now: donning the huge creaky headphones that swallowed her ears, the opaque

Terminator shades that assailed her eyes with light, rendering her deaf, blind, oblivious. He couldn't imagine two hours of anything even denting the obsidian shell of the Black Lagoon, but Will cherished this new time away from her supervision. He'd tried the apparatus on once when she was in the bath, but the blinky light show and left-right pan of surf made him fall asleep and then immediately pee himself, which his mother did sometimes when she supremely lost it, but that was more the Black Lagoon's fault, not the Tapes. Regardless, it seemed to Will somehow simultaneously depressing and thrilling that his entire Outside ordeal had lasted a total of nine minutes.

★   ★   ★

After dinner, Will was wearing his Helmet along with a hooded wetsuit, standing on a chair, and reaching into the stratosphere in London while his mother cowered in the doorway, her blonde chin-length hair framing a pair of dark, insectoid sunglasses. She was snapping her blue elastic band against the velvety inside of her wrist.

'You sure you're okay?' she said, which actually meant, like most things she uttered: *be careful*.

'It's fine, Mom,' Will said, vaulting to his toes, which made his forehead throb. He grasped the lightbulb and twisted, unsure if it was turning or only slipping through the rubberized gloves of his wetsuit. Like all their earthly possessions, they'd ordered the wetsuit from a catalogue, and he'd since drawn numerous ice cube-laden baths to test it. He hadn't tried shocks yet, but the idea was that the rubber insulated against those too.

'I don't know what I'd do without you,' she said, her face tied in a wince.

'Sit around in the dark talking to yourself?' he said, and she smiled.

For weeks she'd worried over this dead bulb in London. She usually had deliverymen do it, but after meeting the boy, Will had begged her to let him try. There was still a moon launch's worth of preparation, including highlightered diagrams she'd taped to the fridge in Paris. If Will were older, she'd probably make him wear a condom, which was like a penis scabbard she told him about for making sex with vaginas safer, but more boring.

She'd been right about one thing: the Outside was indeed steeped with danger. His encounter with the boy had confirmed it. But the Inside could be dangerous too. Besides getting sling-shotted by the amethyst (he'd classified the purple crystal with his encyclopedia), Will had nearly died twelve times in his life — four she knew about, each of which had incited weeklong Black Lagoons. When wet, the tub in Venice got slick as mucus, and Will once almost died from a Helmetless slip that dropped him violently to his butt, which was why they only took baths (they used to share baths but they stopped because of vaginas). Another time he crashed while riding the exercise bike. Once he overdosed on four extra-strength Tylenol. Then he ate yogurt expired by a whole week. Later, he choked on a chicken finger that he tried to push down his throat without chewing — like a boa constrictor, because he just learned about them.

But electricity was one of the premier Black Lagoons: the pain and paralysis, the way it lurked in the walls, everywhere and nowhere, unreasonable, invisible as fear itself. Though his mother stuffed safety guards into every unused outlet, Will had once shocked himself by allowing his wet thumb to linger on the plug of his tape player. He returned to himself across the room with his tongue buzzing and spectral in his mouth. He never told her. Events like that could pack her off somewhere permanently demented.

'Hey, these blades are actually made out of wood,' Will said, now with a good grip on the bulb. The fixture was also a ceiling fan, except she'd long ago hired an electrician to disable this function because if it came unmoored it would cut them to shreds.

'They once made airplane propellers with wood, you know,' she said, with another snap of her elastic. 'Think one of those wouldn't hurt?'

'I guess it would,' said Will.

The bulb turned, and he hated the metal-on-metal sensation, an ungodly grind like chewing sand. The fan rattled a little, and she emitted a clucking sound somewhere between *Oh* and *No*. At the climactic instant the bulb pulled from the socket, she fled the room, and Will couldn't help but feel let down. He nearly yearned for the shock that would blast him from his perch in a hail of sparks and fire, a display he figured the boy would admire, torching Will as dead as the

16

bluejay he'd watched die in the smelly earth so long ago.

That night, after their stew and smoothies, she made him a banana split with BRAVERY scripted along one of the banana halves in chocolate syrup, and he imagined that it wasn't for the lightbulb, but for his covert trip Outside. During their usual bedtime cuddle, he worried for the whole twenty minutes that she could smell his wound or somehow detect the Outside on his clothes, even though he'd changed his cut-off shorts, took two separate baths, and was wearing the wetsuit to bed, which she disliked because she said it made him sweat like a squash player, and he could perish of dehydration.

His mind veered to the day's venture: the wind sashaying around him, the birch trees shaking as though in applause, the gently smoking bomb, the boy's kind, welcoming face, while the preposterous sky flew upward beyond all measurement. He was overtaken with a drowsy urge to describe it to her, this dreadful miracle of the Outside and most of all the boy: Other Will. Even if only whispered in her sleep-blocked ear, Will wanted to somehow administer this information to her like some awful medicine, then watch her vanish into a hurricane of Black Lagoon, the hellish aftermath of both his dangerous venture and the more troublesome concern of the Outside being inside him now, like a stain. But the idea charred him with guilt. And as sleep wafted over from the continent of her body, warm and unlimited beside him, he dreamed of the amethyst striking his forehead again and again, of his own candy-apple blood on his hands, and of the boy repeating that revelatory, heart-stopping sentence — *Nothing can really hurt you, Will* — as if it all had something to teach him, as if it were something he ought to try again.

Relaxation Time

How easy it is for a life to become tiny. How cleanly the world falls away.

The subway platform in Toronto. That was the first. Will was a toddler then. Even today, 'safe' in her bedroom, Diane still couldn't summon the incident in her mind without panic spreading in her like laughter through a crowd. She knew she'd brushed against true madness that day because it was huge and blunt and screaming.

She'd blamed the city, its wilderness of signs and traffic and sounds, its flip book of faces and lightning storm of a million brains. So she packed up their apartment and moved Will north to Thunder Bay, where she'd grown up, where she hadn't returned since her twin brother, Charlie, died at the grain elevators when they were twenty-four.

A year had been the plan, time enough to rebalance herself, perhaps make a film, something personal, experimental, short. She still owned the old house, the one she and Charlie had saved for. Though she was the last surviving member of her family, other than Will, of course, she'd never stored the nerve to sell it.

In Toronto Diane bought a car, something she'd never owned, a robin's-egg-blue Volkswagen Rabbit. She and Will set off in the morning: fourteen hours northwest that they split into two days because after the seventh hour

Will was visited with unbearable silliness and wild irrationality. As they pushed northward, bugs left increasingly phlegmatic blotches on their windshield, and spindly, undernourished trees crowded the road as though trying to mount it, get roots into it, and in this manner escape. They tracked the CBC as its signal lived and died, resurrected town to hamlet to town, while the high, rusty channels dynamited into the roadside granite offered the impression of descending into a mine.

Initially, she dreaded the drive. The ratcheting fear could have resurfaced out there amid all that tree and rock. But she was fine behind the wheel, tranquil even. She sang to her old tapes as Will clapped his orange-sticky hands.

They found the house in neglect and disarray, ten years of woolly grain dust on every lateral surface, everything just as she'd left it, even a few plates in the sink, waiting to be washed for a decade. Her father was never one for photos or memorabilia, but she kept a few things: the old dictionary that had so obsessed her brother after their mother died, some of her own sketchbooks and charcoals she put aside for Will, as well as her father's old work boots — the rest she drove to the Salvation Army.

She always preferred to work in a frenzy, to dash herself upon the rocks of a project — this was how she'd made her films — so during Will's naps she cleaned, vacuumed, polished, painted, plastered, tore back wallpaper, and even sledgehammered half of a wall, swooping about on the skating rink of caffeine, coaxing the house into something that her brother wouldn't have recognized. In a kerchief and some old jeans, she suffered the August swelter and fought the feral yard all the way back to the creek, where Charlie once pulled a thousand silver smelt in one night with just a net and a flashlight. A moving truck brought their furniture, Will's toys, her cameras and books.

The work did her good, and this was a period of reprieve.

It was driving that allowed it back: a grocery run, stopped at a light while traversing the highway, Will strapped into his car seat like a babbling astronaut. When the green came, she shifted her foot, and they bucked then heaved to a halt. She pressed harder, yet the vehicle remained unmoved. Behind her a truck honked unkindly. She peered under the wheel to find her boot planted squarely on the brake.

Then the rushing heart and tingling digits, same as on the subway platform. How could she have confused the two most fundamental controls of the vehicle? Most unsettling was how easy it had been: they were both pedals, so close together, one a golf club and the other a door stopper — yet essentially indistinguishable. And what if she'd done it the other way around? Pumped the gas and jackrabbited onto the highway and the fury of logging trucks and snarling pickups piloted by jumpy, half-drunk hunters? What creature would she find belted into the burning jungle of death and fluid and steel that would remain of their car after the trucks had finished with it?

At first she simply avoided the highway. Routine trips took hours, but she didn't mind. She kept to side roads and residential streets. Houses were a comfort. She'd use their phones if necessary. If what was necessary? Using the phone, she assured herself, plenty of good reasons for that.

Rather quickly, more rules established themselves. No roads over a certain speed limit. No night driving. Then no left-hand turns. She hugged the shore of the right lane, never risking her car in the path of an onrushing vehicle — that leftward leap of faith enough to burn her again with panic.

Each night her mind burbled with the close calls of the day, the inadequate traffic bylaws, the numbers and speeds and physics of it all. And after weeks of this she perceived driving for what it truly was: an impossibly complicated and lethal activity. One that required reserves of faith, confidence, and sheer stupidity that she would never possess.

After she sold the Rabbit and learned that Thunder Bay's public transportation system had died the slow death of depopulation and underfunding, she and Will took taxis. The old trifecta of grocery store, library, and bank they could complete for less than fifty dollars in fares. For a while she'd been able to trust the proven expertise of these old men in mustaches and hats, immigrants mostly, because how could one possibly last as a cab driver without caution? And weren't these soft-spoken men mostly poor? Weren't their cars their very livelihood? Wouldn't a crash scrape the food from their children's plates? What better reassurance was there?

Will was three by this time and loved taxis. He asked the men questions with partially pronounced words that only she understood. 'What means that?' he'd belt out, pointing at their CBs crackling with dispatches. 'Yes, good,' the men would say, nodding.

But soon she found herself advising the drivers where to turn blocks in advance, checking and rechecking their gauges, reminding them of speed limit changes while peering between the headrests out the windshield, blotting the driver's sightline with her alert face. They would glance at her in the rearview with their bushy eyebrows and try to smile.

After she could no longer abide the taxis, her ordering from home began in earnest. She discovered that with the right mix of ambiguity and persistence — 'You see, sir, due to a severe condition I am unable to visit your store' — everyone in town delivered: the grocery store, the library, the pharmacy. Just say 'severe condition,' and deliverymen leapt into their trucks. She was surprised by how easy it was, how efficient. They went through a checkbook a week — good thing they delivered those too. She and Will were free to take walks and do artwork and not be stuck dragging a cart through the shrink-wrapped gore of the meat section every Saturday.

Then the outside closed upon her like the aperture of a camera.

The front yard was more of a decision — a

calculated avoidance of risk — than anything imposed upon her. While shoveling slush from the driveway, she found herself casually worrying that the panic would return, and by the time the dangerousness of this vein of thinking registered upon her, it was already there: the revving heart, the icy sweat, her throat constricting. She left the job unfinished and fled inside, where the symptoms instantly subsided. With no handy explanation this time, no subway doors, no crowds, no city, no mishandled car, only the snarling shovel and the tight cold and her breath a soft crystal in the air, she knew the panic no longer obeyed laws it once respected and would seize any opportunity she allowed it to decimate her. So after that day she would not venture even a few steps from their front door to where she knew it lay in wait.

Then, as she was picking up carrots, coal, and various items that four-year-old Will had used to personify a snowman, it visited her in the backyard, same as the front.

And if she could venture into neither yard without meeting a tempest of dread, how was she to leave? And how to let her son play in the yard if she couldn't go out to retrieve him? What if a stray dog came? Or, God forbid, a man?

So they stayed inside. Thankfully, her son was so obsessed with building and painting and his constant tumult of inquisition that he never seemed to mind. Both Will's father and his uncle Charlie had been solitary boys, content with books and models, words and drawings. It was almost relieving, this simplification, and there followed some relatively peaceful, untroubled years.

Then, around Will's seventh birthday, it came in. She was folding laundry when the air was sucked from the basement, the way water withdraws from the shore before a wave. Terror like lungfuls of knife-sharp fumes choked her, and her mind tumbled. She was on hands and knees when she reached the stairs to claw her way out. She didn't imagine anything truly harmful down there, no ghosts or stranglers, just the immovable fact that panic came for her was enough. She ordered Will a stool and taught him to do the laundry by drawing him a diagram of the controls. She ordered another and placed it at the foot of the freezer.

But the most regrettable by-product of staying inside was losing the capacity to face another human being. The micro-rhythms of conversation, the dance of facial mimicry, the fencing match of eye contact were lost to her once she fell out of practice. She soon ceased answering the door — another chore Will assumed with gusto. She grew lonely, but this, too, dropped away. She no longer yearned for people, other than Will, of course. She sated her social impulses with films, music, books, consoled by the fact that no matter what, the actors and characters could never see how hermetic she'd become, how far she had fallen.

At times she'd considered leaving. Pulling on her olive duffle coat and tramping outside. Perhaps bringing an umbrella. How strange it would be. 'Hello, I've lived next to you for eight years, nice to meet you.' Yet there was never reason enough. She'd always believed that the day she left would be the day she was required to. How that could ever happen she could not say.

If only they could manage to escape, maybe she'd leave the whole mess here behind in Thunder Bay. Back to Toronto, or a fresh start somewhere else, Paris perhaps. Arthur's generous support checks, which surfaced each month in her account as predictably as tides, would bankroll anything she could dream up. But that would mean an airplane — the anticipatory preamble: tickets, packing, waiting, and searching, then the imperativeness of actually stepping through those awful retractable tunnels and finding her seat, with a whole plane watching in judgment. She half-considered hiring some amateur anesthesiologist to put her under for the journey, but she feared needles, and the effects of drugs, and dreamless sleep. Since passenger ships no longer served the Great Lakes (she'd checked), they couldn't even take a boat.

Besides it wasn't that she *couldn't* leave, Diane reminded herself. She was refusing to. Her terms. Years of the *Thunder Bay Tribune* and American news shows had proved what fresh horrors the world invented each day. As far as she could tell, there wasn't much of the Thunder Bay she'd known left. Its industries gone, just strip clubs, strip malls, taverns, and hockey rinks remained — the old Eaton's department store now a call center. The houses were still all aimed at the lake like faces to a coronation, eager for some great arrival, even though the lakeboats had stopped coming and the storefronts downtown, once strung with garlands and signs and teeming with families, were now mostly shuttered and vacant. But it was the knocking of grain-ship hulls from the harbor she missed most — now there was only a spooky quiet over an overgrown industrial ruin that reminded her of Tarkovsky's *Stalker*, a film she'd nearly memorized in college that seemed made for her alone.

No, she and Will were stuck, like the pilgrims who'd built the frames of their houses from the planks of their ships. All they could do now was decorate.

3

Before Will's trip Outside, he'd always given thanks for what their house provided. They filled their lungs with the air of its rooms, drank from its faucets, and were powered by its outlets. They warmed themselves in the abundance of its furnace and cleansed their filth in the waters of its tub.

Lightbulbs popped, went dead, were changed. This was repeated. The vacuum whorled galaxies in the carpet and seasons transpired in their windows like plotless movies. Plants reached from their pots to taste the sun. The fridge murmur-whined in complaint if you opened its door, yet, nobly, it never quit. The dishwasher whooshed plates new as the furnace huffed warm air through the teeth of its vents.

Will and his mother lived as indistinguishably from the house as its appliances and furniture, its lumber, drywall, and brick, dousing time with activities and art. Days were spacious and never-ending. Will painted masterpieces while she played guitar or thwacked paperback pages in her reading chair. They scoured flyers and transcribed codes for what they needed from catalogues — A, B, C, D . . . AA, BB, CC, DD — and the very same things materialized in the arms of deliverymen. Once, a teenager from the grocery store returned with a replacement egg for one he broke, pulling it from behind Will's ear like a magic trick.

Will signed their clipboards with a swashbuckling replica of his mother's signature, and the deliverymen tousled his hair and asked why he wasn't in school. 'Home school,' his mother would say, bending around the corner from Paris in one of her threadbare, translucent tank tops, acting as if she hadn't come to the door because she was cooking, not because she was afraid to touch the doorknob. 'Lucky duck,' they'd say with a conspiratorial wink he knew was more for her, because she frowned.

Will and his mother reigned over their private kingdom with the Black Lagoon as its border. It decreed where they could go, how deeply they could breathe, what shapes their thoughts could assume. It reminded them that the Outside world was dark, pitiless, futile, transpiring only in the windows, in their books and films, in the TV they seldom ignited, that there was no true world but their own. It was perfect.

Until it wasn't.

In the weeks after his jaunt Outside, a clutch of nine minutes Will had rekindled over and over with perfect dives of fragrant memory, the house seemed infiltrated, altered, both unfamiliar and familiar, disgusting and comforting, like a wetsuit he'd been wearing for a year.

Since then, Will could muster no desire to paint masterpieces or sculpt or even sketch during Relaxation Time. Maybe it was an attempt to emulate Other Will's bravery, the way he moved through the ocean of the Outside as though he'd been born there, or maybe his spirit had infected Will somehow, emboldening him. But each day, as soon as the headphones were clamped over her ears and the glasses set over her eyes, Will would descend into Toronto to satisfy a new hunger.

His first Destructivity Experiment involved the G.I. Joe figures that had survived the great toy cull of a year previous, when his mother solemnly phoned the Salvation Army, and an annoyingly cheerful man came to cart Will's childhood away. His mother had already loathed ordering the ammunition-laden figures in the first place. 'We just got this stuff,' she said. 'But that's okay,' she added quickly. 'You're really developing lately.' Will wept when the man plucked his boxes from the foyer, all his soldiers finally sent off to die. 'Killed by the Salvation Army,' he said later, and her laugh spat coffee on the table.

Down in Toronto, with the windows open to vent fumes, he burned the remaining figures into napalm-attack survivors with a barbecue lighter he'd secretly ordered and hidden behind the furnace. They burbled above the flame as drools of plastic slipped from their arms, legs, and — when he'd built the nerve — their faces. They released a purple-black smoke that stuck in his nostrils and pushed his head into somersaults. He shaped the little corpses with popsicle sticks, sculpting mutants, severing their elastics, and undoing the screws that bound their bodies, reassembling them in unholy configurations. Next he managed to start the ancient lawn-mower and ran them over, flinging the soldiers across the unfinished basement, leaving gory gashes in their already mangled appendages.

After a month of Experiments, Will had amassed a plethora of important Destructivity data:

- You can smash a snow globe with a ball-peen hammer and be disappointed that the glass is actually plastic and the snow actually ground-up Styrofoam.
- You can laminate anything by winding it in plastic wrap before a five-minute tumble on Cotton in the dryer.
- You can microwave a lightbulb for nearly twenty beautiful seconds as it turns in there like a pink comet before it finally goes supernova.
- You can safely remove your Helmet and whack your head repeatedly on the drywall, weaving an orange velvet into your vision, before you manage to leave a dent.
- You can cover a wall dent by hanging a masterpiece over it and claiming that you need the work at eye level to properly appreciate it.
- You can simulate immortality by sticking a rubber-handled flathead screwdriver directly into the outlet and only trip a breaker.
- You can ride the laundry basket down the carpeted stairs like a mine cart four times until it catches and ejects you to the bottom, where you strike your elbow and

31

it swells red as a hot-water bottle.

- You can safely light the fluff on your sweatpants with a barbecue lighter and send flame rolling over your legs like poured blue water, leaving a crispy black stubble.
- You can halt a fan if you thrust your hand into the blades bravely — only when you hesitate will your knuckles be rapped.
- You can stick the chilly steel tube of the vacuum to your belly and generate a hideous yet painless bruise, and these pulsating circles when placed carefully can form an Olympic symbol that lasts well into a second week.

Of course his mother's catching wind of any of this would mean a cataclysmic Black Lagoon. But she didn't. Like Will, she was a genius, yet she was also naive. Because everything wasn't only making. When he was a little boy, Will's mother urged him to paint masterpieces of trees, houses, and doe-eyed animals, and then it was impressionistic splatters and loosely patterned blocks of color. But he knew now it had all been meaningless. In his true heart he'd rather draw a fight, a war, a chemical spill pulling the flesh from the bones of the villagers. He torched bugs by magnifying the noon sun that throbbed through the window in Cairo, not because he enjoyed pain, but to witness what would happen, to grasp it. And what was the difference between making something and making it come apart? Painting a masterpiece was also destroying a canvas, sculpting was wrecking a good rock, drawing dulling a good pencil forever.

Even though his Destructivity Experiments charged him with daring, he still couldn't bear to sleep alone in New York — which was supposed to be his bedroom, though he used it as a studio. A single bed would be like a house without a furnace, a body without blood, and without the clean whoosh of her breathing beside him, Will could never settle.

After her Sessions she baked him fresh bread in the bread-maker, read page-turners, or strummed folk songs, her small, white-tendoned hand flexed at the guitar's neck, always seeming too small to corral the thick strings. For someone afraid of everything, she was most fearsome on the stool at the counter in Paris, the stretchy phone cord coiled around her thin arms, where she'd arrange the week's complex schedule of deliveries. Sometimes, when arguing about an overcharge or when met with an outsized incompetence, she'd hold the receiver away from her face and stare at it, her dark eyebrows flexed in disbelief, as though the object itself had betrayed her.

But even when the deliveries went smoothly and Will didn't have accidents, there still remained Black Lagoon traces in everything she did. If he said 'Mom' as a leadoff to something, she'd instantly answer 'Yes?' stricken with alarm, as if he were about to inform her of their recent death sentence.

He knew the textures and temperaments of their house just as intimately as he did hers.

She'd archived his detailed architectural blue-
prints along with his masterpieces in Toronto.
They'd always called the kitchen Paris, his studio
New York, their bedroom San Francisco, the
living room Cairo. She told him it had been his
idea when he was young, yet he couldn't
remember having it. He did recall that she'd
insisted on naming the basement Toronto, which
seemed to please her, maybe because that's
where she'd grown up, even if the Black Lagoon
never allowed her down there. Will did the
laundry and fetched arm-numbing frozen loaves
of her bread from the deep freeze.

Sometimes other rooms would temporarily
close off to her. She'd avoid one for as long as a
month, take the long way around. Will loved
when this was Paris, because they'd be forced to
order in, and he could talk her into off-limit,
choke-prone foods like pizza or Chinese. When it
was San Francisco, Will would pick her outfits
from her closet, mostly shift dresses she'd
crudely sewn or floral tank tops and elastic-
waisted jeans, and they'd sleep on the couches in
Cairo and wake in a whirlpool of sun from the
big window. Luckily it was never the bathroom,
called Venice, because she couldn't pee in the
sink, as Will did sometimes as an Experiment,
because even though she was a mother, she had
a vagina, which couldn't aim. Then, inexplicably
as seasons changing, the Black Lagoon would
relent, and she'd return to the foreclosed room
as though nothing had happened.

Still, the Black Lagoon would never surrender
the Outside. Will sometimes pictured their house

surrounded by crackling electric fences and froth-mouthed Dobermans, sheer cliffs falling from their doorstep to an angry sea. Though he'd never been in a church, he imagined they shared similarities with their house: keeping certain things in and certain things out.

After a day of Destructivity Experiments, Will would try to arrange himself casually on the couch, limbs flung loosely, face careless as a boy who'd never been Outside, who didn't have a friend who fired slingshots and feared nothing, who wasn't already changed forever and only felt counterfeit and hollow. Later, while crunching into a piece of toast he'd puttied with butter, a flavor he knew as well as that of his own saliva, he couldn't suppress the creeping suspicion that staying home was somehow unnatural, something people didn't do unless they were certified cloistered wing nuts like Ms. Havisham or Boo Radley — characters in long books she'd read him that she enjoyed more than he did. He'd always thought his mother was enacting something heroic, like a knight or a navy SEAL, but also something complicated, like how the Vikings had a woman-god called Frejya, who was the god of Love, War, and Beauty all at once, which throbbed his brain to think about.

Everyone went Outside, Will concluded. Everyone leaves. That's easy. Only true warriors and heroes could overcome this weakness, could fortify the stronghold, sit tight, wait it out. But now that he'd felt his gooseflesh stand in the Outside air; now that he'd tempered himself with the true danger and beauty of the backyard and gathered unforgettable data with his Destructivity Experiments; and now that the scab on his forehead had grown dark as beef jerky and started to chip at the edges, Will knew that even though he was her guardian and her only son and their blood was the very same crimson hue, he'd never be as strong as she was.

4

A week later, on a day he knew was Sunday because the newspaper came fatter, Will took the deepest breath of his eleven-year life.

'I think I'm maybe going for a walk,' he said.

'Sure, just let me rinse the blender,' she said running the sink, 'and we'll set up the Ye Olde Strolling Course around London — '

'No,' he said.

' — we could even paint some fresh scenery to put up, like Westminster Abbey or something — '

'Mom.'

' — I've got that nice crepe paper you didn't use for your masterpieces — '

'Outside.'

His mother stopped rinsing, as if Zeus himself had pointed his lightning-powered remote control at her and pressed Pause.

'Out? There?' she said, half-laughing while also breathing distastefully, as though the air itself had spoiled. He could already see the Black Lagoon looming behind her, like a train that had jumped its rails.

'Yeah,' he said. 'Out there.'

She set the blender down carefully, as one would a set mousetrap, then braced the heels of her palms on the counter and threw her head back to examine the ceiling as though hunting for a fresco of helpful words painted there. Then she turned and leveled a pleading gaze, her cheeks lavender welts. 'You don't have a coat,' she said, a shrill warble to her voice.

'It's summer,' Will said, in his mind a vision of Other Will crashing into the woods shirtless and surviving fine.

'Exactly!' she said lifting and dropping her arms as though he'd just agreed.

They waited, a gunfighters' silence between them, while her face pulsed, her mouth a razored line. Water sucked through the drain, and her green irises made small ticking motions as though they had second hands trapped inside each of them.

'I'll be fine.'

'Will?' she said, her face gone suddenly raw and flabbergasted as a spanked child's.

She'd surprised him with his name. She never invoked it, because of course she was talking to him. The only time he ever encountered it was when he signed his masterpieces, and it always looked strange, both too insignificant and too grand. Will broke away and commenced readying himself for the journey, unsure what it all involved exactly.

In the corner of his eye, her thin frame commenced juddering like a shuttle flaming into the atmosphere. She snapped her elastic a few times. Then a few more. This was how it started.

Her phobias were numerous: lightning, fire, electricity, water, accidents, vehicles, animals, the Outside, people. Except it was worse than fear. When the Black Lagoon came, when its bear trap was sprung upon her heart, her eyes went swimmy and blotted with white noise like channel zero on TV. Her body vibrated, convulsed, and burst with sweat, before buckling as if miniature charges had detonated in each of her major joints. Will recalled a thunderstorm and power outage weeks back that had caused her to collapse and pant on the candlelit floor for an hour. But worst of all, during a major episode, it was as though she'd forgotten him completely, as though the Black Lagoon had evicted him entirely from her mind — and this was what terrified him most.

Now she sat in a chair and entombed her face in her hands, silent tears ripping through her fingers and down her forearms. He felt the old rising of guilt, then beat it back. He ransacked himself for the true reason for publicly declaring this walk instead of just creeping out during Relaxation Time again, and all he could drum up was the word *Adventure*. It appeared in plenty of his books and upon the worn sleeves of his VHS movies, though he never lingered on it long enough to appraise its true meaning. He adored the sound of it, a thing to say with wide, mystified eyes. Anyway, it was only a walk. She had to allow it, if only because no forbiddance she could utter would not sound insane.

As if she'd read his mind, his mother seemed to metabolize her fear into a kind of sad surrender, leaning on the drywall beside the closet, while he searched for a coat in the vortex of clothing and masterpiece materials. All he found were tiny jackets he'd long outgrown, goods they'd ordered and never unpackaged. When he extracted a pair of canvas shoes a third his size, he experienced a tattered memory of watching them shuffle and scrape along the scalding pavement of a big city.

'These will work fine,' he said, pulling his slippers over his socks while she regarded his feet as one would twin ticking bombs. She followed him toward the landing.

'Wait,' she said, pulling the oatmeal-hued sweater she'd knitted herself up over her head. He let her yank it down over his Helmet with a pop. Fully suited, he made his way to the door. She tried to follow but stalled a few feet back.

'How about you go exploring like you used to in the basement?' she said, sleeve-wiping a few tears from her cheeks. 'We'll pretend I'm the Queen, and you can go forth, into the wilds, and report your discoveries back to me?'

'Hmmm . . . ' he said. 'Do I have to write anything?'

'No, it can be an oral report.'

'Is there a time limit for the speech?'

'How about . . . one minute?'

Will hated writing. But a spoken report wouldn't be overly demanding, even if a minute was an eternity to talk uninterrupted. He snapped a salute and stood tall.

'Do . . . do you want to bring a snack — I mean supplies?' she asked shakily.

'I just had a smoothie,' he said, reaching for the door handle. 'Remember?'

'Oh, you aren't going out front?' she said, one of those suggestion-questions that he'd only recently begun to classify.

'Actually, I might go see what the creek looks

like . . . not sure . . . I'll figure it out,' he said, tacking on this final uncertainty to emphasize a notion he couldn't put into words. He watched it reanimate something in her face — her eyes egg-soft in the middle.

'But keep to our neighborhood, okay?' she said with a forced breeziness. 'And be very, very careful near that creek.'

'How do I look?' he asked when he was finally Outside, pirouetting in the white blare of sunlight.

She peered through the doorway, still six feet back from the threshold, eyes flashing in the shadows like a burrowed animal. He'd never before looked on his mother from any distance, and it struck him now with a sudden force that she was beautiful. Her sharp chin, her coal-dark eyebrows and gilded hair that she cut herself by collecting a ponytail atop her head and shearing it crudely like a rope, hair that would sometimes channel morning sunshine from the window in Paris and turn so radiant to behold he could scarcely stand it.

'You look good, honey,' she said, her mouth a tight tremble. 'Bright.'

⋆ ⋆ ⋆

He passed through the back hedge into the woods where Other Will had disappeared weeks earlier and gained his first glimpse of the creek that for years he'd heard from his window, feeble compared with the mighty river that roared through his imagination. Rusty-tinged water

41

poured over gray rocks, jutting like foul teeth. After failing to spot any fish, Will decided to follow it upstream.

From behind, the houses adjacent to his looked small and vulnerable, like the underbellies of turtles or someone with their glasses off. Their fences only extended so far, so he figured that keeping to the bank wasn't trespassing.

The air was fresh, exhilarating, dangerous as he remembered. A set of thin poplar lined the creek, their silver-dollar leaves whizzing in the breeze. Tiny birds zipped through the branches like paper airplanes with brains, and deadfall lurched with fluffy caterpillars and crunchy beetles. Reaching out into the bewildering distances for the first time, his eyes burned, and he was forced to lower them every few steps to rest them. Will plucked a waxy green leaf from a bush, stuck it in his mouth, and chewed, then gagged and spat the horrid, bitter mulch into the grass. Examining them now up close, Will decided he didn't care much for trees. Too showy, too unruly, too large — things that had a shape and didn't at the same time.

It took only ten minutes for him to realize he mostly distrusted nature: the wasted bits and pieces everywhere, the lewd odors, the imperfect edges, everything unfinished somehow, as though assembled hastily from what was lying around. Also, the ground was damp, and there was nowhere to nap if he got tired. He preferred the nature in books his mother had read him at bedtime: the ambulatory forests of Middle Earth, the sapphire bathwater seas of Jacques

42

Cousteau. Still, he could sense the moose and bears and wolves in the woods that encircled their town, which she'd called Thunder Bay and that had always left her sullen to talk about.

Will came to where the creek slowed and pooled. Water spiders flicked across the black surface, while insects of unimaginable variety cruised a foot above, each overcomplex as his wildest masterpieces of alien ships.

He tightened the chin strap of his Helmet before placing his slipper on a wobbly rock at the shore and wondered how many Outside boys had already died doing exactly this. Hopping between some even more treacherous rocks, he decided to return later to stabilize them with smaller stones as a public service.

Soon he came to a small bridge, where he climbed a purple-thistled embankment, emerging from the woods onto a street that cut over the water. Will stood with his toes on the curb for five minutes, looking left and right like someone at a tennis match until he found the courage to scurry across the road into a stand of pine.

Again astride the creek, he knew he was nearing a highway because a *shush-and-roar, roar-and-shush* could be heard. Will wondered if he should be spooling out thread as he walked but settled on entrusting the neighborhood topography to his genius-powered memory. Sun seeped from behind a cloud and the creek lit like jewels poured down a flight of stairs. The highway, fenced off atop a berm, roared with logging trucks whisking whole forests away to

Toronto, he figured, where his mother said he was born — to which he'd always jokingly replied, 'Wasn't it damp down there?' The creek ducked through a concrete tunnel beneath the highway; next to it a metal culvert was lodged in the berm, a passage for foot traffic.

There he spotted some boys clustered around a large rock in an adjacent field of sun-crisped muskeg. They were tinkering with something, discussing it, intermittently guffawing. Will squinted, but the distance made him dizzy and he could not find Other Will in the wild blur.

Will puzzled over something odd about the boys until he realized that none of them were wearing Helmets, and despite his dangerous lifestyle, neither had Other Will. Will grasped with shock that nobody in movies or any book he'd read had worn Helmets except warriors, people playing sports, and soldiers. Drawing a brave breath, Will reached up with pincered fingers to disengage the plastic clasp beneath his chin. The straps fell away from his cheeks as he brought his hands to his ears. He steeled himself, hoisting it from his head. A pleasing breeze kicked up in his hair, cooling the sweat that had dewed his brow thanks to his mother's sweater. He set the Helmet behind a rock — noting where his mother had discreetly markered *Cardiel* inside the foam — and planned on retrieving it later.

Will abandoned the path and crunched into some sword grass, half-enjoying the faint lacerations on his calves that he hoped wouldn't bleed profusely. Closer, he could see the four boys were clad mostly in black and dark gray, their shirts like Other Will's: pictures of zombies and fire, with writing in old-time fonts crafted of metal. They had long hair and resembled Vikings in a way that was as exciting as it was fearsome.

'Hi, other kids,' said Will. 'Are you making a masterpiece?'

The boys turned briskly to regard him like deer to a rifle shot. All were still squinting as though they couldn't hear well, while one busily enshrouded something on the rock with his jacket. They had a cooler, along with six or seven coils of garden hose, the bright green of a poisonous frog, stacked neatly behind them. Their skin was dark like Other Will's, and a notion dropped into Will's mind that these boys were Indians.

'So what are you guys doing?' Will said, snapping the tension.

'Do you have any money?' said a tall and gangly boy with an enormous bony Adam's apple.

'No,' Will said, ashamed. 'I left our checkbook at home.'

The tall boy nodded, as though this confirmed a universal expectation.

'What's through there?' asked Will, pointing his thumb over his shoulder to the culvert.

'County Park,' said another, older than the others.

'Oh,' Will said, wondering what park would have such an imposing entrance. 'Are you guys friends with a boy named Will?' he said. 'I gave him a garden hose just like those. We're friends.'

Trucks bellowed past on the highway, intermittently washing away the sound of the creek. 'I don't know anyone named Will,' said the tall one, his throat bucking.

These Outside boys all spoke too slow and said too little, as though suffering from some collective hearing deficiency, perhaps brought on by the highway's roar. At home, Will's mother had cautioned him against rushing through his sentences, so he described Other Will loud and slow, his hair, his scars, his slingshot, highlighting the coincidence of their sharing a name, enunciating the way he did for foreign deliverymen.

'Marcus didn't steal anything from your stupid yard, so you'd better shut it,' the tall one barked.

'No, no, I *gave* it to Other . . . I mean Marcus,' Will said, unable to grasp how his friend could possibly get his own name wrong.

'It doesn't matter because *our* friend Marcus left town a while back,' the tall one said. 'So it couldn't have been him.'

'No, I think you guys may have a hearing problem. It wasn't very long — '

The tall one made a nauseated face. 'That a joke, Will? You hurt my feelings,' he said, palm to heart.

Will had only been officially Outside a short time and was stilled by the idea he'd already done another boy wrong. 'I'm sorry — '

'Hold this,' another boy with big ears said warmly, passing Will something, as though this little gift was the antidote to everything. Will turned the object in his hands. A ball of electrical

46

tape. There was a small hole on top, and it was faintly warm like the biscuits his mother baked in the breadmaker. A ball for some sport, Will concluded.

The other Twin — he saw now they were identical — began flicking matches from his thumb into the dry grass. Beside the cooler and the hoses were scissors and a heap of matchbooks. Though he adored fire — the unpredictable leap of heat, the way it whittled things down, the very thought of flaming arrows — Will had never lit a match before.

The others were still watching the ball he was holding.

'Look, I'm pretty good at art and building things and stuff,' Will said, wary of tooting his own horn, 'so maybe I could help you guys out with — '

' — Throw it in the bush!' the boy who'd handed him the ball yelled, half-laughing, staring at Will's hand.

'What?' said Will.

'Shut *up*, Ritchie,' the big Twin said and Ritchie tightened his mouth.

'Really, what?' Will repeated, keen to align himself with the joke.

'Don't worry,' the other Twin said, 'he lit it an hour ago and it didn't go off, so it's probably definitely not going to.'

Will squeezed the ball between finger and thumb. 'This is, like, a bomb?' he said, half-serious, the smoking wasp-nest husk in his front yard returning to him now.

'Just a little gunpowder and a thousand match

heads,' the big Twin declared nonchalantly.

Will shuddered. He whipped it to his feet and cringed backward. He would've picked it up to hurl it farther, but his muscles were locked. What would his hand be now had the bomb gone off? He remembered how forceful the bang Outside his house had been, how sharp and violent. Will pictured a plate of his mother's slow-cooked spaghetti at the end of his arm and it only looked cartoon-like, silly.

The boys broke into peals of unsmiling laughter.

'I can't believe you *did* that to him!' the big Twin said, pushing Ritchie jovially.

'You should punch him,' the smaller Twin advised Will.

'You want to punch me?' Ritchie said. 'I understand.'

Will couldn't fathom why Ritchie said that. But an understanding had grown in him that these boys did not say what they meant, a trait he'd only previously attributed to his mother, who claimed to be *fine*, even with tears boiling from her eyes.

'I don't want to punch anyone,' Will said thinly, having never struck anything in his life except snow globes with a hammer and pillow dummies with homemade nunchucks.

'But he likes getting punched,' the small Twin said. 'He thinks it's funny.'

'Funny?' Will said, relieved to arrive upon the oasis of a friendly word.

'Look,' Ritchie said, drawing his hand back and whacking himself in the face, making a

48

terrible cold-cut noise with his cheek. He unleashed a lush grin while the white flower of his handprint bloomed beside it.

'Oh, man,' the previously silent boy groaned from behind them.

'It's okay, Will, punch me,' Ritchie said, almost tenderly.

'I . . . won't,' said Will.

'You won't, Will?' the big Twin said mock-sweetly.

'You're a megapussy,' the small Twin said.

'Will you, Will?' the big Twin said, his face now lifeless.

Will had never observed such false, indecipherable expressions on deliverymen, and it finally reached him now — he would not come through this safely.

'I'll punch *you* then, okay?' said Ritchie, stepping closer.

Will's breath went full Black Lagoon as his thoughts veered to the Helmet he'd left in the grass and now longed for on his head. Little good would it do, though — this boy would drill him square in the face, liquefying his nose — but at least he wouldn't have shattered his head on a rock when he dropped.

Ritchie swayed before him, fists clenched, while trucks stormed obliviously past on the highway. It came to Will that he'd never been more than thirty feet from his mother and tears crammed his eyes. When she Black Lagooned, Will could taste his mother's fear if he rested his face in her neck, like tinfoil and salt. If dogs could smell fear, these boys were almost harvesting it from him. He'd spent his life designing weapons, staging intricate acts of toy-on-toy violence, but for this unfathomable injustice he was completely unprepared.

Ritchie drew back his arm slowly, almost as though he'd never used it before.

'He's freaked, Ritchie. Do it,' the small Twin said excitedly.

With his legs too sapped by Black Lagoon to be coaxed, Will shut his eyes and set his jaw. His only hope was that he would not die in an overly embarrassing manner that Marcus would hear about, wherever he was.

'Walk away, kid,' the quiet boy said from behind them, and the others erupted in cheerful argument as Will turned on rubberized legs and made for the footpath, breath whirlwinding in his throat. Emerging from the woods, Will launched into a dangerous half run, half walk, his slippers flying off every ten steps until he settled on carrying them. His lungs shrank and his head swam with stars. He'd done plenty of exercise biking and had often run the loop around Paris-Cairo-London-Paris but had never jogged any straight distance in his life. He could so easily faint and smack his head on the sidewalk, and he cursed himself again for removing — and now abandoning — his Helmet. Coming up his street, he prayed he'd recognize their house from the front, but luckily it was the weekend, and theirs was the only one without a car in the driveway.

He found her in London, pretending to straighten his masterpieces. Her face drained when she saw him doubled over on the porch, his head naked, his hair blown back, and — he realized too late — his forehead scab exposed. She caught him in her arms like a drowning woman would a life preserver.

Relaxation Time

Of course she'd read books. An entire shelf's worth. Agoraphobia. That word. One thing to call it. She'd considered doctors, but that would only mean sedatives, psychotropic drugs, insulin treatments — each cure dropping her a rung lower. A psychiatrist would declare her overdevoted to Will. She needed more relationships. Any relationships. Needed to grieve. Arthur. Her mother. Her father. Her brother. Needed hobbies. A career — that word she'd banished for so long. Get out more. Make another film. Go snow-shoeing. Play bridge. Friends. Men. But the truth was she wanted less. Less world. Less talk. Fewer demands. Less danger. More inside. More herself. More Will.

So she'd tried alternative approaches. Visualization. Flooding. Skinnerian desensitization. A hundred ridiculous diets. She assembled an arsenal of complex breathing techniques to employ at key moments of panic, Olympian-worthy routines of reassurance and relaxation.

None of it worked.

Because here was the ruthless truth, a truth that had cornered her like an animal and would never free her from her cage: to fight panic is to panic.

She'd succumbed to this law only after years of struggle and had been obeying it dutifully ever since. Because when something not only can't be beaten but can't even be fought without strengthening it, when something is so absolute and baseless and mechanical, like death, it can only be avoided, feared, ignored, sunk, buried, deliberately erased.

So her revised goal became to prevent herself from falling too far — each day something to survive. And since it was thinking that tipped her into heart-pounding spirals, her strategy was to quell thinking altogether. She tried pills — Anafranil, Valium, Ativan, Xanax — but their unknowable clockwork of control only made her terror flare more intensely. She tried drinking, big sweaty magnums of white wine, even some of the old grain alcohol Charlie had left in the basement from his days at the elevators, but she worried about her liver, imagined her blood thinning in her veins. Besides, waking with a ringing head to a boy clamoring for cereal and a LEGO partner wasn't exactly anxiety reducing.

There were less intrusive methods. She traded coffee for black tea and read the entire *Thunder Bay Tribune* each day, circling typos she found with a red pen, a shockingly busy activity. She played guitar, sincere old folk songs that charmed her despite their cloying lyrics. Though she never stooped to daytime television, she allowed herself five page-turners per week. Mysteries, romances, spy thrillers — the trashier and more inane, the better. Sure, they were formulaic, wooden, predictable, but they sheltered her mind from itself like nothing else on earth: the softly buzzing pages and freedom from literary interpretation and ambiguity were a comfort. Something about the burning question of whether a person was to be *found* — whether for purposes of justice or marriage or revenge didn't really matter — inoculated her from dread, at least temporarily. Really, the books were only a reason to sit and breathe long enough to watch the sun's orchestral walk through the house from back to front.

Another of her most durable strategies was watching Will paint (she'd tried it herself, but her mind feasted upon itself whenever she shut her eyes to visualize her subject). The way Will's face tensed in concentration as his brush lisped over the canvas always soothed the spastic hive of her thoughts and left her spirit thick and warm. She'd once watched *The 400 Blows* with Arthur at the University Cinema in Toronto, which contained a shot of an audience of rapt children, mouths agape, watching either a puppet show or a magician — it escaped her now, but the image struck her then as the most beautiful ever put to film. Afterwards, when Arthur was filling a chipped mug with Calvados at his endearingly disheveled apartment, she arranged those children's faces lovingly in her mind, and it was then, she later suspected, that her long-held commitment to childlessness was revoked.

Along with her guitar and her books and Will's creativity, she had other tricks to diminish the terror. An agoraphobia expert had suggested the wrist elastic in one of her mostly unhelpful Take Back Your Life! – style books. According to some suspect research, it snapped away catastrophic thoughts, like the arm of a clapboard dropped to

54

end a frightening mental scene. And it did. Sort of. However, she suspected the benefits were mostly side effect: the sting brought a vague annoyance, and the repetition was addictive, which somehow deactivated her brain and held the volcano of fear at bay.

Then last month she'd ordered this Relaxation Machine on a lark from the back of a magazine. Manufactured by a company called NeuroPeace Labs, it was advertised to quiet the mind and 'restore cat-like balance to the consciousness.' She hadn't expected miracles and chuckled at the ridiculous goggles when she first put them on, with their little lights inside like a toy robot. When she clamped the headphones over her ears and began the Session, however, instantly she unstuck from herself and swam out into the bliss of mental oblivion, her mind light and empty as a balloon tied to a child's wrist.

She'd used it every day since and had found the ambient whine of fright in her life greatly reduced. But lately, however, long-sunk memories and unwanted recollections had been intruding upon her Sessions, like water seeping into a hole she was digging with her hands. Even with the volume up to a white roar and the lights set at a dizzying strobe, she couldn't entirely flush the intruders from her mind. What had eased things slightly was using her old reel-to-reel to record herself describing the thoughts that came, in the hopes of turning them loose. Best of all, in the surf-racket of the headphones, she couldn't even hear what she was saying, which was preferable. Much of the contents of her head she wanted little to do with. And maybe one day, when she could stand it, when she was stronger, less panic-stricken, better, she would listen to these tapes, to this voice of hers that she'd couldn't hear, to this stranger telling her own story to an empty room.

Now in the blue strobe of her Relaxation Goggles, she saw again her son bursting into the house only a few weeks ago, winded, terrified, his forehead deeply gouged and already scabbed over, without that security blanket helmet he'd always insisted on wearing, though it did comfort her too.

But he hadn't left the house since. Perhaps he'd learned his lesson? It was Will's gorgeous, overdriven imagination that worried her most. He barely lived in reality, so how could he register its dangers? Who better than she knew how Thunder Bay could reach out and harm a child: the bears and wolves in the woods; the trains, the harbor, and the elevators; the cheap grain alcohol, the highway, the frigid lake, the biblical weather, the hurtling brutality of hockey, all those hard-eyed boys that used to lift Charlie's shirt over his head before pummeling him, the acres of identical birch trees — serene as grandfather clocks — for Will to vanish into.

No wonder she'd allowed him to stay home for so long. But had it been her doing? In all those years, he'd never shown the slightest interest in leaving. Maybe a better mother would've flushed him out earlier. Take your lumps. Play hockey. Crash your bicycle. But what hurts a boy other than lumps? Lumps are brain damage. One lump can drown a boy in a creek, can stop his heart dead as a stone, can rip him from your arms forever.

No, despite his little excursion, she and Will were relatively safe. How many of the world's mothers could claim that? It's not a prison if you've built it yourself, she mused as the Relaxation Tape ground down and the Play button popped, and she unstuck the clammy headphones from her ears and lifted the clunky goggles from her eyes. It's a fortress.

With some baseline of calm restored, she put away the apparatus, went downstairs, and put on the electric kettle for tea. Lately, usually after she did her Sessions, she'd been detecting hints of a worrisome burning odor in the house — plasticky, like wires frying in the walls. She lowered her nose to the kettle to see if it was the culprit, but found nothing.

5

That morning the mailman brought a package. 'You look like you need a nap, Will,' he said. 'Rush delivery. You know where to sign.'

After he'd lied about slipping in the creek and striking his forehead, his mother had been waking him nightly to flashlight his pupils and ask if his mouth was dry or if he had strange dreams. 'My dreams are always strange,' Will said, referring to the hours he'd just spent doubling with Marcus through the woods Helmetless upon a cackling dirt bike.

She'd Black Lagooned ferociously for days after his first official trip Outside. Like an improperly loaded washer on spin, their bed jiggled at night with her panic. Each morning, she lingered under her quilt, sitting up to fingerpick morose ballads on her guitar or spoon the canned soup he'd heated in the slow cooker and presented with a flourish in the clay masterpiece mug he'd once glazed for her birthday. She upped the Relaxation Tapes to twice daily, and, eventually, after a week, her weeping subsided and she started to venture out from San Francisco.

Now Will breached the package with his safety scissors and unearthed the Helmet he'd ordered to calm her, this one traffic-cone orange. It fit perfectly and didn't smell vinegary like his last. He couldn't exactly recall when he started wearing Helmets — always the hockey kind, no face mask. She said she ordered his first when he was learning backwards somersaults as a toddler. When not in use, the Helmet hung from the hook on their bed in San Francisco. In the morning he put it on before his feet touched the floor and even when he shuffled to Venice at night to pee.

Here was the thing about the Helmet: like not going Outside, she'd never exactly made him do it either. But, he found, the ethereal machinery of the house ran smoother with it on. Her shoulders unbunched, her breath passed more easefully through her windpipe. She left him for longer periods of time without checking up on him and even permitted more dangerous actions like running up the stairs or pedaling the exercise bike at full tilt.

Along with the Helmet had arrived other mail, and Will sorted the bills and invoices from the letters addressed to his mother in the usual crazy-person script. He set the others aside and whisked the letters down to Toronto, where he dumped them in a banker's box. Over the years Will had read samplings when boredom had overwhelmed him. They were penned by people in mental institutions and prisons mostly, but sometimes universities and film associations, who all seemed to have memorized her films shot-for-shot. Though Will had never watched any of her films — she said she didn't have prints, which his routine searches of the house confirmed — the portrait he'd assembled was that they lacked actors, or even a story, and were only footage of objects and people she'd shot haphazardly on the thrumming streets of real Toronto — imagine! — with her voice talking overtop. As far as many people were concerned, they were about something called 'modern urban malaise,' which made Will think of city people barfing into open manhole covers, because *malaise* sounded like *mayonnaise*, a forbidden substance because it went deadly poisonous after only a few minutes out of the fridge.

A filmmaker was a person who made movies, but not the ones you'd want to watch like *Predator* or *Die Hard*, which his mother called 'bullet ballets' and limited to special occasions. His mother once said she'd made films that people wrote dissertations about. 'Is that like getting dissed?' he'd said, to which she replied, 'Essentially.'

She made all six of her films in Toronto, where they once lived, which he hadn't remembered at all until he'd gone Outside, because all their years Inside had overwritten it. Mostly his memories consisted of near-death experiences, colors they'd painted the rooms, epic stains in the carpets, whole epochs of furniture configuration. But real Toronto was where his mother had met Arthur, his father, who was a genius architect, except he wasn't really a genius when it came to phone usage. He had a new family and lived in the Netherlands. Will had talked to him a few times, but the calls tapered off because they consisted mostly of long, searching silences. But Arthur's buildings were all over the world, like real Paris and London. The plural of genius

60

is genii. And that's what Will's family was, really, genii, including his mother, except Will couldn't tell anyone that because of the tooting horn. As a boy, Will vowed to use his genius to build them a teleporter so they could go back to Toronto or go surfing in Hawaii, where he would crack coconuts for her with a machete, but she said she'd be too afraid to get into it.

Will slept with the amethyst clutched tight in his fist like a sacrament, the spiky rock somewhere between purple and blue, same as blood when it's still inside your body, before the air coaxes it red. But now that his friend Marcus had left Thunder Bay and those bomb-making twins hadn't exactly welcomed Will into their group, he'd been afflicted with a painful vacancy in the center of his chest that could only be alleviated with two hours of daily exercise biking. With no longer any reason to go Outside, he'd vowed to do only productive activities during Relaxation Time. He bounced balls off the corners where the wall met the roof, performing a hundred catches in a row without a drop. He strained through sit-ups, jumping jacks, and gut-wrenching exercises he invented himself. Upstairs, he crouched over the heating vents like a hunter to dry his sweat-soaked pajamas.

But one bonus of his Outside near-death experience was that it had rekindled the house's wonder. As summer dwindled, days passing like clouds, the sky gas-flame blue in their windows, Will re-counted the stripes in the wallpaper, recalculated the surface area of the rooms, and reached his arms as deep as possible into the heating vents. Again he relished the medieval crawl space, the perfumed confines of his mother's closet, the menacing pig-faced outlets, the raw smell from behind the fridge, the chugging alchemy of the laundry machines. He made recordings on her old reel-to-reel, indoor field studies. Music like John Cage, who was also a genius. 'This. Is the sound of safety. Scissors,' Will said, before snapping them loudly at the microphone. 'This. Is the sound of a garbage. Bag,' he said, rustling. His mother loved his sound collage, and he played the tape for an Italian pharmacy deliveryman, who declared it 'real freaking interesting.'

Mostly, however, Will painted a new series of masterpieces. The totality of his entire artistic output, everything he'd ever painted, con-structed, designed, or slapped together, was archived in Toronto. The magnificence of his masterpieces routinely made his mother weep (not a great feat for someone who literally feared her shadow, admittedly, but she knew art). 'I'm keeping them for posterity,' she'd once said. 'Why would you keep it for someone's butt?' Will had asked. 'That's posterior.' Which was why she said 'for posterior' all the time, because things got tacked to a corkboard inside her head and stayed there. Which, he suspected, may have been her problem. Will harbored a magical hope that Marcus would reappear one day and ping her in the head with his slingshot, just once, hard enough to give her the gift of amnesia. Then she'd step Outside with no clue she was a person who was afraid of everything.

In the evenings they screened films in Cairo, with the VCR or her 16mm projector. Will loved action movies best, which she couldn't stomach. No movies for her with guns or where anyone died, except if it was from tuberculosis or lovelorn suicide. That's what happened in all her favorites, which were in other languages and featured half-beautiful, half-ugly people staring at each other for long stretches of time as though they'd been robbed of speech. They unsettled Will as much as his movies did her.

Years before, for his ninth birthday, they'd watched the 3D version of *The Creature from the Black Lagoon* on the projector. He'd ordered the print from the library, and it even came with 3D glasses that had been retaped a hundred times. He used the leverage of his special day to make her promise to sit through it. It was the most excited he'd ever been.

But she was already breathing funny during the film's opening, repeatedly burying her eyes in her hands and steaming her red-and-blue lenses with hoarse breaths. 'Just make yourself watch,' he said. 'The *Creeetuuure* can't kill you,' he added in a gravelly monster voice, attempting to pry her hands from her face with his fingernails.

'I don't want to make myself,' she said, eyes closed tight as a boxer's fists.

She was fine for a few more minutes as the story was established. Then the murderous amphibian appeared beneath the unsuspecting woman as she front-crawled across the lagoon. He lurked just inches from her, menacing, but also curious, as if he wanted to help her and get sexy with her vagina and kill her all at the same time, as an entire orchestra's brass section blasted away unnervingly, as it did whenever the Creature — or usually only its gnarled, dinosaurish hand — graced the screen. It was more than enough to kidnap his mother's brain.

In old movies when people get afraid — when the killer's shadow seeps through the crack under the door or when the giant radioactive bug crests the skyline — the actors stuff their fists into their mouths like they are eating them. Like eating yourself alive is better than staring down an unmentionable horror. That's what his mother did then, except in real life. Sometimes Will thought she'd eat her whole body if she could somehow get it into her mouth. 'What about my birthday?' he'd called out as she fled to San Francisco and didn't emerge for a whole week. Now whenever she Black Lagooned, he pictured the monster swimming inches beneath her. Except she's the only person who could see it.

★ ★ ★

One morning late in August, his mother was reading the paper in her good green robe, her hair puffed with sleep, when she gasped.

'What?' Will said.

'Oh, nothing,' she said, the Black Lagoon a harried shadow on her face. She rose, neatly folded, then ripped the page into strips, setting them in the garbage instead of the recycling. 'I'm going to do a Session.'

64

When he heard her door click, Will extracted the strips from the trash and reconstructed them on the table. Normally, newspaper stories were of little relevance to Will. He found an article about how it was too expensive to demolish the 'blight' of the old grain elevators by the lake, so the city had to leave them there; an article about some Indian treaty talks that went nowhere; another about a local hockey team that won a tournament.

Then he found it. Small, in the corner near the back. A boy. Missing. It said he lived in a foster home, and they hadn't noticed him gone for weeks. There was a tiny photo, and the boy had the same crooked bangs and bright look as when he'd offered Will his T-shirt to dab the blood from his eyes. Marcus. His friend. His only friend.

That evening, New York seemed shrunken. Insomnia settled over Will, the minutes grinding and endless, quiet as surgery. Will's mind turned with a terrible waterwheel of tantalizing questions: Why had the Twins reacted so guiltily when he approached? Why did they say Marcus had left town? Why the garden hoses and match bombs? And what did any of it have to do with Marcus going missing?

Whatever, sure, brave Marcus had said that day when Will asked if they were friends, a mental reel Will had nearly worn out with replaying. Will looked up this word *whatever* in their old dictionary, the one with the name *Charlie* written in the front, and found that it meant 'no matter what.' At the permanence of this beautiful sentiment Will wept, tears tapping the dictionary's oniony pages.

Even before Will closed the book, his mind had already seized upon a whole new trajectory to aim the Roman candle of his life. He couldn't just go wandering Outside aimlessly like last time. It was much too dangerous. Will needed somewhere to go, a reason to leave. He needed more than masterpieces and smoothies. He needed answers. He needed Adventure. He needed to find his friend Marcus.

He needed everything.

6

The night before his first day of school, Will lay awake, twisting with anticipation. The previous week he'd searched the muskeg where he'd met the Twins — a walk around the block, he told his mother — and found his Helmet gone, no trace of hoses or matches. The next day during Relaxation Time, Will phoned Tom Sprague, the wiry man who'd been doing their yard work for years, and asked if anyone in the neighborhood was missing garden hoses. 'Oh, sure, most of my clients had their hoses stolen at one time or another this past summer,' said Tom. 'Your street in particular. Had to pick up a new one for you.' Will asked whether it was mostly on the creek side. 'Come to think of it, most of them backed the creek, yeah.' After Will placed a call to the police station and was put on hold for an hour until he hung up, he deemed his only move was to go undercover to gather information. He'd known school happened in September because that was when kids trudged past his house in early morning like soldiers with their whole lives stuffed into backpacks.

She'd been reluctant to enroll him, but then he said he would start calling random governmental numbers in the blue pages and tell whoever answered that his mother refused to let him attend school. 'Of course you'd never do that,' she said, more plea than assertion.

Fresh from the bath, Will found his favorite clothes laid out on his bed like a steamrollered boy. He went to his closet and picked his second-favorite clothes as a statement. Over a five-course breakfast of slow-cooked steel-cut oats, fresh bread, eggs hardboiled in the kettle, and sliced pineapple, she warned him of real tests, which were mind games to prove how smart you were. Will looked forward to them. He would surely get As. At home they often did 'Creative Challenges,' which he graded himself, always checking either 'amazing' or 'stupendous' on the evaluation forms she typed up on her Underwood.

In the orange burn of dawn he followed the sidewalk toward the asphalt path that wound up the tall hill on which the school stood. It was an impossibly huge structure, like five entire houses all bound together, encased in cinder block. Other kids were approaching the school, mostly girls in neon swishy jackets. He climbed and entered the colossus randomly through one of its heavy steel doors, into a hallway strewn with tiny dazed children. He wandered giant-like between them until happening upon the office. The perfume-soaked secretary walked him to his classroom.

He hung his coat and lunch bag in the cloakroom, where many of the same kind of jacket lined the walls: felt with leather sleeves and patches. Hockey jackets, he surmised, from their insignias of variously paired stick and puck.

His teacher, Mr. Miller, a gap-toothed man with glasses thick as the double-paned windows in Cairo, ushered him to his desk. This teacher was strange in two ways: one, he was a man; and two, he was old. Will had had little contact with men beyond signing clipboards and writing checks, and the deliverymen were prevailingly young.

'You can sit in Jonah's desk for now,' Mr. Miller said, his teeth whistling faintly. 'But you'll have to move when he returns, if he does.'

Will crammed his legs into the desk as a wall-mounted speaker emitted an amplified breathing. 'This is your morning announcements,' said the quaking voice of a student, who described an upcoming hot dog day and impending hockey registration. Next came 'O Canada,' which Will had heard a few times before, then The Lord's Prayer, which he'd never. Sometimes, when feeling especially chipper, his mother sang '500 Miles,' a song he liked, though it was about being poor and far away from home, a condition he hadn't much experience with, until recently, anyway. When she cleaned she put on *The Rite of Spring*, which sounded like a heinous multi-car accident, except the cars were built out of orchestra instruments. To Will, it was the distilled sound of Black Lagoon.

During the prayer, Will didn't know where to look, how to tilt his head. He attempted a solemn, respectful face. He preferred it to the anthem: juicier words, especially the word *trespasses*, a Marcus word, even if it was something that necessitated forgiveness. There wasn't much of anything in the classroom: no masterpiece supplies, no exercise equipment, no slow cooker. A picture of the queen, who he recognized from the dollar. A map of Canada, pink as a cartoon pig, the top a confettied mess of either islands or icebergs — he was never sure. A pencil sharpener bolted to a shelf near the window. The rest just greenish seas of blackboard.

'And may I introduce Will Cardiel,' said Mr. Miller when the announcements concluded. 'Will comes to us from . . . ' He scanned down his sheet. 'Where do you come to us from, Will?'

'Home,' he said, and the man jumped. Will realized instantly he'd yelled it. He had no clue how loud he needed to talk in this big Inside for so many people to hear him, how to make enough sound to feed all those ears.

'No, I mean which school,' Mr. Miller asked while folding his arms.

'Oh,' said Will, in what he realized was a whisper. Kids were torqued in their desks, and Will hoped they could make out the forehead scar Marcus gave him enough to admire it. That morning, his mother had cautioned him on revealing too much to Outside people about their living situation. 'Um, you wouldn't know it,' he said, juicing his memory for places he knew about. 'It's in San Francisco.' This conjured an image of him cuddling with his mother in their bed, and just as quickly he drove it from his mind for fear everyone could tell.

'Well, well. All the way to old Thunder Bay from Californ-I-A. Aren't we lucky,' replied Mr.

Miller. 'Why don't you say a little about yourself?'

Will was unsure if he was allowed to stand, but talking loudly while seated would feel gross in his belly, so he tried to rise and rammed his kneecap into the metal bar that fixed seat to desk. He lurched to the other side and managed to get upright.

He considered reciting a poem, something his mother taught him by this woman she liked named Emily something. Yet like a burglar in a vacant house, Will's mind found nothing to grab and commenced tearing the place up.

'Whenever you're ready,' Mr. Miller said.

Desperately Will unearthed from his pocket the masterpiece blueprint he'd drawn of his ideal school. She'd called it *visualization* and said it helped with stressful situations. 'But I'm not stressed, Mom,' he replied, to which she knowingly said, 'Not yet.'

Will heard himself describe the blueprint's features, holding it high so all could get a look, especially at its extensive legend, which curved because he'd run out of space at the edge. Mr. Miller was holding a ton of air in his chest as though about to cough. Will raced to sufficiently describe the varying depths of the indoor wave pool he'd included.

' — Okay, Will,' interrupted Mr. Miller.

'Okay?' Will said. He hadn't even described the sniper tower yet.

'Very creative, great, and we've plenty to get through today.' Mr. Miller turned and padded in soft shoes over to his desk as Will's classmates smirked into their laps, shoulders bucking.

'How about I drink chocolate milk out of your skull?' Will said to his teacher, but only in his mind, with black acid foaming in his chest and a hateful heat over him like a hood. Will vowed to burn the blueprint but knew he couldn't do it publicly, which would be the incident's perfect comedic conclusion.

Mr. Miller then commenced a speech about something called the Canadian Shield, which wasn't at all an energy force that protected the entire Outside from alien attack. Will quickly lost track of the speech, instead imagining a shield erected over his house, sheltering it from both meteors and the Black Lagoon. When the bell rang, children launched from their desks like pieces of toast. Will retrieved his coat and followed them Outside. He stood for a while near the doors — the sky huge and ruffled with high cloud — awaiting further instruction. There was only one teacher, a pallid middle-aged woman in a wool beret, covertly smoking behind a playground structure. He stood near her until she shot him an uncomfortable smile, stepped on her cigarette, and walked off across the grounds.

Boys from his class swarmed the rough tennis court, where a road hockey game congealed around an orange ball that sounded hard as ceramic. Will stood at the chain link, unseen, imagining it wasn't because nobody cared about him but because the visible part of him was still Inside and would soon catch up. Then some retarded kids led by another teacher walked past, all wearing Helmets, and Will tried not to think about what cruel comparisons the hockey players would draw if they ever found out he'd only just yesterday stopped wearing his own at home.

Now Will turned from the fence and stood near the doors, where some toddlers trotted in figure eights, screaming at some pretend disaster. Because his house was his way of measuring time, a giant sundial they lived inside, without it Will felt like he'd been at school for weeks. He'd expected more people for him to befriend here, not less, and he wondered if this achy sensation at the back of his skull was what people called loneliness and how long it would last. Already he missed the crisp *thwack* of his mother turning pages in her reading chair, the jet-engine scream of her morning vacuum, how they tangoed expertly around each other through the hall of London.

With still no sign of Marcus or his gang, Will reached into his pocket and retrieved the amethyst. He had to resist the urge to smash it into his forehead in exactly the same spot, in the hope the wound would become a beacon that drew Marcus to him, and he'd invite Will into his pack and teach him how to survive the Outside.

Back in class, Mr. Miller's speech was almost the same, but this time it was called history. To sum up: the French and the English and the Indians all fought bitter battles when Canada wasn't even Canada, and the Indians didn't win much, no matter whose side they took. Then came lunch. Will ate his slow-cooked vegetarian chili silently in the sunless lunchroom. Afterwards he was shooed out for yet another recess, depressingly identical to the first, except for when an excited girl sidled up beside him.

'Hey kid, I'm Angela Gallo,' she said.

When he told her his name, she asked him where he lived.

'Just down the hill,' he said. 'How about you?'

'County Park.'

Already he could feel the schoolyard gaze turn upon them. His only other conversation with a girl was long ago, when two pretty Girl Guides came to his door bearing boxes of chalky cookies. After sampling them, Will suggested they try his mother's recipe for the cookies she made in the breadmaker, but they left in a huff. This Angela looked nothing like those girls or his mother. She had over-large eyes that didn't properly close, flat black hair, and teeth that fanned out like a magician's fingers casting a spell. But the ache in his skull was gone, and there was some faint slippery sound in her voice that he enjoyed, so he kept talking.

'County Park's through the culvert,' said Will, proud of his growing Outside knowledge.

'No shit, Sherlock,' she said, then, pointing to his forehead, 'How did you get that?'

'I fell in the creek,' he lied.

'Huh. Why are you so white?'

'White?'

'Your *skin*? It looks like skim milk.'

'I don't really know what — '

'Here's the deal, Will. I know you didn't move from San Francisco or whatever. My brother was your paperboy, and your mom paid him to play LEGO with you.'

Suddenly Will had a dead porcupine in his throat and a burning under his scalp. He turned to flee, but she grabbed him by the shoulders and spun him around.

'Look, I don't care about that,' she said. 'But can you do me a favor?' Her eyelashes fluttered like the legs of an overturned beetle.

'Okay?' he said, recovering.

'Get me some stuff from the desk you're in?'

'Like what stuff?'

'Oh, papers, but not books. I'm interested in artwork. *Drawings.*'

'Isn't it another kid's desk?'

'Duh.'

'Jonah?'

She rolled her eyes. 'Yessss.' Will noticed that Angela ended all her sentences exhaustedly, as though she was about to faint.

'Uh . . . ' he said, stalling. 'Why isn't he in school?'

'There was a fire at his house.'

'How did — '

'People say he started it, but he didn't!' she said with exasperation. 'It's because he's Native. Even my dad says if you build Indians a house, they'll have burned it for firewood by noon the next day. Jonah's brothers are actually criminals, but they didn't do it either. It was an *accident!*'

'Oh,' said Will, imagining his own house in flames, his mother sitting in a smoke-swirled chair, hair smoldering, content to burn. 'Do you know a boy named Marcus who went missing?'

'Yeah, his foster home is on my street. Marcus and Jonah used to skateboard together. But nobody ever knows where Marcus is. He's always playing tricks and stealing things and running away. He's nothing like Jonah, who's the swee — '

' — Marcus and Jonah are friends?' Will interrupted. 'Would Jonah know where he is?'

'No,' she said peevishly. 'They don't hang out together anymore for some reason. Maybe because Marcus hasn't been to school for, like, years, and Jonah pulls straight As even though he'd rather die than ask Mr. Miller a question. Look, can you do it?'

'Why don't you just grab them yourself?' Will said.

'Because people will see and he'll *know*.'

'Know what?'

'That I'm basically in love with him?'

'Isn't that stealing? Like *real* stealing?' Will fought to differentiate this act from all the times Inside he'd hurriedly mashed brown sugar into butter and stuffed the blissful glob into his mouth before his mother checked up on him. 'Why can't you ask him?'

'Oh, my god, he doesn't talk!'

'In class?'

'No, he doesn't talk. Ever. Look, can you do it or not?' She cocked her hips, tossing her hair even though it was too short to generate much movement.

Will had the sudden notion that Angela was the only person other than his mother or Mr. Miller he was going to talk to all day. 'I'll see,' he said.

After recess the teacher gave more senseless

speeches and squiggled tired diagrams on the board in bleary gray chalk. The first day wasn't even over, and Will had already jammed his frequency completely, like a stealth bomber to enemy radar. To bury time, Will discreetly picked through the desk and removed some papers. A pencil-drawn masterpiece of a skull. The feathery shading, the deep-sea depth of perspective, all done with such acuity to reality he was robbed of breath. It was miles better than any masterpiece he'd ever done or could do. He unleafed another: a perfectly rendered boy on a skateboard flying over a filthy dumpster. Then a less impressive one, what looked like a crudely drawn grid with a number of *Xs* on it. Will slipped them all into his backpack.

After the bell rang, Angela cornered him in the hallway.

'Did you get it?' she said.

'This is all I found,' Will replied, holding up the grid, his least favorite, the one he couldn't imagine Jonah would miss.

'I love *it*,' she said, fawning wickedly, snapping the paper from his fingers and pressing it to her flat chest. 'You're the *sweetest*.'

Studying the drawings later that night, Will knew each of Jonah Turtle's masterpieces made his own resemble enormous unfunny jokes told with paint, all stacked in the basement, kept for posterior. He recalled how many his mother had sent off to galleries in real New York and Paris over the years and nearly imploded with embarrassment. He vowed to hide Jonah's masterpieces from his mother. If she saw them, they'd shrivel, weaken, close over like his forehead, like all wounds when exposed to air. He made a promise to himself to return them to Jonah's desk in a few days, but for now, their mystery, like all his adventures Outside, would remain his alone.

Relaxation Time

She always knew he would go to school, eventually, but she hoped he might be sufficiently gifted to skip all the schoolyard heartbreak, the punch-ups, the crushing report cards, the cruelties and disappointments and failures of life in a Thunder Bay public school — just leapfrog right into a good, safe university or fine arts program when he reached eighteen or so. Juilliard took homeschooled kids, didn't they? As did Berkeley? It seemed like something they'd have to do, for ideology's sake.

But now, given Will's curious nature, he'd soon be retrieving painful morsels of her past like a terrier with a mouse in its jaws. Though perhaps he wouldn't? It was so long ago now, Thunder Bay so different, the hollow ghost of the mythic place she loved as a girl.

She'd hoped it would be impossible to enroll Will so late, but the school secretary said classes were all running at half capacity for lack of students. In Diane's youth, the schools had teemed with children, and she'd loved every dead wasted minute, only because school was slightly more stimulating than the tense drudgery of home life. Though eight-year-old Diane and Charlie weren't exactly popular before their mother, Iola, had been struck by a delivery truck that lost its footing on the ice, afterwards the tragedy clung to them like grain dust to their father's work coat. Their schoolmates began to claim the twins slept together, which they did, sometimes, especially in the blurry weeks after their mother's funeral — a day Diane remembered only for the preposterousness of men weeping and the brass-buckled shoes on her feet — but of course not in that way. After Iola's death, Charlie, who'd always been modest and mild-mannered like their father, responded by dominating their classroom. He thrust his lightning-quick arm at each of the teacher's questions like the reigning champion of a high-stakes American quiz show. He found numerous addition errors in the scoring of his tests, about which he was outraged. Always a thin, bookish boy, Charlie took up sports for the first time, but his asthma would leave him gasping, furious as a kicked beehive, the rage of competition and unaccustomed proximity to other boys often leading to shoving matches with opposing players. Diane remembered how their mother often sat up at night with Charlie, rubbing mentholated ointment into his spasmodic back muscles with soothing words and songs to lessen his gasping panic and how, after she was gone, Diane would lie awake listening to her brother's lonely struggle for air, afraid, unsure how to help him, alleviating her guilt by sketching horses under her covers by flashlight.

On their daily walk home from school, Charlie soon began to fight recklessly with boys twice his size for comments about Diane that he once would've let whistle past or perhaps even laughed at himself. When he wasn't fighting, he tightrope-walked the railing of the footbridge over the creek, stopping Diane's heart. After dinner — now mostly small mountains of heavily buttered potatoes boiled by their father — he ceased watching their favorite programs and sat in a hardback chair to memorize the Oxford dictionary he'd found at the church thrift shop, a stack of recipe cards kept in his pocket for recording unusual words he fancied and pictured himself using to great effect in a courtroom someday. He badgered their father to buy expensive faux-gilded encyclopedia sets, even though there was no money for such things.

When the twins were ten, their father rotated onto a new shift, and with no money for afterschool care, they were forced to walk to Pool 6, the grain elevator where their father worked, to wait until he got off at seven. They assumed the chore of bringing his supper in a tin bucket each night, his vegetables and meat mixing as they walked. With the bucket often frozen by the time they arrived, they'd set it to warm on a donkey engine still used to draw water from the lake. For dessert, Theodore ate two hardboiled eggs whole, unpeeled.

Because of the twins' loss, the men on their father's shift never once bemoaned their presence in the workhouse, even though it meant curbing their swearing and nipping at bottles of grain alcohol on breaks. But soon Charlie hated the elevator even more resoundingly than he hated Thunder Bay and would skulk at a table in the corner like a boy doing penitentiary time, seething over his dictionary while Diane sat sketching, stealing glances to watch the men sip inky coffee as they discussed machines, the vagaries of international shipping, proper bin ventilation, the moisture content of grain, and dreams of summer fishing excursions on secret lakes. She heard them spin complex webs of loyalty and hatred, mostly based on accusations of effrontery, incompetency, or the worst accusation of all: laziness. The elevator workers were mainly sunburned Scotch-Irish or Ukrainian farm boys who'd taken one step up the supply chain or recent immigrants without a word of English that wasn't a curse or a description of grain. Though their father never smoked, Theodore's breath rattled, and he coughed up great whopping solids that he expelled from the window of their truck or into the sink. 'Down the wrong pipe,' Theodore would say. 'Man wasn't born to breathe bread.' After years of grain dust exposure, most of the workers wheezed, and the older men's eyes had hardened to something comparable to amber. Back at home, Charlie would bat the grain dust from his clothes before returning to school the next day, scolding Diane if, after her washing, any dust remained on the pair of Brooks Brothers oxford shirts he'd found miraculously in the thrift shop, shirts he wore alternately each day like sacred robes.

Unlike many at the elevator, their father had a steady, even manner and never competed or quarreled with others at Pool 6. He loved the paintings of Breughel, often staying up late to leaf through the expensive art books their mother had once sold her baking every weekend to buy him, the only books in their home other than the telephone directory, Charlie's dictionary, and Diane's sketchbooks. He took neither coffee nor alcohol — only hot water from a thermos, which he claimed as Science's greatest triumph. But from the workhouse the twins witnessed bare-knuckled fights and daredevil contests of every sort. Men jumping across dizzying spaces between grain bins and iron walkways a hundred feet in the air, balancing sharp pitchforks on their chins and timing reckless dodges through the jaws of the death-dealing machinery. For these reasons and others, Theodore forbade the twins to venture outside the workhouse. The harborfront was a dangerous nexus of furnaces, cables, factories, boilers, switching tracks, shipyards, and extreme cold that came in from the lake like a wraith, and he often spoke of Wheat Pool 5, an elevator that had exploded when its venting systems failed.

Eventually, the twins grew old enough to be on their own at home, and their time at the elevator ended, though Diane still brought Theodore his supper nightly. By then she adored the thunder of trains shunting down in the yard and had learned to distinguish this from the roar of the car dumper as it snatched fully loaded grain cars and emptied them like a child's sand pail. From the high windows of Pool 6 she watched lakeboats crawl off into the blue horizon, toward the canals and locks of the lesser Great Lakes, down to the Saint Lawrence and eventually the ocean. With everything measured on such a grand metric — the thousands of tons of grain and potash and steel and concrete, the enormous boats and stout men, not to mention Thunder Bay's outsized hopes for the future ('Canada's Chicago,' it was foretold then with a straight face) — Diane would return to their house on Machar Avenue and think it better suited for her dolls than a family.

Their father neither struck them nor singed them with harsh words, and Diane was frightened by her brother's growing loathing of Theodore, who she always found pleasantly benign, if only because he was so rarely both at home and awake simultaneously. Charlie began to scoff at Theodore's monotonous descriptions of his work and would sweep up the grain dust that their father tracked in with brisk, agitated strokes with the corn broom. Charlie confessed during a late-night conversation in their room — a time once reserved for surreptitious play: knock-knock jokes, silly drawings, and improvised tales of talking animals told in hushed tones, but now consisted mostly of silent brooding and angry study — that he'd become convinced their father was an embarrassing simpleton and that their only ladder of escape from Thunder Bay would be academics, scholarships in particular, because they'd never have money for higher education. 'You should put down your drawing pencils and pick up your grades,' Charlie said. But since her mother's death, Diane had felt divided from herself, ensconced, drained, mostly brainless, as though her life had become one protracted sigh.

Though she had no mind for schoolwork, Diane advanced into high school mainly because, she suspected, they wouldn't dare split the poor twins up. Charlie continued the fervency of his studies, planting his name on the honor roll each year and drilling himself after school with his dictionary and the door-stopping almanacs of trivia and crossword puzzles that he tore through nightly after completing his homework. It was as though he was burning through their collective ambitions himself, and in some way Diane eased the slow-blooming agony and confusion of losing her mother by taking shelter behind him, behind the battering ram of his anger and drive.

Because Thunder Bay was neither large nor moneyed enough to support a private high school, children from all walks of life were thrown together, and Charlie quickly struck up a friendship with Whalen Agnew, the son of one of the major stakeholders in the grain elevators on the Lakes, including Pool 6 — a tall boy with a high, regal forehead and grades almost as good as her brother's. Soon the two were as inseparable as the twins once were. Charlie would have Whalen over to study, visits for which Diane would spend the week beforehand cleaning, horrified by the thought of grain dust clinging to his finely cut pants as he sat before his potato-mound that she'd tried to enliven with a loaf of fresh-baked bread and a salad.

Then one summer day Whalen called while Charlie was at the library and asked her over to mend the pocket of a sport coat for him. Heart pounding, she hurried up the hill, terrified and thrilled by the prospect of nurturing a secret from her brother, who already demanded a complex, devoted loyalty from his best friend and would seethe if he found out they'd met without him.

They sat in Whalen's lush parlor, and she couldn't keep herself from running her fingers over the varnished moldings of his stately house, with its scrollworked furniture, leaded glass, and bookshelves loaded with fine editions of Victorian novels she then vowed to read someday. It was the first time she'd seen books in any concentration. But beside the glitter of wealth and knowledge, it was something in Whalen's face that gripped her. Or rather something that wasn't. None of her brother's fury or her father's skeptical reserve. Just a welcome blankness, like a pristine canvas she could brush her own story upon. After some polite discussion, she sewed his pocket, the stitches of which, thrillingly, seemed more snipped than worn, and as he was thanking her nervously in the foyer while she pulled on her raincoat, she suddenly took her brother's best friend by the shoulders and kissed him. His lips were dry and fragrant as fresh-sawn fir. This was the first time she'd felt real joy: the helium-filled skull, the thunderous heart, so similar to panic, but in lesser quantities it was pure pleasure. She pressed Whalen into the cashmere coats of the front closet until he shook and whispered that he'd give anything to see her again. She agreed and walked down the hill, flushed, wonderfully guilty of something for the first time in her life.

After that she and Whalen met secretly, mostly in his family's second car, parked in one of his father's disused industrial yards down near the elevators. They'd toss around in the car's mahogany-trimmed interior and scooped-out leather seats, then share American cigarettes afterwards, watching the lights of the moored lakeboats sizzle through the dark. How much of the thrill was sparked by that first betrayal of her brother and how much was her true affection for Whalen, she could not say today, but sitting in his car on those nights, it was as though the long-rusted gears of her own life had finally begun to turn.

Then at dinner one night, just a few weeks shy of their sixteenth birthday, Theodore suggested that upon their graduation the following spring, there would be a spot for Charlie at Pool 6. 'The grain trade is slowing,' Theodore said, 'but there're still more than a few good years left down there, son. It's a right good living.' Charlie excused himself, every little muscle in his face squirming with rage. Diane had watched Charlie send off early applications to the English Departments of the Universities of Toronto and British Columbia — his most sure-footed approaches to law school — and figured his acceptance was guaranteed. 'I want you to have options I didn't,' Theodore called to Charlie as he climbed the stairs.

Her brother may have viewed Thunder Bay as a trap to escape after their mother's death, but

Diane had no such ambitions. Whalen would be taking over one of his father's businesses, and though they'd yet to meet publicly, she believed there was a future for them, especially once Charlie was off at university. How strange it was, she'd often thought since, that she'd be the one to make it out of this place in the end, the one to accomplish things and see the world — only to fall back again, into a place even more dangerous and hopeless than the one they'd known.

Now with her mouth dry and rubbery from what must have been an hour of talking, Diane removed the goggles and clicked off the recorder, ending her Session early. But in the dance of light lingering in her eyes she found the phantom of Breughel's *Hunters in the Snow* — Theodore's favorite painting — a work she and Arthur once saw on a trip to New York: hunters returning to a village with their kill, one measly fox strung up, the rough men either pleased with their catch or gravely disappointed. Either proudly providing for their people or preparing to hunt *them*, one couldn't be sure.

She went downstairs, made tea, and sat in the chair with a good vantage of the front sidewalk. Will's class ended at 3:25. His walk usually took nine minutes. And it was already 3:46, which could mean anything, really, and she tried to pry her eyes from the clock as her mind was already spinning to the creek out back, him in it, wallowing among the rocks, then a flash of him lifeless and pale on the mucky bank, limp weeds and slugs crowding his mouth. She stood, took a long breath, pulled out her wrist elastic good and far, let it go, and assembled some calm in the sting.

Since she'd been scouring the paper for news of that orphan who'd gone missing, Thunder Bay had assumed an even more sinister timbre. Trucks slowing out front for children to pass now seemed menacing, carnivorous, and the woods behind their house, with its dismal, soldierly birches, seemed ever more ready to conscript her son and order him out into the trees. Of course, children went missing all the time in Toronto — yet somehow these tragedies blended into the noise of the city. Here it was close, intimate, like a terrible chime struck in your bedroom.

She walked again to the sink, poured out her tea, rinsed the cup, set it in the dish rack, after this realizing that she'd actually wanted it, so she flipped on the kettle again — for a moment terrified it would shock her — and stood with her hands on the counter, listening to it heat up like a jet fighter approaching from far off.

With a fresh cup steeping, she walked back to the window — *3:51* — her eyes scouring the street, the neighborhood's most attentive husbands already pulling into driveways to help out with dinner, but her son was still out there, and her breaths were coming sharp now, white bolts of fear zapping through her, scalding tea splashing on her shaky hand. She sat again in her chair. What she couldn't seem to evict from her mind, no matter how many Sessions she did, was the vestige of her brother Charlie she saw on her son's face that first afternoon he'd put on his slippers and stepped out the front door: a mere hint of his slanting grin — the slight angle of a pinball machine — and the stubborn resolve and angry ambition that in the end was his ruin — and with that her vision darkened, and her heart was a fist driving her repeatedly square in the chest, and she'd just reached to snap her elastic again when she heard the door come open and her son call out like any normal boy returning from school. Next came the thump of his backpack and the jangle of coat hangers in the hall closet, and she applied these comforting sounds to her black thoughts like a sonic brake pad, which allowed her to see his bright face swing around the corner, his hair so long now, swooping into his eyes, the color of wood grain, of wheat, and then he spoke, this small miracle of biology that for so long was only hers to witness: 'How's it going, Mom?'

7

A month passed, and the fall days chilled at their edges, warm only for a moment at noon. Each morning his mother would press the back of her lotioned hand to his cheek. 'You seem peakish,' she'd say. 'Why not stay home today — your immune system needs time to adapt.' Then she'd hurry off to Venice to fetch the thermometer. Yet despite her best efforts — she ordered once-illicit choke-prone foods like hot dogs and enticing films and art supplies, and even offered to get cable, including the movie channel — he never missed a day.

School itself was numbing, but not unpleasurably so. The building housed and sustained a great oceanic boredom, a boredom so vast it could be tasted. During the most tedious moments, he daydreamed of the freedoms he'd surrendered: languid afternoons of masterpiece painting in New York, his mother dropping a bowl of slow-cooked chicken stew beside his easel; later napping on the sun-warmed carpet in Cairo, the light pouring lava through his eyelids as she picked 'The House of the Rising Sun' at the table in Paris. Still, he loved how school was something all children were subject to, a plague to endure together. There was freedom in this unity. It rescued him from the worry of what to do next that had constantly tortured him at home.

His mother had said schools make you a cog in the machine. 'Another brick in the *wohll*,' she'd slur in a low English accent for some reason. But he liked the idea of being a brick in a wohll. It sounded cozy. Better that than being a brick sitting down in Toronto all by itself.

He enjoyed his morning walk and the din of his classmates, though they seldom addressed him and always scampered off before he'd completed a question. Homework consisted of blanks to put words and numbers in, like writing checks for deliverymen, but easier because you didn't lose money if you botched it. The tests kicked up tiny Black Lagoons that redlined his heart and flooded his mouth with the taste of sour aluminum. So far, As had evaded him because he couldn't scrape all the correct morsels from his mind before Mr. Miller snatched their tests away as though he rightly owned them.

Overall, the Outside was utterly boring and utterly astonishing at once and often exceeded Will's capacity to investigate it. At least once a week his heart bubbled over with beauty and fear, and he'd ask to go to the bathroom, where he'd weep mutely into wads of harsh, abrasive toilet paper. To mask his gaping deficits of understanding, Will's policy was to feign knowledge, to play the part of a normal boy, and nobody seemed to notice otherwise. Still, at times he was hit with a plummet of terror when he remembered he wasn't wearing a Helmet or that his classroom was neither New York nor San Francisco, but these instances diminished with each passing week, so he paid them less and less mind.

His mother was weathering his going to school better than he'd expected. Even so, he'd often return home to find her in Cairo staring blankly from the window out into the backyard, a full mug of forgotten tea steeping eternally beside her.

Marcus still hadn't turned up, and Will continually checked the paper, as well as the woods on his walk home, but came up empty. One Friday after school, Will built the courage to knock on some doors on his street to ask about the stolen hoses. As weird smells wafted from their Insides, several neighbors said the theft occurred around the same time a firecracker exploded on their doorstep. A diversion tactic, Will ingeniously deduced, but what did it have to do with Marcus's disappearance? Did he get caught? By who? Had he ignited himself with a match bomb? And what did such daring boys need with garden hoses anyway?

But Will made other discoveries and had to quell a thousand urges to report to his mother everything he learned. That the cleaning powder the janitors scoured onto their desks was called Comet, which for hours after emitted eye-stinging fumes and left other kids strangely unbothered. That the kids from Will's side of the highway, Grandview Gardens, had full pencil cases, new backpacks, and bright clothes; and kids from County Park, where most Indian kids lived, had pilly sweat suits and markers that dried up in a few days, even if capped religiously.

That, in general, teachers were warmer and more attentive to kids from Will's side, though this warmth didn't yet extend to him. That the many hockey players in his class were all named Tyler or Ryan or Chris, and they sat reeking lightly of sweat because of 6:00 a.m. practices. (Will had yet to detect his own odor, though his mother ordered him a deodorant spray that made him shudder when he tried it.) The hockey players walked stiff and upright, almost daintily, as though still wearing skates. They addressed everyone by last name exclusively and were forever administering a gauntlet of charley horses, punches to the triceps, and trips. They called a fight a 'scrap' and punches 'shots' — as though they were somehow medicinal.

Scraps happened in secret down near the culvert. It was the perfect place to bleed, Will figured, *outside* the Outside, because a kid's blood was something that all adults, not only his mother, couldn't bear. There after school Will witnessed his first real scrap when a blond hockey player named Tyler took a shot at Ritchie, the same boy who'd handed Will the match bomb by the creek. Even though none of the Indian kids at his school played hockey because the Kevlar pads cost a small fortune, both threw their mitts to the ground like on *Hockey Night in Canada* before grabbing collars and wailing. They were left red-faced, gulping tears, mustached with blood, yet somehow they survived. After the fight, Will happened upon Ritchie in the school bathroom, spitting into the sink. 'I think I swallowed some teeth,' he said.

'How many?' Will said, amazed that Ritchie didn't remember him, but too afraid to ask about Marcus. 'You tell me,' Ritchie said and grinned his big, dripping space. 'I don't know,' Will said, leaning in, 'maybe two? Three at the most.' 'Oh,' said Ritchie tonguing the gap, stringy like a carved pumpkin, 'that's not too bad.'

Will had also learned that a gift was a trap, like the match bomb. That 'Up there!' was mere precursor to a finger-thwack to the throat. After his first spritzing with Tahiti Treat offered by a popular hockey player, Will knew free sodas were definitely shaken. That to take bait demonstrated gullibility — the most childish, despicable sin there was.

Angela rallied with Will each morning at the base of the stairs. Since he'd turned over Jonah's least interesting drawing, the one of the grid, she was his sole friend, at least while at school. Best of all, she never asked questions about his mother, questions he couldn't answer without sounding freakish. Despite her low social perch, or perhaps because of it, Angela proved an invaluable informant. She identified the Twins he'd met by the creek as the Belcourt Twins, who were already in a special high school. 'The one for kids who are probably graduating to Stony Mountain,' she said, which was a federal prison in Manitoba and not the mountain-dwarf fortress Will had invented when he was young.

'Why do you care so much about that kid?' she said when Will inquired again about Marcus. She squinted: 'Are you a flamer?'

'No, I didn't touch any of their matches, I

95

swear,' Will said. 'Look, we're, like, friends.'

She scoffed and pushed her eyebrows up near her glossy hairline. 'Doubt it,' she said, then leaned in and whispered: 'But I asked my brother and he said your little *friend* has got himself mixed up with criminals, like *adult* ones? He pissed somebody off, *bad*.'

'How?' Will said, remembering the way Marcus had defended himself so fiercely with his slingshot when they first met. 'By stealing their garden hose?'

Angela drove up her eyebrows again, crinkling her forehead, which she did whenever she thought he'd said something weird, which was most of the time. 'Anyway. Kids say he's not missing. He just hates his foster home. They see him all over. In parks at night and abandoned buildings and under bridges. They say he's living somewhere in the woods and eats berries and drinks deer blood for breakfast.'

'Hiding? Like Outside? Where?' Will asked, fascinated by the notion that the Outside could actually be inhabited for any sustained duration.

'Who knows,' she said, sighing, already bored. 'Anyway, kids are coming and going from his foster home all the time,' she added. 'Maybe he got transferred to another one and they just forgot.' Will would've visited this foster home, but the thought of the journey through the culvert to County Park withered him.

Angela ate her lunch from a long store-bought bread bag — always just four margarined slices, usually including the heel. She didn't have a mother, a condition Will found unimaginable.

96

Her mother had hopped into an old boyfriend's semi-truck cab the very day Angela stopped nursing. Now her father, a former railway ticket agent, spent his days on their stoop soaking his insides with a flammable grain alcohol he procured down near the harbor. 'Why wouldn't he just find you another mom?' Will had asked when she told him. 'There are women everywhere Outside.' Angela's face darkened and she said she had to go Inside for her treatments.

Angela had a disease, something to do with phlegm stuck in her lungs like mortar. Her breath crackled like buckshot on the rare occasions she laughed unmockingly. The school nurse had to go at her chest with a vibrating wand every afternoon during lunch. Whenever Will considered the traffic jam Inside Angela, he had to fight the urge to cough.

'The treatments are okay,' she said. 'I think about Jonah while they do it.'

'Are your hands free to draw masterpieces?'

She gave him another scrutinizing grimace. 'You're weird because you talk too much and say weird things. You shouldn't do that.' Then she asked him if he liked anyone in class, by which she actually meant their vaginas.

He said he was going to wait until someone liked him.

'Girls don't work like that,' she said.

'How do they work?'

'Wouldn't you like to know,' she said, waving her head like a cobra.

What he knew about girls was that they closed ranks and whispered malevolently out of earshot.

They spritzed their architecturally sculpted bangs with complex bottles. There were rumors they had been making bracelets.

Angela said the reason that nobody talked to Will was because he was a pussy and a baby who still slept with his mother, which he did, actually, but he'd set up a cot in New York and could tolerate the occasional night there. He wondered how his classmates knew and hoped it was only a good guess.

While sharpening his pencil, Will often looked out over Thunder Bay, his eyes skiing down the hill and over the steppes of asphalt-shingled roofs, brown, black, and green, each sheltering an entirely different Inside of their own (he still couldn't believe there could be so *many* Insides), then down to the monstrous cloud-wrapped lake and the tired, shabby buildings that kneeled beside it. Like the creek, Thunder Bay had proved smaller than he imagined. 'It was once a charmed place. Now it's just an old rusty ruin' was something his mother said so often it sounded like an official slogan. But he liked the ruined parts, best of all the empty grain elevators that the newspaper called a blight, standing like foreclosed castles near the shore now edged with ice. He decided that if he ever somehow became as good an artist as Jonah, they would be the first real masterpiece he'd paint.

In rare but uncomfortably emotional digressions from his lesson plan, Mr. Miller professed that he'd worked at the elevators to put himself through teachers college and couldn't bear to see them empty today — but Will only caught half of it because it sounded too much like history, which was actually Mr. Miller opining about how much better things were before he got old and had to give speeches to uninterested children every weekday.

Then one Friday morning the janitor brought Will a new desk and placed it in the row beside Jonah's. When Jonah Turtle entered the classroom, Will recognized him instantly as the same boy who'd told him to walk away from Ritchie that day by the creek. Jonah was tall, with thick, swooping eyebrows, and he moved precisely, with a startling elegance, like a gymnast on a beam. He wore a button-up cardigan over old T-shirts and leather old-man shoes, not sneakers. His skin was like gingerbread, darker than Marcus's, and he had close-cropped black hair except for long bangs that often dangled in his eyes dramatically like a cape, which he then hooked effortlessly behind his ear, as if they had been grown expressly for that purpose.

Will observed Jonah during art class that day, which was more like cooking than making masterpieces: Mr. Miller drew the recipe on the board with a meter stick and colored chalk, and the class was expected to replicate it. Today's recipe called for tissue paper to be wrapped over the ends of pencils, then glued in bunches to toilet paper rolls. A Christmas ornament, he said.

Now glue was mixing with the tissue paper pigment and seeping onto Will's toilet paper roll, while Jonah's ornament was perfect, orderly rows of spiraling color. After wringing out their magic in private, Will had finally hung Jonah's masterpieces in New York, and his mother complimented them as 'an interesting new direction in realism.' Will had practiced his own masterpieces of skateboarders and skulls, but they were warped and unconvincing. He could do color fields and free splatters, but never anything real. Lately, Will had begun to question his genius-hood, mostly because there were so many things he clearly sucked at: throwing (anything with his arms), drawing, remembering to bring both his lunch and pencil case to school, math, vaginas, spelling (his mother maintained it was *what you mean* that mattered), and compared with that of his classmates, his cursive looked like an earthquake readout. But if Will did have a special power, it was his ability to see the Black Lagoon everywhere. He could tell that Mr. Miller was actually afraid of his students, and they didn't fear him nearly as much as they did failing a grade and falling behind their friends. And that Angela was afraid both of silence and of having nobody to talk to, and that someday her disease would forbid her to breathe. Will had imagined there'd be less fear Outside, but everyone was afraid all the time: of failure, humiliation, harm, though he was still working out in what order. Jonah, however, in his silence that even Mr. Miller respected, didn't seem to fear anything.

★ ★ ★

100

Later that day at recess, Will and Angela were standing around as usual, drowning the interval with half-meant words. 'I think he'd talk to you,' Angela said, gesturing toward Jonah, who was drawing with fingerless gloves on, his skateboard at his side, near the big rock at the fringe of the schoolyard. 'You have lots in common,' Angela added.

'Like what? Being weird?'

'You're both artistic.'

Will scoffed but accepted it greedily as the first compliment he'd garnered in probably his entire life from someone other than his mother or a deliveryman (those were more for his mother). At home his mother produced praise like water from a tap, and it was just as tasteless.

'Why don't you talk to him?' said Will.

'All I've ever had him do was hiss at me. It was the *sexiest*.' Angela then said Jonah lived in County Park, too, though he didn't take the bus. He skateboarded brazenly through the culvert, which was dangerous because of the hobos and vagrants often lurking there. Jonah didn't have parents and was the youngest of five brothers, who were thieves, thugs, and bootleggers, either in prison, going to prison, or recently released. Angela said a hockey player from the other side of town once whipped Jonah's face with a birch switch. The next morning the eldest Turtle Brother showed up at the kid's house and asked the boy's father to have his son write a letter of apology. When the man refused, Jonah's brother broke the man's cheekbones, as well as those of two neighbors who came to help, then sat on the curb and waited for the police. On the schoolyard Jonah was untouchable, like a hockey referee who never blew his whistle.

'But why would he talk to *me*?' said Will.

'Maybe he'll recognize a fellow artist,' she said.

'Okay,' said Will, already walking.

'Really?' she called after him. 'Don't say anything about me!' she crowed, wringing her hands.

'Thanks for telling me to walk away that day by the creek,' Will said when he reached him. 'You saved my life.'

Jonah's leg stopped bouncing, and his large liquid eyes rose from his sketchbook and fastened calmly on Will's. He had an angular face, as though his features were constructed entirely of wedges.

Waiting for some reaction, Will began to feel even more lost and unprepared for conversation than usual. He already preferred kids like Angela, who commandeered airtime like a seasoned radio host. Jonah blinked slowly, then returned to sketching.

'So why don't you talk?' Will said.

Jonah pumped his shoulders once, leaning into his masterpiece.

'You talk at home?'

Jonah nodded, pencil wiggling.

'You just don't talk at school?'

He shook his head and brought the pencil parallel to the page and began shading. The Indian kids at Will's school all rarely spoke, and when they did it was in voices barely audible and with downcast, skeptical eyes, as though the Outside was one big courtroom in which they were on trial. Will stood marveling at the evenness of Jonah's shadows, their texture, how he knew exactly where light wasn't.

'I like your masterpieces,' Will said.

Jonah looked up again. His face crinkled. He took a breath, then held it and squinted harder. 'My what?' he said. His voice was soft and fast, built entirely of smooth tones like the high notes on a bass.

'Your masterpieces,' said Will. 'I saw some when I was sitting in your desk. They're amazing.'

'Leave me alone, kid,' Jonah said dispassionately, shaking his head as though they'd been conversing for hours, trying to untangle some tricky problem, and Jonah had finally reached his limit. He retreated again to his sketchbook.

Will watched him for a defeated moment before making his way back to Angela.

That night at home, Will let his slow-cooked butternut squash enchiladas cool untouched before him. He saw his mother quake at the sight of his uneaten food, almost savoring this new power of refusal he wielded over her.

'Why did you tell me that pictures are called 'masterpieces'?' he said.

'Oh,' she said, setting her fork down. 'That.' She snapped her elastic, and he resisted the urge to ask why the hell was that question scary. 'Well, because that's what they really are.'

'No, they're not,' he said sharply. Since he'd been going to school, there arrived inexplicable moments when just the timbre of her voice was enough to irrigate him with rage, moments that passed as quickly as they came.

'To me they are.'

'Well, to other people they aren't, like people who are actually good artists,' he said, throwing his napkin at his plate. 'And there's more of them than us, Mom.'

8

Snow fell every day after Halloween, as though the lake had picked itself up and thrown itself inland, snuffing instantly the vivid bonfire of fall. Inside, Will had only felt the cold of the freezer in Toronto, but now immersed in it, he adored the completeness winter brought. Snow made the Outside more like the Inside, a white sheet put over the world, one enormous blanket fort.

Will whiled away hours in his yard, investigating snowbanks, testing their crusts and consistencies, reconnoitering their cliffs and drifts. He discovered snow wasn't tasteless — it tasted like club soda, but not as gross. And slush was so named because of the sound it made. And the sand that plows threw on the road yielded a substance that was half earth, half ice and the deceptively inviting consistency of brown sugar.

His mother had forbidden tunnel forts, so he left his open to the sky. While she peered out from the window in Paris, Will would recline in his burrow, watching frizzy clouds saunter past, wondering if his friend Marcus lay somewhere Outside exactly like this, turning his face to the same endless sky, untroubled that no one was there to protect him. Over the years, Will's mother had read him a thousand stories about orphans torn from their parents and abandoned to the wilds of the Outside. Will had never had that problem. His had been the opposite: too much protection. But like the twelve and the one on a clock's face, he and Marcus were closer to each other than you'd think — 'Other Will,' he'd called him at first. Will had since heard Angela use Marcus's word, *whatever*, to express a complete indifference, but Will could still hear the true tenderness with which Marcus had offered it. *Nothing can really hurt you, Will*, Marcus had said, and Will knew his friend was alive somewhere, Outside, thriving.

★　★　★

Weeks passed. Winter strayed into a truer, purer cold. Will's morning walks were so frigid the ice chirped underfoot like plastic. The air shocked his chest, and a satanic wind bellowed through the elevators up from the lake, now frozen out to the breakwater.

One day before school, his mother began stuffing some packets into his jacket and snow pants. 'What's this?' he said.

'I ordered a box. Hand warmers. Neat, huh?' she said, bending one until it snapped before shoving it into his armpit as though he were a shoplifting accomplice.

His mother knew nothing of winter. To her, the season rendered the world even more predatory. She'd told him about a book she'd read in film school that claimed that because nature was always trying to kill Canadians it made them different from other people. 'In Thunder Bay, you doze off in a snowbank'

— she'd say before making a sharp teeth-whistle — 'that's it.' But he'd napped in his snow fort several times and woken unscathed, which meant both she and whoever wrote that book didn't know what the hell they were talking about. His mother had already exaggerated so many dangers that Will was finding it increasingly difficult to heed her warnings.

On his way to school a hand warmer slipped down into his crotch, yielding the sudden sensation he'd wet himself. Soon he was flushed, dripping with sweat that froze in his bangs like the mousse that had recently materialized in the hair of his classmates. He dumped the warmers along with his gloves, knit cap, and snow pants in the trees before making his way up the path.

At school there was an unspoken contest among boys to see who could brave the frost with the least protective clothing. Their ears went red as stove elements while their cheeks cramped a bloodless white. Jonah — who wouldn't even look at Will after the masterpiece incident — wore just a hooded sweatshirt and old-man shoes, maybe because he was stylish or maybe because his winter clothing had burned in the house fire. Either way, in the school-wide tournament to be the least appropriately dressed yet still alive, Jonah won.

That afternoon, Mr. Miller asked Will to stay after class. He'd seemed a little ragged all day and was sipping from a mug that wasn't steaming and smelled vaguely of the fluid Will's mother used to clean her silver jewelry. 'Will, I wanted to say you're settling in just fine here,' he began. 'Your work is improving. I can even read your printing now, which is a minor miracle.'

Will said thanks and turned to go. Time spent in the direct spotlight of any adult always sent him cowering for the anonymity of a herd of children.

'Another thing, Will. I thought I recognized your last name — who wouldn't in Thunder Bay. But I wanted to say I'm happy your mother decided to move back home from — where was it? San Francisco? I heard she'd done well for herself. 'Course the only way to accomplish that nowadays is to leave,' Mr. Miller said, letting out the fumes of a great sigh that waggled the pink stalactite between his front teeth as he looked out the window to the lake. 'I worked under her father and remember her and her brother from the harbor and, well, it was a shame. What happened. I think all of Thunder Bay . . . Well, we felt for those two.' Then his voice went gravelly. 'Coming back took guts.'

Will did the chuckling thing he'd picked up from Angela. 'Sorry, but you've got the wrong Cardiels, sir,' he said. 'It's just me and my mom. Always has been. And she grew up in Toronto.' To this Mr. Miller apologized, and Will made his escape.

★   ★   ★

When the biggest snow came, a billion flakes corkscrewed slow to the ground. Cars disappeared. Will watched his neighbors dent their truck with shovels trying to locate it. Out back,

Will found the mud on the creek bank flash-frozen and iron-hard like the gravied entrée of a TV dinner. He watched ice creep out from its banks, first like awnings, then with icy fingers across the narrows.

It was thanks to these winter investigations that Will discovered the boot tracks in his backyard. They were too big to be Marcus's, nearly double the length of his own, and fresh. They came up from the creek through a gap in the hedge, then stopped about ten feet from the window beneath San Francisco, right near where he'd found Marcus. The closest footprints were packed tighter than the others, toes aimed houseward. The person had stood in that spot for some time, observing, and at the midpoint of the tread, a distinct hexagonal shape was sculpted deep and clean in the snow.

Will followed the tracks westward along the creek, down toward the lake, wondering if it could've been a yeti — who weren't real, but still — or a deliveryman, or the ferrety gas meter reader, or perhaps one of the gruff, unemployed men who rang their bell with pitifully affordable offers to plow their driveway, men his mother always hired and tipped extravagantly. But what would any of them be doing approaching their house from the creek?

Emerging from the woods near the hockey arena, Will lost the trail in the tire print nebulas of its parking lot.

Relaxation Time

Today she ended her Session early when an image of her twin brother's wrecked body lifting from the black lake cut into her thoughts and left her nauseous. While cleaning up at the sink, she recalled her very first glimpse of Will's blood, in the hospital mere minutes after his birth. A test for blood sugar, the nurse said, roughly squeezing a lustrous ladybug from his pricked heel. Arthur, already depleted by the ordeal and itching to return to his drafting table, went ghostly when he saw it, but Diane's only thought was: *A more precious substance I cannot imagine.* The blood was so recently hers — she wondered if she could still rightly call it her own — and had only become more valuable now that it had left her.

Initially at least, she was happy having a boy. Boys seemed more durable, less finicky. Will's birth somehow eclipsed the tragedies of her past — her chief responsibility now being to ensure he didn't taste abandonment as she had. He fascinated her like no book or film or idea had before. She spent hours watching him in his crib, parsing his overwhelming actuality. Each night she read to him, his eyes waltzing in wonder, until her throat was hoarse, until his book's covers detached, until she'd memorized every word, then until he'd memorized them himself. 'That?' was his first word, said pointing at a page. They spent hours speculating what would happen after the story ended. She ceased reading adult books entirely, her most private thoughts taking the shape of children's stories. Gone were ideas for films, the cinematic visions once gifted to her upon waking or during long walks in the city, but she offered her mind gladly to the chaos a child brought, to the endless tidying and banter, to the horrors these perform on creative inspiration.

Then came learning to walk, all that totter and tumble. Will's first unmoored voyage from coffee table to couch — *relentless* was a word whose true meaning he'd taught her. The cracked heads, bashed elbows, and rug burns; the way Will rose, bloody dirt in his teeth, that little lung-sucking storm before the big show. Motherhood acutely sensitized her to the menaces of the world: the murderous table corners, the seduction of electrical outlets, the friendly dogs that snap gladly at tiny fingers.

How precariously blood moves through us, she thought now soaping her shaking hands in the bathroom. We spring a small leak and lose ourselves to the ground. And how dearly we depend on the lone muscle convulsing in our chests. On the two flimsy balloons that so narrowly rescue us from suffocation. On the wobbly pâté in our heads that preserves our very selves. All of it so ad hoc, so absurd, so temporary.

In the hallway she heard a curious scratching emanating from Will's studio — New York, he called it. A welcome sound. With Will away at school during the day now, like a planet unhitched from orbit, the house had fallen into gloom and silence, even though she'd begun leaving the kitchen radio on and often consulted Will aloud while vacuuming or staking her window-box tomatoes as though he'd never left. Still, the days felt doubly long. She missed his industry and his mind-bending questions ('Is it murder if your friend agrees to let you cut off his hand and then you strangle someone with it?') and had to settle for burying her face in the plush, boyish scent of his bedding several times per day.

She opened the door to New York and found him rubbing 40-grit sandpaper over the grips of the new snow boots she'd ordered, a prisoner's file beside him, blue rubber bits splayed on his easel and already ground into the carpet at his feet.

'What's going on, Will?'

'Oh, hey,' he said, startled for a second. Then it passed. 'Grips are actually really hard to get off,' he continued, returning to the task.

'But Will,' she said, pulling a troubled breath, 'you're destroying your boots. We just had those delivered, and now you're — '

' — Making them better,' he interjected.

'Grips are supposed to . . . what? Any idea?' she said with an ineffectual elastic snap. And in an instant she saw Charlie hurtling down a still-icy Machar Avenue in early spring, pedaling for broke on a bicycle he'd only just learned how to ride, his coarse hair a wildfire in the wind, with Theodore jogging behind bellowing

112

complex instructions and warnings, mere seconds before Charlie would crash into a yellow hydrant, folding his nose flat to his cheek and forcing their family's painful return to the hospital, where their mother had taken her last breath not three weeks previous.

'I'm making them more exciting,' Will said.

'*Grip*, Will. That's what they *do*,' she said.

'Not always,' he said.

'And why may I ask are you ruining your boots?' she said, putting her hands to her hips more to steady them than to appear commanding.

'For nothing.'

'So why, then?'

His eyes fastened on hers. 'Because they're mine to ruin.'

'You remember who buys those boots,' she said, guiltily reminding herself of Theodore.

'So send them back,' Will retorted. He held the boots up, one on each hand. 'I'll go barefoot, then.'

'You are going to snap your neck is what's going to happen. You're going to slide your way all the way down to the harbor and' — she felt her voice go shrill and her blood surge as she watched Charlie descending into a grain bin with only his grin and his daring to save him, then stepping out the door the night that he —

'Stop yelling, Mom,' Will said.

Had she been yelling? She apologized, drawing her hands to her face, fighting anew to keep the images from overthrowing her mind.

'Mom,' he said in a voice so wounded and

adult that it shocked her, 'it's like you're not actually worried *about* me. It's more like you're scared *of* me.'

With that all her panic and anger dissolved. She closed her eyes, preparing a rational, level-headed exhibit of the ways in which her son was sorely mistaken, a response that would assure her dear boy of this notion's utter preposterousness — afraid of *her son*? She was afraid of about everything else! — until a vapor of images swooped again in her, stories from another life, grain pouring from a hopper, a train, a cable, a subway platform, a staccato dream she'd had so many times it had become her: a son torn wordlessly from her breast, dragged back from their house into the woods by phantom figures to be devoured while no one made so much as a sound — neither she from the window, nor he from the dark. 'I'm not afraid of you, honey,' she managed to get out, black spots speckling her vision as she backpedaled from the room.

How could she tell him that to have lost a twin was to be half-erased? To be dead by proxy. That when another version of your very self had failed, had been evicted from the world and pushed back into the dark, what less bitter end could be hoped for, for those you love? How could you ever expect a child to comprehend how easily, *how unnecessarily*, a loved one can be torn from your arms and how it can leave you ruined forever?

So whether she was scared *for* him, or *of* him, it mattered little. Her job was still the same: To build them a world that death could never touch.

114

9

It didn't matter that Will had yet to secure a single Outside friend other than Angela and that he was no closer to finding Marcus or catching whoever was sneaking around his yard, because he had become the most electrifying practitioner in the short but storied schoolyard pantheon of ice sliding.

After the big snow came an oddly brief warming, followed by a temperature plummet of migraine cold that left the hill that butted their school enameled with ice. Originally, he'd sanded his boots smooth to render his tracks untraceable during his investigations, but he soon found alternate uses. When he took a big run and set his feet, not even the best hockey players could match his daring or his distance — the whole hill, nearly to the footpath. Helmetless and unafraid, Will could dance, spin, slide backwards, and do 360s on one foot. For weeks he'd executed the miracles of his slides at recess, the envious gazes of the entire school upon him. Little did they know that to his mother's horror he trudged back up the hill on weekends to practice until dusk, hands frozen talon-like inside his sheepskin mitts.

The only classmate who came close to matching Will's prowess was Jonah. Though he lacked special boots, his old-man shoes served him well, and Will attributed his uncanny balance to that skateboard he kept with him. Though they never spoke, their daring was a bond, a pact. Will now saw something saintly in Jonah's silence. He hid his voice the way Will's mother hid her body, except Jonah had made *himself* the place he never left, which Will envied but couldn't emulate, because having spent his whole life Inside, he couldn't keep his mouth shut.

The day before Christmas break, Will was working on sliding in a squat, one leg extended before him — 'the Cossack,' he called it — as a crowd of students looked on. Jonah watched sagely from the hill's margin, where he stashed his skateboard and backpack, brushing a fuzz of ice from his jeans. As Will climbed again to the summit, a dog meandered onto the schoolyard. It pranced down in the middle section where the hill leveled, the spot where Will liked to unleash his jumps.

Will paced back from the hill, turned, bolted forward, and braced his feet into a slide. As he descended the slope, lowering into a crouch, the dog barked, ear splitting and sharp, then veered over toward where Jonah was. Will heard the supervising teacher call out, backhanding the air in a shooing motion.

The dog paused, then bounded over and snatched Jonah's backpack in its mouth, recoiling exactly into Will's path, a path that, even with his skill and superior balance, was now impossible to alter. As Will thundered closer, the dog grew and resolved, its coat winterized and bristly. Jonah had his hand out and was

116

approaching the dog cautiously. Taking no notice of Will, the dog lowered itself and dropped the backpack to bare its wicked teeth.

Will decided to go down, his first time off his feet in weeks, the ice hot and abrasive through his pants. He dug in his boot heels, traumatizing his eyes with sparks of frost. At the mercy of the ice now, claimed by it, and mere feet from the beast, Will realized that the creature was not necessarily a dog. Trying to draw realistically like Jonah, he'd studied intently the physiology of wolves, their thick, curved backs and rod-straight tails, their teeth visibly protruding from closed mouths, and this creature bore a worrisome resemblance.

Just before they collided, Will clutched a blurry hope that he might befriend this wolf, take it for his own, harness it to a sled or teach it tricks, until he struck its bony legs like a quartet of bowling pins, and in the impact felt skin and fur slide over hard ribs, and the thing yipped, sounding less like a dog, more like an electrocuted man. They slid together, the beast writhing upon him, Will's body a toboggan to it.

Before the next downslope they drew to a halt. Still inverted, the wolf thrashed as though trying to snap its own spine. Then over him, ears flattened, an avenging growl chugging inside it like a lawnmower, its narrowed golden eyes dead as marbles, it lashed and tore at Will's chest, recoiling with a mouthful of white polyfill, his jacket's guts. It jawed the material, puzzled by the taste. Then as Will attempted to roll away came a dull clamp on his thigh. He'd never played with a dog before, had never felt measured play-bites on his arms and hands, so it would've been easy to think that the wolf was playing, except for the sudden dagger of pain that delivered him to the truth. The wolf commenced a series of neck jerks, as if there was something stuck in Will's leg that it rightly owned and was trying to reclaim. The cadence quickened and Will could feel himself coming loose. Searching, he spotted a figure in the fringe of trees, a stout, bald man, and Will tried to call out to him but could not find his voice. It occurred to Will that Marcus could've already died like this, devoured, with no adult to save him, dragged between the frozen trees by a hundred sets of teeth. Just as the pain paralyzed him, the beast relinquished his leg, and Will clutched his neck with interlocked hands, as though performing sit-ups on his side. It sniffed at his neck, breath passing hot over his ear with the sound of blowing over a microphone. Maybe, Will mused in the crude blur, though his Outside courage was growing daily, the scent of Black Lagoon still lingered upon him, the strongest perfume the wolf ever imagined, drawing it to him like a magnet. His mother had read him stories of wolf packs raising lost boys in the Arctic, but they were always orphans like Marcus, boys already wounded, abandoned. Never happy boys. Will wondered for an instant what sort he was. And then a voice, too indistinct to parse, and Will's head knocked terrifically hard, while the wolf yelped and flew upwards in a poof of snow. It walloped to its side a few feet from Will, stopped from rolling by stiffened legs. Over Will was Jonah, posed in the balletic follow-through of a great arcing kick, his old-man shoe nearly shoulder height, hands open and loose beside him like a dancer's. As the wolf struggled, Jonah recaptured his balance, then unleashed a two-footed leap that landed him square on the wolf's rib cage with the sound of dry kindling.

A teacher was over Will saying *my goodness* in repetition, forklifting him from the ground in her arms. A void now in his thigh, more troubling than the pain it replaced, and beyond that, wetness. He watched his blood bounce like beads of mercury on the ice.

A policeman was already waiting in the principal's office. Soon paramedics were treating Will's thigh with an enormous dressing that crinkled like a diaper. Will overheard the teacher and the principal discuss how to manage what Jonah had done, whether discipline was required.

'That Turtle boy left that wolf a sorry sight, but we'd have put it down regardless,' said Constable MacVicar, the one who'd never returned Will's call about Marcus.

'We don't have a phone number on file for you, Will,' said the principal, receiver in hand, 'What is it?'

'No idea,' Will said through his teeth as the stoic paramedic eased him upright.

The principal glanced to the secretary.

'Here, son,' Constable MacVicar said, 'I'll get you home.'

Will passed out for a spell in the police car, the

squawking radio recalling the taxi cabs he now dimly recalled taking with his mother long ago, and awoke levitating in MacVicar's arms as they approached his front steps. 'I remember when your mother and your uncle bought this place,' MacVicar said, examining the golden-lit window in San Francisco. 'Nobody could believe they did it themselves. That was one determined fella.' Then Will's mother appeared, framed by a rectangle of doorway, green bathrobe over what looked like nakedness. As Will rose dreamily up the front stairs she was yelling and also crying, the sight of his mauled leg striking her as though with invisible blows. Soon she was saying the word *lawsuits* while also referring to Marcus, or 'that poor boy who disappeared.' She calmed for a moment and asked why MacVicar couldn't protect her son. 'That's your job, isn't it?' she screeched when the constable left the question unanswered, repeating '*Isn't it?*' as he retreated to his cruiser like a man in a downpour.

'We can't save them from themselves, Ms. Cardiel,' he said at last, popping his door.

Safely Inside, his mother set the deadbolt and embraced Will hungrily, then pushed him back, locking her elbows, almost to ensure he was her son, and not some counterfeit boy, before yanking him close again.

She helped him hop to Venice, where she snipped away the dressing and Will glimpsed two ivory-edged canyons in his thigh before she covered them like an obscenity. After wrapping his wound in a mile of gauze, she dragged the couch from Cairo into San Francisco and

120

positioned it beside their bed. She set up the 16mm projector and brought him snacks and made double-cheese slow-cooker lasagna for dinner.

Later, while they watched a film, she sat close, compulsively testing his bones and kneading his muscles, inventory-taking, pushing the hair from his brow, as though its roughness could harm his skin.

Over the following days, he watched films and swallowed the pain pills she rattled out, drifting into murky reveries of wolves ripping soundless through his school, fast as lava, lifting the weakest of his classmates from their desks, and he saw again the Bald Man he'd spied in the woods while he was attacked. He'd wake in San Francisco to find her tidying, moving things from one side of the room to the other. When she left, he'd call for her, and she'd return within ten seconds; he timed her. She drank tea from her masterpiece mug, and he sipped her special limeade that she hand-squeezed for him, in which he could taste the faint hint of her hand lotion. He requested meat for dinner every night in the belief it would mend his leg.

When he finally massed the strength to hobble to Venice, Will found his mother crying in the empty tub, tears jeweling her eyelashes.

'I cut myself chopping onions,' she said, wrapping her finger with the tissue she'd been blowing her nose with.

'Is it bleeding?' Will asked. 'You need stitches?'
She shook her head.
'Can I see it?'

Again she shook her head shamefully, like Angela the time Mr. Miller asked her for homework she hadn't completed because her father kept her awake all night yelling.

Will hobbled to the fireplace in Cairo and returned with the poker that of course they'd never used. 'Don't worry, Mom,' he said, poker raised, conjuring an image of the boot prints in the yard and the wolf and the Bald Man, 'I'll kill anyone who comes in here, if that's what you're afraid of. A wolf or a person or anyone.'

'Please put that down, Will,' she said wearily. 'Nobody is coming in here.'

Will complied and climbed over the tub's edge and nestled into the crook of her arm, her smell the same as always: yellowy paperbacks and cinnamon and fresh laundry. She leaned in and kissed his hair, the old comfort swirling in him, her clean breath and her pale hands cool on his belly.

'Are you crying about me?' he said, not yet entirely thinking, the warmth of her body and the pain pills loosening the tethers of his tongue, 'or your brother?'

He felt her stiffen.

'What was his name, Mom?' Will said, sleepily.

She let out a long, weary breath. 'His name was Charlie,' she said. 'My twin.'

'Like in my dictionary?'

'It was his,' she said. 'He liked words. Especially odd ones.'

'MacVicar said you bought this house together?'

'We did,' she said. 'Though it was mostly his money.'

'So you lived *here* as a girl? In this house? Not in Toronto?'

'No, we grew up near the harbor, in another house, until we moved here together. But you were born in Toronto, Will, where I met your dad. When you were very little, you and I came back to sell this place, and well . . . we stayed.'

'Why didn't you tell me about him, Mom? Did something happen?'

'Some things aren't easy to talk about, Will. And I didn't . . . I didn't want to worry you,' she said, squeezing him.

'I'm not worried,' he said in his most reassuring voice, smoothing the nest of her hair, struck by the strange sensation that he was at this moment not her son, but her father. 'I'm going to be okay. I may not be a genius, but I'm getting stronger Outside. Nothing can really hurt me,' he said, quoting Marcus. 'Not even that wolf.'

She pulled away, wiped her eyes, snapped her elastic, and shuddered. 'Will,' she said, 'come with me.'

He followed her to San Francisco, where she sat him on the bed. She reached to a high shelf in her closet, producing a yellow envelope, from which she extracted a few papers. Letters from a doctor, she said. 'You were tested when you were a baby, honey, and there is something not quite right about your heart. The valves. Like a murmur, but worse. I didn't want to scare you. That's why I kept it from you all this time. I know I haven't told you much about our family . . . but we aren't the luckiest people.'

123

Will drew his hand between the lapels of his pajamas and palmed his sternum. 'Is that how Charlie . . . '

She shut her eyes and nodded.

'Could *I* . . . *die* of it?'

Her eyes got pained, and she lifted her chin up slow, then let it down even slower with her lips pursed.

'How easy?'

She dropped her head. 'They didn't say.'

'What do you mean they didn't say?'

Her face darkened, and she began to shake, a fresh tide of Black Lagoon cresting in her, shoving her nearer to the shoals of permanent breakdown. 'You'll be fine,' she said. 'I always knew you'd leave someday. Just be careful out there. That's all I ask.'

'I will, Mom,' he said. 'I promise.'

That night after she dropped asleep in his arms in San Francisco, he got up and stashed the fire poker under his cot in New York. One thing he'd learned thus far was that the border between the Inside and the Outside wasn't as impermeable as she liked to believe. He knew that sooner or later, the Outside would want in.

When Christmas break was over, his mother called the school secretary and said Will was going to need more time to recuperate, months, years — the doctors weren't sure. After that they slipped back into the old routine. She ordered fresh art supplies, Will rolling in the desk chair to meet deliverymen at the door, the acrylic tubes still cold in their hands. She ordered Will any

124

food he wanted, even tortilla chips, the choke equivalent of the A-bomb.

She lowered his easel, and he painted while seated with his Helmet on, cranking out a series in the old style — abstract whirls and smears of gold and purple — more to soothe her nerves. He spent more time titling his works than painting them:

- *Sailing a Sea of Wolves*
- *The Surprising Nutritiousness of Jam*
- *Canadian Ninja I: Strikeforce Cobra*
- *Canadian Ninja II: Sais Extra Large*
- *Zeus vs. Jesus: Thunderbolt Rotisserie*
- *Boy, Eleven, Riddled with Spears, Survives Unscathed*

He watched his hunched schoolmates with pity as they passed his house in the dark mornings. The only Outside people he missed were Jonah, Angela, and of course Marcus. But even after their ice sliding and fight with the wolf, Jonah still wouldn't talk to him. One night Will located Angela's number in the phone book, fantasizing about having her over for smoothies and playing her some of his Sound Collages or his Philip Glass-style compositions on the organ (repeating three-note motifs that went on for as long as his fingers could manage) before they'd retreat for some cuddling in New York. But he never called.

Soon his leg grew unbearably itchy, but strong enough to perform his old duties: laundry in Toronto, changing bulbs, writing checks for deliverymen — filling the gaps left by the Black Lagoon. He found his mother weeping less, no longer distracted by a sound he could not hear, like a dog whistle or what was good about jazz music.

He retained his limp past the point he needed, and when he finally allowed it to fall away like training wheels unbolted from a bicycle, he felt her grow tense. But still he made no attempt to leave. Overall, his life Outside had mostly been a disappointment. He hadn't found Marcus or joined any boy gangs or used his genius to solve any mysteries. He'd found only questions piled upon questions, with no connections or sense to it — just Black Lagooned people fumbling around in the dark, alone.

He knew now how selfish it was to leave. His body wasn't only his. Because they were twins, his uncle Charlie's body had been partly his mother's too. And Will couldn't wound her like that again. To be her guardian he would need to protect his body and his heart. As much as it pained him, he would have to leave all the tantalizing mysteries of the Outside unsolved.

Marcus would have to find himself.

Relaxation Time

Charlie. At once a dreadful curse and a holy utterance. Unfortunately for Diane, saying it to Will for the first time, coupled with the sight of his little thigh splayed open, had unbolted a door in her mind.

Yes, she'd lied. But how else could she explain to Will that the reason he had no extended family — no cousins, uncles, or grandparents — was that he descended from a long line of people who died tragically, usually absurdly, with no sense to be made of any of it? That their family tree was one of misshapen branches, bare, leggy — 'Good for climbing,' her father often joked. That historically, the Cardiels were God's crash-test dummies, extras in the action film of history, a people destroyed by what they did. They expired in mine collapses, boat capsizements, log-boom mishaps. They took absurd, Looney Tunes – style falls from the buildings, scaffolds, granaries, and bridges that they'd just constructed. Their sons were the first shot out of the landing boats, the ones collapsed at the lip of the trench, the ones who died in a hail of soil from a shell landing twenty feet from the group of soldiers charging their way to glory. A people terminated in tragedies so senseless they got their own newspaper stories simply because others needed to be reminded that life was only loaned.

Perhaps it was all due to some doomed combination of recklessness, fragility, and rotten luck, or perhaps there was a self-destruct mechanism embedded in the Cardiel line, a kind of discontinuation of the species strategy — she couldn't say — but Will's grandfather Theodore had managed to last longer than most.

He grew up on a barley farm outside Burlington, and after his parents were simultaneously cut to ribbons by the diesel-powered thresher they'd borrowed riskily to purchase, his family fell destitute. Theodore enlisted as a pilot in the Royal Navy when he was eighteen, and only in the last week of flight school was it discovered he couldn't discern red from green. Because the cockpit buttons were color-coded, he was hastily taught to cook and dropped in the galley of a transport ship, where his duties entailed frying breakfasts and pumping up each sailor's daily rum ration from oak casks below. Shortly after, Theodore's ship collided with a friendly destroyer in a fog north of the Isle of Man. As black water poured into the galley, Theodore stripped his uniform and smeared himself head-to-toe with sausage grease. He bobbed in the North Atlantic for six hours, praying the ship diesel splayed on the surface wouldn't ignite, before some Norwegian mackerel fishermen hoisted him out and wrapped him in a red woolen blanket ruined instantly by the grease.

After the war, a shipmate found Theodore work on the docks in Oakland, loading grain boats with willow shovels in order to prevent sparks that could ignite the gases from the grain and blow the entire elevator to the Midwest. Theodore never spoke of it, but Diane knew her father had been to prison around this time: an assault — some said serious, and some said a drunken punch he'd landed with more calamity than he intended — but shortly after his release he met their mother, Iola, who'd worked in the courthouse.

The couple married and moved to Canada, where Theodore secured better employment on the Lakes in Thunder Bay. On principle he chose the largest grain elevator, the Saskatchewan Wheat Pool 6, where he unblocked clogged conveyance chutes and hoppers. 'Walking down the grain,' as it was known — the riskiest job on the harbor, because of the constant threat of live burial. Before he lowered himself into the bins, Theodore would empty his pockets into a tin can — wallet, keys, snapshot of his wife — because if things shifted, if moisture or air pockets were hidden in the grain, a man could be swallowed instantly, his safety cable snapping like a string of spit. 'Grain is neither solid nor liquid,' her father often said, 'so there's your problem.'

After three years, during which frantic coworkers had thrice dug out Theodore's buried and nearly asphyxiated body, each time cutting him nastily with their spades, he was hired as the foreman of an unloading crew. From then on, he minded and coaxed the enormous hydraulic rig that grasped railcars and flipped them over to evacuate them of grain, as many as eight per shift. Theodore was fair and well regarded and men drew straws to work beneath him. If ever the mechanism seized, he did not send the youngest man, as was custom, but climbed into the hydraulics himself, which were, as the saying went, 'enough to turn a boy to a man, and a man to a sausage.'

By this time he and Iola remained childless, and fellow workers left bottles of rye and foul herbal mixtures on their steps, along with cryptic incantations regarding their combination. Iola wrote home to learn that sterility ran in her family and was mutely devastated.

Then one Saturday morning, while doing her shopping, Iola fell down some concrete steps outside Eaton's and spent a month in traction with a snapped pelvis — her 'wishbone,' she later called it. The story went that shortly after her release, Theodore took her on a weekend trip to Onion Lake, where that night in September, after a blistering hour in the sauna, Theodore carried Iola, who still could not bear her own weight, and set her in the frigid water. Iola then declared her intent to swim across the small lake and back. Upon her return, he waded out to meet her in the water.

After the twins arrived and Theodore returned to work, the men on his crew quipped: 'Finally got the cork out, that right, Theodore?' But any linger of needling about his wife ceased eight years later when Iola, distracted by a crying boy who'd been left outside a tavern by his father, was struck by a right-turning delivery truck that had lost its footing on the ice.

Then, when the twins were sixteen, just a

month after Charlie had rejected Theodore's offer of a position at Pool 6, their father fainted — the elevator management claimed it was a bad heart; the union claimed it was overwork; Theodore's close friends blamed the grain dust — and fell into the space between the wharf and a docked lakeboat he'd been trimming. The boat was to capacity with rye and sitting low in the water, so when the gentle waves eased the boat to the wall, Theodore, a man who had survived the North Atlantic, numerous burials in grain, and ten lives' worth of peril, died in a smudge, like nothing at all.

The morning after the funeral, Charlie woke early, took up his father's work clothes, cinching them with twine and rolling the cuffs. 'There's no other way to earn good money in this damn place,' he said, the wrathful resolve he'd gathered after Iola's death now doubled. 'We'll put you through university first. Then I'll follow.' Diane couldn't bear to tell him then that, aside from a vague longing to be an illustrator or an artist of some sort, she had no inclination to attend university and pictured herself staying in Thunder Bay, with Whalen, perhaps working in his office. 'Trust me, I know how this works,' Charlie said as he left that day. 'If we have money, this place can't keep us.' When he reported at Pool 6, his father's men let him stay, purely out of uneasy pity.

After school Diane brought Charlie's supper, as she had her father's, staying long enough to watch him — an oiled bandanna over his nose and mouth like a train robber — descend into the dark grain bins, dangling from his safety line like human bait. She would watch the hole, counting softly to herself with held breath, until he emerged in a blast of coughing and, after that subsided, a whoop. Over the next few weeks, thick envelopes arrived from the universities to which Charlie had applied, but he dropped each in the trash, unopened.

Though everyone said her reckless brother excelled at the job, soon he was hacking late into the night, often to the point of retching, his face a withered sky-blue. Their doctor formally diagnosed his asthma and recommended another line of work, a recommendation that Charlie curtly returned to the doctor. Charlie soaked his bandanna with liquids of all kinds: soapy water, vinegar, herbal tinctures, and, for a time, gasoline. He took pills he bought from a grain inspector on the harbor named George Butler and drank three pots of strong coffee every day from his father's thermos and got some relief.

A year blinked past. Diane continued to see Whalen at night, and after narrowly graduating from high school, she was secretly delighted to be denied by all the universities Charlie had urged her to apply to. Mostly because Charlie was so concerned about money, she took a job at a store near the lake called Pound's that supplied work clothing and boots. She missed the elevator and nearly perished of boredom behind the long rough-planked counter, sick with worry about Charlie's safety. 'Remember,' she warned in their shared Theodore imitation, 'the grain is both like water and like a wall, and you never know what it's going to decide today.'

Often in the evening when the twins were walking home, committed drunks who'd collapsed in hedges or slumped against parked cars made *I now pronounce you* jabs under their breath. But Charlie had grown into a man still unable to abide ridicule or deflect insult, friendly or otherwise. He'd spit on the ground and square off with anyone, wrapping his legs around a big man while striking at his soft parts and riding him to the ground like a tranquilized animal. And not only those in the switching yard or on the walk home: each week new lakeboats arrived, yielding fresh crews — Norwegians, Danes, Finns, Brazilians, Americans, Portuguese — to misunderstand and swing blindly at. Twice Charlie returned home with his nose again grotesquely broken, nostrils nearly inverted, though it healed each time straight as a rifle sight. But things only worsened when he came of age and took up drinking in earnest. She'd often ask Whalen to pry the pint glass from his hand and drag him from the tavern to start his shift.

Then early one morning, Diane snuck home from a rare night with Whalen in a hotel to find a pantless man unknown to her slumped unconscious at their kitchen table, snoring obscenely, the ham sandwich he'd made uneaten before him, their good chopping knife loosely clutched in his hand. She put on her pajamas, then woke Charlie, who gently extracted the knife from the man's hand and, so as not to damage the cupboards, scooped him up like a child, ferrying him onto the lawn, where he proceeded to beat him for some duration. 'We'll get a new house,' Charlie said afterwards, breathing hard. 'Up the hill. Away from the taverns. Beyond stumbling distance.'

The following week, her brother began working nights with Whalen on the car dumper, something Whalen had arranged to help them both earn extra money. On payday Charlie set aside half the hefty wads he'd pull from his canvas coat, then would scamper off for grain alcohol-fueled weekends by the harbor. Between this and the late nights at the elevators, Charlie wasn't sleeping at all, perhaps because of the pills he was taking for his asthma. He'd slink home days later, unshaven, thin, eyes red as wild strawberries, breathing in gasps with a gray pallor, his shoulders twisted with guilt. Always he fell mute when she questioned where he'd been.

But over time the money piled in her bureau, and soon they had the down payment for a house up the hill that backed the creek. Before they moved in, she arranged their meager things as best she could, and Charlie couldn't stop shaking his head when he saw their new home, because it looked so good. But his contentment didn't last. He started working night shifts on top of his regular days. With no time to spend his wages in taverns, Charlie was quickly paying down their house, with the intention of setting her up comfortably before he left for Queen's University, where he'd already been accepted for admission the following year. 'I'll be a lawyer before you know it,' he said confidently.

That week she overheard some workers at Pound's grumbling about what Whalen and Charlie were doing at night at Pool 6, how even if he was Theodore's son, it wasn't right, yet no one would explain the implication in detail.

When she asked Whalen about it one night in his car, he said they'd hired a crew to work nights when the elevators sat idle. 'How come you're making so much from it?' she asked, and he dragged a finger down her spine, setting her to shiver, and said, 'It's an Indian crew from a reserve up north. And they're real good workers too. Charlie's big idea was to pay them a third of normal wages, while telling my father the crew is white. We pocket the difference ourselves.'

'Doesn't sound fair,' she said, doubting Theodore would've approved of such a scheme.

'Oh, come on,' Whalen said. 'Those poor people are starving up there on those reserves. They're grateful for the opportunity. And the extra work is doing Charlie good. When he's gone, we'll finally be able to walk down the street together.' Whalen had always been more leery than she had of Charlie discovering their relationship and had always kept a strict policy of using only notes stuffed into her letterbox to set their next meeting. After Whalen disappeared the night Charlie died, Diane often wondered whether the secrecy was more a convenient excuse than it was born of any real concern for her brother.

★　★　★

The last night she saw her brother alive, she watched him ready himself for work after inhaling his dinner. He said the ice was coming earlier in November than it ever had, and with it came a frantic rush to load the season's last lakeboat before it was ice-locked until spring. She followed him to the door, thinking how after many years at Pool 6 he still looked so unlike other men his age, already bent and puffy with alcohol saturation, fights, and accidents. Other than his lungs, Charlie remained curiously unmarred by life — his eyes shining like polished copper above his sleek, crooked mouth.

She thanked him for all his hard work and passed him the sandwiches she'd packed. 'You and Whalen better hurry if you want that boat loaded before the freeze' was the last thing she ever said to her brother.

How foolish she'd been to think he would stand as the exception to the Cardiels' tragic legacy — that he'd escape their oversized helping of accident and woe. So in some sense, she hadn't lied when she'd offered up Will's spotty immunization record as proof his heart was malformed. It was a metaphor, truer than any fact she could ever teach him. Because the truth was that every second of every life was lethally dangerous. Especially in Thunder Bay. Especially for the Cardiels. Especially for Will.

And to anyone who would disagree, her only defense would be: What is raising a child except lying? It begins with the first *shhhh . . . everything is going to be . . .* and only gets worse from there.

10

'Want to go for a walk?'

Jonah. Eye-level with the window in New York. The Outside, embodied, peering in.

Will had been up late painting while his mother read mysteries in San Francisco. When he'd heard feet scraping on the shingles, Will's murmuring heart had spasmed and nearly quit. He'd been convinced it was the Bald Man — his best guess for who'd left the boot prints in his yard — and was about to take a T-ball swing at his face with the fire poker when he recognized the voice.

'Now?' Will said, watching liquid waves of heat flee into the night.

'Sure, now,' said Jonah, eyes darting sidelong, his face caramel-smooth in the low light. 'I need your help.'

'I can't . . . ' Will said, one hand over his heart, the other setting the poker down discreetly on his desk.

'Why not?'

'I'm . . . uh . . . I'm painting,' he stammered. 'For an exhibit.'

'Your masterpieces?' asked Jonah with a smirk, nodding at Will's color-smeared canvases.

Will's heart nearly drowned. 'They're only paintings,' he mumbled. 'My stupid paintings.'

Jonah shrugged. 'They're cool,' he said, almost smiling. 'Must be fun to go big like that on real canvases — those things aren't cheap. Anyway, that's all right. I thought you were brave from the way you bowled over that wolf. But I guess not. Anyway, I'm meeting Marcus tonight. I heard from that weird girl Angela you were looking for him, and I need someone to watch my back, so . . . '

Will's heart knocked. 'Marcus? You know where he is? You found him?'

'More like he found me. Anyway, sorry to disturb your creativity. See ya around, Will.'

'Wait,' Will said, more childishly than he'd planned. 'Stay right there.'

Will tiptoed from his studio and opened his mother's door with a soft puff, the air inside San Francisco creamy with her scent. She was plunged in sleep, her Relaxation Headphones on, a rare placid expression spread over her face. Will lifted her headphones, uncovering the distant *whoosh* of water, like a toilet running somewhere, and set them on her nightstand. Sleeping with them was new, and he didn't know if this was a good sign or not. He stood watching her, fingering his forehead and kneading the scars on his thigh, his souvenirs of the Outside and now the only evidence he'd ever left the house. And here tonight was the only chance he'd ever get to find his friend. He'd made a promise to stay Inside and be her guardian, but maybe finding Marcus would be the best way to protect her. To prove that the Outside wasn't nearly as dangerous as she believed. That it couldn't swallow a boy whole. Besides, he'd never promised to stay home, only that he'd be careful. He'd make tonight a low-impact Adventure. 'A walk,' just as Jonah had suggested.

★   ★   ★

They could've snuck out the front door, but Jonah seemed intent on coaxing Will onto the roof. The boys managed to disconnect the screen, then detach the window from its track. Will trailed Jonah along the nut-tighteningly high roofline, to where they could jump to the metal shed where Will had met Marcus and shimmy down. Including ice sliding, it was easily the most dangerous stunt Will had ever performed in his entire life, and surviving it broiled him with joy.

Outside, a set of fast clouds raked the stars. Though nearly spring, cold was still stringent in the air, the dead grass hairbrush-stiff with frost, and dwindling continents of snow lingered on the boulevards that edged the bare street. Somehow the snow made the night not as dark, like a day that had misfired. As they walked recklessly in the center of the empty road, Jonah pressed his skateboard against his hip, making no attempt to ride it. The skull graphics on the underside of the board resembled Jonah's drawings, and Will lost himself for a moment in the detail.

'I never got the chance to say thanks for saving me. Again,' Will said. 'I can't believe you killed it. A *wolf.*'

Jonah nodded. 'Felt bad when I stomped him,

but he was done the second he bit you. Were you scared?'

Will kept his eyes forward and weighed his answer. He was unsure if Jonah knew about the Black Lagoon, or if he'd ever faced anything like it himself. Will doubted it. Like Marcus, Jonah seemed perfectly tuned for fearlessness. 'Yes,' Will said carefully.

Jonah spit plentifully on the ground. 'That's a good thing,' he said.

'Were you?' Will said, still unsure if he'd said the right thing.

'Sure, but I just hate wolves more than I like you,' Jonah said, a smile breaching on his lips. After some walking and mental arithmetic, Will concluded that this also added up to Jonah liking him in some measure. Who knew, thought Will, with the warmest gut-sensation he'd had so far Outside, all he had to do was get mauled by a wolf to make another friend.

'Why don't you like wolves?' Will asked after a while.

'They don't think,' said Jonah. 'Plus they steal from my brothers' traps. Plus they run together and attack weak things. They're as bad as men.'

'Your brothers trap? Like animals?'

'Muskrat, beaver, marten — little stuff like that.'

'Do you go with them?' Will asked, floored by the idea.

'No. I'm allergic to fur,' Jonah said. 'And I like the city better. More concrete,' he said, patting his skateboard.

'All I have is my mom,' Will said with a sudden

vision of her throwing back the covers of his cot to find the unwashed clothes he'd bundled there and dying of fright. 'I used to have an uncle,' he added proudly. 'But he's dead.'

Jonah nodded again and tucked his chin to his chest. 'Look, another reason I came to get you is because I need to say sorry. Remember how that wolf went after this backpack?' Jonah said, pulling at the straps with his thumbs. 'Well, it was Marcus who gave it to me to watch over.'

'Angela said you guys used to be friends?'

'Yeah, he taught me to skateboard when he first came to Thunder Bay. He was the best skateboarder I've ever seen outside of *Thrasher*. Smooth as water flowing. But he quit because he broke his board and couldn't afford another one. Then he got into what he called *exploring*. Which meant going into all the places he wasn't supposed to. Abandoned buildings. Culverts. Old mines. He'd find all sorts of things.

'Then a while back he showed up at my house really late. He was shaking, and his face was white. First time that kid actually looked scared. Said he wanted me to hold on to his backpack. He had something important in there. A piece of paper. Figured it would be safe with me because of my brothers. I didn't want to do it, but his being scared scared me. So I said okay.'

'Who was he hiding the paper from?' Will said, remembering again how Marcus hid that day in his yard, and maybe not just because he was stealing garden hoses.

Jonah stopped, squared off, and leaned into Will, his close breath dragging a carbonated tingle up Will's spine. 'I think it was Butler,' hushed Jonah, '*the* Butler. My brothers used to run booze from his stills up to the dry reserves up north. They quit because an old lady, an elder, got struck blind drinking it, and no money was worth poisoning our people like that. But even my brothers are scared of the Butler. After the elevators shut down, he hired every desperate dockworker and hard-ass former railway man down there. Plus he breeds wolves. Keeps them with him always. Kids around here say you should never forget anything in the woods. Once the Butler's wolves get your scent, they'll follow you all the way into your bedroom.' For a moment Will's mind flashed to the Helmet he'd left behind beside the creek. 'The thing is,' Jonah said, 'I think he sent that wolf to get Marcus, and it picked up his scent on this backpack. Would've got me if you hadn't body-checked it like a true Canadian hero.'

'Jonah,' Will said. 'I saw someone when that wolf was on top of me. A bald guy. In the woods. Short and stocky.'

'Hmm,' Jonah said. 'Not the Butler. He's got a full head of hair, all electrocuted and snow white. Probably one of his men.'

Will inflated with pride at his genius contribution and fought to contain his beaming as they scuffed their feet into the hushed night. After the wolf attack, his mother had ordered him new boots with grips like dirt-bike treads, even more acutely embarrassing now with the snow essentially gone. Will was suddenly aware he had to pee. To his horror there were no

142

bathrooms Outside at night. Anywhere. He hoped dearly there would be one wherever Marcus was.

Jonah clattered his skateboard to the ground and hopped upon it, all regal grace and fluidity, zipping ahead under the propulsion of his left leg. He rolled through a temple of yellow streetlight, his hands open and searching, as though feeling the pavement's texture as it passed. Then he crouched, frozen like a cat stalking a robin, before cracking the rear of the board down, rocketing himself upward with the apparatus clinging impossibly to his feet like a burr. After this, the silence of flight but for the sibilance of wheels spinning, then a growling return to the asphalt and his lackadaisical ride-away.

This tidy morsel of magic that Jonah had performed seemed almost another trap to test Will's gullibility, another shaken pop can or match bomb, but Will couldn't resist.

'What was that?' he said reverently, when Jonah button-hooked back.

'What?' said Jonah.

'What you just did.'

'That? It's called an ollie.'

'But how do you make it jump like that?'

'I don't really know,' he said, smoothing back his bangs. Will wondered if his brothers cut his hair like that, or if he did it himself. 'It just works. I taught myself by reading *Thrasher* and watching Marcus. You jump and slide your front foot and it happens. I don't even understand it. It's better that way.'

143

'Do it again.'

As Jonah cracked off a series of identically lofty hops over manholes and storm drains, equal measures of recognition and rapture struck Will like sheet lightning. It was an act of such miraculousness that Will felt unworthy of it. Every dance performance and action movie and Destructivity Experiment he'd ever known seemed to be contained in this one gesture, this *ollie*. Will's legs itched to try, but somehow he understood the sacrilege of asking for a turn on Jonah's board. Plus, he had to take it easy on his heart.

'How long have you been . . . doing that?' Will asked.

'A few years. My brothers pitched in and bought me a board. Believe me, I'm not that good.'

'Looks like you were born on it.'

Jonah let go a rare laugh. His teeth were crooked, cool crooked. 'My brothers were always shoulder-checking me, tripping me down, shoving snow in my face. You get good at staying on your feet.'

Then, as though to contradict him, a grinding sounded from beneath him, and Jonah was hurled to the half-frozen pavement with a naked *thwack* of palm and hip.

'Jonah!' Will said rushing to his side. 'Can you hear me? Are you okay? Do you want an ambulance?'

'I'm fine, Will,' Jonah said through pain-gritted teeth while rolling over, then lifting himself incredibly into a sitting position on the ground.

144

He kicked away the small pink stone that had thwarted his wheel.

'Don't get up,' cautioned Will. 'You may have a spinal. Or a concussion.'

'Chill *out*,' Jonah said, laughing, as Will was casting about for a phone booth.

Will fell silent as Jonah rose and they resumed walking, quietly loathing his mother and the Black Lagoon for so thoroughly screwing his understanding of what constituted a catastrophe.

'Why don't you talk at school?' said Will, hoping Jonah wouldn't stop talking all over again.

'They expect Indians not to,' he said. 'So I don't want to disappoint them. Talking only digs you deeper in that place. They handcuff you with your own words. You ever say anything that brought you good there?' Jonah asked.

Will remembered describing the visualization blueprint he'd drawn on his first day and shook his head.

'I talk all the time,' said Jonah, his limp diluting with every step. 'I talk to myself. I talk to my brothers. I'm talking to you. I talk when I want. But when I'm there, I keep my mouth shut, do my schoolwork, and go home.'

Will noted they were nearing the path to the culvert. 'So where's Marcus?'

'He left me a note written in blood on birchbark. Said he wanted to meet. Typical Marcus. I heard he was living on his own in the woods, stealing things for the Butler to make money.'

'Garden hoses, right? You guys use the match

bombs as a diversion while Marcus steals the hoses from the backyard.'

Jonah did a little palm-clap. 'Very good. But I only taught them how to make those bombs. That was it. I don't need money. My brothers are working at the call center now. Anyway, you can't buy your way out of Thunder Bay. I'm leaving my own way.' Will was about to ask how when the mouth of the culvert yawned before them, black as deep space, and a force overtook him, denying the obedience of his legs. He watched Jonah plunge into the soupy dark. Will's heart was double-bumping lethally, but more than his nascent Outside bravery, it was the mounting distress in his bladder — now a stingy jellyfish spreading its tentacles across his pelvis — and the prospect of relief that pressed him into the eeriness of the tunnel. The dark was pure as the linen closet in London with the door shut, and Will's eyes gulped it greedily, the borders of his body lost to him. He put one foot in front of the other, and the opposite opening approached like an inhospitable planet.

'Come on, Will,' Jonah beckoned from the woods when he emerged. After he walked through a stand of pine, five flashlights snapped, and Will found himself surrounded by a Stonehenge of boys.

'You again,' said Marcus, his eyes incandescent with mischief and bravery. 'Couldn't resist coming out for another taste of the world, huh, Will?'

Will slyly watched Jonah's reaction to see if his

146

household's situation was common neighborhood knowledge, but found no confirmation on
his new friend's face. Marcus's hair was longer
than before, now well past his eyes, greasy and
matted with leaves. He wore a filthy one-piece
snowsuit — a cross between caveman and
spaceman. On his feet were snowmobile boots,
much smaller than the hexagonal tracks in Will's
yard.

'I've been looking for you, Marcus,' Will said,
speaking quickly. 'I'm going to school now. And
I'd got really good at ice sliding until a wolf — '

' — Too much talking,' the biggest Belcourt
Twin said, the light of a calculator watch flaring
on his wrist. 'Time is nigh,' he added.

Marcus rapped Jonah's skateboard deck with
his knuckle. 'Are the Home Ranger and the
Rolling Indian up for a little visit?'

Will and Jonah followed the boys, romping
deeper into the woods, the only sound a faint
rustle of highway. After a while, their amber
beams reached out to define a structure in the
scrub, a shack, crafted of corrugated metal
rusted oxide-red, a few wood scraps, and a tarp
worked in somehow. One wall was comprised of
a huge green road sign — TORONTO: 1376 KM
— which reminded Will momentarily of his
basement.

'Like my place?' Marcus said, unhitching a
padlock with his scarred hands and ushering
them inside. 'Built it myself,' he said, swiveling
his light and their collective attention around the
interior. Will had expected the trappings of
delinquent boys — discount sodas, firecrackers,

147

various Destructivity Experiment material — but it was surprisingly neat. There was a camping stove, a few chairs, a bedroll, and a single book, titled *Great Lake Navigation*. Nearly fifty garden hoses hung from nails everywhere, green, black, and orange. Stacked on a shelf were hundreds of tins of sardines and many pint boxes of blueberries. Struggling to disguise his envy, Will was thrilled his theory had proven correct: Marcus *had* been living Outside. In an Inside entirely of his own making. Wonderfully alone. Beyond the reach of adults, with nobody to worry over him or bombard him with guilt — it seemed to Will a tremendous luxury.

'You approve, Will?' said Marcus. 'I already heard about your little tangle with that wolf. Impressive. Thanks for helping to keep my stuff safe.' Will resisted the sudden urge to embrace Marcus and tell him everything that had happened since they first met in one great typhoon of description: his Destructivity Experiments, the taste of the leaf he'd chewed, the boring excitement of school, his blood bouncing on the ice, his dead uncle Charlie, Jonah's miraculous ollie. 'Oh, and the Twins saved this for you,' Marcus said, pointing to the old Helmet he'd left by the creek. Will didn't know if it would be worse if he ignored or acknowledged it, so he settled on a meaningful nod.

'You've got a ton of hoses in here,' said Jonah. 'You still selling them?'

'Haven't seen him in a bit,' replied Marcus. 'We've built up a surplus. But hoses don't matter anymore.'

'Haven't seen who?' asked Will.

Marcus looked at the Twins. They nodded.

'He used to work for the Butler,' Marcus said. 'But not anymore. Nobody knows his name. He mumbles and never really makes sense. He salvages metal downtown. Tears out the guts of all this city's old industrial pigeontraps. That's where I met him. We leave him hoses, and he leaves money in grocery bags.'

'But why does he want hoses?' said Will. 'Is he a gardener?'

'Who cares?' the big Twin said.

'Does he wear boots?' said Will.

'Question time's over,' said Marcus. 'Look, it doesn't matter, because now that Jonah's got my bag for me, I'll be leaving rotten old Thunder Bay forever and won't need to touch another garden hose again in my life,' he said, rubbing his hands together like a cartoon villain.

'But where are you going?' Will said, his eyes misting at the notion of Marcus leaving forever. 'What about this place you built? And — '

' —Yeah, Marcus, the thing is,' Jonah began. 'I still have the backpack, but I don't exactly know where your paper is. I had it stashed with my drawings, and then they all just . . . disappeared.'

Marcus's eyes sunk into black pits, and he sat down on a crude wooden bench and pressed his palms to his cheeks, pushing back his bangs into a kind of crown. The scars on his neck grew red as stoplights. The Twins inched to the edges of the cabin. 'It's okay,' said Marcus in an ineffective, self-consoling way that reminded Will of his mother. 'The Butler still can't find me here. Neither can his wolves.'

'But Marc,' one of the Twins said, 'he *knows* it's you who took it.'

'You could give it back,' said the other Twin nervously.

'It's too late for that,' said Marcus grimly, setting his forehead on the table.

'Look,' interjected Jonah. 'Maybe Mr. Miller snatched it from my desk. I could ask him?'

At the mention of Jonah's desk, Will's stomach dropped and a milkshake of bile rose in his throat. Thrust before him was his first Outside crime: the drawing he'd stolen and given to Angela on his first day of school. How could he now risk his only chance at friendship by telling Jonah he'd taken it? He had to get it back from Angela. He could only hope she still had it and hadn't boiled it down to make a Jonah-scented perfume or something.

Perhaps it was the thrill of finding Marcus, or the bulge of guilt in him, but by this point Will's bladder was on the cusp of detonation. Any second he'd shower everyone in Marcus's cabin with a boiling brew of blood and urine. Afterwards, surgeons would have to fashion Will an artificial one out of something gross like a sheep's stomach or a gall bladder — whatever that was.

'Marcus, where's the bathroom?' Will said.

Marcus lifted his face and cast his eyes around the cabin theatrically. 'Now where did I install that lavatory . . . ' he said, hand on elbow, two fingers to his chin.

'Are you fucking kidding?' the big Twin said.

Jonah leaned into Will. 'Just go outside, Will,' he whispered.

Will exited through the rickety corrugated door, listening to the Twins' snickering wane as he plunged into the brush. He walked until he found a stump that was vaguely toilet-like — hollow with one section risen up at the back. He fished out his penis and brandished it, but nothing ensued. He'd never peed anywhere other than Venice or the strange urinals at his school that reminded him of children's coffins made of porcelain, all tipped up on end. He was thinking about how reckless and unlawful it was to deface the forest this way, especially since lately he'd started liking trees, when a thick arm tightened across his neck.

'Stay still, prawn,' a wheezy voice said. 'I'll twinkle your throat like a stripe. Don't entertain whimsies about it.' Another arm grappled his waist, squeezing the effervescent jellyfish of his bladder, which was now crawling electric up his back.

'Who're those zygotes in utero?' he said, nudging Will to the shack.

'Who?'

'The mini-titans, rooting through the ground-swell!' the man yell-whispered, his breathing textured with tiny pops and wheezes like the embers of a dying fire.

Will managed to rotate his head but the face was sallow and scooped out by darkness. 'Just boys. One of them lives there.'

'Oh, so that's the differential, is it? Well, what's my address?' the man hissed. 'Quick!'

'I . . . don't — '

'Okay smarty-pepper, what's yourself?'

'My address?'

'And don't conjure me that swimming in pool six.'

Will whimpered the name of his street as he released a painful zap of urine into the brush, squeezing it to a halt.

'Your name, pipsqwuak!' he panted. 'Put your groundhogs behind it.'

'My name is Will . . . ' he said, straining.

The man emitted a little gasp, loosening his grip momentarily. He drew close to Will's ear, and his tone softened. 'You'll operate best by vacating here, chummy. This venue is the worst refuge. *He's imminent.*' Then the man ratcheted his arms again and began to drag Will into the woods. For a moment, Will felt nearly calmed by the man's force, as he sometimes did when his mother Black Lagooned so bad that her before-bed cuddles bruised him. And it was amid the sanctum of this thought that release arrived, full-steam and warm, deflecting off the man's coat and whooshing over Will's legs, splashing into his dropped jeans and trickling through his cuffs like downspouts.

'Orchard fire!' the man bellowed, releasing him, and Will landed in a flat-out sprint, hoisting his pants as he crashed through a barbed wire of branches, the moon swinging overhead in the night sky like a scythe blade loosed from its stick.

He soon dashed into the culvert with sweat scorching his face, his still-healing thigh tearing away from the bone. He dropped his arms to

152

pump at his sides through the tunnel. When he was two doors from his house, the air snapped with a new injection of cold, and tiny flakes were sent to spiral into the air, almost not falling at all.

Bursting through the window into New York, he shucked the urine-soaked pants from his legs and camped under the covers of his cot, his chest thudding like a speed bag, on the brink of going Black Lagoon supernova. He lay awake for what felt like hours, waiting for his eyeballs to pop and his heart to perform its last kick and his life to ebb. But soon Will grew leaden, and before long he crashed headfirst through the plate-glass window of sleep.

11

Will lay low until the following Monday, when he woke early and departed for school before his mother emerged from San Francisco.

'Happy to have you back, Mr. Cardiel,' said Mr. Miller glumly, wiping his glasses on the hem of his golf shirt before draining the noxious contents of his mug. When the bell rang, Jonah wasn't at his desk; neither was Angela. Will approached Wendy, Angela's next-closest friend, and learned that Angela had been sent to Toronto for special treatments. 'They don't have the right machines in Thunder Bay,' Wendy said grimly, revealing a glimmering briar of braces when she spoke.

With the school bell still in his ears Will jogged back through the dripping catacomb of the culvert, this time with only a tickle of fear, and plunged into the woods on the other side. After some searching he found Marcus's shack between two wooded hummocks. It was half-dismantled, the corrugated metal and chip wood splayed outward on two sides. The garden hoses had vanished, as had the sardines and blueberries and camp stove and bedroll. Will failed to find any boot prints in the hard dirt around the shack, which was crisscrossed with roots, but he did turn up a few lifeless chickadees and grackles on the cabin's perimeter.

The streets of County Park were narrower and less treed than those of Grandview Gardens. The driveways harbored pickup trucks, mostly, all with tool-bearing racks and locking containers. Curiously, there were no power lines overhead, and every third house had a green box out front that read DANGER! BURIED CABLE! aside the image of an electrocuted man, twisted in rapture.

Will located the address Mr. Miller gave him in a battery of brick townhouses. After a spell of complex unlocking issued from behind the door, it was opened by an enormous shirtless man with the same handsome gauntness and precise athleticism as Jonah, though he was stouter, with thick crow-black hair to his shoulders and the voice of a giant, as if his chest doubled as a furnace. A tattoo of two black, red, and yellow eagle feathers strung with barbed wire curled around his thickly muscled ribs. He rumbled that his name was Gideon and showed Will Inside.

Will watched the big man relock the sheet metal-reinforced door, further bolstered by three deadbolts and an iron crossbar. Inside, the house was nearly empty, all linoleum floors with no carpet and minimal furniture, scant artwork on the walls other than a large photograph of a black bear standing on the hood of a car at a dump. Perhaps because no mother lived there to decorate, Gideon's tattoos and some beaded moccasins lying abandoned by the door, yellowed and stiff as stale bread, were the only ornamental things around. They must've lost everything in the fire, Will thought, but even so,

155

it seemed so temporary, as though they could pack up and leave at any moment — a stark contrast to how his mother crammed their place with books and furniture and wallpapered it with Will's boring paintings so that they could never leave, even if they tried.

'The Doc's in his office,' Gideon said, directing Will down the back stairs into a barren unfinished basement. At its center hung four pieces of fabric from the ceiling, establishing a tent-like rectangle.

'Why weren't you in school? I was worried about you,' Will said, drawing back the fabric to find Jonah reclined on a neatly made mattress, reading. Will tossed some paper-clipped sheets onto Jonah's bed. 'Here, I brought your homework.'

Jonah looked up from a large hardback book and smiled, black bangs cast over one eye. 'I was worried about you, too, Will. I mean more than usual,' he said. 'I got my brother Enoch to call the school this morning so I could sleep in. Last time it was the house fire, this time I have scoliosis.'

'You never had a fire?'

'No. I just wanted to stay home for a while to study and draw. I learn twice as fast when I'm not in that classroom. But I was, like, 'Enoch, you could've just said I had mono, dumbass.''

'Sorry about leaving you. I was supposed to have your back,' said Will, before launching into an account of his puzzling and frightful encounter with the Wheezing Man, playing up

156

the adventurous drama of his escape, omitting the pant wetting.

Jonah said that after Will left they were waiting in the cabin when there was a knock at the door. 'Marcus thought it was the hose guy, but then there was some growling outside, and he freaked and kicked a hole in the opposite wall and told us to scatter into the trees. I was running with him for a while until we hit the creek and he yelled for me to run through the water to put off the wolves and he'd lead them the other way,' Jonah said, lowering his eyes. 'That was the last I saw of him.'

Will slowly unzipped his backpack and handed Jonah his drawings. 'The important one is missing, isn't it?' Will said, his throat tightening. 'I took them from your desk for Angela. But now that she's in Toronto,' he added, 'there's no way we can get Marcus's paper back.'

'So that's how you saw my masterpieces,' Jonah said, shaking his head. 'I'm not mad. I never should've held Marcus's stuff for him. I always told him that Thunder Bay was just itching for a reason to see us dead or in jail. But he couldn't stand school. Said being inside for that long made his legs shake and his head hurt. Anyway, it was his mistake for crossing the Butler like that. Now he's on his own.'

'But why does the Butler want it so much? It was only a grid with some Xs on it.'

'Marcus was going to use it to make money,' Jonah said, shrugging. 'Enough for him to leave Thunder Bay forever, which he always talked about.'

'You said you heard growling before everyone ran. Do you think the Butler and his wolves got him?'

Jonah lowered his head. 'I don't know. It was dark ... Marcus is quick. He knows how to disappear. He probably got away ... ' Then Jonah's eyes defocused.

Will sat on the bed. 'Except what, Jonah? It's important.'

'Yeah,' Jonah said softly, 'well, I heard him call out.'

Will waited.

'But he yells things all the time,' Jonah said. 'He's always faking dead and crying wolf for a joke. And I was still splashing through the creek — but sure, he said something, something I thought I'd never hear him say.' Jonah took a breath. 'It was *help*.'

'We need to find Marcus,' Will said, fighting a sudden storm of tears.

Jonah scoffed. 'And how are we going to do that?'

'Ask questions. Search the Outside. Investigate.'

'I don't know, dude,' sighed Jonah, slumping back on his mattress. 'Indian kids go missing all the time. Especially orphans. Nobody in Thunder Bay even blinks.'

Will took a moment to examine the train of burgundy-spined medical books — exactly like the one Jonah had been reading — arranged on a shelf of cinder blocks and boards, the only furniture in his apartment other than his bed. Will recognized them because his mother often consulted theirs whenever the Black Lagoon made her think she had a terminal disease. 'You're not sick, are you?' Will said.

'No, I'm just interested in how people work,' Jonah said. 'I'm on the second last one. My brother Hosea stole them from a house he broke into because he did some yard work for a doctor who refused to pay him. Hosea thought there'd be one of those money stashes cut into them. Lucky for me there wasn't.'

Will was astonished Jonah had somehow mustered the energy to read all those books *himself*, with no mother to do it for him. Then he leaned close. 'Doctors are supposed to save people, right?' Will said. 'And Marcus helped you that night. Now he needs us.'

Jonah picked up a green urethane skateboard wheel, pinched its bearings, and swiped it into a blurry spin, watching it for a while. 'How about this?' he said when the wheel slowed. 'Since Marcus quit, I've been skateboarding alone. And after witnessing your ice-sliding skills, I've been meaning to tell you to get a board.'

Will recalled again the sheer divinity of Jonah's skateboarding. He'd known desiring a board immediately would speak poorly of him, would degrade the seriousness of the endeavor. But now here was Jonah offering the green light and Will nearly buckled with excitement.

'So before we do anything,' Jonah continued, 'you're learning to skate. Because I'm not rolling around with some White kid speed-walking behind me all summer. And after you become a skateboarder, I'll become a detective.'

'It will be the perfect cover for our investigation!' Will exclaimed.

Jonah's face pinched. 'How come you're always so excited about everything? It's like you've never done anything before.'

'Sorry,' Will said, fighting to camouflage his joy.

Jonah laughed and swept his bangs from his eyes. 'Deal?' he said, lifting his hand and aiming his fist at Will with his wrist cocked.

'Deal,' said Will, his eyes welling again with gratitude and excitement, resisting a profound urge to tackle and cuddle his friend. After a second Will realized Jonah was waiting on him to do something. Will lifted the same right fist in exact imitation and nodded his head knowingly.

'That'll work,' said Jonah, dropping his hand.

To his mother's relief and delight, the next morning Will claimed a fever and stayed home from school. When he heard footsteps on the front porch he ripped open the door. 'I want you to stop bringing these, okay?' he said to the teenage carrier about to tuck a bagged newspaper between the doors, as they'd arranged long ago.

The boy pulled out a little notebook. 'You're paid up until the end of the year, Will Cardiel.'

'I'll give you a hundred dollars if you stop, like forever, no matter what your boss says.' The paperboy's eyes lit, and Will darted for his mother's checkbook.

After that Will went to Paris and filled a pitcher with water, which he toted to Cairo and poured in its entirety into the vent in the back of

160

their television. Then he did the same to the kitchen radio. Even though he wouldn't be able to watch VHS movies any more, it was a reasonable sacrifice. If any news of Marcus or the Butler or their investigation reached his mother, the Black Lagoon would sweep her over a waterfall of terror. But more than his old familiar fear that she'd be banished somewhere and lost to him forever, Will had something new to worry about, something real. He couldn't let her interfere with their investigation.

12

The following weekend, with his mother's credit card, Will ordered a complete skateboard from the back cover of one of Jonah's near-holy *Thrasher* magazines. At first Will fancied a board called the Vision Psycho Stick, until he clued into the dubious connotations it might cast upon his mother, or himself, so he picked a Santa Cruz, Jeff Kendall's pro model, mostly because he liked the picture, which depicted a ruined, burned-out city, where up from the smashed concrete rose a pumpkin-headed monster borne into the air. Will was struck by a deep, piercing resonance, both with this image and with Jeff Kendall, a man he knew nothing about, other than he lived in California and was a skateboard wizard. Will chose Independent trucks (the metal braces that attach wheels to board, Jonah told him), both because Jonah had them and because when he said it repeatedly, the word sounded like an unstoppable train charging forward.

When the box arrived, the air it released was humid and fragrant of ocean. With Jonah's help Will assembled his board on the worktable in Toronto, after which they charged berserkly to Will's front sidewalk. With spring in high gear, the neighborhood drains gushed, the water syrupy with silt, and the sun seemed boosted — as though now properly charged.

It took no more than five seconds for Will to

ascertain he would be forever cursed as a pitiful skateboarder. It was nothing like exercise biking or ice sliding or painting or Destructivity Experiments. Constantly he was flung downward, the board tomahawking off in the opposite direction, his knees and elbows quickly bashed and gored by the tyrannical pavement.

'You're putting too much weight on it,' said Jonah as he executed spritely ollies up the curb near Will's driveway. Will knew of no possible way to stand on something without putting weight on it and told Jonah so. When he later questioned Jonah on the secrets of the ollie, a feat Will was in no position yet to even attempt, Jonah only offered: 'It's sort of like riding a bike — your body learns the rules, but your head doesn't.' Will neglected to inform Jonah that the only bike he'd ever ridden only had one wheel, which didn't touch the ground.

Will spent the ensuing weeks dumped to the pavement with demoralizing repetition, flaying the tender flesh of his lower back, knees, and hips like an invisible monster was dismantling him cell by cell. He stymied wave after wave of hot tears. In the mornings when he awoke in his cot in New York, his body was a symphony of aches, he found himself clumsy as an infant, as though during sleep he'd misplaced his ability to walk.

Sometimes while skateboarding Will spotted his mother's dark shape in the window of Paris, rereading her page-turners and heating soup in her electric kettle, and the sight of her, shipwrecked there, stabbed him with a pocket

163

knife of guilt. Will knew his mother viewed skateboarding as the worldly equivalent of going snorkeling in the Black Lagoon, but so far she'd only hung his new orange Helmet from a nail near the door, right beside where he kept his skateboard, leaving unmentioned the fact he never touched it. Jonah didn't need a Helmet, so Will didn't either.

After two weeks of flagellation, nearly quitting hundreds of times, Will was able to ambulate somewhat safely on his board without cracking a kneecap, and Jonah agreed to set off on their first investigation.

'We need to make sure Marcus isn't back at his foster home, hiding out,' said Will while they rolled toward County Park on the asphalt footpath.

'Was there anything else you remember about the dude who grabbed you?' Jonah asked.

'Like I said,' Will replied, 'he wheezed like crazy, like he could barely breathe. But he was fast and strong, and didn't make any sense when he talked. It was like a junk drawer of words. I don't even remember half of them. But I'm sure I felt hair on his head, so it wasn't the Bald Man.'

'And the Butler's pretty frail,' Jonah added, 'so that rules him out. Must've been that scavenger who bought their hoses. Marcus said he was hard to understand.'

'Could be. Oh, and when I got home, my coat was covered in this dust that was really hard to get off,' Will said. 'But the Wheezing Man is definitely our prime suspect.'

The boys kicked up their skateboards (Will's struck him painfully in the knee) in front of Marcus's foster home — a box of mildewed stucco with a ratty, slumping tin roof. They heard a miniature wailing and realized it originated from the burgundy minivan angle-parked in the driveway. They peered inside. A little Indian toddler was strapped in a car seat, his mouth a perfect O.

'Are you my new boys? Where's your paperwork?' called a woman's voice from the doorstep.

'Sorry?' said Will in an embarrassing sonorous voice he used to employ for deliverymen. 'No, we're friends of Marcus, and we have a few questions.'

She invited them in with a solemn finger wave. They removed their skateboard-chewed shoes and ambled to the living room. Will spotted a few little Indian kids peering shyly from the rooms down a dim hall. The air in this particular Inside was viscous with dust vapor, and small plastic bits of toy paved the moldering carpet like autumn leaves. Sad-eyed collectible Eskimo dolls peered down from high shelves in tiny fur coats with plastic harpoons in their hands. The boys sat on a toy-laden couch, and the woman thrust fruit punch-flavored juice boxes upon them without asking. Marcus's foster mother was White, with a heavy, pale face, both the hue and shape of an uncooked turkey.

'Sorry if this is hard for you,' Will said. 'The police must've asked you lots of questions already.'

'Police never asked me nothing,' she blurted. 'They came and searched his room for drugs and alcohol. Was about it.'

'Okay,' Will said, extracting his notebook from his kangaroo pocket. But he didn't know what to write, so he began doodling a skateboard ramp. Jonah watched him and shook his head. 'Did Marcus have any enemies?' Will said.

'Only anybody with ears connected to half a brain,' she said. 'That boy's mouth soured about every last person in town in the few years I had him. Except most didn't stay ticked. He has a way like that. Mine was the sixth foster home he been through.'

'Did you say *sixth* foster home?' Will said, scribbling notes he knew instantly would prove worthless because his cursive was still awful.

She nodded gravely. 'The second wasn't kind to him. Some pastor and his wife, his worker told me. Kept him in homemade chicken-wire shackles at night. Took a curling iron to him. A cordless drill. Worse things best not said.' Will remembered the lace-work of scars on Marcus's hands and torso when he'd offered his shirt that first day Outside. ''Course he didn't want to talk to nobody about it, certainly not me.'

'Do you have any idea where he is now?' Will said, as Jonah turned away to peekaboo with a little girl with huge eyes and dancing pigtails who'd crept to the edge of the room in a filthy purple leotard.

The woman shook her head. 'He was always staying out, sleeping outside in forts he'd built all over. He brung things back for the other children

166

here: toys and candies and such, roasts and potatoes for me to cook. I pitched most of it 'cause I knew he didn't have no money.' Suddenly her breathing thickened. She touched her tear duct with her finger as though to manually press it closed but a tear slipped past.

'At first I thought he'd gone up north to look for his mother,' the woman continued in a sputter, 'he always claimed she was alive, said he saw her in visions. Used to draw these pictures of her, all these colors swirling around her — you know how the Indians draw, with those energy lines? Except his worker was certain she was killed hitchhiking just after he was born. Still, that boy could see to himself. That's a true fact. His uncle taught him to hunt and fish before he was murdered by his best friend — one of those liquored fights over some misunderstanding. I know one thing: Indian boys go sideways staying inside. Marcus was the same. Gets worse as they grow. They don't care for the indoors the way the White ones do.'

'Don't *they*?' Jonah said, annoyed. 'Is that why you made Marcus stay out of the house from nine to five every day? Even if he was sick?'

Will shot Jonah a wide-eyed, imploring look.

She was sobbing openly now in her pouchy armchair, and Will's mind flashed to his own mother. 'He was driving this house half-crazy,' she wept. 'Teaching the young ones to light campfires and carve little wood sculptures with knives. They worshipped him. I needed to protect *them*.' Then her voice sharpened. 'Maybe you'll have kids yourself someday and find out how there's no way to keep certain boys from jumping off cliffs.'

Ignoring her, Jonah plucked an Etch A Sketch from the toy-drecked floor and after a quick flurry of knob twisting, showed the little girl a delicately rendered horse in full gallop. She squealed and clapped with delight.

Will leaned toward the woman and spoke calmly, realizing that if his time Inside had taught him anything, it was how to soothe. 'Ma'am, did Marcus leave anything suspicious behind? Phone numbers? Papers?'

'Why, did he swipe something of yours?' she said, dabbing her sludgy mascara.

'No, I don't mean — '

' — Alls he came to me with was an old shopping bag of hyperactive pills he refused to take and a chocolate bar his social worker had bought him because she was done with him. That was it. Not even pictures of his kin. Plus, I mean he shared a room here with three other boys, sometimes four, and to tell you outright, I'm not sure what's his and what ain't. Mostly a slew of boy things in there: bits of slate and amethyst, wood swords and slingshots, skate-boards, and dead things they find. Broken things they keep and want to fix but don't know how.'

After draining his juice box with a gurgle, Will thanked her and stood. Out front they found the child in the minivan fast asleep, its little eyes smashed shut in the seat as if it were preparing for some kind of impact.

'One more thing,' she said, taking Will aside

while Jonah practiced kickflips on the sidewalk. 'An old, white-haired fella came by a while back asking about Marcus. Said he was a social worker. Seemed real official. A right good talker. But he was lying.'

'How do you know?' asked Will.

'He had an old hockey helmet he said he wanted to return to Marcus. That boy never wore one of those things in his life.'

★ ★ ★

'So we know Marcus has either been kidnapped or he's back hiding out,' Will said, pacing New York with his hands behind his back like a lawyer. 'But where? Another shack? Or if the Butler or his henchmen did get him, where're they keeping him? And why?'

'I asked Ritchie, and he doesn't know anything. And Gideon said the Belcourt Twins dropped out of school and went north,' said Jonah. 'So we're out of luck there. But he did say the word is the Butler is offering a drum of Neverclear to anyone who finds Marcus, which might mean they don't have him yet.'

'What's that?' asked Will.

'Neverclear? The Butler's newest gift to Thunder Bay. Gideon said it's a blend of high-test grain alcohol he mixes some kind of solvent into,' said Jonah. 'Apparently it presses the reset button on your head, wipes you clean as a blackboard, something all the old wastoids here are looking for, believe me. Maybe Neverclear is what Marcus interfered with somehow. Tell me again about that sheet you gave Angela?'

'Like I said, it was just a bunch of Xs on an empty grid, like a big game of tic-tac-toe with only one person playing. And there's no hope of getting it back with Angela still in real Toronto.'

'Looks like a dead end,' said Jonah. 'Oh well,' he sighed cheerily, lacing his hands behind his head while examining Will's art supplies, 'there're worse places to be. And why do you always say *real Toronto*, anyway? Of course it's real.'

★　★　★

When the spring rain came, Jonah's basement filled with water the color of chamomile tea, and the creek behind Will's roared wrathfully. Unable to skateboard, they whiled away their weekends at Will's house.

'No wonder you never left,' Jonah said through a mouthful of grilled cheese they'd made themselves (Jonah had removed the heavy architecture books his mother had stored in the oven, plugged in the stove, and instructed Will on how to turn it on). 'This place is unbelievable.' They sat on the couch in Cairo, watching an old Buster Keaton film called *Sherlock Jr.*

'It'll get to you,' Will said pulling a cheese thread from his chin, 'like anywhere, believe me.'

'You know what?' Jonah said later, as Buster Keaton was being pitched around by a hurricane and slammed into walls. 'You look like this dude

170

when you skate. I'm serious. You're like crazy and careful at the same time. You even fall like him. It's funny.'

'It doesn't feel funny,' Will said, struggling to unclench his teeth.

'Whoa, don't get mad. It's a good thing,' he said. 'You look invincible. Even when you're falling. It never looks that bad.'

Inside, the boys gorged themselves on skateboard magazines and lore, poring over arcane details, savoring every square inch of photography. They memorized Jonah's skateboard videos, *Streets of Fire, Hocus Pokus, Video Days*, the way the academics and inmates had memorized his mother's films. They picked their skate gods — Will's was Natas Kaupas, and Jonah's Mark Gonzales, or 'The Gonz,' as he was known — and tried to mimic their styles. They learned skateboards were constructed of 7-plys of rock-hard Canadian maple, which left them proud. To think Thunder Bay's boring trees were trucked off to California to be shaped and screen-printed and returned as magic totems, as myth. The boys painted and drew in New York, covering Will's walls with renderings of skateboarders and skulls. 'You think I could have a go at one of those canvases?' Jonah asked. 'I feel a masterpiece coming on.'

They played the rap and heavy-metal tapes Jonah borrowed from his brothers, which well-articulated the Outside's menaces, much more than the saccharine Inside songs his mother had sung with her guitar in Cairo. Slayer, N.W.A, and Dinosaur Jr. made *The Rite of*

Spring sound like a lullaby.

In New York, Jonah talked incessantly, with an almost automatic exuberance. But he again fell dead silent when Will's mother entered with lunch, watching her with transparent awe. She would clatter forks on Will's desk and say the same old thing she always did: 'Gentlemen, draw your swords.'

Lately his mother was washing her hair and wearing actual clothes, perhaps because Jonah was around, and seemed insulated from the Black Lagoon. Once she touched Jonah on the back in a half-hug, and he grimaced like she'd sandpapered his sunburn. Will had never seen his friend touch anyone before. Occasionally Will would still break down and indulge in a prolonged before-bed cuddle with his mother, and he envied Jonah his fortitude.

Before long, spring leapt into summer, liberating the boys from school. After months of daily flagellation, skateboarding grew kinder to Will. Though the pavement still regularly hurtled upward for reasons he couldn't decode, he was inching toward stability. He could roll without tenseness in his legs, without winging his arms in big hysteric circles.

In the convection of July, a heat that reminded Will of the Destructivity Experiment where he pointed a blowdryer at his face for as long as he could stand, Will and Jonah patrolled the neighborhood, half-searching for Marcus, half not wanting to go home. They memorized every street, parking lot, staircase, curb, storm drain, fire hydrant, and sidewalk square in Grandview

Gardens and County Park. They scoured the backyards along the creek for empty swimming pools, like in *Thrasher*, but those they found were squared with no transition, just abrupt walls lining a deep pit. It was another example of California's overwhelming superiority — they had the sense to properly construct a swimming pool.

At first Will was distraught when the pumpkin-head design on his board became scratched. He'd seen advertisements for plastic guards that protected the precious graphics and was preparing to order them when Jonah told him, 'You don't need any of that stuff.'

'But I'll lose the picture,' said Will.

'That's what it's *for*.'

'For what?'

'Getting ruined.'

Nightly, Will drew himself hot baths in Venice to ease his tenderized muscles. By now his skin, especially at the apexes, was crammed with scabs, welts, rainbows of bruises, and the cursive of scars, like collages made from the pages of Jonah's medical textbooks. Beneath these floated tiny chips of bone that prickled in his flesh.

There'd been other changes too. Maybe it was the effect of the sultry Outside air, but Will's voice had burst like an engine run without oil, leaving a warbling parody of a young delivery-man. He'd also begun to notice certain emerging roundnesses evidenced by girls his age, especially Angela, his memory of her anyway, who, he realized with shock, he missed terribly.

There in the steam of his bath, to keep from

173

tumbling into black, gut-churning thoughts of the Butler's wolves with their snouts buried in his Helmet, memorizing its vinegary scent, or the Butler finding the name Cardiel markered in it and then dropping by for a visit, Will reread the *Thrasher* magazines that Jonah had loaned him. He especially liked the interviews with skate-boarders, who were always irreverent and brave and strange and always reminded him of Marcus.

Now the door in Venice came open. 'Just a sec,' Will hissed, hurriedly reaching for the bubble bath, squeezing a long ribbon into the water. 'Sorry,' he heard her say, shutting the door again, as he swished the water frantically, kicking up a thick flotilla of bubbles that stung his scrapes. 'Okay, you can come in,' he said, sinking to his chin to hide his abrasions under the foam. He could only imagine how she'd inspect him like a piece of fruit, her tongue clucking at the roof of her mouth.

'I'm always going to knock from now on,' she said entering meekly. 'You're older now. You deserve privacy.'

'Sure,' Will said, with no idea what she was talking about.

She sat at the edge of the bath. 'Jonah go home?'

Will nodded, blowing bubbles from his bottom lip.

'He can stay over anytime he wants, you know, I won't mind. I don't love the thought of him going through that culvert at night. We could set up another cot.'

'Jonah can't sleep if he's not at home,' Will said. 'He doesn't feel safe.'

'Well, we've got that in common,' she said, laughing with her eyes shut. 'I really like him,' she added. 'He livens this place up. It's so good you two are friends. It wasn't always like that in Thunder Bay, Will. Your uncle and I didn't have Native friends. It just wasn't something people did. Actually, with those skateboards of yours, in a way you boys both remind me of your uncle.'

Will fought the urge to sit up. 'What was he like?'

'He was smart. And funny. And daring,' she said. 'And angry.' She gave a quick smile.

'What was he angry about?'

'Oh,' she said, scooping some bubbles in her palm, 'I suppose he was mad about losing our parents, and at the way things were here. And he didn't know where to put it. He could've done so much, gone to university somewhere or created things. He was brilliant, like you. But when our dad died, he had to stay to take care of us. At that time people in Thunder Bay didn't have options the way people in other places did.'

'They still don't, Mom.'

She shook her head as though to clear it. 'But you're happy out there, aren't you?'

Will nodded. 'The world is really big,' he said. 'It's hard to believe. It just keeps going and going.'

'I remember that,' she said.

'Mom, I heard that people die in their houses way more than anywhere else,' he said, 'making this, like, the most dangerous place in the world. At least for us.'

She put her wrist over her eyes. He could see her body tense like a bow drawn with an arrow. 'That's because people are in their houses more often than other places,' she said. 'It's just statistics, Will.'

'But it still means you're safer if you go out and do stuff,' he said. 'That's the truth. That's not just statistics. Everybody Outside knows it.'

They sat for a while in silence, and she seemed to let it go.

'Mom, is it because of Dad? Or is it because of Charlie?'

'What, Will?'

'The . . . Black Lagoon?'

Her eyes were open and searching.

'The reason you can't go Outside,' he added.

'Is that what you call it?'

'Sometimes.'

'I don't know,' she said. 'In some way, I guess. I do miss them both. For different reasons. But it also comes from . . . me.'

'Then you can stop it. If it's from Inside you.'

'It's not that easy, honey.'

'Being brave is never easy. That's why it's good for you.'

She cocked her head and sighed but didn't say anything.

'What if we built you a shack in the backyard and brought all your stuff out there, like your bed and your books and guitar? Wouldn't it be basically the same?'

'It's more complicated than that.'

'But if we painted it exactly like your room and got — '

'Look,' she said, her voice cutting, 'sometimes I'm scared to *breathe*, Will. The more I fight it, the worse it gets. But I've been doing better lately. This Relaxation business really helps.'

'Why be scared of breathing, Mom? Breathing never killed anyone. It keeps you *alive*. You just think about it too much.'

'I've tried to stop thinking about it. Believe me.'

'You need something to *do*. Like solve a puzzle or something. Find a mystery. Get a hobby. That's what I'm doing.'

'Honey, I don't think crossword puzzles are going to fix this.'

'But what are you *actually* afraid of? Dying? Kids at my school have scraps all the time, and they're fine. It's *actually* pretty hard to die, Mom.'

She snapped her elastic. 'Oh, please don't say that word,' she said. 'You've come close before, believe me. You just can't remember.'

'I got amnesia?' Will said, excited at the potential territory of himself previously unmapped.

'No, you were young. When we were in Toronto, the sub . . . ' — she seemed to weaken for a moment — 'you nearly fell — actually, you did slip . . . on a pool deck, and cracked your head.' Her elastic thwacked twice. 'You bled like a faucet. They had to clear the pool because it went pale-pink.'

'You took me to a pool?'

'You were young,' she said in a long quivery

breath. 'Oh, Will,' she said, shutting her eyes. 'What I'm most afraid of is breaking apart and losing everything.'

'Aren't you already broken apart?'

'Not completely.'

'Well, maybe you just need to get it over with,' he said, 'like I do in skateboarding. If I'm scared to try a trick, I need to fall once really bad, and then I'm not scared anymore.'

'You and Jonah going skateboarding tomorrow?' she said, turning to examine her face in the mirror, except her eyes weren't looking anywhere.

'Yeah, probably,' he said, then, just to scare her: 'We might go find some hills to bomb downtown.'

Her breath caught, and she stared at the bubbles for a long while. She pulled back the elastic at her wrist but didn't let it go.

'Could you do something for me, Will?' she asked, avoiding his eyes.

'I'm never quitting skateboarding, so don't even ask — '

'No, no, it's not that. Promise me one thing. Please don't go downtown to the harbor. Okay? It's just . . . very, very dangerous down there. Even more so than the creek.'

Though he'd never admit it to Jonah, he was still reluctant to leave the neighborhood anyway, because of the Butler's wolves and the possibility of the Wheezing Man's bear hug breaking all his ribs like sticks. 'Sure, Mom,' Will said, and she put her hand in his wet hair and they sat like that for a while listening to the bubbles fizz.

Relaxation Time

It was July, and she'd been daring to open a window in her bedroom, letting the delicious air slide over her skin, amid nothing more than a manageable stitch of anxiety. Perhaps she had absorbed a little of Will's courage, or perhaps all this talking into her reel-to-reel was helping to loosen panic's grip on her, finger by finger, word by word, memory by memory.

Both the radio and TV had gone dead, and there hadn't been a newspaper delivered in weeks. Even after Diane had berated the profusely apologetic circulation office for an hour, still the paper did not come. At first these had seemed terrible omens, but now she was enjoying the quiet. It cheered her to be free from the *Thunder Bay Tribune*'s ever-depressing editorials, all those missing children and dour forecasts of a worsening economic future. She was reading *Great Expectations* and watching old films on her 16mm projector Will and Jonah had set up. Even sketching a little and taking some still photos here and there — mostly when some regular household object caught the sunlight in such a way that the light seemed to originate from within it.

Will had started sleeping on his own in Charlie's old room. Sometimes she still woke in the dark and listened hard for his breathing but found no little warm engine of a boy beside her, only the unearthly roar of night. To compensate, she'd ordered an extra quilt to put atop her old one. Tonight she vowed to check on him only twice — a hard-fought number. It was as high as ten previously. Poking her head into his room was like diving into a pool of his sweet breath. She loved to watch his perfect chest rise in the half-light like smoke. But she'd been sleeping better on her own. Now whenever she was troubled by a dream, she could click on her reading light without fear of waking Will.

Summer meant Will was again a constant presence in the house, and so was Jonah. He was a quiet boy, and at first she'd worried he was somewhat morose, but now that he was opening up she could see something lustrous in him, a vein of brilliance that in some ways reminded her of Arthur. But Will was smitten and rarely ate when Jonah was over, the surest sign of adoration. Initially she was unable to watch their skateboarding — this machine without seat belts or protection of any kind, upon which her sweet, tender son, his legs like finely sanded sticks, hurtled through traffic and over concrete. But on her better days, she liked to watch them out front. Mostly it was to see that old determination on his face, the same zeroed-in look he'd get while painting — something he hadn't done in months. Though she'd never tell them, she found skateboarding as beautiful as any dance, with its arcing turns and graceful little leaps. (She could only imagine what Arthur would say about how these disenfranchised boys were reclaiming their inhospitable urban environment in creative ways.) It transported her back to the hours she spent in the workhouse at Pool 6, watching in fascination the displays of balance and daring and one-upmanship: men swinging from safety lines, leaping from high perches, dancing through dangerous machinery. As long as Will stuck to their neighborhood as he'd promised, and he and Jonah didn't start hurling themselves down staircases and sliding across banisters and curbs like the boys in the magazine pages that now wallpapered his room, she'd do her best to contain her fear. Hadn't Charlie been equally reckless after the deaths of their parents? Fighting, scaling high trees, riding his bike like a demon, working like a man possessed — why must boys terrify the world to know it loves them?

But most heartening was to see Will and Jonah together. In the Thunder Bay of her youth, Native people still mostly kept to the reserves and to themselves. She suspected that was the real reason the other elevator workers had grumbled about what Charlie and Whalen were up to at night at Pool 6. When a rumor went around that they'd let the Native workers use the common mugs in the workhouse, the men smashed every last one, and the thought of this now left her ill. From the paper she knew more and more Natives were living in the city these days, mostly across the highway in County Park (a subdivision that hadn't existed until after she'd left) and down by the harbor — a good thing, she supposed, as long as they weren't forced from the reserves, as they'd been forced onto them. She recalled the silent scorn and derision heaped upon the Native students at her school, worse than she and Charlie ever got it. How they were never called upon by teachers in class. How at recess they were literally spit upon and ignored. How White children washed their hands if ever they happened to touch a Native student or pass one a handout. It was so easy to misplace details like these because they tasted so foul in the mouth, were so quietly vile. And it would be easier to say that Theodore was kind to Natives they'd pass on the street, which he was, but Diane also remembered her father expounding that old Thunder Bay adage that Natives were averse to work — to him life's greatest virtue, making idleness life's gravest crime. Diane could still see him flushing her and Charlie from the house, as though their idle presence on a weekend afternoon was unclean. 'I don't huff grain dust to finance a couple of homebodies,' he'd say. Any man spotted in taverns or sitting on his porch on a weekday was less than an insect to Theodore. But it was worse if they were Native. 'I understand these people were given a raw deal,' he said once while driving in his squeaky pickup. 'Who hasn't. Look at us Cardiels. But they need to just forget the past and get to work.' She wondered now what he'd have said about the crew that his son had cheated out of their fair pay? Or of all the hours Will and Jonah spent together painting and skateboarding? And what would her father think of her now? The very definition of a homebody. Living off Arthur's support checks and her meager royalties. Moping around the house. And what would he make of her films? Had it been work to create those? To Theodore work meant huffing grain dust or loading trains or framing a house. Work was defined by one thing: a punched clock. A payroll. Diane hadn't worked in decades by his definition. But wasn't everything that demanded care and effort — painting, growing up, skateboarding, reading, filmmaking, hiding — also equally important work? How much damage had this narrow idea done to people in Thunder Bay? And to Charlie, who would've given anything to set foot on a university campus or to make a film, as she had? How much more damage would this idea do?

It is hard work to be destroyed, she heard herself say out loud to the image of Theodore floating in the lights of her goggles as she pulled them from her face and removed her head-phones, uncovering the soothing clatter of skateboards out front. No, that first glimmer of Charlie in her son that had so terrified her when Will first stepped outside wouldn't land him where it had landed his uncle. These two boys tearing around together was proof enough that things didn't only get worse in Thunder Bay. Maybe recklessness would be the very thing that would save them.

13

While Will was in Paris duct-taping the hole in his shoe that his futile ollie attempts had chewed away, the phone rang. 'Angela's back from Toronto,' Wendy said conspiratorially when he picked up. 'She's at Our Lady of Sorrows. She wanted you to know.'

To reach the hospital, the boys piloted their skateboards through tributaries of street and sidewalk out beyond the preposterously expansive golf course on the outer limits of Grandview Gardens, drawing Will farther from home than he'd ever been. From the peak of Hill Street, he was rewarded with a closer glimpse of the grain elevators, which were even more decrepitly majestic than ever. When they reached the hospital, the sign outside put Will in mind of his mother. 'My Lady of Sorrows,' he said to himself.

Inside, the building was a spaceship, all gleaming metal and glass, with a clean smell with an undertow of decay, the way fresh white paint put over rusting iron eventually bubbles and bleeds orange. Will had never been to a hospital. He'd never been sick, either, if you didn't count choking on the chicken finger and the expired yogurt. Was there a machine here that could fix his heart? Had his uncle Charlie been brought here when he was dying? Had one of these people failed him?

As they were looking around, a stethoscope-wearing man with a crisp collar blooming up through a buttery V-neck sweater bent down to examine Jonah's swollen elbow. 'That's a nasty one, son,' he said. 'Are you okay?'

'Yeah, it sort of stays like that,' Jonah said, his eyes wide. 'It's just a moderate contusion. But it seems to be resolving fine.'

'You're quite right,' the doctor said, letting go of his elbow, impressed. Then he leaned in close to Will. 'Is your friend safe at home?'

'Oh, yeah, he's really safe,' said Will. 'He's maybe the safest person I know.'

The doctor directed them to Angela's floor on the children's ward. That there could be enough children in medical peril to fill an entire wing nearly sent Will running back Inside. The boys heard a sound from down the hall like a seal's bark, and they found Angela in her bed, her body braided with coughs, her face a swimming-pool hue. There was a thin white tube snaking into her nose, taped to her cheek. Will had the sudden fluttery urge to sneeze.

'Hold on!' she said when she spotted them, making a bowl with her lower lip, as she kicked off her blankets and rushed to the bathroom, dragging a rolling pole of swinging fluids behind her. They heard guttural sounds of expectoration while Will examined her room: a vase of chrysanthemums, a sparkly purse, a few teen magazines, and some pictures hung in frames on the wall. Will recognized one as the same grid he'd given her from Jonah's desk.

'Don't worry about this,' she said, pointing at

her nose as she emerged with her hair spray-sculpted and dark eyeliner dragged raccoon-like across the inside of her eyelashes. Though she was right in front of them, her voice seemed underpowered, distant, as if she were speaking through a thin pane of glass. 'It's a feeding tube,' she said. 'I don't need it to breathe or anything. My CF grows fibers in my intestines, so if I don't get like four thousand calories a day I lose weight. Hey, Jonah,' she said sheepishly.

'Hey,' he said. 'I'm happy you're okay, Angela.'

Angela's jaw dropped. She looked at Will. 'That's the most he's ever said to me!'

'I fixed him,' Will said proudly.

Her face lit like an old person's birthday cake, and words tumbled out of her. 'My dad's convinced all the grain dust hanging in the air made me sick. Actually, my doctor said the childhood asthma rates in this city are through the roof, but CF is totally genetic. You can live to thirty-five, but mine is the worst type — there's no way I'll make thirty. So I'm just like *whatever*. Thirty, eighty, same difference.' She arranged herself again on the bed. 'I can't have babies because I won't be there for them,' Angela continued, shooting a surreptitious look at Jonah. 'And I'd feel bad getting married and then just, like, dying, or whatever.' She sighed like a bored movie star. 'I'm what they call *doomed*. But it's okay. I can do what I want. Have fun. Plus I'm never going to get wrinkles!'

Will tried to take comfort in his and Angela's mutually doomed fates, and wondered whether he could even expect eighteen more years from his heart. But such magnitudes of time had a similar underwhelming effect as when his mother first taught him that every single star was actually another sun just like theirs. They created a *humph* — then nothing. Some information was too enormous to cram into your mind.

'But it's *so* good to see my *best* friend again,' she said to Will, brushing his back in a way that made his penis hook uncomfortably in his underwear. 'You look . . . different.'

Will felt his cheeks flame under her gaze. A summer of daily skateboarding Outside had left his hair sun-streaked, his body dark and slender, tempered by asphalt and concrete. His legs cracked like twin bullwhips when he jumped, and his right calf, the pushing leg, was significantly larger and more rigid than his left. Even his bones felt different: strong and flexible as aircraft aluminum. 'Jonah's been teaching me some things,' Will said as a nurse entered the room with a blocky machine on silent wheels.

'Angela, it's time for your percussion,' she said, setting out a cup of pills that Angela snapped into her throat with unbelievable ease. It still took Will an hour of gagging to swallow a Tylenol.

'You guys can stay,' Angela said, leaning forward for the nurse. 'I do this every day. It loosens the mucus.'

'Angela, I have something I need to ask,' Will said as the nurse velcroed her into a vest that reminded Will of a flak jacket. Angela coughed a few more hoarse seal barks and spit some blobs into a cup.

'Sorry,' she said, an embarrassed look directed at Jonah.

The nurse hooked two tubes from the machine to the jacket, and as Will was about to speak, the machine roared and the jacket inflated like an airplane life vest. Angela began to shake. The nurse checked her watch then left the room.

'Angela,' Will began nervously, speaking loudly as he did on his first day of school. 'You know that drawing of Jonah's I gave you? Well, he needs it back.'

She frowned while her bottom lip wobbled with the shaking.

'He said he'd draw another one for you?' Will added, turning to Jonah, who nodded.

'But I love that drawing,' she said, her voice warbly like a sheep saying *baa*. 'I see it when I *wake up*. It keeps me going.'

'We . . . need it, Angela. It's important.'

'Yeah,' Jonah said. 'That one's not even good. I'll draw you anything you want.'

'So . . . ' Angela said, 'you wouldn't have come if it wasn't for this thing — '

' — No, that's not it!' said Will.

Suddenly the machine stopped, and it felt like the whole Outside had never been so quiet before. Even the distant beeping and institutional hush of the hospital was lessened.

Angela thought for a moment before horking brazenly into a cup. 'Okay, boys, I have an idea,' she said.

Will and Jonah spent the next day setting up an ersatz crime lab in Jonah's basement, opposite to where Enoch kept his weight set. They'd considered setting up in Will's house (better art supplies and lighting), but Will knew their investigation would unsettle his mother, plus Marcus's grid was safer here. Despite their fearsome exterior, the Turtle Brothers spoke softly and made a point to eat together every Friday night, the boys all sitting down to either a big stack of ordered-in pizzas or some fried whitefish that Gideon pulled sizzling from a cast-iron pot with a wire scooper. They always waited for Will to take his share first.

Once after supper Will asked Jonah if he'd ever tried the Butler's grain alcohol. 'No,' he said, then tapped his temple, 'I'm keeping this baby pristine for med school. My brothers don't touch it either now that they're working at the call center.' Jonah's brothers spent their days convincing people to increase their credit limits, and the thought of these powerful men talking all day into tiny headsets gave Will a headache. Jonah said that when they first moved down to Thunder Bay from their reserve, his brothers started a roofing company. They put an ad in the yellow pages, bought a truck, tools, and an air compressor for their nail guns — but their phone sat quiet as a rock. Gideon even took the phone back and demanded another at the store. But the new one didn't ring either. At the unemployment office the man asked Hosea what they were thinking. He said Indians don't know the first thing about roofs. 'He said homeowners in Thunder Bay knew we haven't lived under them for long enough,' Jonah said.

'Why do your brothers call you Doc?' asked Will.

'Because I've always sewn them up with dental floss whenever they came home gashed up,' Jonah said. 'Those medical textbooks are how I learned to draw real people. Studying anatomy.' With an image locked in his mind of Jonah with a loop of dental floss in his teeth bending over his grimacing brother's split eyebrow, for the first time in his life Will wished he'd had siblings.

'Is that how you're getting out of Thunder Bay?' Will said.

At this, Jonah grew shy. 'Yeah, maybe. I'm going to fall back on medicine if my pro skateboard career doesn't work out,' he said with his usual smirk.

It took only a few days in Jonah's Inside before Will decided he preferred it to his own. Here nobody was watching you, and the most ghastly horror films elicited only laughter and glee, and the Black Lagoon did not reign. It was during this time Will noticed water-swollen porno magazines nestled beside the upstairs toilet. The hairstyles of the women were huge and souffléd, and upon their orangey faces he found an exact replica of his mother's Black Lagoon look — as if they'd all been struck by some great, unknowable terror. Will realized then with horror that penises were Outside and vaginas were Inside, and the import of these connections sent him lunging from the bathroom.

The boys rush-ordered a fingerprinting kit and practiced on themselves, applying latent powder with the impossibly fluffy brush, lifting the print with tape and fixing it to a backing card, pausing only so Jonah could occasionally wipe his mouth with his sleeve after his kiss with Angela. She'd said she would surrender the drawing only if they both French-kissed her in her hospital bed for a count of thirty seconds each. 'I want to be fair,' she'd said, which Will hoped was more than evidence of her charitability. Angela removed her feeding tube, and after Will sufficiently coaxed him, Jonah went first, tucking his bangs behind his ears, as he brought his lips to hers, Angela wide-eyed. The sight of his two friends mouth-locked was both unbearable and dazzling for Will to behold. When Will's turn came, it was like his face ollied down twenty stairs and landed in a tub of warm oil. Jonah had lasted only twenty-five seconds before pulling away, but Will couldn't venture how long his kiss was. He could still taste the flavor of her mouth, acidic, apricot-like, the best thing the Outside had offered so far.

One night, they were fingerprinting Marcus's grid when Enoch came over to their worktable after an hour of grunting beneath his barbells. 'Why're you tools putting makeup on that map?' he said, breathing hard, toweling his face with a shirt.

'It's not a . . . ' Will said, before locking eyes with Jonah.

''Cept it doesn't have any fucking street names on it,' Enoch continued. 'Some map. But looks like the harborfront, to me. That's the only part of this shit-pile town built in a grid.'

14

September arrived the following week and demanded their begrudging return to school. The boys claimed the rearmost desks, where they whispered about the map they'd yet to decipher and the byzantine skateboard tricks they would someday master. Their new teacher, Mrs. Gustavson, wore a beach-worth of shell jewelry, smiled emptily, and spouted in a sugary voice lots of his mother's words, like *creativity*, *gifted*, and *self-esteem*. Will trusted her about as far as his mother could go for a jog.

In the first week, when Will was picking up an exercise he'd narrowly passed from her desk, he said, 'Thanks Mom,' instantly scorching himself with embarrassment.

At recess, Mrs. Gustavson asked him to stay behind. 'I couldn't help but notice what you said there,' she said.

'Yeah, sorry,' said Will. 'Old habit.'

'Oh, I don't mind. In fact, I'm quite flattered,' she said, pausing as if something was sinking in other than the death knell of boredom and the senseless squander of recess time.

'You know, Will,' she continued, 'I must confess something to you. I'm a great admirer of your mother's work. And your father's, of course. But I saw *The Sky in Here* when I was in university, and it made an indelible impression on me,' she said, as though they were sharing some great secret.

'I've never seen it.'

'Really?' she said, shocked. 'But you must be very close?'

'You could say that.'

'Well, she's modest, I'm sure. But I know some people who will be very pleased to hear Diane Cardiel is safe and sound and back living in Thunder Bay. She must love having a bright, creative fellow like you around the house,' she said, smiling falsely, and Will bristled. Jonah had more creativity in his right leg than all the students at his school combined, and though she was brand new, Mrs. Gustavson already acted as if he wasn't there.

'Is this over yet?' Will said, wounding her visibly, before racing outside to find Jonah.

Now that they were in the seventh grade, their classmates talked of group trips to the roller rink and declared doomed loves in bubble-lettered notes and three-party phone calls. None mentioned how last year's grade eights had disappeared like planes into the clouds of high school, an ascendancy death-like in its impenetrability. Happily, the mysteries of what to wear and say and when to put your arm around a girl and how to properly manage a vagina were of zero relevance to Will and Jonah, who were content with the mystery of Marcus and how, exactly, one could possibly ollie over a fire hydrant.

To endure the flavorless hours, the boys reacquired the necessary talent of kill-switching their minds, slowing their pulses, holing up in private mental dens. They perfected a communication exclusive to their eyebrows, while lazily doodling skateboard graphics and complex ramp arrangements on their velcro-flapped binders. In class they were cheetahs napping, borderline catatonic, preparing for the bell's merciful peal.

At lunch they shunned the cafeteria to go skateboarding off school property. These days Will could manage the occasional weak ollie — the trick's true alchemy still outpacing his understanding. There in the parking lot of the grocery store that still delivered his mother's food, Will drank a throat-searing two-liter carton of iced tea while Jonah practiced heelflips, landing again and again on his sideways board, folding his feet in half and pouring himself to the oily ground.

'You always get the same thing,' said Jonah, 'ice tea and salt-and-vinegar chips.'

'I know what I like,' said Will, though the truth was the towering neon of the grocery shelves and the sheer glut of choice they presented baffled him. While they ate, some high-school-age hockey players shouted 'Skater fags!' from a gunning pickup truck, almost obligatorily, kept at bay only by the fearsome legend of the Turtle Brothers. Rather than the designer sweatshirts and safety pin-tapered jeans of their peers, the boys donned the flannel button-ups and work pants that abounded in Thunder Bay's thrift stores. The pants were constructed with thick polyester that survived their worst spills and were cheap to replace when they didn't. At school, hockey players had started to sneak up behind

Will to yank his pants down, so they both wore webbed belts cinched tight around their bruised hips, even though Jonah was never subjected to the indignity.

After school, with the map folded deep in Jonah's backpack, the two ventured downtown, into the crannies of the city that no upright citizen had reason to frequent: loading bays, alleys, abandoned industrial buildings, check-cashing places, the parking lots of windowless strip clubs, closed gas stations, and listless strip malls. The concrete and the bustle brought forth new memories of days spent careening around Toronto with his mother, the glint of subways, the towering buildings, his hand caught warm in hers.

'So if the lines are streets, the Xs must signify something, because there are like thirty of them,' said Will, sitting on a bench, turning the map over and over in an attempt to orient themselves. 'But what could be possibly valuable enough for Marcus to use it to leave Thunder Bay forever?'

'Ain't no buried treasure anywhere down here, Long John Silver,' Jonah said, gesturing to a squalid apartment block with crotch-yellowed underwear hanging from the window like the flags of surrender.

Will had made no mention of the solemn promise to his mother he was breaking by coming to the waterfront. But he'd seen plenty of boys his age walking around, and none of them looked immediately endangered.

'Think we need to worry about the Butler's wolves?' Will said later, fighting again to keep the image of a fanged snout clamping over his other thigh from his mind. Lately, each time he left the house, he'd been liberally dousing his entire body with deodorant, in the hopes it would mask his scent.

'Bah, we're small potatoes,' said Jonah. 'Plus we can outrun his wolves on our boards.'

They tried penciling various street names onto the lines, but, frustratingly, downtown Thunder Bay was a grid with no defining abnormalities. Each time they thought they'd located an X, what they found was uniformly unremarkable and decrepit: another abandoned building with an old, plateless car parked out front. The boys rifled the glove boxes of the cars and staked out the buildings with no luck. 'Some treasure,' Jonah said.

But when riding his skateboard, even the 'rusty ruin' of Thunder Bay sparkled with vitality and potential in Will's eyes. While investigating the map, they happened over perfect skateboard terrain: painted curbs surrounded by smooth concrete and perfect sets of stairs with no cracks at the top, where the boys would return again and again after security guards had shooed them away. Surfers rode waves, which were already beautiful, but skateboarders *made* things beautiful: the ugly, discarded nooks and leftovers of a place, the abandoned, unused architecture that people preferred to ignore. Beneath their wheels, these dead places became sites of wonder.

At times Will wondered what special genius allowed Jonah to nimbly launch himself from the summit of any stair set without a stitch of Black

197

Lagoon in his body. It had something to do with the possessed gleam he'd get while maniacally attempting a trick for hours until he'd mastered it. Jonah was channeling something. Will figured. An anger, maybe. Equal parts joy and fear. He resembled the skateboard titans of *Thrasher* more and more each day.

Will couldn't discern if it was the sight of a White kid and an Indian kid together or the velocity with which they disregarded every traffic bylaw and trespassing ordinance on the books that caused pedestrians to recoil as they zoomed past. As much as it seemed like a suicide attempt to passersby, skateboarding was precisely the opposite: it was about mastery — a *seizure* of control, not a loss. That the board did their bidding — danced or flipped or spun successfully beneath them — afforded the most sublime pleasures of their short lives. Even after his most crushing falls, Will was learning to greet the pain, to wade out into its eddies and unexpected pools. To feel it pull parallel with another, worse pain inside him — born of the fact that his mother was wasting her life Inside or that his heart could give out any minute. And these pains aligned themselves, matched tempos, a kind of duet. Will would listen to the minor chord of it ring in him and find comfort in the sound.

After spending every weekend downtown, the boys grew well acquainted with Thunder Bay's maniacs, its miscreants and castaways, those wandering its alleys and vacated streets with nothing better to do, and Will was terrified and fascinated by the harm the Outside could inflict.

198

There were the drunks, some Indian, most not. Many were friendly, overly friendly, and Will would shake their hard, smelly hands while Jonah always kept his distance. Fresh and noxious with Neverclear in the early afternoon — they either came from distant reservations or once worked for the elevators, the railway, the mills, or the lakeboats. They often called to Will and Jonah with equal parts admiration and contempt. 'Let's talk to youse two boys,' they'd slur with dim mustardy eyes, waving them closer. Some would even ask to try their boards, claiming they'd possessed great balance in their day. The boys watched solid, railway tie-driving men drop to the pavement like toddlers. Sometimes they'd ask for change, which Jonah hated most of all. 'How about you *change* your clothes first?' he'd mutter after they'd left.

Then there were the crazies: the man who believed he was a policeman and wrote them fake bylaw infraction tickets for skateboarding on donut shop napkins; fixed to his jacket was a sticker — THIS ACCIDENT HAS BEEN INVESTI-GATED BY THE THUNDER BAY POLICE — which he'd push forward like a badge. The woman who only walked backwards, peering over her shoulder with a smudgy makeup mirror. The withered guy who had a voice like a child and strung sentences together like beaded necklaces: 'Who are you what are you doing where's your helmet why are you here you boys are going to kill yourselves.' The carnival-size woman they called Anti-Old Lady because she hated everything. 'Do you want a hug?' they'd call to her from safe across the street. 'I hate hugs and I hate you!' she'd screech, shutting her eyes with pure loathing. Will listened intently to them all, marveling at their variety, noting their voices and syntaxes, but despite their shared insanity, none bore any resemblance to the Wheezing Man.

But then their first stroke of luck: Will spotted the Bald Man hurrying along the sidewalk with a rolling dolly, on it a small steel drum. Silently the boys lifted their skateboards and followed at a distance, soon arriving upon a spot on the map they'd investigated previously, where they'd found a sun-faded purple car, the color of diluted wine, out front of a shuttered brick laundromat. The Bald Man pulled his dolly beside the car, taking a quick glance around before levering open the gas tank and feeding the mouth of a section of green hose into the tank. He put the other end to his lips, spat, then stuffed it into the barrel at his feet. He waited like that for a few minutes, glancing around, the boys watching him while tucked behind a used car lot's sandwich-board sign. Then he capped everything up and pushed the dolly off toward the lake.

When he was gone, the boys approached the car and opened the tank.

'Why all the secrecy for siphoning some gas?' said Jonah, lowering his nose to the opening. 'At least now we know what those garden hoses were for.'

'I have an idea,' Will said, searching a garbage-strewn alley, where it didn't take him long to find some discarded drinking straws. He crumpled the ends and fit three together into one long tube. 'One time I made the Eiffel Tower like this,' he said. 'My mom loved it.' He stuck the straw in the tank.

'After you,' Jonah said with disbelief.

Will pursed his lips and sucked. Into his mouth flooded a gulp of burning death and antimatter and the purple fumes of a hundred melting G.I. Joe figurines. Will gagged and nearly vomited while a good amount continued to napalm his throat and claw its way down into his belly. 'When is this going to stop?' Will said weakly, doubling over, a lingering aftertaste like whatever was in Mr. Miller's mug.

'Ah, give it a second,' Jonah said pinching the straw from Will's grip. 'You don't have Indian tastebuds.' He took a sip and smacked his lips. '*Whew!*' he said. 'That right there is grain alcohol like I've never tasted. There's something extra to it' — he clacked his tongue — 'A kick. Like nailpolish remover and model glue. Neverclear, I'd bet anything.'

'Butler must be hiding it around the city in the gas tanks of abandoned cars!' Will said hoarsely, now feeling as if his mother had duct taped a few dozen hand warmers to his belly.

'Okay, so Marcus was stealing hoses for the Butler. Then he got the idea to take the map so he could use it to find the Butler's stashes of Neverclear and sell it himself. Something like that would generate enough money to kiss Thunder Bay good-bye forever.'

'Maybe it worked. Maybe Marcus did it?' Will said, still recovering.

'Then why is the Butler still offering a reward?' said Jonah. 'No, the Butler and the Bald Man must've remembered where this one was without the map, or we would've seen them do this weeks ago.'

'But if all those Xs are cars with Neverclear stashed in them — '

' — it means there are gallons and gallons of this stuff out there,' Jonah said. 'Which means the Butler still really, really wants it.'

Jonah cinched the straps of his backpack.

'Shit,' Will said, swearing credibly for the first time, but still too afraid to enjoy it.

Relaxation Time

With Will back at school and afterwards riding his skateboard out who-knows-where — she was mentally replaying his promise to avoid the waterfront thirty or forty times per day — Diane had been forced, under threat of starvation, to answer the door herself. While signing for a large, heavy box, she made the mistake of glancing over the courier's shoulder, out into the white radium glow of the pavement, at the brown delivery truck chuffing in her driveway, and the desolate infinity of it threw up a squall in her chest. But she felt her knees hold, and no icy sweat broke over her like that first time it came while she was shoveling the driveway.

Triumphantly, she dragged the box through the hall into the kitchen. Normally she left packages in the entranceway for Will to open when he returned, but the heft of this one intrigued her. She fetched the key from its hiding place, unlocked the knife drawer, and removed a small paring knife. After carefully splitting the tape, she lifted a stack of film canisters from the box, each entombed painstakingly in foam, all battleship gray or mint green — six in total. Next she unearthed a newly minted hardcover book, published by the National Film Board, entitled *Diane Cardiel: A Filmography*. Inside were lushly published still images from her films and many

essays, including one called 'The Constructed-
ness of Public Space in the Age of Anxiety.'
Folded into the book was a letter from the
director of the NFB, stating that they'd
reissued her entire filmography two years ago
but had been unable to locate her. Until a
former student of his named Penny Gustavson,
who was now an elementary school teacher,
had recently informed him that Diane was
living back in Thunder Bay. Perfect timing, he
said, because the NFB was mounting a running
retrospective in Toronto and Montreal next
spring and would like to invite her to speak. 'I
understand, however,' he added tactfully toward
the end, 'that travel may be problematic.'

A *retrospective*? Weren't those for the dead, or
at least the near dead? It struck her that she was
now widely regarded as a relic, an oddity. But
had she been away that long? Long enough for
the mildew of enigma to grow upon her? Even if
she could make it there, somehow, people would
ask what she'd been doing all this time, what
work she'd done. 'Oh, hiding in my house,
watching my son paint,' she'd be forced to say.
Of course she'd write the director to say she
couldn't go, but as she turned the book in her
hands, she couldn't avoid feeling some blush of
pride at the crisp handsomeness of it, and at the
care and delicacy the director had exhibited in
his letter, which seemed intended for a person
much more eccentric, fragile, and important
than herself.

While reboxing the canisters to hide them in
her closet, Diane noticed that Jonah and Will had

left the 16mm projector set up in Cairo. Though it was nearly time for her usual 10:30 Relaxation Session, she found herself threading her first film — *The Sky in Here* — into the take-up reel. She made tea, snuffed the room's lamps, drew the curtains, and coaxed the projector into a clatter.

As the film played, Diane sat quietly, her mind not so much absorbing the images as turning inward to reconstruct the person who'd shot this film, who'd synced the sound and spoke the now precious-sounding voice-over, astonished by how foreign to herself she'd become. After the first film ended she loaded another, watching them in the order she'd created them, fascination creeping into her, each film a missive from a dark region of her self she'd left unconsidered for so long.

She had such feeble command of the period after she'd watched them pull the first tatters of her brother's body from the lake. Oh, how did she ever survive it? In the days following, she'd cried with such force she learned to navigate their house by feel, a grief so fierce and depleting her whole body felt like a turned-out pocket.

When she gathered the strength, she phoned Whalen's house and spoke to his father for the first time. He said his son hadn't been home since the accident, and he begged Diane to tell him where he was.

The number of the funeral home sat on her table for a week. Arranging her brother's burial was the kind of task that grief should impel a person to do, but she couldn't lift the receiver without fear of screaming into it, and was too proud to ask her father's old coworkers for help.

There was still no sign of Whalen. The truth came out about how they'd been swindling the Native crew, and though Whalen's father claimed he hadn't laid eyes on his son since the night of the accident, the common belief was that to avoid scandal he'd changed Whalen's name and packed him off to a university dorm somewhere back east, his head now buried in a law book. On some level she'd been preparing for Whalen to abandon her all along. As she suspected now she would have done herself had Charlie made it to university, and they lost the thrill of secrecy, left only with backgrounds and lives that could never be properly woven together.

It came then to Diane that with both Charlie and Whalen gone, and with no real ties to Thunder Bay left, for the first time in her life she was completely free to do as she pleased. She could leave, tonight, and though she wouldn't have Charlie to answer her questions or roll up his sleeves and fight her battles, she also wouldn't have him watching over her and correcting and interrupting and sucking the light from every moment either. It pained her to say it now, but a long-crushing weight had come off her chest, and while she hadn't known it at the time, her brother's accident assembled inside her a kind of engine of courage.

She packed a bag, locked the house, and walked along the creek to the highway. For months she hitchhiked south and west through a series of uncelebrated American roads. During that time she slept beneath interstate overpasses, drank from eaves troughs, ate wild raspberries and plates of all-day breakfast she'd treat herself to. She had sex with an unhappily married civil engineer who smelled like Whalen in a long aqua-colored car, then a few others as easily as talking to them. She rented weekly-rate motel rooms in a few insubstantial towns, inventing new names for herself in each one. It was during this period she'd made all of her life's most monumental mistakes, seizing every possible occasion to endanger her mind and body, as though Charlie's death had stripped her of the capacity to fear for her own safety. But like a plant that benefited from rough treatment and neglect, she felt more herself than she ever had in Thunder Bay.

From a pawn shop she bought a Nikon camera and a 50mm lens. She preferred photography to sketching: the immediacy, the immersion of seeing, the endless hunt for the perfect subject. She shot empty taverns, derelict train cars, abandoned bicycles, crude underpass graffiti, broken people milling around Greyhound stations, all of it — she wouldn't realize until later — somehow touched by decay.

Eventually, after a time living with a separated beekeeper outside San Francisco who measured his food with a hanging scale and refused to orgasm for spiritual reasons, she made her way back to Canada and enrolled in some arts courses while working at a city-run day care in Toronto. She bought a smelly wool duffle coat from a thrift store and an acoustic guitar, which she plucked nightly until her fingertips hardened into thimbles. In her classes she painted murky watercolors, molded lumpy sculptures, stained glass, fired ceramics, even crocheted — her capricious interests dragging her from one artistic disappointment to the next. An instructor told her that she was cursed with the aesthetic sense to know her work was dull but lacked sufficient skill to fix it. Yet she was not discouraged. It was so much easier to fail without her father or her brother peering over her shoulder.

She came across a book on the history of cinema and after reading it in one caffeine-fueled gulp, she enrolled in film full-time. Her dedication captured the eye of her instructor, yet when called upon in class, either her voice faltered or she talked in tight, senseless circles. Near the middle of the semester, a friend from class brought her to a club popular with U of T grad students, where breathtakingly awful poetry was read as they quaffed Pernod and water. Arthur was an architecture student with tortoise-shell glasses and a clumsy girth. He had a Beach Boy wholesomeness that in a sea of Dylan and Sartre imitators infantilized those around him. Without her brother to speak for her, Diane had become a blurter — offering too much, too quickly, her sentences like a verbal yard sale — and found Arthur's habit of thinking long and hard during conversations soothing. That night she fell into his circle and drifted to a party at an off-hours theater space, where Diane drained six cans of a tasteless beer popular in Thunder Bay that Arthur's friends drank for its 'working-class authenticity.' Soon after, she kicked Arthur in the side of the knee — hard enough to topple him to the carpet — to prove some point about pain tolerance and gender. Minutes later, she was dragging him to a secluded futon with such verve that her mind didn't return to her body for days after.

It was a mutual friend who later told Diane that Arthur was married to a woman who'd been his English professor when he was an undergraduate. In a rushing daze Diane called this woman at the university, impersonating the dean's clerk. Her office was slated for renovation, Diane said. When would she be next out of town at a conference so they could schedule accordingly?

Diane waited weeks until the proper time to ring his bell. Her reward was a week of cab rides to converted lofts in the East End, where they smoked hash from comically large faux-Arabic pipes. Arthur got drunk enough to stand on couches and say, 'Friends, countrymen. This is *essential*,' launching into speeches with full awareness of his own silliness, the discussions always devolving into the drug-addled men questioning meaning itself, which went down the conversational drain of Derrida and deconstructionism before the women cradled them off into the night.

Unlike Whalen, Arthur was so brazen with their meetings, it wasn't long before he parted from his wife and Diane quickly fixed herself at his new apartment. His fridge was full of Polaroid film and homemade pickles bought from a Polish neighbor, sketches of cities and plazas spidering over every square inch of wall. He sang her 'Factory Girl,' complete with a Jagger fish-mouth, and delighted in her working-class tales of Thunder Bay. He surprised her with a photo of the old elevators — including Pool 6 — in Le Corbusier's *Towards a New Architecture*, who admiringly wrote that they were 'the first fruits of the New Age.' It was as disorienting to her as finding a portrait of Theodore or Charlie displayed prominently in a museum.

She hungered for Arthur every waking minute, and when he left to fetch Korean takeout or cigarettes, she would count seconds and watch his apartment door with the same rising panic as when watching Charlie drop into the grain bins. Arthur's world tolerated her as a pretty curiosity. His stature, both physical and intellectual, was enough to shelter her from comments on her attendance at an unremarkable college and her dearth of artistic accomplishment.

The nights shrieked with drugs and sex and overcomplex conversation that ended in screaming matches as often as bed. Everyone was making a film, writing a book, the air a stiff meringue of ideas. It was as though you could pluck one down, staple your name to it, and attain national recognition by that time next week. She set up a desk at Arthur's place and dared to construct a few poems, little bowls of word-salad she threw together hastily enough to disavow attachment to them. At Arthur's urging, she read them to a few slit-eyed friends dozing on a shag carpet.

Then for her birthday Arthur gave her a 16mm camera, a Bolex he'd bought in the park from a smacked-out chess player named Steve. She wandered the city alone, shooting quick bursts of whatever caught her eye, recording snatches of sound with a reel-to-reel slung over her shoulder. A streetlight, some trash, people on benches. At the time she was enthralled by Richard Avedon's photographs: coal miners with blackened faces shot against white, angelic backgrounds, the effect rendering his subjects eerily otherworldly, transcendent. Everyone is worth noticing, the images said and always put her in mind of Charlie and how even today she'd give everything for a photo like this of her brother, with his light-chipped eyes, slanting grin, and grain dust in his coarse hair.

Then one September day she walked to Union Station, closed her eyes for nearly half an hour, deciding that the person she saw when she opened them would be her first subject. She threw her eyes open and asked a young woman if she could film her face, dead on, looking into the lens. The woman kindly complied and after some nervous smiles and hair fiddling, gave her thirty golden seconds of raw vulnerability. She repeated this with twenty others.

When the film was developed, however, a good portion proved unusable: a milk of ghostly light spilled over each frame. Diane was devastated. She'd changed the canister improperly, and light had leaked into the black felt bag while she switched reels.

Arthur pulled a favor and arranged some free

late-night time on an editing machine at the National Film Board. 'Make *something* at least,' he'd said. There she found some usable clips and a few nice frames she managed to duplicate as stills. But it wasn't enough. Then, on her way to the bathroom, she spotted a nest of cut footage in a waste bin nearby. Nearly in tears, she asked another editor if she could use it. 'Knock yourself out,' he said.

She spliced these unwanted clips, intercutting them with her own shots of the city and people at Union Station. She laid the sound she'd recorded of a crowd roaring at a hockey game over a shot of a person sleeping. The sound of a fistfight over lovers walking, a baby gurgling over documentary clips of a bullfight, trains shunting over shots of trash. It was the public invading the private, the inside invading the outside, and the effect was disorienting. When she showed it to him, Arthur declared her film genius, adding that it was about anxiety and public space and love and dread, which confused Diane but still flushed her with pride.

A premiere was organized. The film, which she'd titled *The Sky in Here*, drew effusive praise from those who cared about that sort of thing. They said that it had captured the 'anxiety of the age' and compared it to Joan Didion's essays and the films of Arthur Lipsett, both of which Diane had always loved. She won a first-film award and quickly made a few more works in a similar vein with money from the Film Board and the Arts Council, garnering still more awards and praise.

During that time she and Arthur discussed marriage at length and decided against it. Reasons like resisting the patriarchy and his previous marital debacle were tossed around, but in truth, they were both skittish about commitment, the drift toward entrapment. Though she never found words to tell Arthur about Charlie or her parents, she suspected he knew she couldn't stand to do any more losing.

Arthur had gone to private schools and had never held a job, something the closeted Marxist in him hated to admit, but after graduation he landed an office remodeling, then a small park and a community center. He soon developed a name, which he snidely claimed was the only thing one actually *built* as an architect. Then came the plaza in Copenhagen, and almost overnight Arthur was inaugurated as the high priest of plazas — the great facilitator of urban renewal and community. He was described as visionary, a 'starchitect' — a word they had once only used with the tongs of irony. He designed increasingly significant structures: galleries, libraries, public buildings, first in Europe, then throughout North America, Asia, the Middle East. Arthur would do anything to get his projects built: spew flurries of pseudo-intellectual claptrap, employ the theories of far-flung psychoanalysts, the folklore of African hill tribes — anything to entice funders and investors. It was during this rise that she'd become pregnant, and Arthur did his utmost to hide his trepidation.

'What about your work?' he said. 'Your next film?'

'I can come back to it,' she said.

After Will was born, Arthur tunneled deeper into himself. Increasingly, he preferred life rendered, sketched, blueprinted — better yet, modeled in balsa wood or viewed from a plane, high above the disappointing actuality of place. He applied the same aerial view to Will, reserving his energies for the greater questions: where he should go to school, in what neighborhood would they live. He spent more and more time away, at his drawing table, off in the stratospheres of theory. In truth, Arthur had never enjoyed people. Even Will he treated like a project he was overseeing, checking in every so often like a foreman in a white hardhat to ensure construction was on schedule. Then came their separation, the subway platform . . . but here she was rooting around again in the past, and with that her thoughts gained traction in the slapping of her last film in the take-up reel, the projector blasting pure, empty light on the collapsible screen, and for the first time in years Diane was battered with the sense that though the cupboards of her self had been abundantly stocked with determination and some modest store of talent, she'd made so little of these ingredients to set upon the table of her life. These six canisters of celluloid and one marvelous boy were the totality of her life's output. Her mind writhed with specters of conversations she could've participated in, words she might have combined, films she could have

214

cut together, the howling ghosts of ideas she would never have.

But maybe there was still time, she thought, rising to kill the projector. Her panic was lessening each day. Who was to say it wouldn't continue? Perhaps by spring she could make it to the retrospective, at least the one in Toronto. And just so she'd have something to talk about, she could shoot something new. At home. Nothing grandiose. Maybe some time lapses of the sun swinging through rooms like a pendulum. Plants growing. Dust fuzzing the tops of books. Carpets speckling with lint. Will painting — if he ever did again. And these tapes she'd been recording during Relaxation Times, maybe she could work them in somehow, cut them up, cobble the better snippets into a voice-over. She'd pulled those unwanted filmstrips from the trash to make her first film; who was to say she couldn't do it again with the trimmings of their life here? That settles it, she thought, dragging the box upstairs to her room. She'd ask Will to fetch her old Bolex from the basement when he got home. She only hoped it still worked.

15

The next Monday, Will asked Jonah to accompany him to the police station downtown. 'I won't let anything slip to MacVicar,' Will said, 'but we need to see what he knows about Marcus.'

'Sounds like a solo mission,' Jonah said, flung laterally across the armchair in Cairo, eyes boring into the latest *Thrasher*. 'It's a fact they have great difficulty letting Indians leave that place.' He then reminded Will how Social Services can steal a kid from their parents any time they please, just uproot you from your house like a brown tooth. 'They do it all the time,' he said. 'They did it to Marcus. They tried to get me.' Jonah said Social Services nearly took him after Hosea went to jail for hunting deer within city limits. But his other brothers hid Jonah in the basement and said he moved up north. 'I stayed down there for a month memorizing medical textbooks and eating tinned salmon.' Since then, Jonah's little basement tent was the only place in the house he could sleep. 'But they don't only do it to Indians, Will,' Jonah said, lifting his eyes. 'They do it to White kids, too, if their parents are messed up enough.'

'What's that supposed to mean?' said Will.

Jonah lowered his voice. 'Look dude, I love your mom. I'd quit skateboarding in a second if I could live here and read and paint pictures all

216

day, like forever, but I'm only saying. Be careful what you tell those people.'

★ ★ ★

'I'd like to see the constable,' said Will in a somber voice to the peevish officer standing at a long counter. 'I have important information. Pertaining to a kidnapping . . . '

'Well, if it isn't our little Jack London,' said MacVicar jovially when Will was admitted to his office. 'How's the leg, son? Back on the hockey rink yet?' In his coarse uniform MacVicar loomed tall and had a lean, muscular face like an astronaut. Will remembered his mother berating him in their doorway after Will's wolf attack and now wondered if MacVicar had considered whisking Will away from his transparently deranged home environment.

'Constable, I need to know if you have any leads in Marcus's disappearance.' MacVicar squinted.

'Marcus? The *orphan boy* who went missing?' said Will.

'Right. Right, we're looking into it,' MacVicar said. 'He wasn't a friend of yours was he?'

'Yes, he was,' Will said. 'And he's been missing for *months*. Don't you have anything yet?'

'Son, anything related to that case won't go public before the investigation is concluded,' said MacVicar, his good cheer draining.

Will was instantly overcome with the tsunami of exasperation that so often accompanied his Outside interactions with adults. 'This is bullshit

. . . ' he murmured uncontrollably, crossing his arms, accidentally kicking the side of MacVicar's steel desk.

'Look here,' MacVicar said, his face concrete, 'Will, the only reason we're talking right now is because I knew your family. My father worked with your grandfather Theodore and then your uncle Charlie down at those elevators, and I for one know you come from a good, hardworking family, so I'm cutting you some slack. But as I said: these particulars are confidential. And they're going to remain that way, am I clear?'

Will sneered and turned his head to the window. He hated how in books children were always undiscovered geniuses or princes who inherited rolling green estates at the end. The Outside had laid bare his mother's great lie: Will wasn't even in the neighborhood of genius, and a soaring inventory of questions stonewalled his understanding. Just once Will wanted Outside things to go as smoothly as they always had Inside. This idea closed Will's throat, and he unleashed a low, flabby sob.

The constable sighed and pushed forward a box of tissue. 'Can I get you anything, son?' he said.

Will shook his head, unlatching a few more tears that dappled his shirt.

MacVicar rose and poured himself a cup of coffee from the machine on his filing cabinet.

'Can I have one of those?' Will said, sniffing.

The constable paused, cocked his head. Then shrugged. 'How do you take it?'

'Pardon?' said Will.

'Black?'

Will nodded, even though he knew coffee was actually dark brown. His mother only drank black tea because coffee 'rattled her cage.'

'Look, Will, I know things haven't been the smoothest for you and your family,' said MacVicar, handing the cup to Will. 'How is your mother? She getting out?'

'She's good,' Will lied, remembering Jonah's warning about Social Services. 'We go to the movies every week and on long walks and stuff.'

'Good, good, Will,' said MacVicar, before they took matching slugs of coffee. Will nearly gagged — the taste was cheap hot chocolate mixed with the moldy soil of a neglected houseplant.

'And I know how tragedies can unsettle a community,' said MacVicar, easing back into his chair. 'I'm sure your mother must have told you about your uncle's accident and what a blow that was to everyone in Thunder Bay. I was there that morning. A terrible thing to witness. It makes a kind of sense her being leery of things and all.'

'You were there when my uncle's heart gave out?' Will said.

'His heart?' said MacVicar. 'That's an interesting way to put it, son. But I don't blame her.'

'For what? said Will.

'You'll have to ask your mother that question, Will. Listen, my point is, nowadays we've got boys like Marcus going missing *monthly*. Mostly they scarf Valiums or oxycodone before getting gunned on their dad's hooch or their sister's hair spray and then go winter swimming in the lake is my experience. So pardon me if our top investigative priority isn't a lazy delinquent whose natural proclivity is for getting himself lost.'

'Marcus wasn't lazy,' Will said irritatedly. 'He built a cabin. *Himself.*'

'That shack near the highway we found?' said MacVicar. 'On *Crown land.* Which I shouldn't have to point out is stealing.'

'He was hiding,' Will said.

'From the truant officer,' scoffed MacVicar.

'From *the Butler*,' said Will, with either his anger or the coffee loosening his tongue. 'It was his wolf who bit me. And he's a bootlegger,' Will added. 'I have proof. And I think he kidnapped Marcus.'

MacVicar sighed deeply. 'So there's the big fat chunk of information that brought you down here, huh?' He walked over to the window and looked out at the water like the captain of a ship. 'Son, there're some things about Thunder Bay I don't expect you to understand yet. It's different than it was in your mother's day. At that time, things made sense here. We put the bad guys in jail and sent the good guys to work. But once the grain stopped coming on those rails and went east to China, things took a turn. Now we've got the highest crime rate on the Lakes, outside Chicago. The only grain people're interested in is the fermented kind. The pourable version. The kind that helps you forget the better times and hunker down into the new. Will, just because you survived that wolf bite don't mean you'll come through whatever else this city can muster up for you. People here aren't in the habit of minding manners, if you go poking into their affairs.'

'People like *the Butler*?' said Will. 'That's what he does, right? Makes grain alcohol? And now Neverclear? And you already know this, but you don't even stop him?' Only halfway through his coffee, Will already noticed his jaw trembling and thoughts piling in his head, like a thousand people waiting to pass through a narrow exit, and his mouth felt more comfortable moving than at rest. No wonder everyone Outside drinks it, he thought, coffee makes you brave.

'It may not be pretty,' said MacVicar, 'but George Butler keeps order down there among all those hobos and miscreants. Man hops off a train or a lakeboat, perpetrates something wicked, hops right back on. How do I trace that? Then there's our Indian troubles to complicate things, with more and more coming down from the reserves for opportunities we can't even offer *our own* sons anymore. So as it stands, George Butler performs a vital function here. Keeps a lid on things. You don't know this yet, but there is nothing more dangerous than a person with nothing to do.'

'If you won't find Marcus, then I will,' Will said defiantly. 'For starters, I want to make a formal request for a list of all escaped mental patients within a hundred-mile radius.'

'And what are you going to do with that?' asked MacVicar.

'Investigate.'

He let out a long breath. 'Careful, Will. I suspect the first name on that list would be

221

yours.' Will threw himself to his feet and started off. 'Look,' MacVicar said. 'For years I've turned a blind eye to what's been going on over at your place, the irregularity of it, so don't try my patience. But what worries me most is how boys, even good boys like yourself, can end up in the same places as our society's less exemplary members.'

'Kinda like my being here?' Will said.

'You know why that is?' MacVicar said, ignoring Will's jab. 'Because kids and bad people have one thing in common: they both prefer to be alone.' With that, MacVicar stood and opened his door. 'It's been a hoot, Will,' he said, 'but I have an appointment at two.'

Will looked at the wall clock, which was also a stuffed walleye. 'But it's not even ten?'

The constable took a sip and nodded as he swallowed.

'Oh, and Will,' the constable called out across the reception area. 'What about your safety equipment?'

'I don't wear Helmets anymore,' Will said, clutching his skateboard to his hip. 'You can write me a ticket if you want.'

Titus

His new life commenced where another had ended.

With the bang of the cable still knitted in his ears, he told the Indian crew to leave or there'd be trouble for them and watched as they walked mutely back to their tents and their vans and their wives and their babies — all woken and set wailing by the sound — where they packed up camp and made off.

Alone now, he knew she'd heard the cable snap. The whole town must've. This was a sight she couldn't withstand, so he carefully shoveled his best friend into a plywood handcart and rolled it from the loading bay to the slip and pitched him over. Afterwards he scrubbed his hands and arms with reeds at the lakeside and carried on, dazed, with an empty and ringing head, down the waterline away from the elevator, while trucks bounced over the tracks in the distance, careening toward Pool 6.

He soon came to a pier where a foreign lakeboat lay at anchor. He climbed the gangway onto the high deck. The boat was a long, flat bulker — a twenty-story building out for a swim — and its posted signs and safety warnings were presented in some overwrought alphabet he couldn't deign to read. It was nearing morning and pale pink had exploded beneath the horizon, underlighting the clouds that night had stranded over the lake. He made his way to the bow, where for some time he stood, his pained chest against the rail, eyes cast into the ice-strewn harbor, contemplating his quick plunge over, how the water would vacuum his life in a welcome instant. But he figured this was still too close to his best friend's remains — the state of which he held himself responsible — so he pulled at a nearby hatch in the deck, and when it came open he dropped himself into the dark, equally prepared to accept a fifty-foot plummet to the iron hull as he was what he did receive: a shallow landing in a soft puff. He rose, brushing something from his trousers, then pulled the hatch closed with a neat bang, unable to fasten it down from the inside, leaving in the sky of his crypt a crescent moon of dawn.

He lay himself down on what he knew were oats, from the nutty smell and tender feel. There was a deep warmth rising up from within them, and he scooped some over himself into a kind of blanket. He recalled how, at the elevator, cars would arrive on the receiving tracks from the prairies frozen shut and how they had to blowtorch them open, how the grain was always still warm at the center when they unloaded it. Oftentimes they'd find animals mixed in, like coins in a child's cake — prairie dogs, deer, barn cats, beasts large and small swept up by threshers or trapped by bins — and human parts, too, the lopped fingers, arms, and legs of farmhands. He soon lost touch with himself and woke into another time, amid a cataclysm of engine sound. His overworked body was somewhat replenished, so it must've been more than a few hours later. The boat shuddered and began to move. He could catch the occasional hoarse bark from men above. A horn blasted intermittently, the sharp sound blunted by the deck, before the engines ramped up. He'd let this boat carry him out to where he'd cast himself into the deep of the lake, because he didn't deserve to drown anywhere near his home.

He guessed they'd sailed beyond the breakwater when the boat listed and the oats drifted over themselves with a hush like driven snow. After an hour of rocking, sleep took him again, this time more delirium than rest. He yelled soundlessly at a misty replica of his own face for some duration, before he was troubled by a vision of himself as a boy, running on a hot dirt road, but only the back of his head, never turning. He followed the boy to where he came upon all the people he'd known gathered together in a green field, dead but standing, mute but singing low in broken voices. The boy went unnoticed, though he shouted for a while before he started picking up stones from the gravel and throwing them. A stone struck his own father beneath his hatband, but he remained indifferent, a lisp of blood spitting to his collar. Another struck her arm but left no mark. The boy threw stones like that for a while, shattering cups of lemonade and pinging off the eyeglasses of the pastor, until his arm tired and he lay out in the grass to count clouds.

'I thought these are ghosts,' came a voice from within an eye-piercing circle of light above him. 'I'm the watching on the deck at night. I heard this wailing and find this hatch open. I'm thinking grain was wailing. Or ghost in grain. I am happy because it was you and not this cargo. That would not be appropriate. But I have the best hearing. For my hearing you are lucky. And you are lucky we weren't full steam. No hearing would hear then. Not even me. Very unlucky.'

As his corneas adjusted with dual unscrewing sensations, there resolved a man squatting over the hatch, a boot on either side, a sparse yellow fuzz clinging to his head.

'I am fifth mate, Vadim,' he said. 'What is your?'

Heaving the inert clumps of sleep from his mind, he couldn't understand how this man could be so completely unaware he was a dream.

'Never mind this,' said Vadim. 'Here, you're hurt. I will lift.' He stretched his hand down into the hold. 'If this was wheat, the dust would have suffocate you by now. This oats is another luckiness.'

Still he did not move.

'Come,' Vadim said, extending his hand deeper, 'except know that Visser will not turn the boat around for a clumsy trimmer. He is crazy to escape the Lakes before the freeze. But our next call is Sault Sainte Marie. There you depart.'

Fully awake now, he shook his head and made a shooing motion.

Confusion took Vadim as he retracted his arm. His face was thickly creased and featured a handful of lumpy moles, though rather than dark, they were the same color as his flesh. It was an untroubled face, a boy's face, except for his nose, which was like a stepped-on cherry.

'You were loading boat, yes? You are grain trimmer? Thunder Bay? You fell?'

'Not exactly,' he said.

'Good! You talk! I was worried you hit this head or were too stupid. Still, you go ashore at the Sault. Otherwise, you go farther than you want.' Vadim extended his hand again into the hold.

'I'm comfortable here,' he said, patting the heaped edges of his nest. They still weren't far enough out for him to jump.

'But this is salted,' Vadim said.

'This is what?'

'I thought you worked the Lake?'

He didn't answer.

'I'm meaning this is ocean vessel.'

'Look, don't fuss over me,' he said, 'I'll find my own way off soon enough.'

'In North Atlantic? Don't you care to know your heading?'

'No.'

He laughed. 'A fatalist.'

'How do you mean?'

'It means you are someone who does not worry forward. Look, I am from Ukraine, Odessa, but this is Dutch boat. This oats is a backhaul to Africa. Then our last port of call is Delfzijl. Trust me, fatalist, you do not want to make vacations there.'

'No difference to me,' he said. 'Best way to help me is to forget me.'

Vadim's face darkened. 'It is no good for you to do this stowing. You do not want to be discovered by Visser.' Then Vadim lowered himself to sit on the edge of the hatch and related a story of Visser, the ship's chief mate, a Dutchman who once found a stowaway on a saltie outbound from Singapore and kicked each of the man's teeth out, including molars, before pitching him into the water with his clothes in shreds. 'You don't want to know what he would do to yourself. On the ocean there is no law. And Visser is worse than nothing.'

Someone called to Vadim from up on the deck, and he leapt up and answered in a language that was different still from his accent.

'Oh well,' said Vadim squatting again. 'Even fatalist ghosts require water. I bring water.'

'I'm fine.'

'No, no, you'll be murdered by thirst. Say no to refusing. This I will do for you.' He took the hatch in his hands and swung it half closed. 'Sorry, it must be locked for the grain is kept dry. If not, I will become in troubled. But I won't linger.'

'Dark suits me fine,' he said.

'And sir?' Vadim added. 'Don't sink.'

'Isn't that your job?'

'No, no. In there. Stay flat! Like ah, how do you say . . . snowshoe? Don't flip around too much,' he said and shut the hatch.

He spent that night spread-eagled on the surface of the oats, allowing himself only a thin layer to banish the chill, not because he wanted to live, but because he'd been buried in grain many times before and didn't want to die with oats stopping his nose and throat. He was certain he deserved something much, much worse.

★   ★   ★

The storm started as a hungry wind drumming the hull. He'd heard sailors oftentimes declare November on Superior a war of wave and fog and sleet, home to a cold that could freeze eyes into cubes. Next came hail on the deck above like buckets of ball bearings dumped out to be sorted. He stuffed oats in his ears to dampen the racket.

After a few hours of pitching, nausea arrived, hot and delirious. Despite his time at the harbor, he'd never been on a boat other than weekend fishing jaunts on small, tepid lakes. When his mouth flooded with saliva he crawled away from the hatch into the deeper dark and emptied his stomach into a hole he'd dug in the oats.

He waited for the sickness to pass, his back propped against the curved wall of the hold, trying to stabilize the brain in his skull with placid thoughts, thoughts of her, but couldn't keep the vileness in him now from touching her image, so he punched the steel hull until his mind shut off. With so much vomiting, his thirst had reached a deadliness even he could recognize. *You'll die of thirst on a mountain of food*, he thought, and this set him chuckling.

An uncountable time later, his stomach settled into starvation, and he stewed up spit in his mouth for an hour in order to get some oats down, but they sat in a lump low in his sternum like he'd swallowed an apple whole. After eating, he attempted sleep. Hours in the vacuum of dark had opened his senses wide and his eyes took on another purpose. With nothing to land upon they concocted visions, like old prisoners telling stories to keep sane. Soon his eyelids flared with something near light, and amid these specters he watched himself put his own ear to that cable as though to a shell. He'd known it was weakened and tapped at it with a screwdriver, like he knew what he was listening for, while the Indian crew waited, speaking in low tones next to the half-unloaded grainer. 'It's fine,' he'd assured them, well aware the lake could freeze any minute, holding up their scheme until next year. 'What are you boys afraid of anyway, a little grain?' he said to his crew, then told his best friend to fire up the car dumper, which he did because they trusted each other like brothers — and a second later the air broke open with the lung-sucking sound of the frayed cable whipping through his friend, his remaining arm clutching at his crushed chest, trying to unlock it, his face scrambled like a painter's palette. Then his wrecked flesh dimming to white, the life lifting from the pieces of him like frost from the earth on a warm morning.

When the visions ceased, he fell through sleep and wakefulness, as though through the floors of a skyscraper made of mist. When he awoke, the storm had passed, the engines silent. He stood, ready for his last swim, and reached upwards for the hatch, yet even when he stretched tall, his fingers discovered only air. He could tell by the way his voice bounced that the ceiling was much

232

higher than before. The oats must've settled in the vibration of the storm, he concluded. He pushed some into an incline and managed a mound from which he was able to graze the hatch with his fingertips. But there was no way to open it from the inside.

Thirst had returned, and he feared it would weaken his capacity to refuse the visions, so he sat telling himself knock-knock jokes he'd shared with her — *Lettuce. Lettuce Who? Lettuce in, it's freezing!* — until sleep took him.

★　★　★

'It was all hands last night. There was no way I could come. Then we must go ashore. This was important. But now I'm returned.' It was night, and Vadim was backlit by a needlepoint of stars. The bright smell of alcohol wafted into the hold. Vadim was drunk, and it made his accent harder to unravel.

'I thought: But Vadim, he has oats!' he said raggedly. 'And then I remembered: the water! So now? I've come.'

He tried to speak but only croaked, dragging his tongue like a dry mop over his lips in a futile attempt to moisten them. Vadim tossed down a jar of water and it landed in the oats with a whump. He couldn't resist throwing himself upon it but drank conservatively, trying to disguise how pressing his thirst was.

Next, Vadim took out a flashlight, and it was possible to make out some gaps in his grip. 'I lose these in the winch,' Vadim said grinning, wiggling his two remaining fingers like a man giving an obscene gesture. Then Vadim directed the flashlight into the hold, stinging his vision. 'Ah,' Vadim said, 'there you are. Oh no no . . . you have bleed on your face. Is this new?'

He thought he'd washed it all off in the lake. 'From before,' he said. He captured a handful of oats and scrubbed his face with them, unwilling to waste any water for this purpose.

'Well, I've heard you with these complex words in your sleep. No doubt you read: Bill Shakespeare?' asked Vadim, sitting.

'Who?'

'I studied Englishman's literature in Odessa. I like him most so I call him Bill. We are familiar this way. Titus Adronic was a man who saw many bloodsheds. He was drenched in this. For his whole play, he's bloody. It is very hard for him. His family. He kills them. Some of them. No one likes this play, this Adronicus. But I do. This is Ukrainian play. So! I call you: Titus' — he said, rhyming the word with 'noose' — 'because you remind me of this blood man.'

'Okay,' said Titus, after surfacing from a long pull of water. 'Call me whatever the hell you want.' Anything that would toss an extra shovelful over the grave of everything he'd left behind was fine with him.

'Oh, it is too bad you cannot see the world with me, Titus. So much ports! Shanghai the girls are burning hot but expensive. Bangkok the girls are burning hot but cheap. The problem with cheap is dick remembers how much pockets pay! Do you understand this?' He laughed until

234

it degraded into a cough.

'So, Titus,' he said, wiping his pink eyes, 'if you were no grain trimmer, who then?'

'I worked. Inside the elevator,' Titus said, holding a small sip in his mouth to soak it. 'Pool Six. Unloading grain cars. At night.'

'Ah,' he said. 'Dangerous work this.'

'What isn't.'

'Yes, yes. This is a yes thing. Well, we are moored here tonight. Then tomorrow we go through locks. Tonight you would like drink that is not water? This is dry boat but there is much grain alcohol. If you have money. Maybe you want girl down there in your bed of roses, Titus?'

'I'm busted,' he said, though he had a thousand dollars of the Native crew's pay in his wallet. 'But maybe you can get me a bigger container of water?' He'd had his heart set on drowning, not expiring of thirst, and jumping while still in a harbor would guarantee he'd be found. He would spare her that sight too.

'Ah! Now you're caring about your well-being self!' Vadim declared drunkenly. Then he seemed to fatigue and rubbed the back of his neck with his palm. 'But I'm sorry, Titus, I cannot. This jar is already so much. There would be people noticing. There is not much vessels to go around on this ship. It is best way.'

'Why are you doing this?' Titus said, trying to keep the hatch open a little longer, if only for the starlight.

'What?' said Vadim, momentarily affronted.

'Helping me.'

'Oh! Well, Titus my friend, there is a beautiful,

beautiful Ukrainian proverb: 'He is guilty who is not at home.''

'That makes two of us.'

'Yes! This makes all sailors guilty. Which is true. And maybe everyone is guilty who lives with their matinka no longer,' Vadim said mirthfully.

'Suppose so,' said Titus, half-smiling, the other half of him dedicated to preventing a treacherous idea like *home* from finding purchase in his heart.

'Oh, who is this Diane?' Vadim said as an afterthought when he was about to shut the hatch, and Titus's breath stopped, as it does whenever another man reads your mind.

'You cried name Diane in your sleep,' said Vadim. 'Is it goddess? Girlfriend? Dream?'

'Yes,' said Titus, fighting to blockade her from his mind, 'a dream.'

★   ★   ★

After another formless interval of sleep Titus became aware of the ship's brush against steel, scraping its way into the locks. This continued until a rumbling began, and he knew the boat was being lowered. Titus tried to feel the descent but could not. He'd heard crews discuss these locks, a freshwater staircase that carried ships from the Great Lakes down to the Saint Lawrence as gently as a child putting a boat in a slip of rainwater.

The hold grew stale and drowsy. His thoughts mixed and wandered. After years in the elevator,

236

he knew grain released gases, carbon dioxide, mostly, but also others over time, and he worried the oats were deranging him in some manner. He closed his eyes and looked again upon the Indian crew in their ragtag clothes, overalls and perma-pressed shirts worn alongside garments of fur and hide, most of them in steel toes — or soled boots for that matter — for the very first time in their lives. They walked tentatively, as though the cement was soggy spring ice on the lake. They'd brought them down from a remote reserve, Ojibwes — or Ahnisnabae was their word for themselves. Many couldn't manage a proper English hello. The elevator's regular crews had long refused to work nights, so no trouble there, but what irked the men most was how the Indians had brought their families along, how their women were camped in a lot near the railroad tracks in the harbor, babies strapped to them in beaded carriers, sage and sweet grass burning most of the time, laundry all hung up like flags of an invading army — a disgrace, some called it. In their eyes, some crucial separation was not being observed, and they revved their trucks near the camp during the day to disturb the night crew's sleep. When one got his hand sliced by a shovel, an elder came and sewed him up with some animal gut. Titus and his best friend were relieved not to require a doctor. But overall the Indians were cautious, methodical workers, unlike the daytime regulars, drinking and fighting and carrying on. Altogether the Indian crew managed ten cars a night. Every night. 'Those ones are industrious,' a grain inspector named Butler had remarked at shift change, 'despite their lazy heritage.' Titus wasn't proud of paying them so little, but they were poor, desperate for work, and his partner had convinced him they were doing them a favor.

Traversing the locks seemed to take a day, though of course he couldn't be certain, and Vadim didn't appear. Titus rationed the water, allowing himself a teaspoon from the jar for every five hundred breaths he took, and before long his water was down to the amount of beer a man would abandon in his glass without thinking a thing of it.

Luckily, before the nightmares returned, the hatch popped. Night again, starless this time, and the lights on the deck cut sharp angles into the hold. Vadim was sober and seemed hurried, gruffer, as though embarrassed by the camaraderie they'd shared last time. 'I've come to tell you we pass Montreal in two days,' he said whispering quickly. 'You can get off there. This is the last port call before ocean. Okay?'

Titus said okay. Somewhere in the dark hours alone, he'd lost his conviction to drown. But Montreal seemed as good a place as any to die.

'We are not docking in Montreal, but I know a tugboat man who hauls there. He brings supplies. Booze and other things. He will return you into the harbor.'

Titus thanked him. Vadim looked like he was preparing to go. 'Any chance of some more water?' Titus said. 'Or even something to eat? These oats are twisting me up.'

Vadim sighed. He put his hands over his face.

'You know it is not easy for me to get this water,' he said sharply. 'It does not look good carrying jars about. It looks like I am loafing. Or with moonshines.'

Titus told him he could tie it to a string and dip it in the lake. 'I'm not picky,' he said.

'This is not the point,' said Vadim wearily, shaking his head. The wheedle of gulls could be heard in the air above the hatch, and for a moment Titus thought he would like to climb out, throttle this silly man, then go swimming.

'Okay,' Vadim said after some consideration, 'toss up this jar.'

Vadim caught it and put it under his arm like a football.

'This tugboat, in Montreal,' Vadim said before he shut the hatch, 'this is not free. He is my friend, but he must make a living.'

When Titus started digging for his wallet, Vadim shook his head. 'There is a man,' Vadim said, shifting his weight and checking over both shoulders. 'He is from the center of America somewhere, Ecuador, Panama — who knows. He has a name, but this is not matter to you. It's a poison on the tongue. He is causing many problems for me. For your friend Vadim. He is a vile man. A nastiness. Like in Bill Shakespeare, or a novel by Charlie Dickens — yes! A man like Sikes.'

Titus nodded. He couldn't keep his eyes from the empty jar under Vadim's forearm.

'Well, this man has been stealing from me, Titus. He tells me I owe him money when I do not. He tells me we have made bets that no crew has witnessed. At night he comes to me when I sleep. He whispers that he will cut my a killings tendons. You know these?' Vadim made a slashing motion over the back of his leg.

Again, Titus nodded.

'So this is this thing I need helping with. You see I am small man. I am watchman. I watch. But you are not, Titus. You are a man who does not only watch. Who has seen much bloodshed. I tell this by your face. You have scars. You are a hardness. So, I'm hoping for this. Help this man fall from the boat. That is it. Like Bill Sikes. Give him what is his own. It would save me from so much . . .' His gaze fixed on the edge of the hatch as he trailed off.

Titus took a breath. 'I'm sorry, Vadim,' he said. 'You've been real helpful. And I appreciate it. But I don't think — '

'No,' Vadim barked and grabbed the hatch. 'I knew this. This is okay. This is my problem. You have your problem and I have mine. These are separations.' He said he would return with the water, then closed the hatch. Later Titus woke to find two jars of water had been tossed down into the hold while he slept. They were murky with green bits spinning in them like tiny meteors.

* * *

Maybe it was the sight of his best friend's blood dripping from the handcart he'd used to transport him or the limited oxygen or some mysterious fumes, but the texture of Titus's mind had altered. There in the dark hold he

240

watched time pour time down the drain indifferently, lying for hours, unchafed by boredom or unwanted visions. He played chess with old friends and directed theater productions entirely in his head. He remembered whole texts he'd read as a child, enough to recite them backwards. His time in the hold had nearly turned pleasant — empty spaces like a stack of newspapers printed blank, nothing but dates at the top of every page.

He ate oats soaked in one of the jars and reserved the other for drinking. Soon from the scuffing sounds he knew the ship was again in a series of locks. Then for a period anchored. With the engines quiet he heard more voices above, some footfalls, then nothing. In the dead quiet he listened to the rustle and snap of himself blinking.

Then the engines roared again. The ship sounded its foghorn. The boat rocked. After a while he detected a briny scent skulking into the hold. After another day he heard a tapping at the hull. All kinds of clean notes like a glockenspiel: ice, he soon realized. The water in both jars was gone when Vadim came again.

'I'm sorry, Titus,' said Vadim sorrowfully. He was drunk again, his face rosy with blood.

'We're the sea's music now, aren't we, Vadim?'

'This is what I've been *trying* to tell you,' he sobbed. 'But you don't making sense when you speak. It looks like you are taking vacations after all.'

'What about Montreal?' Titus said, elevating his voice, less concerned with his own well-being than a man's adherence to his word.

'I have job here, you know,' said Vadim. 'I had to paint winches. Grease chains. Low work, you must think, Titus, beneath you. But it must be done. And my tugboating friend did not come. It is not all easy for Vadim. He does not get to slumber all day in a soft bed.'

Titus clenched his teeth and once again considered piling up a mound of oats so he could climb out and throttle the man, though now the hatch was even higher. Perhaps Titus was eating his way down.

'But there is another problem,' Vadim said sheepishly. 'This man I told you about. The Panamanian. Titus, I told this man about you when I have been drinking. A mistake. I am a talking friend, Titus, my weakness. And now he is going to Visser about you. He said this with his mouth. About how you have stolen your passage and have been eating the cargo. This is not good. He is also a rapist, this man. He boasted to me last night, as though I would applaud?'

'Okay,' said Titus, 'get to it.'

'If you don't deal with him soon, I don't know if I can come again. Too dangerous for me.'

Titus understood now his position. That he'd rid himself of his desire to die and attained something near peace in the dark hold meant nothing. He would not go unpunished for everything he'd left broken behind him. It seemed fitting now that the price for no longer yearning to cast himself overboard would be to further degrade himself, but he'd already constructed the armored vault in which to put all the vile things he had left to do in his life, and its dragging weight meant there would be no more good days for him, no more comfort or kindness.

'When?' Titus said.

'He is on watch tonight, before me,' said Vadim, his eyes on fire. 'I will fetch you when the time is clear.'

Later, a knock came and the hatch opened, and rain fluttered in as Titus heard the slap of feet retreating on the wet deck. Titus had hoarded a large pile of oats that allowed him to grasp the lip of the hatch with two hands and hike himself up.

On the deck, he drew the sweetness of sea air into his body. No stars, only a tin roof of cloud and waves crashing like shunting trains. He removed his work boots and set them beside the hatch, which he closed but did not fasten. He crept in bare feet along the railing in the dark toward the bow of the ship, as rain swept in fizzy sails overhead. He spotted the man: short, but sturdy looking, copper skin like an Indian, smoking, sparing the tiny ember from the spray with a small cave made with his hand. He stood exactly where Titus had weeks before, the morning of the accident, when he nearly plunged himself into Thunder Bay's harbor, which he'd now left so far behind.

With the sweet air in his lungs and his head clearing, Titus came to the knowledge he could do this man no harm. He'd picked up some Spanish while gambling with sailors laid up in Thunder Bay and was sure he could piece together enough words to inform the Panamanian of Vadim's plot. Then Titus would throw himself at the mercy of this Visser. Titus had been beaten plenty in his life, and the thought of it didn't quicken his pulse in the slightest. At worst he'd be thrown overboard.

The Panamanian couldn't hear Titus when he called, so Titus touched him kindly on the shoulder. The man spun and his eyes cracked open and popped with panic and he started yelling in a guttural tongue that Titus had no acquaintance with. The words came faster the more he spoke, the way an avalanche gathers speed. He was something closer to black, light-skinned, but black. *Tranquillo*, Titus repeated a few times, until the man clenched his fist over his cigarette with a hiss and swung. Titus half-ducked and took it hard on the ear. They grappled. Perhaps it was his time in the hold, or the lack of oxygen, or his oat diet, but Titus did not find the strength he'd expected. They scuffled for some duration, each trying to upend the other, slipping wildly on the slick deck. When exhaustion took them, they spent some time in a clinch. Each instance the man made to cry out, Titus squeezed his chest and killed his breath. Titus tried every word in every language he knew of to reach him, even making some up, as the man breathed in his ear like a dog, but none of it registered inside him. After a period of rest, the man commenced thrashing in earnest and wailing his fists. Blows landed on Titus's chin and face and neck. The man was strong and pinned Titus to the rail. Titus grabbed the seat of his rubber pants and desperately hoisted upward. Upended, the man clutched at the air and caught hold of the railing with a leg and an arm on his way over. Clinging there, he started calling in his inscrutable language toward the rear of the ship where the wheelhouse was. People's names, sounded like, and Titus wondered momentarily if they corresponded to his parents, or friends, or crewmates. Panicked, blood and voices howling in him, Titus struck once at the man's bulging throat and it yielded and instantly he lost all wherewithal to breathe. He choked like he'd swallowed a box of fishhooks, dangling there, before strength abandoned him and he dropped into the dark roar.

★ ★ ★

The next day Vadim came to the hatch with a grin. He lowered down a bucket on some twine. In it was cabbage, fried beef, potatoes, aromatic as anything ever put before him. 'You have saved me, my friend,' Vadim said.

Titus sat looking at the bucket but did not touch it.

'But I must tell you. Visser is not happy about the losing crewman. He said he was sure-footed. Seasoned. And that he does not believe in falling accidents. So, Titus, they are searching the ship. And it won't be long before they see the holds.'

'I'll entomb myself here,' Titus said. Sculpting an old word in the air with his tongue comforted him.

'Don't be stupid. There is weeks of your shit down here. They'll find your traces.'

Titus looked beside him. Blood from his nose and face from when the Panamanian had struck him had left clumps in the oats like cat litter. 'I knew this would transpire,' he said, unable to believe Vadim couldn't tell he was already dead.

'Come, Titus. I've found you a new place.'

A great weariness came over each of his muscles. 'I need to wash,' Titus said with a sudden distaste for his hands, the blood that had been on them.

'No, no, no — ' Vadim began.

'Either that or I ring Visser,' Titus interrupted.

Grumbling, Vadim led him to the lockers at the base of the wheelhouse. Titus stripped, set the shower as hot as it would go and kept his head down, water hammering his neck as he hissed every word he'd ever known into the steam. He put his clothes at his feet, letting his own steps and the runoff clean them. He shaved with a razor he found hanging from a screw in the scummy tile. After, he wrung his clothes over the drain and pulled them on wet before returning to the hatch. He lay down, the oats coating him like batter.

Back in the dark, finally clean, Titus turned his soothed mind toward the walks he used to take with her to find the blue and yellow prairie wildflowers that grew all along the tracks that snaked their way east to the elevator. Sown by seeds that the threshers inadvertently swept up along with the grain, the flowers were found all the way down the line in high summer. The thought of this set him weeping.

Vadim returned that evening and helped Titus climb up onto the deck. He threw a line and looped it over a lifeboat hanging from some rigging high above. 'They've already searched these, so they should be safe. And here,' Vadim said, handing Titus a laundry sack filled with oats and three jars of clear water. 'I found some more vessels,' he said quickly.

Titus took the line and shimmied up to the boat. He snapped away the vinyl cover and crawled beneath it. The bench seats of the boat made it so there was nowhere to lie flat, and the wind rattled the craft as though it was airborne. He shivered when night came, piling the oats in the driest corner and wrapping himself in the laundry bag, missing the muffled gloom of the hold, the warmth of his nest like the afterglow of a lover.

The next day, he discreetly opened the part of the cover that faced outward and bathed various parts of his body in a triangle of sunlight. He tossed a few oats to the seabirds that followed in the ship's wind, listening to their gorgeous shrieks, until a crowd began to form around his hiding place and that was the end of that.

⋆ ⋆ ⋆

It was the following day that Titus sighted the green shoulder of land. He tried releasing the lifeboat, but the mechanism was padlocked. Hurriedly, he drank all the water and sealed air in the jars as tight as he could manage and tied them up with his money and boots in the laundry bag. He drew back the vinyl cover and jumped as far out from the ship as he could manage to clear the engines. He bobbed for hours in the high waves, clutching the jars, which weren't enough to buoy him completely but lessened his labors.

When he emerged from the seawater onto a mucky rise he was met by black men on rafts preparing some cylindrical traps. After he'd finished vomiting from exhaustion, one of the men prodded his chest with a fishing rod, probably to see if he was a ghost. But Titus could find no handhold in the sounds they made, could make no order of their faces. He walked inland from the dock and followed a baking dirt road for hours until he reached a disorienting city. There he found a bank. He handed them the money from his wallet and the smiling woman handed back colorful bills in a wad so enormous he had to distribute them among the pockets of his trousers.

He bought half of a barbecued goat and some yellowish fruit chunks in a plastic bag and brought it to a public sitting area. As he ate, garbage burned in a wire incinerator nearby, and the smell pleased him. He rented a room in a squalid hotel he felt he deserved and walked for hours each day, finding the Panamanian's face in the crowds, as well as his best friend's, speaking out loud to himself, happy at the incomprehensive looks he received in return. After a week of wandering, he asked for directions to a port where he contracted on a ship carrying chemicals out of Liberia.

After that he signed with other boats. Years passed at sea, quick as a shudder. Aughinish. Hamburg. Latvia. Antwerp. Murmansk. Vancouver. Shanghai. Rotterdam. New Orleans. Nagoya. Amsterdam. Hay Point. After all his time on the water, both stowed away and now as crew, he attuned himself to loneliness, to the captivity of oceangoing, to a life spent between ports. Visions rarely troubled him. Though he still disliked the talking required with the other crew, minimal as it was, and frequently retreated to his cabin to read and whisper into his pillow.

But over the years, his whispering became harder to contain, and he managed to offend a Polish first officer and was let go. Sitting beside an American in a beachfront drinking establishment in Shanghai, just a long table under a bale of thatch, he overheard the man say he'd signed a contract on a bulker to the Great Lakes. Titus followed him to the wharf and signed his name.

He rode again through the locks, this time climbing them like a long staircase. But he learned from a crewmate that Thunder Bay got very little grain traffic these days. So he hopped off and caught freights back and forth across Canada, east and west, each time sailing through Thunder Bay, unable to locate the courage to jump off. In his new life he could pass days like a blink and months in an afternoon. He found he preferred rail travel to shipping. On trains he met every manner of low creature, tucked away in all the nooks and crannies that railcars accidentally provide. A man who injected grain alcohol into his veins with a hypodermic needle, who could attain pure, shambling drunkenness with a capful of cheap vodka. Another man who snorted brown powder from a baby food jar and slept twenty hours of twenty-four. People missing half their heads, half their hearts; people who'd stabbed their families, and who'd been stabbed — by their families and otherwise; people who'd been raped and had raped, not necessarily in that order. There existed a crude system of exchange between American and Canadian currency, cigarettes and jugs, the rates for which were maintained collectively in their heads. They passed around the ugliest money he ever laid eyes upon. Bills soaked in blood, urine, semen — animal and human. Money begged for, killed for, hidden and squandered and stolen a thousand times over. He never raised a finger toward any of them, because none was worth helping or hurting, and he received the same indifference in return.

Then one day while catching out of Steinbeck, Manitoba, he climbed onto a gondola car loaded with big packets of lumber that already sheltered a bedraggled man. 'Room for two, fella,' the man said, and Titus tucked himself into the space beside him. Titus nodded but didn't speak. Since he'd been riding trains, the whispering had worsened, and his words were further jumbling in his head, as though someone had taken a sledgehammer to the card catalogues in the library of his mind.

But after a day of watching the prairie rip past from their nook on the highballing train, the man zeroed in closer with a finger in Titus's face. 'I recognize you. The elevators. We worked an unloading crew,' the man said. 'I heard you was dead.'

'Things . . . change,' Titus managed to get out right.

'Sorry I can't rightly place your name there, fella,' the man said squinting. 'But welcome home besides.' Luckily, by the empty closets of his eyes and the way decades of cloudy brandy and sleepless transience had carved from him all glimmers of vitality, Titus could tell this was a man accustomed to ghosts.

After that Titus hopped off in the yard near Pool 6 and considered going to her straightaway, but first he wanted a look at the elevator. He needed to take it slow, as though he were coming up from the deep ocean. Finding the elevator abandoned, he slept overnight there, and despite the sickening sight of the water out front that had swallowed his best friend, he found comfort in its smells: train diesel and the linger of grain dust. From high in the workhouse he'd look up to Thunder Bay and scarcely recognized it after all those years. But it was good to be near where she was. Better even.

Then one morning he shaved and washed up and regarded himself in a rearview mirror he'd pulled from an abandoned truck. With his skin tanned and eyes clear, he looked like something not quite dead, something almost worth forgiveness, even for the worst things, especially by someone as good as she was. He followed the creek up to her house and found it dark. Part of him was proud of her for leaving. He returned each Sunday night for years, watching, until one day the lights were on, and he saw her, twirling a little boy around, dancing together in the lamplight among the furniture, and it was then he realized a wall had been built between him and the world of houses. Between him and the world of calendars and dancing and dinners steaming on tables and children drinking glasses of milk with two hands. He could not track his mess into their house. Into these bright, buoyant lives. He belonged to a different world now. Outside hers.

The
Outside
In

16

One October afternoon Will returned from skateboarding to find something pasted to the outside of the picture window in Cairo:

please go back inside for your own good, or else, there will be turmoil.

He rushed out and snatched it down before his mother saw it. The words were crudely formed on a flattened carton, ballpoint pen dug into the waxy cardboard.

'Why the hell would a threatening note say 'please'?' said Jonah later when Will brought the sign to their crime lab. 'Doesn't make any sense.'

'And does it mean, like, there will be 'turmoil' no matter what?' Will wondered. 'Or does it mean 'or else there will be turmoil' and the period was like an accident?'

'No clue,' Jonah said.

After some further discussion, they brushed the sign for prints and came up empty. The boys returned to Will's house and searched the soil under the window. There they discovered the same boot prints Will had found the previous winter, same hexagonal imprint, right where Will had watched the bluejay die. This time Will ran inside to fetch his mother's old Polaroid camera from behind his boxed masterpieces in Toronto. 'I have an idea,' he said.

The boys rolled downtown to a workwear

store called Pound's that they'd often skate-boarded behind that summer, which, judging by its mustiness, dated signage, and general disrepair, had been open since well before Will's mother last breathed fresh air.

'Yup, used to sell those,' said the aged, squinty clerk when Will showed him the photo of the boot print, forgetting all the times he'd shooed the boys from his parking lot. 'Not anymore, though. Used to assemble them right here in Thunder Bay. But I sold my last pair years ago.'

'Any idea who wore them?' asked Will.

'Workers mostly,' he said. 'A popular choice. Lots of fellas wear them. Miners, boilermakers, grain trimmers, loggers — you name it.'

'Right,' said Jonah once they were back Outside. 'So we're looking for someone who's insane, can't breathe, collects garden hoses, has poor grammar, and wears old boots nobody sells anymore. Awesome.'

'Every clue counts, Jonah,' said Will. 'But that last word of the note really does seem like something the Wheezing Man might write.'

A week later, while doing laundry in Toronto, Will pinched a pelt of dryer lint from the trap and tossed it in the trash. Remembering that his mother had asked him to fetch her old Bolex for her, he stood on an overturned bucket and retrieved the camera's dusty case from back near the wall where he'd stashed Marcus's bloodied shirt. When Will was younger, she'd taught him how to use the Bolex to make a short Claymation movie of a volcano erupting and engulfing a village. Will realized now that he and

256

Jonah could make their own skateboarding movie, like the Californian skateboard videos they worshipped, and resolved to do it once they found Marcus and everything went back to normal. Will yanked aside a box, crashing masterpieces to the floor, and something caught his eye.

'Where did these come from?' he said, setting the pair of work boots down on his mother's comforter, boots that had sat unremarkably in Toronto for as long as Will could remember, the exact hexagonal pattern he'd been searching for embedded in the tread.

'Oh, those,' she said absentmindedly while writing in a notebook. 'They were your grandfather's.'

'Why do we have his boots?'

'Will, what's wrong?' she said, putting down her pen, her eyebrows knitted. 'Why do you look so worried?'

'I asked a question.'

'And I answered it,' she said. 'They were your grandfather Theodore's. We got them when he died. They were all that was left of him.'

Will was about to let the whole thing drop when he noticed a chalky substance had flaked from the soles onto his mother's navy bedspread and everything clicked. 'Did *you* write it?' Will said. 'Have you been *wearing* these, Mom? Outside?'

'Will, what's wrong with you?' she said plaintively, with a snap of her elastic. 'Please lower your voice.'

'Well, have you?' he said, picturing her

sneaking secretly around the back walk to paste the note to the window, exactly as he'd done when he first met Marcus what seemed like eons ago. And just like her to write a guilt-inducing *please* on something that was supposed to be threatening.

'You must be kidding,' she said.

'Then why are they dirty?'

'That's grain dust, Will. Both your grandfather and your uncle worked at the elevators. It coated everything they owned: their clothes, their hair. Your uncle hung his work clothes outside the door and showered before dinner, it was so bad. Want me to show you the hook? It's still there.'

Will was heartsick with all her lying and acting and faking, and at that moment some part of him turned inside out: all the pity and compassion and responsibility he'd once felt for her had finally compacted into a molten core of disgust. She'd already squandered her own life, and now she wasn't brave enough to let him live his own. He'd conquered his fears by forcing himself Outside and going to school and skateboarding and making a friend while she cowered in her bed and lied about everything that mattered to him most. The truth was, she could leave anytime she wanted, except she didn't care to, because she was selfish — and for this more than anything he loathed her.

In a red haze Will dug into his pocket and held up the note he'd found. 'Look familiar?' he said. Her eyes flicked over the crudely arranged words — the strange *please*, the odd *turmoil*, the contentious period and barely scary TV cliché threat — and her jaw dropped open like a glove compartment. He watched as something in her tipped over and terror flooded in to replace it. Then she shuddered in panic and exploded with a million questions. 'Forget it, it was only a prank,' Will said. 'Some hockey players at school.' Before fleeing to New York, where he locked his door and yanked on headphones, setting Public Enemy to a teeth-numbing volume.

She might have questions, but he was drowning in them. Questions like how Charlie really died, and where Marcus was hiding, and what the Butler's wolves would do to him when they finally picked up his scent. Maybe she didn't write the note. Maybe she hadn't been wearing the boots. But at least now he had proof. Proof of what, Will couldn't exactly say. But their investigation must be on the right track.

He and Jonah had somebody worried. Somebody other than his mother, for once.

Relaxation Time

It had been a reckless mistake to spout her life history into this reel-to-reel and to watch her anxiety-stricken films and go tromping around willy-nilly in her past with such abandon. Something had come unstuck — some psychic retaining wall, if there were such a thing. After Will had shown her that note he'd found (had he made it himself to scare her?), her memory became impossible to corral, turning again and again toward the past like a crippled airliner spiraling to the ground.

Before the images overwhelmed her, Diane removed her goggles and found she had been struck blind. Panic clamped her chest. She ground her fists into her eyes but still they failed her. It wasn't until she saw some sunlight leaking from behind her thick bedroom curtain that she knew the lightbulb had died. She fished around in her drawer for a flashlight and snapped it on.

Will had claimed that note was a prank, but why would he have accused her of writing it with such outrage? And there was something more troublesome about it. *Turmoil.* Such a strange word to choose. The kind of overwrought word Charlie would copy down from his dictionary to use after their great escape from Thunder Bay. Also, the printing itself had reminded her of the cryptic instructions Whalen would slip into the

260

vents of her locker to schedule their secret meetings.

She went downstairs and found that Will had left. She made tea and took up her guitar to calm herself, but it lay dead in her arms. No matter how hard she tried, she couldn't sustain any fingerpicking pattern for more than a few bars, so she put it down.

The house had seen better days: plants choking of thirst in their pots, underwear she'd washed in the tub dangling from the pot-hanger in the kitchen to dry. With most of the lightbulbs on the main floor out, too, and no Will around to change them, she'd been moving lamps from room to room, plugging them in with dish gloves on. The house had assumed the particular disheveled sadness she'd always associated with closed amusement parks.

This house. What would Arthur think of it? *Unremarkable*, she could already hear him say. Though she never told him, she hated architecture. Of course she didn't hate buildings — how could you, especially if you're a shut-in — it was more that she hated the *everywhereness* of architecture. That, like a labyrinth, it could never be escaped. That she must sleep and eat and raise her child within it. The very definition of oppressive.

Diane took a nectarine from the fruit bowl and began paring it with a knife, lifting the wedges of fruit from its edge with her lips. Then she realized the dangerousness of what she was doing and locked the knife in the drawer. She pulled back her elastic and snapped it soundly, the pain only further agitating her.

Who was she kidding? She'd never make it to that retrospective. She couldn't even sit in the dark alone for a while without terrifying herself. They'd have to find another caged curiosity to trot out. She walked to the kitchen counter and crumpled the NFB director's letter and dropped it in the trash. She would've burned it had the thought of fire not caught her breath and set her hands tingling.

She returned to her bedroom with a new table lamp but couldn't yet dare to plug it in, even with her dish gloves on. She couldn't risk another panic. She got under the covers and read by flashlight — as she had all those nights as a girl — and silently decreed her five page-turner limit hereby null and void. If the Relaxation Sessions had stopped working, these silly books were the only barricade left between her and ruin.

But after she'd read her eyes dry and sore, and her mind dipped toward sleep, a memory knifed up from the past: the bang that had lifted her from this same bed long ago. An apocalyptic sound she later learned was heard as far as fifty miles outside Thunder Bay. Diane took her father's old truck, her bare feet on the rough pedals, over the tracks and down to the harbor. Men arrived in coats over their nightclothes, leading her to the loading bay, where an overturned railcar had dropped to its side, a thick support cable lying sheared and slack near a good quantity of spilled oil — she hadn't known it was blood until she saw the way the others avoided it. A search of the area was conducted, men with naphtha lanterns slicing the dark, projecting the shadows of giants onto the towering concrete of Pool 6. After a few hours, in the very same water from which they'd pulled Theodore years previous, one of the men spotted something that belonged more to the lake than to the land. The men had no idea how it got there, with wounds too mortal to carry itself. She helped them drag twine nets through the harbor throughout the night, but her brother was never recovered in his entirety. Though Charlie and Whalen were the same size, had the same haircuts, and had worn the same canvas coveralls, and though the body was shredded by the frayed cable's whip, the face a ruin, it was the terrible confirmation of Charlie's fate — the expectedness of it — that convinced her that night of exactly who she'd lost. She knew her brother never would abandon her to the world if he could help it — a loyalty she never would've expected from Whalen.

Yet what drove her panic today wasn't that her brother had died at the elevators, just as her father did, or that her mother died a young woman. It was that anyone did. Anywhere. That tragedy made no distinction. That it claimed equally those who invited it and those who didn't. Those treasured, and those ignored. That there was no protection, no spell. It knew every face. Every address. That doom, as Emily Dickinson wrote, was a house without a door.

She knew she was supposed to be optimistic, was expected to hope, that hope was a mother's great gift, and that she was betraying Will's bright future if she could not accomplish this most basic self-deception. But what she felt was the opposite of hope. It was only a matter of time before he would break his little bones. Before he would become drunk, diseased, delirious, deranged, and one day — whether she was around to see it or not — he would become like Charlie: only parts of himself, undone.

If only there were some way to teach him that everything is lethal. That injury, sickness, calamity, death — these things follow us like a white moon whipping in the trees beside the highway. And that it is more insane to forget this, even for a second, than it is to remember.

17

That night in New York, Will shot up in his cot, his heart kicking like a bronco.

Grain dust.

It had been a week since he'd confronted his mother with the dusty boots and she'd said his grandfather and uncle were always covered with it from working at the elevator. It must've been what the Wheezing Man had left on Will's coat after he grabbed him.

'I can't believe we were so stupid,' Will said to a drowsy Jonah after he'd phoned and had Enoch rouse him from bed. 'Everything points to the elevators. The boots. The dust. Plus the creek runs from where Marcus went missing right down the hill and empties into the lake exactly where the elevators are. The Butler must be using the creek to get around the city undetected.'

'The harborfront is the only place we didn't search,' said Jonah.

'Maybe Marcus is hiding in one of those abandoned buildings down there. Or the Wheezing Man.'

'Or maybe the Butler is,' Jonah said sleepily. 'But fine, we'll take a look. We might find a dry place we can skate when winter comes.'

The next morning Will filled a pop bottle with tap water and dropped it into a backpack. Next, he went to Paris and retrieved the secret key from the top of the doorframe that he didn't know about and unlocked the knife drawer. The selection was limited, but he took the wickedest-looking blade, a long serrated thing with a blunt tip that his mother used to slice her fresh loaves, and stuffed it into his hoodie.

'Is everything still okay, Will?' asked his mother as he was pulling on his skateboard shoes. She was in her bathrobe, her toenails long as teaspoons. Like half-buried jewels, her eyes had fallen deeper in their sockets during the past few days that they hadn't been talking. 'I'm worried about you,' she said.

'Imagine that,' he said, hitching his laces tight.

'You're always in such a hurry these days. And that note, I just hope you and Jonah aren't in danger — '

'Everyone's always in danger,' he interrupted while fixing his pants cuffs. The way they met his shoes had recently assumed great significance to him.

'Sure,' she said, retying the sash of her robe as though trying to cinch herself calm, 'but are you in more danger than normal?'

'Are *you* in danger, Mom?' he said, standing. 'Right now?'

She frowned. 'That's not fair,' she said. Her face melted, and she began to drip tears, again.

'Sure it is,' he said, willing himself to stone.

'I don't know how worried I should be. Can you at least tell me that?' she said.

'I've got it under control,' Will said, flinging open the door.

'Being anonymously threatened is under control?'

'Better than you're doing,' he said. 'You don't know who's threatening you either.'

She went to say something angry but turned her head slightly to the side and shut her eyes. 'You're just . . . never home anymore, honey. I miss you. I miss watching you paint. I miss your voice in the house.'

Looking into her eyes that were green and bright as alarm clock digits, her yellow hair over the neat cockles of her ears, he felt the old Inside parts of him soften for a moment and ached suddenly for her to enfold him. 'I miss you too,' he conceded.

'You're growing up so fast,' she said, putting her cool hand on his cheek. 'It's like you don't need me anymore. We used to take such good care of each other.'

Will felt these words bulldoze his heart, and he shut the door and fell into her arms with a great heaviness, a feeling not unlike when he used to stay in the tub in Venice until all the water had drained out, leaving him heavy, sedated, and blissful, as if he'd narrowly survived a drowning. They lowered themselves to the floor, coming to rest side by side against the wall. He tried to breathe again in the old way, in exact synchronization with her, but because his lungs had grown Outside, matching her breaths didn't spin his head like it used to. How could he explain now that even though boys could trip and punch you, and wolves could feast upon your flesh, and blood could gush from your body and bounce on the ice, and some kids didn't even have parents to worry about them, and a boy could disappear from the world and nobody would care, Marcus had been right — the Outside wasn't all that dangerous. It was worth leaving for, if only to see it up close and to make a friend for a short while.

They sat like that for a spell. Then he rose, kissed the top of her head, threw his backpack over his shoulder, took up his skateboard, and again walked out the door. He was already late.

18

Will met Jonah in the parking lot of the hockey arena, amid the throngs of fathers shouldering corpse-heavy bags of gear and calling their sons 'Buddy' while leading them inside.

'You're going to roll around with that in your waistband?' Jonah said when Will covertly displayed the serrated knife he'd brought for protection.

'Good point,' Will said. He wrapped the knife in his sweatshirt and stuck the bundle in his backpack along with his amethyst and the Neverclear map.

As they started out, Jonah turned inexplicably angry. 'What're you going to do with that knife anyway? You think Marcus got kidnapped by a loaf of French bread? All kinds of things took Marcus,' he yelled over the cacophony of their wheels as they began bombing a hill. 'None of them you can stab.'

Downtown, the fall cold had herded everyone inside the taverns, leaving the sidewalks barren. After kickflipping perfectly up the curb of a closed gas station and then improvising a magnificent ollie over an overturned trashcan, Jonah's rage seemed to dissipate, or at least resubmerge. 'I could see if my brothers could get us a hunting rifle,' Jonah said. Will liked the idea but figured it would be difficult to carry inconspicuously. Will asked Jonah if you could saw a rifle off like a shotgun and Jonah said he didn't think so. 'Maybe we'll hold off for a while,' Will said.

The waterfront itself was the only section of the city they hadn't searched by skateboard because it was all condemned industrial land, just broken concrete strewn with junk and rubble, impassable for their wheels. With boards in hand they crossed the tracks and discovered a deer path through a tough thicket of fireweed and brambles. They passed a rusting washer-and-dryer set that stank of putrid water, then followed a tangle of lesser rail tracks that ducked through a fence into a junkyard.

Hidden amid the landscape of discarded trucks and train cars and garbage were a few shacks and lean-tos, less sturdily built than Marcus's had been, constructed mostly of derelict metal, plastic sheeting, and wood scrap. Two men were sitting near a steaming paint can hung over a smoky fire, one of them armless, the other weeping like a child while holding a tiny radio to his ear. The boys sighted some wolves or dogs — again they weren't sure which — stalking the doorway of a distant burned-out shed across the yard, and Will's heart ricocheted around in his chest while he cursed himself for forgetting to apply his deodorant that morning. But the wolves seemed otherwise occupied or at least didn't catch his scent.

'So you think the Butler hides out down here?' Will asked, hiding his trembling hands in his pockets.

'My brothers said he's rich, lives in a log

mansion near the border. But he comes down to load Neverclear on trains and the occasional boat. So what exactly are we looking for, then? A big cage with Marcus's name on it?'

'Anything,' said Will, scanning the bleak moonscape. 'Everything.'

Soon they arrived at the foot of the largest of the elevators, twelve enormous concrete cylinders stood on end, all fused together like a pipe organ or a clutch of giant shotgun shells. Attached to the cylinders rose a towering structure connected by a bridge, looming two hundred feet overhead, high as the castles of Will's encyclopedias. Painted on the side of the desolate structure in enormous flaking white lettering: SASKATCHEWAN WHEAT POOL 6.

'Hey!' Will exclaimed, 'I think the Wheezing Man said something about 'swimming in pool six' when he grabbed me that night.'

'Okay,' Jonah said, craning his neck upwards. 'We'll start here.'

After tracing the perimeter of the elevator, they found an unblocked entrance near a covered area where the tracks spanned over a massive steel grate amid some brutish, disused machinery. 'This's where they unloaded the grain, I think,' Will said.

Jonah walked out over a rusted metal grate. 'No bottom,' he said, peering into the black beneath his feet, setting Will's stomach aflutter.

Inside, the floor was heaped with something strangely soft underfoot like moss, sweet-smelling in an unsettling way. It wasn't until Will heard the burbling of thousands of pigeons overhead that he realized it was a carpet of droppings. Giant concrete pillars suspended a vaulted ceiling that sprouted with various mechanisms, sheltering their nests, while, below, a battlefield of metal scrap was scattered on the floor, all of it rusting, as if a great demolition derby had taken place long before either of them was born.

Everywhere was the smell of bricks, oil, metal, and wood, coupled with the stench of spilled beer dried to stickiness. They investigated a few doorways — control room, bathroom, locker room — and the instant they stepped inside, a hundred pigeons whooshed upward like dirty phoenixes to the closest smashed-out window. In these secluded nooks Will spotted half-busted bottles of fortified wine and malt liquor, a few limp mattresses that stunk of Neverclear, scattered with rank morsels of food.

Pressing deeper, climbing over broken-down doors, through ribbons of metal and wire, around open grain chutes in the floor that disappeared into nothing, the boys came upon a set of foursquare wrought iron stairs leading upward, high enough to vanish. Sunlight slashed through the shattered windows of the stairwell, illuminating rusted vents and hundreds of galvanized pipes that snaked about like a jungle canopy made of dead iron.

'Why did they have to build this thing so big?' said Jonah. 'It's like a demented cathedral.' As Will agreed, there came the sound of heavy footsteps on the stairs.

Will froze, as though the embodiment of the

Black Lagoon itself was at this very moment cascading down toward him like a herd of demonic horses. Then a hard tug on his shirtsleeve as Jonah dragged him into a crouch behind a large overturned table.

'Think he was telling the truth?' They heard a gruff voice echo through the staircase. 'That he did what you told him?'

'Who can say,' came another, softer voice, enunciating like someone interviewed on television. 'But I truly regretted that. Unfortunately, words really aren't much use with old Corpsey.'

'Maybe another of those kids has it? Like the one who left his helmet?' the other voice said. 'I checked the phone book for that name like you asked and came up empty. But I bet Corpsey knows where he is. So why's he protecting them?'

'He's got a soft spot for the younger set, it seems,' the soft voice said with a sigh. 'Corpsey used to be such a good resource. But I'm afraid he's overshot his expiry date.'

When they passed, the pungent smell of Neverclear wafted behind them. Will riskily peered at their backs and could make out a short bald man, accompanied by a slender one, white hair, at least a foot taller.

'Were you able to see their boots?' said Jonah after they were gone.

'There was too much bird shit on the floor,' said Will. 'But that was definitely the Bald Man from the schoolyard. And my guess would be the other was the Butler.'

The boys made their way to the stairs. After

the shot of adrenaline and the stair climbing, Will's heart seemed to gear down into an unstable and dangerous cadence. Exhaustion soon tugged his face into a grimace, *The one who left his helmet* replaying in his mind mercilessly. They must've looked up *Cardiel* in the phone book, but of course his mother kept their number unlisted. Will's stomach contorted, and he drove back tears as they crested the stairs and emerged into an enormous chamber that contained more droppings and disused machines. Huge windows lined the walls, providing a view of what seemed the entire world. Over the braying wind Will heard a groan and then a choked wail, halfway between a laugh and a shout.

Something was dragging itself across the floor.

'Hey,' Will said, approaching the heap cautiously. Rebar lay beside it, three pieces interlaced like pick-up sticks. A bearded man, barefoot in a dirty fur-lined parka, his thick jeans smattered with oil and mud, large lateral slashes in the fabric, the skin beneath a color past purple, before black.

'Are you okay?' said Will.

'Returning to the place. I spoke of that once,' the man whispered, his forehead pressed into pigeon droppings. The familiarity of his voice launched a flock of chills up Will's spine.

'Jonah, let's go call an ambulance,' Will said, still unable to move.

'No!' the man hissed with coals in his eyes, and both boys backed up. 'This is an uncomfortable setting, Aurelius,' he said, twisting onto his back,

274

sweeping the palms of his big-knuckled hands above him. 'Those cruelties may revamp,' he added with a wheeze, then fought to rise, smearing more blood into his jeans.

'Please don't move,' said Will. 'You're bleeding.'

The man chuckled. 'The sound is perpetual. I've surrendered to it.'

'Still bleeding, dude,' said Jonah. 'You should get your legs elevated.'

'I've surrendered to it,' he repeated, as though the middle syllable contained a special malevolence. By now the man had managed to stand, wobbly as a bear on a ball.

'My quarters,' he said, eyes on Will.

'What?' asked Will.

'Sorry buddy, we don't have any quarters for you,' said Jonah.

'My quarters!' he howled, pointing his elbow at a door across the room. 'Aurelius, invigorate your blood bank,' he said, now pointing at Will with a defocused expression.

'I think he wants us to take him somewhere,' said Will.

'He's already there,' said Jonah.

The man shambled forward, painting a bloody masterpiece of his progress on the concrete. He threw open a heavy door and lurched Outside. The boys followed cautiously through the doorway and onto the high platform they'd glimpsed from the ground.

From this height Will could see all the way up the hill to his school and Grandview Gardens. Between this landing and the other tower was a

275

rusted wrought-iron walkway and the man plodded out upon it. Will tested the bridge with his foot, trying not to see through its gaps.

Jonah joined Will at his side. 'So this guy wheezes like a busted vacuum and is not making too much sense. It's him, right?' he said.

Will nodded. 'It's the same voice. He's got plenty of grain dust on him, but he's not wearing the boots. We can follow hi — '

'Will! This is crazy,' Jonah pleaded. 'Maybe he deserved to get beat like that. Who knows? Let's just go. This is plenty of information to offer up to your constable buddy. Or we could come back with my brothers and make him talk.'

Will met Jonah's eyes. 'He could've broken my neck that night he grabbed me. But he didn't. You heard the Bald Man himself say this guy was protecting kids. And he just said Aurelius. I remember my mom reading a book that was supposed to make her less scared of the world written by some emperor guy named *Marcus Aurelius*. What if the Wheezing Man thinks I'm Marcus? Or wants to lead us to him?'

They watched the man continue over the bridge on wrecked legs to a faraway doorway, into which an immense black iron boiler was wedged, making the way impassable. He swung open the heavy door with a rusted wail. He stooped, then stuffed himself inside, fitting narrowly.

'Come on, megapussy,' Will said, then bent his head, took the cold railing, and stepped out, without glancing back to see if his friend would follow. Frigid squalls launched themselves into

276

his eyes, and the high, rusty bridge turned Will's knees to gelatin. When he reached the boiler, he set his skateboard inside, then crawled through the soft ash and through the identical opening on the other side.

He emerged, swatting ash flakes from his pants, into a grand room high above the harbor with huge windows and plank floors without an ounce of pigeon droppings. There was a scattering of old furniture and small rugs, a few plants. Judging by the large desk near the window and the shelving on the walls, it was probably once an office of some kind. No sign of garden hoses, or Marcus.

By the time Jonah wrestled himself through, the man moaned and collapsed to the floor, clunking his head soundly on a table leg. Will hurried to his side. He pulled his sweatshirt from his bag, unrolled the knife, stuffed the shirt under the man's head, then stashed the knife back in the bag. Will got a good view of him now, mid-thirties, except he looked older and younger at the same time, his long hair graying, the skin around his hollow eyes thin as lavender petals.

'Those two men did this to you?' Will asked. 'Was it because you're protecting Marcus?'

'You're right, Aurelius. They're unconglomerated,' he said with the hollow gaze of a man recently subject to an explosion. 'But you'll be tacking in the rip soon,' he continued as his teeth hissed and chattered. Then he coiled with a violent cough, his legs smearing blood like a gory snow angel.

'Why's he shivering so much?' said Will.

'He's in shock,' said Jonah. 'Textbook. We need to keep him warm.'

Will surveyed the room and spotted an old woodstove obscured by a stack of old books. 'I'll start a fire,' he said, scanning for matches and finding none, vowing to stuff his G.I. Joe — torching barbecue lighter in his backpack the next time he went Outside.

'This castle!' the man belted loud, straining up with a gurgle, 'is full of gas — the grain, rotting. You'll sail us to the ether!'

Will regarded Jonah quizzically, and he shrugged.

'Okay!' said Will, nearly yelling in the man's face, hoping to lodge the words in his brain through sheer volume. 'Do you have any blankets!'

'Abysmal,' the man said, cinching his eyes closed.

Jonah found a heavy-duty sleeping bag on a mattress set atop some pallets. Rather than risk getting too close by attempting to shove the man in, Jonah unzipped the bag and draped it over him. Soon the pace of the man's shivering slowed. Will cracked the water bottle he'd brought and set it beside him on the floor.

'Will, will, will, will you find me again?' the man called with a strange tenderness. 'Is that my voice?' he said. 'I've been eating birds for so long — ' Then he began to retch. Will held the bottle to his lips, allowing him a long, desperate slug.

'Pththththththt . . . ' he said spraying the liquid broadly, aerosoling it in the sunlight.

'Pestilence!' he shrieked.

With this rebuke the man seemed to have burned up a final reserve. His wheezing slowed before slipping into something near sleep, a rest unsettled by winces of pain and his mouth's own involuntary workings, emitting sounds halfway between word and dream.

Jonah put his fingers over the man's wrist, then lowered his ear near his mouth. 'His vitals are fine,' he said. 'But looks like we won't be finding Marcus tonight.'

They sat cross-legged beside the man, collecting themselves while monitoring the buzzy, tortured lift of his breathing and listening to the bleat of gulls and the rumble of the occasional train that ran without stopping through the yard far below. Through the window they could see dozens of birdfeeders made from old oilcans fixed outside the window to the concrete. The air was thick with the tang of rust, the funk of wharf, iron, and blood. Will knew about iron in blood because sometimes his mother had claimed hers was low and made them steak, slow-cooked for an ungodly duration until it became something closer to jellyfish. Before long the sun dipped behind the hill and the sky ignited orange. The man's sweat had already soaked his sleeping bag like a dishrag.

'I think we should stay the night,' said Will, cutting the silence.

'You're kidding,' Jonah said.

'What if we come back tomorrow and he's gone? We won't be able to ask him about Marcus. Plus they hit him in the *head*, too,

Jonah. You know concussions better than I do. What if we leave and he doesn't wake up?'

Jonah regarded him seriously. 'One thing I've learned is that there isn't enough help in the world for some people.'

'Come on, Doc, you don't really believe that,' Will said. 'Or are you planning on choosing all your patients?'

'It's called triage, Will, look it up,' Jonah said. 'I want to be a family doctor,' he added, 'not a mortician.'

For a quiet minute the boys watched little birds flit in and out of the birdhouses, brimming with seed and grain. Will had once believed Jonah was fearless, but lately he'd detected in his friend a coastal shelf of fear sunk to a depth to which no person could hope to dive.

'Please, Jonah?' Will said, trying not to sound pathetic like his mother at the door. 'You didn't have to tell me to walk away that day by the creek or jump on that wolf. But you risked yourself then. And Marcus did the same for you the night he went missing. This might be our only chance to save him. But I need you. I have this feeling that we'll be safe as long as we're together, that nothing can really hurt us.'

'You're sounding more like Marcus every day,' Jonah said shaking his head, half-smiling. Then he grimaced with disbelief at what he was about to agree to. 'Won't your mom be worried?' he said.

Will laughed. 'Naw, she'll be fine,' he said.

'Well I'm not crawling into one of those,' Jonah said, gesturing to the remaining sleeping bags on the mattress. He took a drag from an imaginary cigarette, then blew a puff of frost toward the ceiling. 'We'll need heat,' he said. 'There's plenty of burnable wood down there.'

'But do you think what he said about the gas from the grain is real?' said Will. They both regarded the man again, his rough mouth hanging wide and loose, his skin papery with scars and caked grain dust.

'I don't think so,' said Jonah. 'An elevator blew up down here like forever ago. But we'd know about it if it still happened.' The boys marched back downstairs and returned with an armload of scrap wood, Jonah passing it to Will through the boiler.

'Maybe they haven't blown up because nobody is in them, except people like him . . . ' said Will, thinking of his dead uncle Charlie as Jonah was loading the stove, cursing himself for not paying more attention to Mr. Miller's history speeches.

Jonah stood with his lighter held up in the air, thumb poised. 'Ready?' he said.

In an instant Will was looking at the match bomb Marcus had set off in his front yard, the life-changing bang that had started it all, and he realized now that if he'd learned anything, it was that the Outside was one gigantic Destructivity Experiment. 'Do it.'

Then came a raspy flick that made Will's scalp prickle and his throat swell like a stepped-on balloon. Jonah waved the flame aloft and made the sound of a roaring crowd. 'Thank you, Thunder Bay!' he said, then killed it with a quick puff.

With the stove lit and the windows mostly intact, the room grew warm. For a while the boys talked in the glow of the small fire, mostly about skateboarding — tricks they were amassing the courage to try, legendary falls they'd withstood — in an effort to normalize the situation. Will knew that boys their age would default into a discussion of girls at these moments — a comparison of their respective kisses with Angela, perhaps — but this subject never arose between them. Lately at school, a few girls, weirdly entranced by the boys' apartness, their withdrawal, their griminess and scars, had been slipping notes into their desks. Though sometimes just a glimpse of a girl's velvety collarbone under her tank top strap was enough to force Will to tuck himself discreetly into the waistband of his pants, Will and Jonah tore the notes to bits. While Will retained a secret loyalty to Angela, having an actual girlfriend seemed an unjustifiable risk, if only because she could turn out like his mother.

Before long, Jonah drifted off near the stove, his head propped by his skateboard and neatly folded jacket, his breath precise and easy. During the Wheezing Man's patchy sleep and fugues of muttering incoherence, sometimes his eyes would bolt open and fix blankly upon Will as he called out strange names. He murmured of birds and ghosts, of cables and wires binding him, of ships and trains, of blood and water, of people being hurt, healed, and hurt again. Will lay there, remembering all the times he'd coached his mother down from the panicked summits of

Mount Black Lagoon, the times he'd found her babbling on the floor in Venice, baffled with terror, her nightgown soaked in her own urine, and he detected the familiar tenor of her voice in the Wheezing Man's raving, a sound that was oddly comforting. He thought then about his Outside life — how vividly he could conjure all that had happened so far, how at night his dreams were dazzling carnivals and his days lasted years — and felt so lucky that he nearly exploded. Even if his mother was right and the Outside was unthinkably dangerous, he was desperately in love with all of it.

After a while, Will gave up on listening and let the man's words flood over him. And as Will's own eyes drooped, he felt as though he could be just as easily thinking these things himself, the man's pained dreams tinting his own like paint upon his palette, now sitting so far away in New York.

19

The boys woke in the chilled morning, the Wheezing Man still chloroformed with sleep.

They loaded the stove silently and lit it. Parched, they considered drinking from Will's water bottle, the same one the man had sipped from and refused the previous night, but decided against it because of AIDS. Jonah stood watch while Will examined the man's things but found nothing he could imagine had been Marcus's.

Eventually, his eyes shot open and he struggled upright. 'I reckon I can commence smoking tobacco again,' he said when he noted the coals flickering in the stove. He tried to stand, then looked down at his legs and seemed surprised by them. 'Some specter put a crushing on me a doctor wouldn't forget,' he said.

'It was the Butler who beat you,' Will said, approaching him cautiously. 'Because you helped Marcus, and he thinks you know where he is, right?'

Some kind of confusion took him when he saw Will's face. He managed to nod.

'Do you know where Marcus is now?' Will said, speaking slowly.

The Wheezing Man shook his head. 'Met Aurelius scurrying around this structure. Exploring, he termed it. Took a shining to him. Sheltered him for a spell. Gave him some tribulations. Hauling, shoveling. Paid him

284

staunchly for it. One day he said he had a thing to accomplish. Promised to resurface before he set out. But since then been no word. No dissertation. Nothing,' he said before shutting his eyes and murmuring incoherently into his pillow.

'So he could come back anytime?' Will said excitedly. 'But what if the Butler finds you here? You're helpless.'

He shook his head. 'Doesn't survey this little dwelling. His wolves drop the scent over that bridge and the ashes in the boiler. That doesn't mean you boys shouldn't vacate.'

'His bleeding has stopped. And he doesn't have a concussion,' Jonah said.

'Do you have food? If we leave you?' asked Will.

The Wheezing Man glanced at the window near the birdfeeders. 'I'll do fine,' he said. 'But what'd keep me propped up, boys, would be some unblighted for my substrates.'

'Un . . . blighted?' said Will.

'Lakes aren't all one water,' he said, dragging himself up over to the window. 'This cove is all taint. Solely rats and sicknesses imbibe themselves here. You boys trample up the shore to where the factories and the wharves discontinue. There you fetch me some unblighted.'

Will looked at Jonah and Jonah shook his head.

'Okay,' said Will.

'And then we're gone,' said Jonah. 'There's a science test this afternoon, and I need to go over my notes.'

★ ★ ★

Back Outside at the foot of the towering elevator, the boys halted beside a rusted-out car near the shore, in which, judging by the blankets and cardboard pad, people were recently camped. Beside the car the lake water foamed slightly with a rainbowish film.

'Let's just use this,' Jonah said, dipping the bucket the Wheezing Man gave them.

'I think he meant pure, Jonah.'

'You think he can taste it?'

'You think he can't?'

'Whatever,' said Jonah, dumping the liquid from the bucket.

The boys continued down the shoreline, lowering their gazes when they passed a mean-looking man hanging a slippery skinned animal from a leafless tree, then an Indian couple locked unconscious in each other's arms beneath a torn tarp propped up by some old skis stuck in the dirt.

★ ★ ★

When they returned to the elevator an hour later with water from at least a mile up the shore, the man was asleep. They set the bucket beside him and left.

Will approached his house from the creek and snuck in through the back door. His stomach stewing with hunger, he tiptoed into Paris to fix a snack. At the table sat his mother, both palms pressed against a steaming mug of tea, beside her

Constable MacVicar.

'And look who it is,' said the constable, as though speaking to a girl who'd had her birthday party canceled. 'Out for some overnight mischief, like I said.'

Slowly his mother looked up from her mug, her face blanched and drained. 'Is that you, Will?' she said, her voice croaky. 'You're here?' For the first time Will noticed white strands surfacing in her hair. But her eyes were still leaf-green, and he resisted another sudden boyish urge to crash into her arms.

'In the flesh,' said the constable. 'And where were you, Will?'

'Jonah's,' said Will. 'We fell asleep watching horror movies. Sorry, Mom.'

'Jonah Turtle?' asked the constable, quickly.

'Yeah,' said Will. 'His phone wasn't working, so I couldn't call.'

'Okay,' MacVicar said, perturbed for a second, before he reattained composure. 'Well, you're fine now. Home. Safe. That's what matters.' He clapped. 'Anyway, Diane, I'd better be going. See me to the door, Will.'

After the constable pulled on his zippered boots, he set a big hand on Will's shoulder. 'I want you to steer clear of that Indian boy, Jonah. That Turtle family is no good. I know you've been riding those boards of yours around downtown, trespassing and damaging prop-erty — '

Will kicked into his best surprised routine. 'What do you mean?'

'Save the act. That boy's dangerous, son. A

287

magnet for calamity. Most Indians don't know how to conduct themselves in a city. Jonah and that Marcus are cut from the same cloth. You need to make sure you don't turn yourself into one of those kids I haven't much interest in finding.'

Then he gestured gravely to the kitchen. 'That woman in there has had enough distress in her life,' he said. 'She doesn't deserve any more grief from you. Look, I know you lied to me in my office. Your mother hasn't left this place for years. But if she slips any further down, I'll have to ask Social Services to step in, Will. And I don't want that. Which means your job is to prevent me from making that call. Do I make myself clear?'

Will mumbled something to get him out the door, then retreated to New York. He lay on top of his comforter on his back, his room darkened by blankets he'd plastered over his windows, studying the ghostly pages torn from *Thrasher* that wallpapered his room as completely as they did his imagination.

Some time later came a soft knock on his door. With his head buried in the pillow, Will felt the bed cant under her weight. 'You don't have to go to school today,' she said from beside him. 'You can stay home with me. I'll slow-cook us a lasagna.'

'Sure,' he said, his voice muffled.

She snapped on his bedside lamp and let out a tiny cluck when she saw the scars on his arms that he'd forgotten to cover with a long-sleeved shirt. 'Oh, honey,' she said, turning his elbow, 'do they hurt?'

'They're fine,' he said. 'Scars don't hurt, Mom. They're *healed*.'

'They don't look fine,' she said.

Suddenly he couldn't tolerate her hands on him. He tore away and rolled to his side. 'It's just skateboarding,' he said.

'But you'll ruin your career in elbow modeling,' she joked, but Will didn't laugh, because there was still guilt stashed somewhere in it.

'My skin is mine to ruin,' he said. 'Or did you only loan it to me?' He reached and angrily clicked off his light, wreathing them in near darkness.

'Will,' she began again after a while, 'when you didn't come home last night, I called Jonah's place and no one answered.'

'I told you their phone was broken.'

She took a deep breath, then drew back her elastic and let it go. 'And the constable mentioned you'd been down to visit him at the station? Down at the harbor?' she said, her voice gaining in pitch. 'Asking about the boy who had . . . who had disappeared? Is that true?' She sobbed out the last word.

Will said nothing.

She wept then for some time, the bed jiggling like the ride you put coins in at the mini-mall where he and Jonah skateboarded at lunch. He could sense her soggy face hung above him, as dangerous to behold as a solar eclipse.

'How am I supposed to trust you now that you broke your promise?' she said, regaining some composure. 'After you've been lying to me about where you and Jonah go all day?'

'Not nearly as much as *you've* been lying to me, Mom. Like why you're so afraid of the harbor? But you know what? It's fun down there. I like it.'

'It was dangerous then, and it still is, Will,' she said. 'Maybe worse.'

'That's where Charlie died, right? Of a heart attack? Right? Constable MacVicar told me he died in an accident.'

She shut her eyes. 'Oh, Will,' she said, 'I'm so sorry.'

He scoffed. 'And there's nothing wrong with my heart, is there?'

He watched her take five slow breaths. 'It was a metaphor,' she said.

'A metaphor for what?'

'Our family, Will. The Cardiels. Your grandfather, your uncle, me — we don't have the best luck. I wanted to tell you that you need to be especially careful, but didn't know how . . . '

'My friend Angela,' Will said, 'she's *actually* going to die, Mom, like for real. There's nothing anyone can do. And you know what? She's not even scared. She enjoys the time she's got left.'

'Will — '

'So what. I've lied to you like crazy since I've been going Outside. I've nearly died more times than I can count. And there are going to be more. There. Now we're even.'

They sat again in silence, and Will fought against synchronizing his breathing with hers, waiting to breathe in when she breathed out.

'I feel so far away from you now,' she said, her voice emptied out.

'That's how it's supposed to be, Mom,' he said.

'I suppose so,' she said. 'Just please let the constable do his job. That's all I ask. You work on growing up. That's dangerous enough.'

★ ★ ★

Will waited until Relaxation Time to go spelunking into the most neglected cupboards of Paris for dusty-lidded cans that his mother wouldn't notice missing: beets, herring, coconut milk, water chestnuts (whatever those were), fruit cocktail comprised mostly of soggy, tasteless pears, as well as a bag of uncooked oatmeal and some past-stale hunks of bread she kept for croutons.

'Are you going back to the harbor?' she said while he was putting on his skateboard shoes, an unimpressive sternness to her voice.

'Aren't you supposed to be 'relaxing' right now?'

'I asked you a question, Will. Did you hear me?'

'I'm going *out*,' he said, swinging his upturned palm at the door as though to indicate the whole world.

She started shaking, then stiffened, and drew her hands to her hips. 'Will, I *forbid* you to leave this house.'

'Okay sure, Mom. And I *forbid* you to stay home.'

'I'm serious.'

'Or what?' he said, stepping backwards through the open doorway.

Her anger opened into a pleading look like a flower blooming. 'I don't know what will happen to me if you go,' she said pitifully.

'You'll be fine,' he said, taking another step back.

She started walking toward him, arms outstretched, stepping onto the tile landing. 'Don't go, Will.'

'You're going to have to come get me,' Will said with another backwards step down the stairs, which he knew she thought was dangerous but actually wasn't at all.

She minced forward, slippers shushing on the tile, unsteady as a woman with no handhold on a speeding train. For a moment Will cheered her on, promising himself that if she could only step Outside now, he wouldn't need to go back to Pool 6. She would fix everything. The same way she berated store managers on the phone. He pictured a whole new life beginning for them: sitting in those white-tableclothed restaurants he'd whizzed past downtown, watching the rain hit her coat as they walked under trees, him reassuring her that lightning never hits you, even if you dare it to. But as he watched, her face constricted as though she'd received devastating news, and she quivered and slowed before stopping, still two feet back from the opening. When tears flashed in her eyes and her body shook, conquered, Will turned and walked away. Because nothing would ever change. She'd always be this way, and it was a waste of precious Outside time to wait for her.

Tears are salty water, he thought as his skateboard roared over the sidewalk beneath him like an entire pack of wolves growling at once. Like sweat. And who ever heard of a person sweating too much. It was good for you. Natural. Maybe people were born with a finite amount of tears Inside them, and all a person had to do was let them all fall, and then they'd be free.

⋆ ⋆ ⋆

He found the Wheezing Man sitting up in his pallet bed with an enormous book split in his lap.

'You want me to spritz us with a passage?'

'Okay,' said Will, unshouldering his bag. Despite the man's limited mobility, Will remained leery of getting too close.

The Wheezing Man began to read, but the words and sentences he produced seemed too confused and unrelated to one another to be published in any book. From the spine, Will noted that this volume was supposed to be about shipbuilding and various lakeboats, yet the man talked mostly of dark clouds and steel cables, about people weeping for years and animals giving birth in a river. After a while he switched to another book that was supposed to be about the Napoleonic Wars, except he held it upside down. He managed to say the word *blood* ten times in one sentence, pausing only to recapture his wheezy breath or to draw slow, careful slugs of water from a tall glass that he sat down carefully like a fine jewel.

'Where did you get all this stuff?' Will said after the Wheezing Man stopped, gesturing to his bookshelves and the room's lavish furnishings.

'Happened over the bulk of it in the garbage,' he said. 'Procured some of it. Fashioned the rest. You wouldn't fathom what citizens turf nowadays.'

Will pulled a can of coconut milk and another of beets from his bag and set them beside the bed, vaguely regretting that it was food he wouldn't dream of eating himself. He placed the bag of dry oatmeal on a nearby table.

'How salubrious,' the Wheezing Man said, leaning over to tuck the oatmeal into a drawer, shutting it carefully.

Will passed him a hunk of his mother's bread, which, even though it was stale, Will hoped was his most appetizing offering. The Wheezing Man took a bite and shut his eyes. A look of contentment overcame him, and Will worried he'd dropped to sleep.

Will took a deep breath. 'It was you who grabbed me that night in the woods, wasn't it?'

His breathing quieted down. 'I was fixed to warn Aurelius, but I couldn't pinpoint him,' he said after a while. 'Luckily the old man's wolves missed too.'

'Why's he called the Butler?' Will asked.

'He's the worst version,' he said, chewing. 'Only assists himself. But he used to be a bona fide man. University man. Escaped Thunder Bay for two years at Queen's but had to boomerang back to care for his simpleton sister. Came back quoting Wordsworth and all things. Worked in a white coat checking grain boats for weevils and worms. Until he took a loading boom to his head and surrendered half of himself.'

'What half?' Will said.

'The good one,' he said.

'I once perpetrated for him,' he added, finishing his bread. 'Squirreling out good grain from this old hulk for his Neverclear.'

'And you and Marcus were getting hoses for him, right? For his gas tanks?'

'Principally,' he said. 'Then young Aurelius went and nose-dived into a volcano.'

'He stole the Butler's map, right? To make money? But what if I can get it back? Would the Butler leave him alone?'

Dismay crossed the man's face. 'Wouldn't account much,' he said. 'The Butler's already brewing up more of that coffin varnish to satiate his clientele.'

'What was Marcus planning to do with the money?'

'He was itching to flee this latitude. Dreamt of a little sloop. A one-hander he could wind himself.'

'You mean a boat?'

'A cabin. A little outboard. Said it was a habitat he could cart with him. Like a turtle. Never again get lodged anyplace he didn't care for.'

'Do you think he did it?' Will asked. 'Made it out?'

'Not yet,' he said, pulling at his beard.

Every day that week, Jonah and Will ditched school to trudge through the fresh-fallen snow to the harbor with cans and food scraps for the man, who said his name was Titus. Will was astonished by how much it took to sustain him, the sheer weight of it. Jonah contributed some sausages that his brothers had made from a bull moose they'd brought down last spring, and the boys had to convince Titus not to eat them raw.

After all those years caring for his mother Inside, Will slipped effortlessly into the caretaker role — fetching food and 'unblighted' water, filling the voids in his faltered abilities — and was warmed by that old thrill of domestic usefulness that sustained him for so long Inside. Will felt oddly at ease with Titus, despite everything. He was more like his mother than anyone he'd met Outside, probably attributable to their mutual craziness.

That Saturday Will coaxed Jonah into redressing Titus's legs, which now bore long scabs, black as slugs. More worrisome, though, was how both his calves were hot to the touch, swollen tight as Jonah's moose sausages.

'Erythromycin,' Jonah said, tossing onto the table the rattling vial he'd fetched, his cheeks pulsing after a breathless run up to County Park in the frigid air. 'Two times daily with food. My brother Gideon got them after a tattoo of his got infected. Expired two years ago, but they'll have some fight left in them.'

Apart from the possibility that Marcus would reappear at Pool 6 and the opportunity for Jonah to practice his medical skills, the snowfall was how Will had convinced Jonah to frequent the elevator. Will's second winter Outside had been nothing like his first. Gone were the thrills of exploration and novelty. This time it was all drab light and frozen-footed walks down to the harbor. Because skateboards required dry pavement, winter for an obsessed skateboarder was a time of despair and unimaginable yearning. Will secured Titus's blessing to build some skateboard ramps in the large room where they'd found him beaten, the Distribution Floor, he called it. They extrapolated the design from *Thrasher*: ribs placed laterally, curving upward on a template, bent plywood surfaces screwed down over those. The wood they found in abundance around the harbor, two-by-fours used as concrete forms, tool sheds, and old beached dories they busted up. It took them a week to sweep up the bird droppings, and Jonah launched ten sagging garbage bags' worth out onto the lake ice, where they sat like periods.

Jonah had Enoch write him another note, and after years of signing his mother's checks, Will found forging his own a cinch. While their classmates sat deadened in their desks, the boys rode their ramps each day, high above the lake, threading their way between pillars and hoppers and conveyance vents, back and forth at breakneck speeds, grain dust gummy in their eyes. There they withstood unplanned splits, shinners, debilitating knee whacks, wrist tweaks, bent fingers, hippers, elbow bashings, back scrapes, rolled ankles, and chin abrasions. Despite the injuries, or perhaps because of them, Will's skateboarding was further improving. His new favorite trick was the 'disaster,' which entailed ollieing 180 degrees while on a ramp, then, instead of landing safely back in the curved transition, hooking his rear wheels on the lip. Only through a finicky rocking motion executed immediately could he escape being hurled to the concrete floor. It was like picking a lock, pure joy when it worked, pure mayhem when it didn't. After trekking back up the creekside, Will would return home, stinking of pigeons and wheat, hacking up dollops of grain dust like little uncooked loaves, spitting them with delight into the sink in Venice.

'So what are you Icaruses training for? A tournament?' Titus said, after dragging himself from the workhouse over the high bridge to the Distribution Floor for the first time to look on. His antibiotics were nearly done, and his infection was improving. Lately he'd been calling them 'Icarus Number One' and 'Icarus Number Two,' for reasons they didn't grasp.

'No tournament,' said Will.

'So what's the schedule then, the import-export?' said Titus.

'Just to do it,' said Will. 'To get good at it.'

'I can't help but sustain that you boys should've been wagering your necks down here in another epoch: unblocking grain bins, leaping between freights, doing a usefulness, rather than bleeding for no account whatever. But very least you're putting this old maid to use with your roller toys,' Titus said, patting the bricks. His beard split with a smile. 'That's a sunshine.'

'They aren't toys,' Jonah said.

'What's their frequency, then, Icarus Number Two?'

'Skateboards are . . . they're like . . . tools,' Will said.

'For what career description?' Titus replied skeptically.

Will took a moment to think. Unable to find the right words, he blurted the first thing in his mind. 'For falling,' he said.

'Well,' Titus said, shaking his head. 'Every youth needs a war. I found mine. This constitutes yours. But don't overshoot it. Smashing through those windows will earn you a two-hundred-and-twenty-foot blitzkrieg to the wharf.'

Later that day, as though on cue, Jonah careened off the edge of the ramp and sunk some ragged metal in his palm. 'We'll see what we can accomplish,' Titus said, holding up a pair of needle-nosed pliers he'd boiled in a pot on the woodstove. Jonah, mute with pain, surrendered his bloody hand to Titus, while Will fetched the serrated knife from his backpack and stood beside them, just to be safe. Titus dug with the pliers, and for a moment it seemed like he was torturing Jonah, and Will was trying to imagine attacking when Titus backed off. 'The woodland only hurts you because it loves you,' he said, flicking the shard at the wall.

'Your ancestors mind you filleting yourselves

up like this?' Titus said later when they were heating some cans of beans on the woodstove.

'Who?' said Jonah.

Titus shook his head. 'Your' — he strained to produce the correct word — 'parents,' he said.

'Father? Is that you?' Jonah said, eyes turned upward with his hands clasped at his neck, scanning the filthy rafters as though communing with angels. 'Am I going to be all right?'

'Roger that,' said Titus. He put his head down. 'How about you, Icarus Number One?' he said, almost too quiet for Will to hear.

'My mom doesn't like me skateboarding. Or coming down here. But it's my choice.' These days she was scarcely leaving San Francisco, and the boys had even stayed over at Pool 6 again twice more and she never said anything. Will figured she was too Black Lagooned to check his room at night. 'Anyway, that's her problem,' said Will. 'My mother cares too much. About everything. She's basically psycho.'

Titus stared at the ground for a while with his jaw set and embers burning beneath skin. 'That's not a thing to say,' he said flatly as he rose. 'My pins are twinkling, Icaruses. Think I'm fixing to pay my taxes.' He hobbled to his bed and zipped himself into his sleeping bag.

At times the boys would stifle laughter when the randomness of Titus's utterances landed in the realm of the comic, yet sometimes a switch flicked inside him and his moods took dark swerves, his hissing voice assuming a too-loud, desperate quality, the way people speak when they're wearing headphones. At these times the very same words became frightening, portentous.

While Titus slept, they'd searched every inch of the workhouse for clues: the hexagon boots, handwriting that matched the sign, any trace of Marcus — yielding nothing. But despite its desolation, Will preferred the elevator almost more than he did Jonah's house. Maybe it was because his uncle and grandfather had both worked and died here that Will felt some manner of bone-deep connection to it. Or maybe it was because there was nobody to tell them what to do or to worry about them. MacVicar had said that boys frequented these abandoned places — old mills, mines, and derelict cabins — because they needed to be alone. Which was probably the only thing he'd ever been right about. Because, Will was discovering, the Outside's most forgotten areas were both the perfect places to hide and the perfect places to grow up.

Relaxation Time

It was loosed upon her now. Like that day on the subway platform, floodgates blown open, her thoughts a maze with no openings or exits.

Her son returned home each day from school smelling like Theodore and Charlie had after work: grease, sweat, sawn lumber, and grain — the only explanation was that her fear was inventing this. But canned food had been disappearing faster than she could order it. Perhaps Will was donating it to a shelter or some organization that ministered to the poor. Though she doubted it. She'd even found the bread knife tucked in his backpack. But what could she do? Forbidding him hadn't worked. If he ran away, she couldn't even go out and look for him. She'd have to rely on MacVicar, whose track record for locating children wasn't legendary.

All her tricks to deactivate thinking had failed, like old clunky jokes that nobody laughed at anymore. The elastic. Will's artwork. Her guitar. She could no longer read. Not even page-turners. Certainly not mysteries. It was like trying to soak up water with a piece of plastic wrap. The terror was as ceaseless now as her heart beating.

She'd tried to appease her spiraling thoughts, reason with them, flee from them, but her methods had betrayed her in the end. Fear had been festering inside her, and all her efforts to contain, quell, and suppress it had only incubated and nourished it.

So it came to this. It would be no permanent thing. Not like the basement. She simply felt safe in her room. She'd been wearing the same malodorous robe for a week, unwashed dishes tucked under her bed, a greenish frizz around the dregs of vegetable soup, toupees of blue floating in unfinished yogurt cups. She'd carted the phone to her night table to order groceries. With Will gone, she convinced the regular deliveryman to accept a key so he could place the bags far enough inside the door that she could reach them. She'd innovated a method to get to the washroom or retrieve packages without falling into a hole, which involved drinking half a bottle of codeine cough syrup — luckily they delivered these by the case — and darting for the door.

But it wouldn't be permanent. Eventually fear would release her, would retreat as it always had before, and she'd be bold enough to again roam her own house as freely as her son now roamed the outside world.

That night, panting in her bed with no Relaxation Apparatus or other means to defend herself, she was accosted with the sense that there were parts of the story she'd been leaving out. The night before Charlie died. She remembered walking at Whalen's request up the hill in a bedlam of sleet to his house. His father was away on business, so he brought her inside. They sat in his dressed-up parlor on separate chairs. He made no move to embrace, blaming the dusty work clothes he already had on, identical to Charlie's, but she could see now that this was an excuse, that the private world between them had already started to close.

Whalen said that according to the crew who worked the day shift that morning, there'd come an odd pinging from one of the cables that held the grain cars aloft while they were flipped, like the high strings of ten violins plucked once. There'd been a heated debate over whether the entire counterweight mechanism had lowered an inch. Whalen said he'd told Charlie, but her brother wasn't worried. 'He's determined to get this boat loaded before the freeze,' Whalen said. 'He said it's the only way he'll get the money to take care of you when he leaves for school next year.'

Whalen took her hand and kissed her, and she told him she'd try. On her walk home she realized that with no engineer in Thunder Bay, they'd have to call one in from Duluth to check the cable. And even with an engineer, changing a cable of that gauge meant two days of downtime. If those two didn't unload that boat tomorrow night, for another entire year she'd be bringing Charlie's suppers, enduring his angry tirades, listening to his sad wheeze, all while sneaking around with Whalen as the secrecy of their meetings poisoned them for good.

She returned home and said nothing to her brother about the cable. The next day, she thanked him for all his hard work and packed him two of his favorite sandwiches. 'You and Whalen better hurry if you want that boat loaded

304

before the freeze,' she said, her eyes fixed on his dust-covered boots.

Yes, she'd done her part to doom Charlie, she admitted this now while weeping into her sheets. But please let her not fail Will. Let her not be selfish like she'd been that night. Her son was too full of life, too robust, too valuable, to be taken from her. But too valuable not to be.

How was it that to give a child life was to, on the very same day — even before you could lay eyes upon their slick, purple bodies — have already given them their death?

20

Whether it was because Titus had beaten his infection or was eating regularly or drinking unblighted water, or simply that the boys had grown accustomed to his pureed speech patterns, Will couldn't say, but he was making more sense. 'I been out of people practice,' he offered once when Will was fixing him a sandwich on his mother's freshly thawed bread, which Titus always requested. 'I got a hard time sticking words into things, sticking things into words.'

With his wounds mending and the swelling reduced, Titus could stand with crutches he'd fashioned from two oars, though he still seemed an inch from collapse. Jonah had eyed Titus's recovery closely, as one would a rousing sea monster. Then the day came when Titus could ambulate with only one crutch. 'Remember when you said that once he's better and completely dangerous again, we're out of here?' said Jonah. 'Well, he's better.'

'But what if Marcus comes back like he said?' said Will. 'What if he gets the money for his boat and needs Titus to help him?'

'Marcus never said anything to me about a boat. So who knows if Titus is telling the truth. He may have hallucinated the whole thing,' Jonah said. 'By now Marcus is either already dead or he's left Thunder Bay forever. There's not much room left in between.'

'He could still be hiding? Another shack, farther out? We could go exploring.'

'Have you got any letters from school lately?' Jonah said.

'My mom is afraid of mail, remember?'

'Well, I have. They're sending me to Templeton next year — you know, the school for future inmates? They said I'm not participating and missed too many days. So I'm out.'

'What about medical school?' Will gasped.

Jonah shook his head, and his face flushed. 'I don't think Templeton is an institution that really screams *doctor material* on your application,' he said, his head hanging. 'It's mostly Indians there, so they'll probably take their time before they ship you, too, Will. But it'll happen soon enough if we don't go back.'

'Let them. We'll be together. You can teach *yourself* to be a doctor,' Will said. 'I never liked school anyway. I only went there to find Marcus. But now Titus is our *only* lead. Something's going to happen soon. I can feel it.'

'We did a good thing and took care of him. You were right about that. But anyone who talks about blood that much doesn't have at least a little on their hands. What if in one of his moods Titus did something to Marcus and doesn't even remember? And even if he didn't, he's still dangerous. So I'm out of here, and you're coming with me.'

At the thought of losing his only friend, Will was swamped with a great weariness. He'd been investigating the Outside for so long, but he knew he still lacked the courage to face it alone.

'Okay,' Will said. 'You're right. He is more dangerous now. We can stake the place out, watch him from a distance.'

While they were packing up their tape player and tools and backpacks on the Distribution Floor, Titus crutched his way in. 'Getting scarce,' he said nodding. 'I do appraise you Icaruses tending to me while I was downtrodden. That was a queasy one. And I've liked spectating this little war you've manufactured for yourselves,' he said, gesturing to the ramps. 'But I divine that you Icaruses might be interested in some extraneous travails before you scatter.'

'You mean work?' said Will. Beside him, Jonah crossed his arms.

'Here is three hundred dollars each,' Titus said, pulling six bills from his parka. 'That's for deeds you already completed. You boys can appropriate some new roller platforms.'

'Skateboards,' said Jonah as Will plucked the bills carefully. It was more cash than he'd held in his life, not counting his mother's checkbook.

'And I'm financing each Icarus three hundred more when this new act's through,' said Titus.

'What's the job?' said Will.

'Stealing from people's yards?' said Jonah, and Will shot him a look.

'Not succinctly,' Titus said. 'A task Marcus didn't stay put to see out. But I'll have to exhibit it to you.'

Will dragged Jonah aside. 'We can save the money for when we move to California to skate all year long,' Will whispered enthusiastically. 'If

308

anything happens, we'll run. This could be what we've been waiting for.'

'I'm just curious when exactly you got *crazier* than Marcus?' Jonah said, shaking his head, running the money between his fingers, before he agreed.

They exited the workhouse through the boiler and began their climb down, during which Titus coughed and spat from every open window. After a few flights, Titus's breathing grew increasingly pained, his face ashen as the elevator's walls. At the bottom, Titus doubled over and muttered curses between long gasps. When he recovered, they passed an open grain chute that Jonah kicked a piece of rubble into. A chilling sound issued from deep below, like rushing water.

'Rats,' said Titus. 'A majority in the bins now. Only takes a pair to tumble down to birth a hive. With no exit they're chomping their way to the floor of all that forgotten grain. When they arrive there they'll have at each other. Don't go falling in, Icaruses. After nothing but stale wheat berries for decades, they'll be game for some protein.'

They trudged Outside through muddy snow, past the towering disused iron-ore dock and the shuttered shipbuilding yard down by the river mouth. During the walk, Titus fell quiet, carefully planting his crutch in the slush. Soon they passed another elevator, like Pool 6 in design, but smaller.

Titus pointed his crutch upward. 'I toiled down here as a whelp. A single of those bins can hide the yearly output of a hundred farms. That's millions of bushels — all told,' he said asthmatically. 'During the war, we were the only zone shipping wheat anywhere. Feeding the entire sphere! How's that, Icaruses?'

'Fascinating,' said Jonah, and Will was relieved that Titus's particular insanity made him mostly numb to sarcasm.

'Now look at us,' Titus said, gesturing incomprehensibly. Will wasn't sure if he was referring to himself or Thunder Bay. 'Only enough grain to keep the Butler's stills going.'

'Wait, you worked here? In the elevators? My uncle and my grandfather both did, too,' Will said as they walked. 'Did you know my uncle, Charlie Cardiel?'

Titus nodded and dropped his gaze.

'What was he like?'

'Oh,' Titus said, 'he was tethered. And he banged up some of the populace he shouldn't have. But he was just a colt. And would've atoned for it if allowed the timeline.' After that he fell quiet again. They pressed farther, crossing a rail junction where some men with a few large dogs communed next to a pile of burning garbage near the tracks, stealing predatory glances at their group.

'Is that the Butler?' Will said, flash frozen, hazarding a glance in their direction.

'Nope,' Titus said without looking over. 'Those hobgoblins don't exist.' Then he coughed loudly, his breathing a burst air mattress. 'This is us here,' he said, leading them into an abandoned structure of crumbling brick, a hundred feet back from the lake. Inside was a busted ecosystem of garbage and gears and

310

decomposing gulls and rusty clutter, as though the factory had been perfectly repurposed to manufacture squalor. They passed through a warren of unlit hallways and came to a steel door, on top of it a small window.

'Who yearns for a boost?' Titus said.

Will and Jonah regarded each other.

'Is this the job Marcus was supposed to do for you?' said Jonah.

'A fashion like it,' Titus said.

'Well,' Jonah said, 'let's get this over with. Safer in there than out here with you two nutters.' Will lifted Jonah's foot, and he vaulted gracefully through the opening above.

Will stood in the hallway, body tensed and ready to sprint, while Titus swayed like a chopped-at tree.

'You needed Marcus to unlock this from the other side, huh?' Jonah said when he opened the door before them, but Titus didn't answer as he plunged Inside. Long tables and rusty chairs crowded the big room, which may have once been a cafeteria. Some windows overlooked the junk-drawer factory floor through which they'd just passed. 'Those rubber?' Titus said, pointing at their wrecked skateboard shoes that they insisted on wearing throughout winter. 'Hope so,' he said. 'Still some living wires snaking about.'

Titus hobbled over to a tarp and drew it back to reveal a large stash of garden hoses — mostly green, some black, and a few orange — coiled neatly together. 'I need you Icaruses to link these up. The lot of them. These go betwixt,' he said, tossing a paper bag of what looked like hundreds of rubber gaskets. 'At conclusion I want a mythic snake. No leaks, so make sure to twist tight.'

'Marcus got you all these?' Jonah said.

'He was a persistent helper.'

'But what're they for?' asked Will.

Titus turned to the wall. 'A chore I should've perpetuated a long time ago,' he said with an empty look, as though reading some instructions on the inside surface of his eyes. 'But I got an agenda to communicate with,' he said making for the door as the boys began untangling lengths of hose. 'Rally in the workhouse when you're through. The work should do you a kindness,' he said, leaving.

Wordlessly the boys set to their task. Maneuvering the hoses while keeping them from kinking or twisting was difficult, and getting the threads to match up required more precision than they'd expected.

'I knew it would be the hoses,' Will said, thrilled.

'We're still leaving after this,' Jonah said, lifting a heavy coil.

'Would you rather be listening to Mrs. Gustavson talk about how creative her cats are right now?' Will asked, referring to the art class they'd endured the last time they'd attended school for a full day, two weeks ago now.

They worked through lunch, until hunger left them and their stomachs fell into an eerie quiet. 'You ever sleep Outside in the woods like Marcus?' Will asked, to keep his mind occupied.

'No,' Jonah said. 'Gideon always wants to take

me up into the bush to teach me stories and hunting and traditional medicines, but I don't like camping. It's too creepy. Too exposed. Skateboarding and school are the only reason I go out.'

Exhausted, they left the job partly done and didn't see Titus again that day. The boys cut school for two consecutive days to finish the project, their forearms deadened from hand-screwing the hundreds of coils together. On the last day, they discovered six crisp hundred-dollar bills rolled up and tucked in the final hose. They jammed the money into their underwear before gathering their skateboards and venturing back out onto the harborfront.

'The real mystery here is what Darth Hobo plans to do with the mother of all hoses,' Jonah said.

'That's what I can't figure out. Maybe he's going to turn Pool Six into one big vegetable garden,' Will joked.

'Pfffffftttt,' said Jonah as they turned the corner against a brick structure, its paint detaching in scales. 'Not likely.'

'Be careful there, boys!' a man said sharply after they'd nearly run into him. 'What's the big hurry?' He had white hair and a soft voice and two leashless wolves panting at his heels. The Bald Man was beside him, shovels clutched in each of their hands, sharpened silver by use, bright as starlight. Near them another man pushed a wheelbarrow with something large in it, covered by an electric-blue tarp. Will mumbled an apology and made to go around.

'You two boys look tired,' the Butler said, stepping in front of Will with a look of concern. His skin was pale as halibut, his hair, a tempest of ivory cowlicks, like an illustrated ocean in one of Will's old storybooks. Despite his age, his face was strangely boyish, with an underlying pinkness and baby-soft cheeks that appeared polished. 'Don't they look tired?' he said to the Bald Man. 'Been working hard, have you boys?' asked the Butler. 'Parched? Would you care for some water?'

Worried the Bald Man would recognize him from his encounter with the wolf, Will tucked in his chin, taking the opportunity to note nothing boot-like on either of their feet: the Butler in dress shoes and the Bald Man in trashed sneakers. 'We're fine, thanks,' said Will. When he made to take another step around their group, one of the wolves growled with the same lawnmower chugging as the one that bit him, electrifying Will's scalp.

'Sss . . . tas . . . stas . . . niabo . . . bo . . . vich,' a voice from the wheelbarrow murmured, a leg hanging out from beneath the tarp. It sounded like the deliveryman who used to come to Will's house who was from a country that ended in *ia*.

'Sorry you have to see this, boys,' the Butler said. 'I don't want to judge . . . however, I'm afraid this particular fella has overdone his schnapps. But gosh, it sure is good to see some fresh young men down here, isn't it Claymore?' said the Butler. 'Hard at work. Just like the old Thunder Bay.' He stuck his long owlish nose, stiff with cartilage, into Will's face. His gaze

314

sharp and fearsome, and the high smell of Neverclear seeped through his teeth. Then the Butler raised a long, parsnip-white finger. 'Say,' he said, 'you wouldn't happen to know a fella, lives down here somewhere — can't breathe too well, unfortunately — was having a little trouble with his legs?'

Will swallowed the acorn in his throat. 'No, we wouldn't,' he said, his eyes on the wolves, who seemed to be inching closer though their feet weren't moving.

'Thing is, he was supposed to contact me, and we're a bit concerned about him, this particular man,' said the Butler. 'We're worried he might've gone somewhat misguided in the head.'

'He said we don't know who you're talking about,' said Jonah with that snarl that often arose without warning whenever he spoke to adults.

'I know you, don't I?' the Butler said to Jonah, creepily delighted, as though they were old friends reconnecting. 'Ah yes, you're one of the Turtle Boys. The youngest, I assume. Good to see MacVicar hasn't quite yet locked all of you up. And how about you, son?' the Butler said, turning to Will. 'You don't look quite as hardened as your friend. Do I know your family?'

'The girls are interested in him,' Claymore said, as the wolves began sniffing Will's shoes. 'What's the matter, kid?' Claymore said gruffly. 'You don't like puppies?' Claymore was like a cannonball that had sprouted limbs, with knuckly ears stuck perpendicularly in his head like fleshy rivets. Though he'd run out of deodorant, all Will could do was pray that the smell of Inside Will on the Helmet they'd found at Marcus's shack was vastly different from the Outside Will he'd become since he'd removed it. 'Maybe you'd like a little Neverclear to settle your nerves,' Claymore said. 'Or maybe your friend would?' he said to Jonah.

'We don't drink,' Will managed to say.

'That right?' Claymore chuckled, still staring at Jonah, sharing some joke with the one pushing the wheelbarrow. 'Well, he's got a whole lifetime to change his mind.'

'Let's go,' Jonah said, pulling Will by the arm.

The wolves growled, and there came an increasing wail from beneath the tarp. Claymore reared and whapped the highest point of the plastic with the flat of his shovel, as one would firmly tamp down the dirt of a hole they'd just filled. When the tarp kept stirring, Claymore struck again, harder this time, sounding like an aluminum bat hitting a base hit with a lemon.

'Where was I?' said the Butler, patting the breast pockets of his shirt as though he'd misplaced his glasses.

Sand filled Will's throat and his head felt like it had been microwaved. Including scraps on the schoolyard and their most hideous skateboard spills, Claymore's shovel strike was the most violence he'd ever seen a person endure.

'Yes, well this man,' the Butler continued, 'this *friend* of ours, has been hiring boys to do his work for him. Dangerous, dirty work. Boys close to your age, in fact. And well, they aren't always safe around him, I'm afraid. So I'd suggest, for

316

your own safety of course, that you two steer clear of this man.' Then he turned to Jonah. 'And as for you, since your brothers are no longer in my employ, don't think anything could keep my wolves from paying a midnight visit to that squalid little duplex of yours in County Park. Just to ensure you and your brothers are keeping well. Understand?' he said.

The boys managed to shake their heads affirmatively, Jonah's breathing gone pure Black Lagoon at the mention of his house.

'Good,' the Butler said. 'But if you do have the misfortune of encountering this poor, belea-guered fellow again, I'd like you to pass along some information for me.'

The boys nodded robotically.

'You tell him that things will be much safer for him when he brings me my *proof.*'

'Got it?' said Claymore, pitching his shovel over his shoulder, the wheelbarrow dead silent beside him.

21

'Here,' said Jonah at Will's front door, holding up a sealed plastic baggie of fingerprints pressed neatly onto squares of cardstock, 'I lifted these from your water bottle that first night we met Titus.'

Will removed the cards and examined the prints. Good definition on the whorls and crisp detail for each digit. 'Looks like you managed some really good pulls.'

'I wanted you to have them because I'm finished,' said Jonah.

'But we're getting so close!' said Will. 'We'll go down to the elevator tomorrow, tell Titus what the Butler said and see if he talks. Don't you want to know what this *proof* is the Butler is looking for?'

'Will, last night after we met the Butler I got scared and told my brothers what happened and they freaked. They're talking about leaving Thunder Bay, moving us to some little lake up north where our auntie lives. I had to promise them I wouldn't go back down there to keep them from packing the van.'

'That's easy. You'll sneak out when they go to work. They can't — '

'Will!' Jonah yelled, his face hard with disbelief. 'He knows who I am! And from the way those wolves were sniffing at you, they've probably already figured out who you are too.

Something bad is going to happen. I know it. I've had dreams about it. I just can't risk it anymore.'

'Something bad is *always* going to happen,' said Will, stepping Outside and shutting the door so his mother wouldn't hear. 'No matter where you are or what you're doing. You're starting to sound like my mom.'

Jonah shook his head somberly. 'You know what Indians do best in movies?' he said. 'We die. It's like our job. We look pretty, then scream and get shot from a brown-spotted horse with no saddle. I watched all those movies growing up and I thought dying in a hail of rifle bullets seemed . . . I don't know, like . . . natural. Something I'd do one day, same as having a kid or leaving Thunder Bay.

'But you know why I really stopped being friends with Marcus?' Jonah continued. 'It wasn't because he broke his skateboard. He could've bought ten more with the money he was making from the Butler. It was because I was sick of worrying about him. Sick of lying awake all night while he slept somewhere outside, sick of watching him set bombs or taunt the biggest hockey players or skate out in front of cars just to see if they'd stop. I already worry about my brothers enough.

'That's why I started talking to you,' Jonah continued, 'because you were different. Cautious. Safe. Even when you did dangerous things, I never worried about you. Until lately.'

'But he's still our friend,' Will said. 'He should be here. Like we are.'

Jonah shook his head. 'There's no such thing in the world as 'should,' Will. Haven't you figured that out yet? There is only whatever happens.'

'But maybe you're wrong. Maybe we can still help him leave. We owe that to him.'

'You know I've always meant to ask you this,' Jonah said, his voice rising. 'You think Marcus was your *friend*, but he shot you *in the head with a rock*, then stole your garden hose the first time you met him.'

'He didn't mean to hurt me. He was . . . afraid. Just like you are now. It's not good for us to be afraid. Trust me. Marcus taught me that. And finding him is the only way I can prove that everything Outside is actually safe.'

'Prove to who? Your mom?'

'To everyone.'

'Well, brace yourself for it, Will: it's not.'

They stood in silence for a moment.

'You actually want me to say it?' Jonah continued, his voice quiet now. 'Okay. You're right. I'm scared. For you. For me. It's hard enough for an Indian to make it to eighteen in this place and still have a pulse. Even if you're doing everything right. But I refuse to vanish like Marcus. Or end up like that guy in the wheelbarrow. Call me a megapussy all you want. But skateboarding is as close to danger as I need to get.'

'We won't even have to go near the elevators,' Will said. 'We can still investigate from a distance, like we said.'

Jonah sighed and swiped away his bangs. They

both sat on the top step. 'When I was a kid and we first moved down to Thunder Bay,' Jonah said, 'I used to think White people were trying to kill me, not just the social workers who tried to take me away — like all of them. For a while I didn't leave the house, exactly like your mom. I'd stay in the basement and imagine them coming in the windows like zombies or vampires, trying to suck my blood, eat my brains with teaspoons. I used to concoct ways to defend myself against them. I'd practice judo and draw all these diagrams of explosives and guns and knives. I made traps, snares, and machetes hanging over the windows — that's how I learned to make those match bombs. It was around that same time I stopped talking because I felt like my words were feeding them, giving them strength.'

'Nobody's trying to kill you, Jonah,' Will said after some silence.

'You sure?' Jonah said, making to leave.

'You don't want to help me anymore, that's fine,' Will said desperately. 'But winter's going to last for three more months. What're you going to do? Play hockey?'

Jonah shook his head. 'I'm going home where it's safe, and I'm going to stay there — I'd like to see those two try to come get me. Then I'm going to drink some hot chocolate and read two hundred books and have every known human disease memorized before spring comes. Then in a few years I'm going to get a crappy job like my brothers and save some money and go to med school in California and skateboard every single damn day with a big stupid grin on my face and I won't ever think about Marcus or Thunder Bay or old Titus, not once.'

'Wait,' Will implored as Jonah backed down Will's steps, 'I have an idea . . .'

But he was out of ideas. Since he'd been Outside, he'd learned that fear was only a default setting, like how the TV always starts at channel 3 when you first turn it on. That everyone is born afraid of everything, but most people build calluses over top of it. His mother didn't have calluses because she never touched anything, never even tried. Of the things Will was most afraid of — bees, wolves, witches, getting kidnapped, the clunking noise the dryer made when it stopped, calling Angela and telling her he'd liked their kiss, the Butler, the Bald Man, rebar, shovels — he was most afraid that, even after all his bravery and scars and near-death experiences, he still couldn't survive the Outside without Jonah.

Jonah set the small vinyl case containing their fingerprinting kit on the bottom stair. 'See you around, Will,' he said.

22

The following day, Will wrote to his principal as his mother to say there would be no need to send him to Templeton because they were moving back to San Francisco. Then Will spent the morning alternating between practicing fingerprinting, crying into his pillow, doing jumping jacks, and reading the *Thrashers* Jonah had left behind.

To cheer himself up he practiced pulling prints from difficult places like the toilet bowl and some trim in London. Then he stood on a chair and pulled one from the light fixture in New York: large prints that weren't his own, yet looked oddly familiar. He compared them with the small library he'd amassed so far in a photo album, prints belonging to the mailman (doorknob), the grocery deliveryman (milk bottle), his mother (glass of water beside her bed), and now Titus (from the prints Jonah had given him), which matched exactly those he'd pulled from the fixture. Will recompared the prints ten times in tingly disbelief, but there was no question they were the same.

Titus had been in his room.

It was concussive, thunderous, his two worlds colliding like brakeless trains — the Inside and the Outside — and in the great crash Will knew that he'd been wrong about everything. Jonah was right, Titus had done something to Marcus in one of his black moods, and concocted that story to cover it up. And Will and his mother were next. Titus had been watching them from the yard for months, maybe longer, peering at them through the windows, writing that note, but now he'd come Inside, and any night he'd creep up on their beds and grip their throats. With horror Will remembered now how Titus always got shifty and red faced whenever the subject of his mother came up. Maybe on some level his mother had sensed his menace all along — maybe Titus always was the real reason for the Black Lagoon, and suddenly an idea parachuted into Will's head. Though he had settled long ago on not being a genius, he was smart enough to know exactly what measures he had to take to set everything right and keep everyone he held dear safe.

★   ★   ★

'Can I get you anything, Mom?' His mother was sitting up in her bed in San Francisco, staring into the darkened wall like it was the grille of a speeding truck.

'No, thanks, Will. But it's good to hear your voice,' she said, her breathing quick and shallow, as if her lungs were tiny as walnuts and located right beneath her neck. Will realized he'd never seen his mother take a deep breath in his life. 'I've missed you,' she said.

Will sat on her bed. Their bed. He could barely see her in the dimness, except for her eyes, green and crystalline. Most of the bulbs in

324

the house were out now. At night it was like the Middle Ages. He'd thought she would eventually get fed up and change them herself, but she used lamps until they burned out and then ordered flashlights and a headlamp that she wore whenever she forced her way into Venice.

'Want me to change it?' he said, pointing to her light fixture. 'I could, but I'm not wearing the wetsuit.'

'Would you?' she said, animating slightly. 'I didn't want to ask. Everything I say makes you so mad lately.'

Will returned with a new bulb, and soon the room jumped into light and she winced and shut her eyes. Sitting on her bed again, turning the dead bulb in his hands, he watched light surf down through her bedraggled hair. She shifted and a smell puffed from her covers like turned milk.

'Was that Jonah I heard at the door yesterday?'

'He and I might not be friends anymore,' Will said.

'That's a shame,' she said. 'I like him.'

Will nodded, and they sat for a while, her hand on his thigh, as Outside trees sifted the wind. It was the first time in months he'd felt any sympathy for her. Will recalled how he used to find her at the window when he was still Inside, sighing, looking not down at her book but out into the streetlights. He wondered if she had any idea what she'd given up, what she'd wasted all these years Inside, what she had yet to waste. If she had any idea how beautiful she still was, how many people there were Outside for her still to meet.

'Have they found that boy yet?' she asked after a while, smoothing his hair. 'The one who was missing?'

'Yeah, they did,' Will said, mercifully. 'He was camping and didn't tell anybody.'

'Oh,' she said, 'that's a relief.' But if she relaxed further, Will couldn't tell.

'I remember a time when you were very young, maybe three or four,' she continued, picking at the duvet fabric with her pale fingers. 'I pulled you from the bath and stood you on the mat. I stepped out to the linen closet to grab a towel, and I returned to find you looking down at your little wet body, and you were sobbing. You said, 'My body is crying.' It nearly broke my heart. I wasn't sure I could take something that sweet and sad at the same time.'

'But it wasn't,' Will said. 'I was wrong.'

'You've always been such a sensitive boy, honey. I never wanted to see you hurt.'

'Mom,' Will said, 'you won't need to worry about me anymore. There's just one last thing I need to do tomorrow morning. Something I left behind that I need to get. But after that I'm staying Inside again. Like you said, I'm too sensitive. It's too much for me Outside.' She brushed his ear with her thumb, and suddenly a sadness overtook him. 'I hate Thunder Bay,' he said in a sob. He was so tired of being endangered and watched and confused.

'Oh, please don't stay home on my account,' she said. 'You were right not to let me hold you back. I've been selfish. I needed you too much. I never should've brought us here from Toronto. This place is so dangerous for a boy.'

'Can't we leave?' Will said into her chest. 'We could go tonight. Can't you just make yourself get on a plane?'

'I wish it were that simple. Years ago, maybe. Not now.'

'We could knock you out? I could get you some grain alcohol or give you some drugs and put you in a car, and you'd wake up someplace you weren't afraid of?'

She shook her head. 'That place doesn't exist, Will.'

He could have tried explaining the mess with the Butler and Marcus and Titus. Other mothers would have called the police. Demanded action. Sorted it out. Or left town. But not his. She'd been Inside too long. And it was only getting worse. The truth would destroy her. All that remained was the sick feeling that if only he'd kept painting his stupid masterpiece that day and not been lured out by the bang of Marcus's match bomb, everything wouldn't have gone so terribly wrong. The Outside wouldn't be ruined if he hadn't been there to ruin it.

But he said nothing, and soon sleep wafted over from her body into his, sharing it.

Relaxation Time

That morning she woke, marooned in bed — her only lifeboat now in a sea of panic. Will was gone, his imprint still rumpled in the sheets beside her, the doorbell ringing, *had been* ringing for some time. She knew instantly that to set foot on the floor today would mean risking everything.

It rang again. Deliverymen were rarely this persistent. Will had locked himself out. Or it was Jonah, wanting to make up after their fight. Or some official, here because something had . . . she threw the sheets from her body, reached and guzzled an entire bottle of codeine syrup, then snapped her elastic twenty-five times and drew six deep breaths. Just as the codeine slid into her bloodstream like liquid lead, she dropped to the floor fast enough to keep the panic from grabbing her ankles and darted through the towers of paperbacks and trash and unopened packages and mail to the door. She threw it open and before her stood an older man, in a suit and topcoat, with a tempest of white hair and an apologetic smile.

'Sorry to trouble you, Ms. Cardiel,' the man said warmly, 'but I went by the school today, and the principal informed me that your son, Will, hadn't been there for some time. So I thought I'd stop by to chat with him here.'

'He's out,' she said, the codeine a cold

smolder in her now. Was she swaying or was it the wind in the trees?

'Oh. Out?' the man said. 'Any idea where?'

'No, I don't,' she said, bracing her hand on the doorframe, fighting to keep her eyes focused upon his, and not the pure disorientation and terror that lay beyond him.

'You don't know where your son is?' he said, surprised.

Her mind gluey, she nearly told him that she'd begged Will to stay, but he just wouldn't listen, then stopped herself. Who did he say he was? Had he?

'You don't look well, Ms. Cardiel,' he said. 'Are you feeling ill? Perhaps I should come in?'

'Wait,' she said, resetting, trying not to sway. The codeine made the floor impossibly soft beneath her feet, like turned earth. But he was familiar somehow, with his theatrical face, like someone from a Fellini film. 'Who are you? And why are you looking for my son?'

'Oh, my apologies,' he said with a wide smile. 'My name is George Butler. And, come to think of it, I remember you and your brother as children, down at the elevator in the old days, bringing your father's supper.'

She placed him now. He was the grain inspector at the harbor, who Theodore called 'the bug man.' In snow-white coveralls he'd go around checking lakeboats for pests, weevils and worms, before giving the okay to ship them out. He was educated and knew grain as well as Theodore. He was also the one selling Charlie those pills for his asthma that kept him up every night.

'It was truly a shame what happened to your brother. But I have a feeling that wherever he is, it's a much better place,' he said. 'You were living away, I remember? Of course I'm in a different line of work now,' he went on. 'You wouldn't recognize very much on the harbor these days, I'm afraid, Ms. Cardiel. Unfortunately, child apprehension is currently the only growth industry in Thunder Bay.'

'Wait, did you say child — '

'Oh, no,' he said, putting his hand to his heart, 'that's certainly not why I'm here, Ms. Cardiel. But I am afraid your son has found himself mixed up with some boys who are currently on my case-load. Will's got a bit of his uncle's — shall we say — moxie? But I'm here to ensure his safety.'

Everything was going too fast for her. She'd expected a deliveryman, a quick exchange. Her mind was sliding. This man's mouth didn't match his words.

'Are you sure you don't know where your son is?'

'He said he had something important to do today,' she said thinly, shutting her eyes to keep the light out.

'Did he, Ms. Cardiel?' he said, leaning closer. 'Like what?'

'He said . . . ' She felt a great itchiness under her scalp; the codeine was already waning. She wasn't sure how much more of the blinding doorway she could stand. 'He said he'd left something behind, and he had to go get it.'

'Maybe he was referring to this?' From behind his back he raised Will's old helmet, dangling from his finger by the chin strap. 'We found it in an abandoned shack frequented by criminals. It has your last name written in it, Ms. Cardiel. At first I thought it belonged to another boy in town, but now based on what you're saying, I'm convinced that your son is in grave danger. Think hard for me, please: do you have any idea where your son went today?'

She braced herself against the door, everything churning, the subway platform finally closing over her, and into her tumbling head came all the smells she'd been finding on Will's clothes when he returned home from school: grease, sweat, blood, sawn lumber.

Grain.

23

Will found him sitting in a straight-backed chair in the workhouse, the woodstove roaring like a cast-iron dragon. Titus had shaved, his half-grayed hair dangling at his unlined cheeks like slips of smoke. Beardless, his face was even more fearsome, all diamond-cut angles and the scars of hard Outside living, but younger than Will had expected. Closer to his mother's age. Titus sat with eyes glazed and fixed, sweat sheening his brow, both hands plunged in the pockets of his parka with large coils of wire wound around the sleeves.

'It's you, Icarus Number One,' he said, clearing his throat and twisting his head with a queer surprise. His voice was hoarse, and Will pictured him awake all night, yelling at ghosts, Marcus's included. 'Sturdy choice of headgear,' he said.

Will tugged at the strap under his chin. It was tight, but his orange Helmet still fit, though the cranial pressure had him feeling a touch dazed. Perhaps all that he'd learned Outside had made his head bigger. 'Felt like I needed a little extra protection today,' he said.

'And your compatriot?' said Titus.

'Don't know,' Will said. 'He won't be coming down here anymore.'

Titus's face fell and he shook his head. 'I wasn't ever in much danger of triumphing as his favorite citizen, but that Icarus could piss his name in a sheet of plywood,' he said. 'You two should congeal together. Especially if you insist on perpetuating more ventures to this jurisdiction.'

'Well, this is my last time coming down here. I came to ask you some questions.'

'Allow me one last suffrage,' Titus added, standing. 'If you're capable. Plenty of time for exchanges as we venture.'

'What do you need me to do?'

With a twitch, Titus turned to the window to regard the sun-dazzled water. 'There are ocean salmon in there. How they established is nobody's purview. Stowaways likely. Salties suck 'em up as ballast and dump 'em here. When I was a youngster you could catch whitefish right off the piers. Baitless. Clean as a whistle. Fish lined up and bought tickets to get a hook in their lip, like it was fashionable. Now this juncture is so chocked with heavy metal and sick outflow, you're better off snacking on your chemistry set than some fresh-pulled whitefish.' Behind everything Titus said was a monologue of murmur, a faint whistle, like the ghostly scrapings of his mother's fingers on the strings of her guitar.

'Is that why you won't drink the water? Because it's polluted?' Will asked, but from there Titus tipped into nonsense, every so often pausing to lurch at something, like a dog snapping at an invisible fly. He cleared his throat for long periods while mumbling, just angry syllables hissed under his breath.

In the pocket of his hooded sweatshirt, Will

gripped the handles of the garrote he'd constructed that morning. He'd removed a string from his mother's guitar and tied it between two pieces of dowel he'd once made nunchucks with. On his walk to the harbor, Will tried to buttress his courage with the image of Titus pinning Marcus down near the creek and inflicting him with more scars, like that pastor and his wife had done, but it wouldn't resolve. So Will settled on picturing Titus Inside, rooting through their drawers, perusing Will's masterpieces, thumbing his mother's page-turners, watching her sleep in San Francisco, poised to smother her with one of her malodorous pillows.

Then a rustling came from Titus's coat pockets, and this seemed to evict him from whatever reverie he'd been lost in. 'Let's flitter,' said Titus.

They descended the stairs to the water's edge, where Titus, breathing desperately, tugged a sheet of tattered canvas away to reveal a wooden skiff lodged in some reedy mud near a clutch of unidentifiable rubble. Titus lifted a pair of boots from the hull, stepped out of his foul shoes and put them on. Will didn't even need to examine his footprints for the hexagon shape to be certain they matched, same as his grandfather's.

'We'll load her trim and even, so she doesn't capsize or go to toothpicks,' Titus said, tugging the massive hose that Will and Jonah had assembled out from a thicket of goldenrod nearby. As they worked, coiling the hose into the small skiff like a noodle onto a plate, Will saw a fish carcass bob near the shore in a blizzard of flies. Titus also tossed into the boat several grocery bags full of stones. Soon Will began to sweat, and he scratched at his hair, itchy under his tight Helmet.

'Hop in, Icarus Number One,' Titus said after everything was loaded, pointing to the small area they'd managed to leave clear at the front of the vessel. 'We'll chatter while we venture.'

Pure terror riveted Will in place.

''Course you're not impelled to,' Titus said. 'Not everyone's chopped up for seamanship. Marcus quivered at the outset.'

'You took Marcus out on the lake?'

'Taught him the rigging I know. He rightly flourished. But sailing wasn't my teacup. Mine were lakers. Salties mostly. But we need to endeavor this quick before the cove ices to the breakwater,' he said. 'Won't have another swing this year.' Will thought it best not to remind Titus it was spring, in case it agitated him.

Will knew this was his last chance to get answers from Titus, and his stomach felt like a swimming pool with a thousand maniacal kids in there, all splashing and screaming. Titus cleared his wrecked throat as the skiff bobbed at Will's shins. A song his mother used to sing with her guitar came into his head: 'Lord I can't go a-home, this a-way . . . ' meaning poor and naked and destroyed, and Will felt the same way. His real life Outside had been short, but he'd already managed to lose everything dear to him — Marcus, Jonah, Angela, skateboarding — and if he didn't confront Titus, how long would it take for his mother to fall deeper into herself, until she was not much more than a shadow, a wraith? How long after would MacVicar call Social Services, who'd whisk him to some foster home, perhaps even the one where Marcus had lived, where Will would share a room with four other sad, abandoned boys? But if he could force answers from Titus, nobody would need to be afraid, not Jonah, not his mother, not Will. The Butler would call off his wolves. Maybe even Marcus would return. The Outside would go back to how it was, before Will had ruined it. Who better than Will understood that those who were not brave, who didn't perform dangerous feats, wound up imprisoned in a bedroom somewhere, staring at the wall, terrified to breathe.

'It's a good thing I told everyone I know where I was going today,' Will belted out confidently, even though he didn't have anyone left he could tell. 'Otherwise, they might be worried.'

'Sturdy hypothesis, Icarus Number One,' Titus said with an undisturbed face. 'Can't be over thoughtful, specially bobbing on the water.'

Will climbed into the seat, and Titus pushed off and pointed the skiff at the gap in the breakwater a mile out, the skiff's bow clicking against the meager waves. The water looked frigid, and Will wished he'd worn his lightbulb-changing wetsuit. Titus lowered the outboard and began yanking the starter ferociously. When it caught, he blared the engine, and the roar buried the ambient hush of the harbor.

As they plowed away from shore, the skiff low in the water with the weight of the hose, the air whisked with impossible freshness across Will's face, recalling to him that first walk along the creek, when everything was still amazing and shot with wonder. He watched the water darken from blue to black beneath them like a bruise. Aside from that time his mother said he'd once smacked his head on a pool deck, Will had never been immersed in water deeper than their bathtub. Swimming was an activity he couldn't even consider. He only hoped the protective foam in his Helmet would keep him afloat if it came to that.

Looking back at Thunder Bay, Will recalled a painting his mother showed him in an art book she said had belonged to his grandfather. Ships in a harbor, some carts going alongside a cliff. 'See anything?' she'd said. When Will replied no, she pointed to legs sprouting from a tiny splash in the corner like a flower. 'I don't get it,' Will said. '*Icarus*,' she said, indicating the splash. 'He flew so high the sun melted his waxen wings and he fell to Earth. Except nobody noticed. Nobody cared. The world's like that sometimes, Will. It's too heartbreaking to look at.'

As they cruised farther out into the bay, Titus began rummaging in the pockets of his parka. He produced something, seemed to reject it, then placed it beside him on the bench seat. Will recognized it as a chickadee, except it wasn't moving. Then Titus took out a wicked-looking fish knife and set it beside the bird. Will tried again to force himself to imagine Titus slicing Marcus, his throat, his chest, but he still couldn't stitch the vision together in his mind. 'Those elevators're the tallest strivers for hundreds of miles!' Titus yelled over the motor's white roar, pointing back at the harbor. 'In my era, men came from all over, either to toil in them, or to toss themselves from the top! Some sad souls secured jobs only to perform that!'

'Why are your fingerprints in my house?' Will heard himself yell. And when Titus didn't react, Will knew he'd only whispered it into the snoring of the motor. Soon the skiff passed through the southernmost gap in the breakwater — a giant's version of a stone garden wall, car-size chunks of granite fitted together, all of it submerged hundreds of feet below — and Will knew that this passage had altered something fundamental inside him, that he was finally something different from a boy. Titus yelled about the millions of pounds of stone that went into the breakwater, the equivalent of five pyramids sunk beneath the lake. 'Indian labor built it, mostly!' he said. 'They put up a hefty chunk of Thunder Bay, but nobody honors their exertions!'

Out on the unsheltered water, a chop kicked up. No other vessels were on the lake except for a giant lakeboat anchored miles past the breakwater that Titus yelled was from Brazil and carried potash. Then Titus cut the engine and set the skiff to drift, the weight of their cargo dragging them on. The vessel lapped through the waves with the sound of slapping someone's wet belly. A powerful inevitable feeling stood up in Will and informed him that he had this situation under control: he'd been training for this

338

moment his whole life — all his Destructivity Experiments and brave Outside acts had prepared him well. He'd be as brave as Jonah jumping on that wolf, as brave as Marcus snatching the map from the Butler. He'd overwhelm Titus, not head on, but sneak up, garrote him, and force him to reveal where Marcus was. Already the man could barely breathe, so Will imagined strangling him would be something like popping a balloon with his bare hands or trying a new skateboard trick, scary and unwieldy at first, but easy once you barged through and tried it.

'You hungry, Icarus Number One?' Titus asked.

When Will shook his head, Titus lifted the dead chickadee from the bench and neatly stuffed it into his mouth like a pastry. He sat chewing, silhouetted by open lake. Stunned, Will listened to Titus's soft crunches, his graying hair flying in the wind and eyes somewhere near gone. It occurred to him that Titus was leagues crazier than he or Jonah ever suspected and had suffered damage more titanic than anyone he'd ever met Outside. Titus swallowed, sucked air through his teeth, and stood. The skiff wobbled unsteadily under his weight and that of the hoses and the shopping bags of rocks, and a few pints of water splashed over the gunwales. Will tightened his grip on his seat as gulls whirlwinded overhead.

'Those resemble seagulls, but that's negatory!' Titus said pointing upwards, too loud, as though the motor was still going. 'They're lake gulls!' He whirled around as they passed over, and the skiff tipped beneath him.

'Can you please sit down, Titus?' said Will.

'Gorge themselves on garbage all the livelong day! Riddled with blight, metastatics, and parasites!'

The skiff teetered worse, and a larger slap of water came over the side. Will saw it pooling beneath the labyrinth of hose. 'Titus!' Will said.

'I took a cruise once,' he said, pointing to the anchored laker. ''Course that was another era. Best to leave it in the water.' Then he drew another, larger bird from his pocket and bit it bloodlessly in half, a tuft of down clinging to his lower lip.

As he gripped its dowels in his pocket, the garrote seemed suddenly ridiculous and toy-like in Will's hands. Which string had he selected to make it? The highest or lowest? He couldn't remember. Hadn't his mother broken these strings while strumming the gentlest of folk songs? So how could this grown lunatic of a man not be able to do the same? If Titus turned hostile, Will's only hope would be to shoulder-check him overboard and start the engine before he could climb back in. He'd never make it to the breakwater. He could barely climb stairs.

Then Titus began to hop up and down at the back of the boat, whooping at the gulls. More water swamped into the skiff, soaking Will's shoes. 'Sit down!' Will yelled. 'You'll sink us!'

Suddenly Titus produced a sound near shrieking, and it poured slush down Will's spine.

He barked splinters of sentences and incantations as a diabolical force overrode his face, an amalgamation of surprise and sorrow and rage. But it was Titus's avoidance of Will's eyes that was most worrisome. Titus's meeting his gaze seemed to form the last vestige of Will's safety.

'No epoch but the current!' Titus roared, bending to pick up the fish knife, his eyes lustrous and blazed with gold. He pointed the tip to Will and stifled a chillingly girlish titter, then pointed the tip into the dark waves that flapped like fabric in a gale. 'In we tumble,' he said.

'I don't know how to swim,' Will whimpered, a small boyish utterance, as a great shaking overrode each of his muscles. 'My mother never taught me.' What Will would give to be with her now, to be watching her snap a fresh sheet in the air over their bed, waiting for it to descend like a sweet parachute.

With that some dark spell was counteracted inside Titus, and at long last he met Will's eyes. 'She didn't, did she?' he said. 'I'm sure she had some silver explication. She's too buoyant for it. It's a risky businessman, swimming.' Then Titus chortled, and Will couldn't decide if it was mirthful or maniacal.

'Be brave Icarus Number One,' he went on. 'You can perform a life entire without ever getting wet.' Then he lowered himself and dipped a cupped hand into the rough water. He brought it to his lips and slurped long and loud with his eyes smashed shut in rapture.

'Here,' he said, in one long breath of relief. 'This is the meadow.'

Titus set down the fish knife and began unwinding a length of wire from his arm, which was wrapped tourniquet-tight and made the veins of his thick hands bulge. Then he picked the knife back up and began snapping pieces of wire in short lengths.

Next Titus grabbed one of the many bags of stones and fixed it to the end of the hose with wire. He kissed the hose mouth like a beloved rattlesnake and tossed it from the skiff. Will watched the white bag disappear into the deep like a fleeing ghost.

Titus started the motor. 'Come back here and take the tiller,' he said. 'Fly us in sleepy as you can.'

Will minced his way, hands still gripping the garrote in his pocket, to the back of the boat, passing Titus in the middle, who clutched the knife at his side. Will took the motor's vibrating handle.

As they crept toward shore, Titus fastened rock bags intermittently to the hose with wire and sent more of the coil overboard. With his own Black Lagoon subsiding, at least temporarily, Will allowed himself the momentary pleasure of piloting a boat for the first time. No wonder Marcus wanted one.

'So why are we doing this?' Will said over the low rumble of the engine. 'Is it some kind of art project?' He'd nearly said 'masterpiece' but caught himself.

''Spose you could dedicate it so, that is if you sought some verbiage.'

'Can I ask another question?'

'I'm in an interrogative mode,' Titus said.

'I met the Butler and he said he wanted *proof* of something from you. Proof of what?'

'He's dilated,' said Titus, as Will guided the skiff nearly to the shore. 'Bring her in over there,' Titus said, pointing to some rubble at the foot of Pool 6. Will piloted them up on a patch of rocky sand, mostly hidden from the water. Will felt like kissing the ground when he stepped out. There he saw a shallow trench already dug, running up toward the elevator. Titus laid the hose in the trench and buried it at the waterline, then dragged the remaining length up the embankment. Following the trench, they reached the outer edge of the elevator, where Titus took the end of the hose and stuffed it into a protruding conveyance chute.

Will followed Titus at a safe distance into a chamber of the elevator he and Jonah had never explored. Inside, Titus pulled the hose from the chute and began attaching it to an ancient machine. As Titus kneeled to fiddle with its settings, Will recognized this as his final chance, and with tingling, fear-deadened hands, he extracted the garrote, pulled it tight to his belly, and for a second it rang out a high sound. Will crept noiseless as he could toward Titus.

Still crouched, Titus pulled a cord, starting the machine like a lawnmower. It puffed a foul ball of smoke and shook, running a few seconds before water burst from a spout.

Right when Will was about to hook the wire around his neck and demand Marcus's whereabouts, Titus pursed his lips and applied them carefully to the stream. He took a long drink with his eyes shut with such profound pleasure Will felt the moment was nearly too intimate to observe.

'Superior,' Titus said, swallowing deeply. 'Eventually, I'll run this unblighted up to my quarters, but this donkey engine'll suit for now.' Titus pushed a bucket under the stream, and it began to fill noisily.

Will laughed aloud, jamming the weapon back in his pocket, half-overjoyed, half-terrified. 'This was what you were doing all this time? Trying to get pure — I mean unblighted — water?'

'I'm not as strong as I once was to fetch it myself, and I can't go relying on you or Aurelius to do it for me anymore. I'm falling weaker each day. But I'm aiming to habitate this old premise as long as permitted. Which is why you should tumble home now, Icarus Number One. You've saved me in more methods than you're privy to. But you're a gold necessity to your mother. Boys don't fit down here. It's only septic things. The Butler included. I can't shield you like I could've once.' Titus stood and wheezed, long and tired. He thumped at his chest violently with his big fists. 'Sometimes I suspect my whole damn condition is that my head isn't privy to enough air,' he said pitifully, 'because of these old wind bags. And that's why my nut goes turbulent.'

'Can I ask you a question?' Will said backing away cautiously.

Titus looked up and nodded again.

'Promise not to take it the wrong way?'

'No such right way here down by the bay.'

'What does it feel like to be crazy?'

Titus watched him for a moment with an unreadable expression. 'So that's what has been wobbling on your vector top this whole operation?' he said.

'Yeah,' Will said. 'I guess.'

'Well,' Titus said, cutting the pump's motor and standing there on legs bowing as though they might snap. 'A ripe comparison would entail trying to fix a radio. Except the only tool that comes to hand is another busted radio. You scavenge me?'

'Is that why you helped Marcus? Because he's a busted radio, like you?'

'I nurtured him because Aurelius has been through Hades and still managed to till some good acreage in his soul.'

'Yeah, well, I have one more question,' Will said with a throb of mounting courage, turning his feet to bolt for the door. 'If you were so busy helping Marcus, why did I find your fingerpri — ' and it was then Will heard the dull scrape of metal behind him.

Relaxation Time

At the subway station, she canted the stroller and wheelied her son onto the escalator, holding him prone as they descended. He frowned and threw the worlds of his eyes wide, thoroughly baffled by her upside-downness.

They emerged onto the grimy, gum-spackled tile of the platform. Always tile! she mused playfully, must public transit take place in one enormous bathroom? As though all the tunnels were slated to someday be flushed?

She and Will awaited their train, the air close and thick, her son babbling fragments only she could piece together, most related to food and the construction scene they'd witnessed earlier that day: a section of pavement torn out, exposing the multifarious cables and pipes beneath, densely packed as a wrist. Workers had cut into the pavement with a tremendous saw, a blade the size of a café table, throwing a rooster tail of sparks into the tepid morning air. It was a spectacle of noise and destruction no boy could resist, so she'd held him up to watch over the fence. When the sawing ceased, leaving his eyes braziers of wonder, aflame with the knowledge that, like wood, pavement could be sawn, she resisted a gushy urge to crush him in her arms, to feel him squirm but hold him fast.

Now in the cool of the tunnel, she could feel the lick of perspiration at her neck's nape. It had been a long day of walking, of submission to the pedestrian rapids, to the dueling scent of exhaust and hot dog cart — how long would these smells last if either were outlawed? A year? More? She'd once heard the street scene called a ballet, but she disagreed. The president of some arts foundation had once mailed Arthur tickets, but Diane fell dead asleep, only to be poked awake by the pin of her thrift store brooch. 'No one ever falls in the ballet,' she'd said afterwards, one of her famous remarks.

But is there a greater, more sustaining joy than walking in a city? She could wring all that she needed from the sight of men shaking hands, the cooperative swerving of cars, the incredible garbage arrayed curbside for collection. What a thrill it was to move through it all, unharmed, like sipping tea in the splayed jaws of a lion, then stretching out and napping there, waking only to linger in the lion's warm breath for another minute.

She'd imagined strangers as houseguests to introduce to her son, adoring the combination of indifference and tenderness commingling in their faces: a man with a thudding radio perched upon his shoulder like a parrot; phalanxes of businesswomen in imposing shoulder pads and high, fortified hair; a man in red leather pants and futuristic shades like the human version of a sports car; another man rummaging through the trash with a baseball mitt. Even the ugliness was important, the seediness, the homeless, the filth — it needed to be acknowledged, even to children, so they didn't grow into princes. If she wasn't with Will and she'd had her Bolex, there wasn't a single part of it she wouldn't have loved to capture.

A day of ticked-off errands: produce shopping in the thick compost funk of Kensington Market, the post office to forward Arthur's mail to his latest PO box in Milan, and a visit to her lawyer. To avoid conflict of interest she'd found her own counsel, a woman that their lawyer (who Arthur kept — old U of T classmates) had suggested. She took the fact that she had toys in her waiting room as both a good sign and something terribly sad.

Had she really just signed those papers? Wasn't this business the reason they'd remained common-law? Legally, however, it was the same mess. A 'trial separation' — whether this meant a tryout or a formal ceremony of judgment and sentencing she was unsure. It was terrifically amiable, almost maddeningly so. She wondered if he was paying full attention. The house was hers. As was Will, whom Arthur adored, theoretically, but had always viewed more as a side dish to the main course of himself, as he had her, she supposed. In truth, she felt nothing: neither longing nor onrush of freedom, only an emotional beigeness, as though hydroplaning on the surface of her life, something close to those reckless months after Charlie died. But she expected life without Arthur would closely resemble life *with* Arthur, who was either at his drafting table or attending the architectural conferences and colloquia of the world.

Finally the train arrived, and she wheeled a

now-napping Will into position. Bodies pushed to line the tracks. All these people, she thought, as the train stormed past their noses, so content to stand inches from their deaths. When the doors parted, casually, with no warning, like the tiniest snag on the otherwise flawless surface of her confidence, she realized that she might be somewhat afraid to step onto this particular car. With this thought a knuckle of fear slipped into her throat, unswallowable.

She chuckled. Afraid the doors might pinch her behind? Of going the wrong direction — as she and Arthur so often had, rapt in the conversation of their early days? Was this feeling even real? She'd ridden hundreds, thousands, of subway cars — though she'd never loved the black rushing of tunnels, she'd always endured them, cheerfully even.

Yet her heart insisted on racing, like an oil-doused bird flapping for its life in her chest. Other sensations, too, unmistakable as neon: a dull pain throughout, a soreness to her blood, a twisting in her gut, stardust in her fingertips. It would pass, a mere miscalculation of an errant brain that found danger where there was none, that saw a lion instead of the lamb before her.

People pushed past as she breathed hard and fought to reset herself. She needed only to regain the mental ground on which she'd stood a moment before, only one step back, a gathering of balance, but the fear — it was fear, she admitted now — would not abate.

She refocused her eyes, saw the car still split before her like an offering. A chime sounded. The doors jumped shut and the train dragged itself away. She laughed, more for those she imagined watching, then glanced around the empty platform. Everyone had done what she couldn't. She must look lost, or more probably insane, as if she'd remembered her pressing appointment with God in the other direction.

She drew Will away from the tracks. Passengers arrived clueless of how narrowly they'd missed a train. She took a long breath and decided she would simply make herself, through sheer mental force, board the next train, and the inevitability of this comforted her. Soon her heart slowed. Tingling ceased.

She waited with a bullied, yet sturdy, calm. A warm breeze emitted from the tunnel, carrying with it the fragrant innards of the city. Wheel grease had affixed itself to everything down near the tracks, leaving all the mechanics and gadgets a flat black, like the backdrops of those experimental theaters Arthur loved. Only the tracks themselves were clean and silver-smooth, like the palms of hands.

She was composed now, solid even, and her foundation — all she'd done, the dangers she'd braved, places she'd traveled — had returned beneath her. Maybe it was the sight of the steel subway tracks, but suddenly she was a girl looking on the grain cars from the workhouse of the elevator in Thunder Bay, sitting like notes on a musical staff of steel far below. It was those same tracks that brought the cars that both her father and Charlie unloaded. Their weight that broke the cable that swept her twin brother from the world like crumbs from a table — oh, she wished a train would arrive this instant! If the doors opened before her now, she could surely step in and leave all this nonsense behind. This was but a tiny blockage in the flow of her day. The only mercy was that no one would ever know it happened.

She was exhausted. That was it. The lawyer, the heat, the walking, the city, the hectic day with Will — and look, here was another train blaring into the station. They were quick during commuting hours, thankfully. Why was she thankful? Couldn't she have waited longer?

The train's wind flicked her bangs from her face and puffed her cheeks slightly, a film of dried sweat tightening her skin. As she pushed Will closer to the tracks, she was forced to admit that this particular train seemed fiercer, more indifferent than the previous. It wept and screeched as it halted like a tortured thing. The doors blew open and people erupted. More passengers this time, nearly rush hour. Will would be starving when he woke.

She would step onto this train, but the fear of another failure stayed her. Figures pushed past. To buy time she searched her purse for nothing in particular, imagining what she'd lost. She grasped her house keys and squeezed them until her hand shot with pain. Then, impossibly, the doors shut, after hardly enough time for people to board. Had there been a mistake? An impatient operator? The train lurched forward, fitting into the dark like a glove.

She retreated. Her knees were water boiling. Her limbs crawling and tingling as though Arthur had slept on them. She could leave, cart Will back up the escalator and hail a cab to deliver them home. But how would she manage without the subway? She'd have to lie, hide, make excuses — it would be dreadful.

She leaned against a plexiglassed advertisement hung on the brown tile wall, inhaling deeply, blowing out her panic like a birthday candle, but it only leapt back, fed by each breath, with a thicker, more lustrous flame.

She could hear her tongue scouring the roof of her gauze-dry mouth. Her throat constricted — how small a windpipe is, she thought, how minuscule an area we must keep clear to survive. Her heart thudded in her eyes. The word *pulmonary* entered her mind like a cruel rhyme. What word did it usually go with? Ebola? Embolism. What did that mean? Why did she think what she didn't even understand?

Then someone speaking in an annoying, distant manner. Oh, she couldn't bear assistance. Not now. She needed to weather this. Alone. But the voice persisted. She decided to listen, only enough to gather what was said in order to properly repel it. The words were a man's. For how long had men talked in her direction, wanting something? She held the words at arm's length. Every part of her felt unfounded, jumbled, questionable, open to invasion and disarray. She would not let him alter her, enlist her. He wanted his fingerprints on her organs. If she wasn't careful, he could tell her that her name was any old word in the dictionary and she would believe it.

'You said you're all right, right, yeah? No need for help?' he said earnestly, like someone, Whalen, but not him.

'I did?' she said. She could feel her face betray her, twisting and sweaty, her eyes two flushed toilets.

'Did you?' he asked, somewhat flirtatiously, which left her exhausted and ill.

'I'm all right,' she said, willing a smile, an expression not attainable by those on the doorstep of losing their minds.

'Cute,' he said, nodding his head toward Will.

She waved him away, and he retreated, no doubt convinced of her madness. That was what they wanted anyway: a functional madwoman, crazy enough to excite, not too crazy to be a burden. He turned back and said something else, and she realized then that he had no idea that he was as intangible as smoke. She let loose an enormous current of breath and blew him away before feeling herself stagger. She set her bags on the floor and yearned to join them there, but gravity had become a villain. She could feel death — real, cold death — snapping at her ankles like a black lapdog that could tear her to pieces with needle teeth if she fell. A thought stood up in her mind: go under here, and you will die or awake crazy. Crazy enough for them to take Will.

From her.

Her son.

A mere whiff of this notion sent the

dimensions of the tunnel sliding together. Her balance vacated her, wracking her with tremors of such ferocity they seemed to originate outside her. Sound ran together like the paint of children. The light died. Spots bloomed like mold in her vision. She peered into the tunnel and saw that it was the blackened esophagus of a giant, a monster. She knew then that she had been swallowed, as her brother and father had been in another life that was still hers, whether she'd left it behind or not. The platform crowded again. Another train, a throb of steel and glass, the lewd screech of wheels, a symphony of hissing and chuffing. Did it ever stop?

Time slow as poured honey. She'd sat down but had not died. Will was awake now, fighting the straps, mewling in his stroller, the sound recalling his birth: all that breathing, an ocean of air through her, and his first breath — not breath — gasp, how greedily he'd come. Mercifully, she undid his buckle, and he stepped free from his bondage, plodding forward out into the empty platform, unsteady, half-made.

Suddenly she looked down to watch a slow-motion darkness bloom in her dress, the accompanying release, the patter of urine on the platform. She considered wiping it with one of the diapers in her bag. No worry, when the tunnel was filled with fire, everything would dry and the city would crumble like dead paper and the sky would blow with cinder. She heard a rumbling and didn't know which train it was, Charlie's or her own. Boys loved trains. Why was that? The noise? The speed? The single-mindedness? Why wasn't hers here? They'd been walking today, in the heat, so long ago now. She had a son, didn't she? Yes. Blond. Not wholly blond. Hair like wood grain, the tint of wheat. She'd misplaced him, but he resolved before her now on the platform. A rushing thing close behind him.

Perhaps, she thought breezily, it would be better if she crawled over the edge and into the track bed. Put herself in the clank of gear and wheel, down where her brother was. How would its thunder register in her chest, where on her body would the kiss of wheel and track come? How insignificant those on the platform would look.

She watched this perplexing, curious shape stumble onward near the edge of the tracks, right to where she'd been standing so recently, mesmerized by the noisy mechanics and the searing lights and the dark tunnel, and, yes, of course she would lift herself from the tile and go to him, scoop him to her breast, protect him. This was her duty.

She was a mother. *His* mother. But even though she was a mother, *his* mother, she would not go to him, could not protect him. She would fail at this, as she had failed to protect her brother, because she would remain here, in her lair, burrowed, sapped, doomed, because this weakness had always lived in her, disguised, hiding like septic marrow in her bones, as it had lived in her brother, taken her brother. She fought to rise but couldn't and knew balance would never again return, that her name would be the sound of her own weeping. She'd been pierced by the lion's jaws, because the jaws had finally closed.

What did it matter that this helpless morsel of boy had that day spent an uncountable time mere inches from the yellow line, silhouetted by the pure, apocalyptic motion of a train blasting through the station, his hair a wildfire of gold, his jostling cheeks iridescent, before turning to toddle back toward her and plop down at her feet as if nothing of consequence had transpired while she'd sat frozen in panic. It was what she couldn't do that had ended her life that day. She'd failed him so thoroughly, so completely, as she had her brother, and now here he was, imperiled once again. *Right now your son is in grave danger*, said that strange man on her doorstep, who seemed so much more menacing in retrospect.

And here she was, trapped in her bedroom, preparing to fail him again.

24

'Nice of you to return my boat, Corpsey,' the Butler said as he crushed Will around his arms from behind. 'For a while I thought you and your little crewmate were going to perform your best submarine imitation out there.'

Will kicked his legs wildly in the air and yelped. Titus grew stern and spit on the ground and had put up his big fists to advance on Butler when from behind Claymore appeared like a phantom and drove him flat across the back with his shovel. Titus collapsed as though his body had momentarily teleported from his clothes. He lay in the pigeon droppings, heaped, breathing shattered.

Will struggled to retrieve his garrote, but his arms remained pinned. Then the Butler seized his wrists and offered up his hands to Claymore, who bungee-corded them behind his back. When the job was done, the Butler let go, and Will took a jumping kick at Claymore, who dodged it easily.

'Careful there,' Butler said, tapping at Will's Helmet with his own sharpened shovel. 'When my friend here loses his temper, he doesn't find it for two weeks.'

Titus was bound and hauled to his feet. They dragged Will and Titus through the elevator's lower catacombs to the iron staircase. 'Up,' Claymore growled, kicking Will in the flank.

As they climbed, Titus was soon drowning in the clogged pond of himself, coughing and retching and sucking voluminous gasps that never were sufficient to sate him. Will's thoughts turned to Angela grinding out coughs in her hospital bed, to his mother hyperventilating on the kitchen floor. At last they crested the stairs and passed through the Distribution Floor, where Will and Jonah's skateboard ramps sat unused like monuments of a fallen civilization, a world Will now doubted he'd ever inhabit again.

'It's a clever security system, Corpsey,' the Butler said out on the walkway, swinging open the boiler door with a rusty peal. 'But we found your hidey hole all the same. Thanks to a mutual friend of ours,' he said to Will with a grin.

With his hands bound behind him, Will was pushed onto his face in the ash and was spitting it out when he came through the other side into the workhouse. There Will saw another of Butler's men, the one pushing the wheelbarrow that day, watching over Jonah, who was bungee-corded to a chair, his head dipped, bangs hanging in his face like a fox tail.

When they were all inside, the Butler took out a small bottle of amber fluid and had a long slug. Claymore walloped Titus again across the back and he buckled to the floor near his pallet bed.

'Don't,' Will said, nearly sobbing. 'He can't breathe.'

'Oh, he's used to it,' said Claymore, unwinding Will's wrists in front of Jonah, who looked up to Will and offered a weak smile. 'Doesn't take care of himself is his problem.'

After Will was tied to the chair beside Jonah's, the Butler left, and Claymore and the other one started tearing the workhouse apart, unearthing plants and throwing Titus's hefty books around, plunging their heads into the cupboards and shelves.

'They asked about the map,' Jonah whispered. 'But I stuffed it in my underwear. Luckily they're not perverts. But I do wish I wore my helmet.'

'Shut up,' Will said, smiling despite his clunking heart.

Then the other man left, leaving only Claymore, who was turning over Titus's mattress and peering into the birdfeeders Outside. Titus remained unconscious, crashed on his face, hands bound behind him. By then his breathing had quieted and sounded trifling as a fire flickering out. Soon Claymore gave up his search and sat across the room thumbing through Titus's books, smoking a hand-rolled cigarette that smelled of creosote.

'How did you get here?' Will whispered. 'I thought you were done?'

'Because I couldn't sleep. I knew you were crazy enough to come back down here. I figured you'd be needing some medical attention.'

'Jonah,' Will said, leaning as close as he could manage. 'You were right about Titus. He did do something to Marcus,' Will whispered. 'I think he might have sunk him in the lake during one of his moods. But I don't think he remembers. For some reason I'm not convinced he meant to. I can't explain it, but whatever he's done is what's making him insane.'

'Well, our best bet is to give the Butler his map and leave Titus to them. He deserves whatever's coming for what he did to Marcus,' Jonah said, managing to dig in his pants, extracting the map and balling it in his fist.

'But it's not *just* Marcus,' whispered Will. 'Today he was wearing the exact hexagon boots. And last night I found *his* fingerprints *inside* my house.'

'That's not possible,' said Jonah, shaking his head.

'Where. Were they?' Titus said, suddenly awake, neck straining upward in agonized rapture.

'Where were what?' said Will. 'The tracks? Right behind my house. Made by the same boots you're wearing.'

'The fingerprintssss . . . ' Titus said, his lungs letting go.

'Doesn't matter where they — '

'In. My room?'

'No,' Will said, 'they were in *my* room.'

'I watched. Her paint. Everything. When she returned. Where. Was it? Up high?'

After matching the prints, Will had dusted other surfaces like the doorknob and the light switches and moldings, and he'd found plenty of his own, even a few of his mother's, but the prints on the light fixture were the only trace of Titus he found. 'Yeah, so what, what does it matter?'

'Wouldn't get. Wiped. There. Not unless. A neat freak. Which she never. Was. Exactly,' he said heaving.

360

'Will,' Jonah said, before leaning in to whisper that he remembered studying a passage near the end of their fingerprinting manual that said latent prints left on ideal surfaces like glass or metal when kept in a climate-controlled environment could last for years, sometimes indefinitely.

'But why were you in our house?' Will said.

Titus managed to roll onto his back, and his breathing came easier. 'After. I saw you both in the. Window,' he said. 'I waited. For her to come. Out. But she never did. I knew. Something wrong. So I watched. I would. See you. In the window. Icarus. Number One. You always looked. So busy. I liked to observe. You. Paint.'

'So you *were* watching us,' Will said angrily.

'I told Marcus. To leave your. House alone. That it. Was vacant. But he. Didn't. And then out. You. Came. I knew you. Were hers. The night. At Marcus's. Shack. Recognized your name. From. Paintings. You threw away.'

'Then why did you write that note trying to scare me into staying home?'

'Too dangerous. Down. Here. For you and Icarus. Number Two. Didn't want to draw you. Into this. Thought she. Would keep. You home. But you came. Back. Your decision. I knew she'd never. Forgive me. But you brought. Her bread. And I liked. You Icaruses. Here. Selfish. Now look. I'm. Sorry.'

'Okay, okay,' Claymore said, nudging Titus's ribs with his foot. 'Normally I knock people around to make them blabber, but today I may have to do so in the interest of quiet.'

361

Then the Butler returned through the boiler, a tall glass of water balanced between two long fingers. 'Sorry for all the hubbub, Corpsey,' Butler said in mock sympathy, standing over Titus. 'It pains me to say that this has all grown more convoluted than I'd have preferred. But that's why I left my girls at home in their kennels today, because I want to resolve this peaceably.'

Then he turned to Jonah and Will. 'You see, this old ghost here was supposed to do something for me.'

'I've always. Done,' gasped Titus. 'What you asked.'

'The problem is,' said Butler, still addressing the boys, holding the glass of water. 'Now that our trust is broken. I can't be sure.

'You see, me and Corpsey here are old friends,' the Butler went on. 'And I was glad to see him return to Thunder Bay after so long. I promised to keep it under my hat, especially with respect to particular acquaintances of his, if only he'd do me favors now and then. Tell the boys what you do for me, Corpsey?'

'Asked you a question,' said Claymore, dinging Titus's head with his shovel. Titus buried his face.

'Did you think he pulls those crisp bills he pays you with from the trash? And it's not just finding me good, unsprouted grain in old Pool Six for my operation or procuring me hoses on the cheap, is it Corpsey?' said the Butler, his eyebrows vaulting suggestively. 'No, he loses things for me, too. Don't you Corpsey? You see, a lot of people down on their luck on this fine harborfront aren't exactly Jesuits, if you understand. And sometimes, due to their own miscalculations of course, they end up in need of — shall we say — disappearance?'

'Like that guy in the wheelbarrow?' said Will defiantly.

'Sure. I mean, who can blame someone with so few prospects who'd rather remain woefully inebriated for their life's sad duration than suffer the humiliations of unemployment and dashed expectation,' the Butler said. 'Well, I can ensure it's done safely. For one. And I can ensure it's done affordably — which is why Neverclear is crucial to Thunder Bay. Especially given how things have turned out.' Then the Butler noticed the glass in his hand. 'Speaking of refreshments, you look parched, Corpsey. Stand him up,' the Butler snapped at Claymore, who dragged Titus to his feet.

'You boys know where I got this water?' he said, examining the glass sidelong like a suspect diamond. 'I got this water on our very doorstep. Right down where all those beautiful grain boats used to tie up at Pool Six. But old Corpsey here is picky. Yes, unfortunately this beggar is choosy. He says it's polluted, but you boys know why Corpsey here *really* doesn't care for this particular water?' The Butler tapped the glass with his clipped nail. 'Well, he and this water have some history together. His pop died right down there, crushed like a chestnut by a ship in its berth. I saw it happen. A tragedy. And then old Corpsey here went and dumped his poor, poor friend in that very same water. But your pop and your best friend aren't the only secrets sunk in that wharf are they, Corpsey?'

The Butler stepped closer to Titus, glass held high. Titus turned his head away, and from behind him Claymore wrapped the shaft of his shovel around his throat and pressed.

'You see,' the Butler went on, 'what Corpsey *really* excels at is sinking. Always has. And recently there was a certain boy who decided it was a good idea to sneak into one of my storehouses and steal my property, then mocked and disrespected me by offering to sell it back. He was setting a bad example for good, honest, hardworking boys like yourselves. So since they knew each other so well, I asked old Corpsey here to fix our problem, for the good of everyone.'

'I did. What you asked,' Titus said, straining against the shovel. 'Leave these. Icaruses. Be.'

'Marcus trusted you!' Will heard himself cry out.

The Butler shook his head. 'Thing is, now *I'm* the one having trouble trusting Corpsey. I'm worried that perhaps he didn't manage things quite in the manner I would prefer.'

The Butler had the glass close to Titus's face as Claymore tightened his grip. 'Now you'll show me proof that you did what I asked,' the Butler said, lifting the glass an inch from Titus's lips, 'or else you're about to take a nice, long drink of history.'

Titus glanced at Will, his face veiny crimson and for a fleeting moment innocent and soft, the same vulnerability Will had found on his

364

mother's face a thousand times Inside, and even despite what Titus had done, Will couldn't help but pity him.

Titus turned his eyes to the water and shuddered.

'Show us,' Claymore growled in his ear, 'and we'll leave you all be.'

Slowly, Titus extended his lips and put them on the glass, slurping loud and long. He closed his eyes and gulped, his throat constricting as the Butler tipped it up, spilling water over his cheeks until it was empty.

'Tasty,' Titus said with a stifled shiver.

The Butler threw the glass, smashing it on the wooden floor. 'Downstairs,' he said.

They untied the boys, bound them again by the wrists and dragged them back down the stairs.

'All this concrete,' the Butler tutted as they descended the staircase, 'not even worth the money it would cost in dynamite to blow them up.'

When they came to the lower level, Claymore pushed Titus to the ground amid the mangle of animal remnants and industrial litter. Then the Butler gave a nod, and Claymore grabbed Jonah roughly and dragged him over to one of the yawning grain chutes. 'Okay, Corpsey, since you clearly don't care much about yourself . . . perhaps this will persuade you,' he said, crouching over Titus. 'How about we drop your precious workers into the bins. Just for old times' sake. Starting with the Turtle boy?'

Claymore roughly pushed Jonah backwards

over the hole then grabbed the belt that held up his baggy work pants, leaning him back on his heels. Somewhere down in the chute came a sick rustling, and Will remembered what Titus had said about rats craving protein.

'Don't,' Will pleaded, with a painful lurch in his gut.

'Don't be scared, son,' Claymore hissed at Jonah.

'You should stay off the Neverclear 'cause your breath is like a gallbladder right now,' Jonah said, but it was weak, his words suffused with panic.

Will watched Jonah's arms swing to recapture his balance and remembered his drawings and his basement tent room and how neat his bookshelf was kept and how fearful he'd been of dying before Will had dragged him down here, and it broke Will with despair. 'Your map is in his hand,' Will cried out. 'Take it and leave him alone.'

'Oh, that doesn't matter anymore,' the Butler said, sighing as Claymore retracted Jonah and ripped the map from his grip, stuffing it in his own coat. 'The merciful thing about my business is one never has to worry about demand, only supply,' the Butler said as Claymore drove Jonah back over the hole. 'Luckily, our stills have already caught up.'

'Remember the old days, Corpsey?' the Butler said to Titus. 'When men used to line up for the privilege of going down into those bins. You were particularly skilled at it, if I recall. Had a few scrapes with an early burial. This old elevator has been swallowing Thunder Bay's bravest young men since time began.'

'You hurt. That boy,' said Titus from the floor. 'I'll see you buried. In the ground. Where you stand.'

'In three feet of concrete?' said the Butler, scuffing his shoe on the floor. 'Not likely.'

Claymore released Jonah's belt and grabbed the pelt of his bangs, leaning him farther over the hole. Jonah cried out and grabbed Claymore's hand to keep his hair from being torn out, shutting his eyes, his foot knocking a rusty bolt down into the hole with a long clatter, and Jonah let out a pitiful screech.

'Oh come on, you're tough boys. I watched you two fight off my wolf that day at the school. Didn't realize it till after we ran into you down here,' Claymore said to Jonah, letting out some of his hair. Will had watched his friend withstand skateboard falls that would've shattered seasoned gladiators or stunt men, but he knew his friend had never fallen nearly this far.

'Oh, Corpsey,' the Butler said, his palm over his open mouth mockingly, 'I'm afraid someone *else* is about to have a terrible accident at Pool Six . . . '

'Stop,' Titus barked, his face pained. 'I didn't. Sink. Aurelius. Like I. Told you. I buried. Him. Unbind me and. I'll unearth. Him.'

'Didn't want to sully the old harbor any more than you already have, huh Corpsey?' the Butler said, grinning as he leaned over to untie Titus, still holding the shovel at his side, ready to swing. 'Show me.' Claymore drew Jonah back

367

upright, cinching his bristling arm around the boy's throat.

Titus crawled over to a large hopper, fed by pipes that snaked from above like some terrible musical instrument. 'Buried him in the grain, did you?' the Butler said. 'Isn't grain marvelous?' he added, addressing Will. 'The way it can build a city like Thunder Bay, the way it can earn a man a good living and feed a family? And the way it can aid the forgetting when all that is lost.' Titus rose to grab a wooden lever and dropped it. A spout leapt open and out burst a stream of golden grain that Will couldn't identify. They watched it quickly build an enormous conical pile in the center of the room. 'He's. In here,' said Titus when the hopper had emptied and the taupe tornadoes of dust had dissipated. 'But I'll need one. Of those shovels.'

'Not likely,' the Butler said, taking a quick swig from his bottle. 'Dig with your hands.'

Hacking and blue faced, Titus climbed painfully up the side of the mound and began scooping grain like a dog preparing its bed. 'Still champagne wheat in here, isn't it, Corpsey?' the Butler said, running a handful through his fingers. 'Not even sprouted after all these years. Shame nobody wants it. All those starving children in the world. But I'll find a use for it.'

Titus dug as Will fought a mist of tears and strained against his ropes to no avail. Then Titus uncovered a large, green canvas duffle. He blew the grain dust out of the zipper before grinding it back as the Butler approached, his eyes zapping with delight. Titus reached inside the bag and drew out a large glass jar of water and a stack of paintings that looked curiously like Will's masterpieces. 'He's gone,' Titus bellowed. 'I put him on a lakeboat. A saltie. A favor from. A man I once knew. You'll never find. Aurelius. He's safe. Now.'

'That's unfortunate, Corpsey,' the Butler said and Claymore grabbed Jonah by the shoulders and with wrath in his eyes prepared to send him headfirst into the open hole.

'Will, what's going on?' said a woman's voice from behind them.

Everyone turned, and Will saw before him an unsteady figure that was familiar in such an overwhelming manner that it was impossible to grasp completely. Her face was fierce and shining, and she looked afraid in her old nightgown, filthy from the elevator's walls. The Butler scoffed and started pacing toward this person, this woman, and at that moment Will saw something grand and terrible cross her face. As he drew near, she reached and snapped a bracelet on her wrist, her eyes stewing with fright, but also indignant, furious, her body coiling, about to cry out, either in pain or in fear or in rage — it was impossible to tell. And it was then that Titus exploded from the pile of grain toward them. Since he'd been Outside, Will had seen people grab cats in this way, but only at the back of the neck, never the front, and cats seemed to enjoy it, because there was so much skin back there, or they didn't have any nerves there, or it reminded them of their mothers. But Will didn't think the way Titus grabbed the

Butler fell into this category — from the front, his fingers closed over the Butler's windpipe like a bit of garden hose. The Butler dropped his shovel, and his pale hands flew up into the air like twin doves. Titus walked him back toward the opening of a chute. 'I'll make a wonderful. Mess. Out of you,' Titus said through his ruined lungs. 'You reconnoiter that?' The Butler's stricken face was unmoving, but his eyes blinked in agreement. Titus drove him to the ground, pinning him on his back almost gently.

At that moment, Jonah dropped through Claymore's arms, sidestepping him, then gracefully kicked him with a skateboard-hardened shin in the back of the knees, dumping the man to the ground.

Behind the woman burst in two of the Turtle Brothers, and they charged for Claymore, who cowered backward, away from Jonah as if he were a lit match bomb. 'Look, I got no trouble with you Indians,' Claymore said, brandishing his palms.

'Indians?' said Enoch, the one with a black crew cut, short as the lip of a soda can. 'I look like Gandhi to you, motherfucker?'

Claymore got to his feet, shaking his head like a chastised boy.

'Because we're definitely not feeling all that nonviolent right now,' said Gideon, beads tied into tightly drawn pigtails and tattoos twining up his neck. 'Get your ass outside, Doc,' he said to Jonah. 'We won't be requiring your services.'

The woman rushed over and untied Will's hands and took him in her arms. While Titus and

370

Jonah's brothers bound the Butler and his men, she led the boys out from the elevator to where the Turtle Brothers' van was parked. Silently, they sat on the torn vinyl seats, the boys rubbing their wrists while they waited. Will wasn't sure if Jonah was shivering beside him because of fear or cold, and his mother put her arms around them, and they both leaned into her and shut their eyes.

'I can't believe you're here,' Will said, still not quite able to look at her.

'I was worried,' she said with disbelief.

'How did you know where we were?'

'That terrible man came, and I told him where you were — for some reason I knew you boys would be in this elevator. But I got a bad feeling afterwards — I mean worse than usual — so I called Jonah's house. But his phone still wasn't working, so I walked there to find you. His brothers brought me here.'

'You went through the culvert?'

'Yes,' she said, exhaling, puffing the marigold-colored bangs from her forehead. 'I realized that even though I'd already lost you, you could still use my help sometimes.'

25

Jonah had once told Will that if you drop a penny off a high building, like the ones in real Toronto or New York, it ends up falling so fast it can zip right through a person's whole body from skull to feet before driving itself six feet into the pavement. Will took this bit of magic to mean that his mother was sort of right: everything was dangerous if it falls for long enough, even the littlest things. Will knew now that the worst calamities that happened Outside were unremarked, things that nobody noticed, like Icarus plunging into the water, or children who went missing without a soul looking for them. Outside was still chock-full of questions Will couldn't answer, like how his uncle Charlie got the way he did, or his mother, or why Angela was doomed and other girls weren't, or what had made Marcus push the Butler as brazenly as he did. And even though in the end Will hadn't solved its mysteries, he still loved the Outside so intensely that he worried he could die of it.

According to the Turtle Brothers, Constable MacVicar never did make it down to the harbor to arrest Butler and Claymore where they'd left them, and nobody ever found all the Butler's Neverclear. The rumor was that after they were through with him, whatever malevolence that Titus said had overtaken the Butler when he was hit by that loading boom had been reversed, or at least muted. They heard he dismantled his operation, and the following summer Jonah and Will saw him once while skateboarding near the harbor. He was wearing slippers on the sidewalk, staring blankly into the window of a vacant store, now just another of the damaged faces that the boys rocketed past. In Will's 'bullet ballets,' they always caught the criminal boss last, but seeing how the Butler didn't exactly fall into that category, Will supposed that in the story of him and his mother, the real Outside bad guy was harder to pin down and definitely wasn't something MacVicar could lock up in jail.

For a while Will had difficulty believing that Titus was his uncle. His mother said that it was actually some friend of theirs named Whalen who'd died in the accident at the elevators, not Charlie, but it made little sense to Will. Maybe it was because he'd never had any family other than his mother, so it wasn't easy to scrounge up a room for Charlie in his mind. Will had already stuffed it with so much since he'd left the Inside, the whole family thing would have to wait until free space became available. Still, Will liked having him around. Somehow Charlie made the Inside fuller, less claustrophobic.

At his mother's request, Charlie had moved into Toronto, where they set up a suite for him, at first so he could heal the three broken ribs that Claymore had given him with his shovel. But after that, he stayed. The basement wasn't called Toronto anymore either. Now they called it 'the Apartment,' or sometimes his mother called it 'Charlie's Crypt,' except never in front of him.

Charlie brought along his furniture from the workhouse, and Will's mother had even started going down into the basement again. She and Charlie would sit at an old table where they'd drink tea and play cards for dirty pennies. Will often heard them laughing exactly the same laugh and remembering a million things from when they were young. Will and his mother ordered Charlie a water cooler that they could hear gurgling all the time like a big underground stomach. Now that he wasn't in the elevator huffing grain dust and living on birds, his breathing had improved, and he was making more sense. When he read books to Will, what he said seemed more like something that a person could've written.

But it wasn't all perfect. Sometimes Charlie didn't come upstairs for weeks, which, for their house anyway, wasn't overly unsettling. That is, until he'd start claiming items in their basement were trying to suffocate him, and he'd send up paranoid screeds scrawled on scraps of Will's old masterpieces. Once Charlie dismantled the furnace in the dead of winter because it was recording his thoughts and sending them through the air ducts, pouring some kind of poison gas into their bedrooms that could hurt Will and his mother. But most of the time he was all right. In the spring, he used a net to pull hundreds of smelt from the creek, which stunk up the house when he fried them whole on his hot plate. In summer, he and Will built a new fence in the backyard, sinking the four-by-four cedar posts deep into the soil with a giant corkscrew that Charlie could turn one-handed. On the weekends he went off to collect cans and things he'd fix up, like radios and tools nobody wanted. Charlie had also put up some birdhouses he built near the fence, but whether they had traps in them was one of those things the family didn't talk about, like how the Black Lagoon used to be. But when Will woke in New York in the morning, where he had a proper bed and even a dresser now, along with the soothing gurgle of the creek, Will heard the music of his uncle's birds and it always made him feel like going Outside.

His mother still got the Black Lagoon — that didn't go anywhere — but after she'd rescued him at the elevator it was like somebody had permanently turned down the volume. Will liked to imagine that her bravery that day had built at least a bit of a callus between her and the Outside. She was baking bread in the oven, into which she'd put a large flat stone Charlie had pulled from the lake. She even called her fear the Black Lagoon now, which always made him laugh, like when she swore, which sounded overdubbed and fake. Will and his mother went on a short walk once per week, lazy jaunts around the neighborhood, walking slow and careful under the trees, during which the sunlight went wild in her hair as if it were made of fiber optics, and Will held her hand, not because she needed it, but because it felt good.

Once during their walk Will asked what it was

like having her brother back. 'He's completely different,' she said. 'Yet he's the same. But watching the people you love get hurt is part of the deal, I'm learning. That's the mistake I made with you, honey. And somehow, despite getting hurt, Charlie managed to hold on to the kindest parts of himself. It's the only way we can survive what the world will do to us.' When she saw him losing interest, she finger-poked his ribs. 'But the good news for you is: he's very brave about changing lightbulbs.'

Another time they walked all the way to a thrift store, where she donated her old Relaxation Machine. 'I've got a new one,' she'd said to the clerk, patting the Bolex that now hung constantly at her side, which she'd bring on their walks to shoot things that caught her interest. After that, Will urged her to venture again outside their neighborhood, downtown, or the culvert again, but she refused. 'Trust me,' she said. 'Our street is enough danger for me.' So he let it drop. They were going to Toronto on an airplane for something to do with her films the following fall, so he'd just have to trust her.

People Outside say someone is 'losing it' when they get scared, but Will wasn't so sure. It was more like his mother had been securing something during all that time Inside, clutching at it, like those people on TV stuck in a blowing tube, trying frantically to catch the money fluttering around them, except the bills were actually pieces of her. Even though it didn't look pretty, from now on Will had to trust that she'd catch at least a few of them.

Jonah did get sent to Templeton, but he and Will were going to the same high school next year if he kept his marks up, so it wasn't the end of the world. By now Jonah could recite his medical books backward, but Will hadn't told his mother yet that they were both taking a year off after grade twelve to move to real San Francisco and skateboard professionally for a year before Jonah started med school. Will hoped for her sake that the Black Lagoon would be gone by the time that happened, but if it wasn't, she'd have to build some more calluses.

Angela was doing better, and Will often skateboarded to the hospital for visits. When her breathing permitted, they'd wedge the door of her room shut with one of her vibration machines and lower her bed flat. Then Will would take off his shoes, and they'd lie for a while and kiss and clamp their pelvises together and stroke each other's hair while listening to the whooshing and beeping of the hospital.

All that summer, Will and Jonah filmed themselves skateboarding with the new Bolex they earned working for Titus. They met some other skateboarders downtown who'd ventured forth from their own neighborhoods and driveways: a Chinese kid who bruised easily and had to hide both his bruises and his skateboard from a strict father who taught chemistry at the college; an only-child girl whose father was the city's best hockey coach; a motor-mouthed Irish kid who used to be a soccer prodigy but quit when his mother died. Even the Belcourt Twins had returned from up

377

north and somehow had acquired skateboards, though they were more interested in opportunistic mischief and hash smoking than doing actual tricks. But despite their outward differences, Will had observed that skateboarding was a contagion a certain species of kid was susceptible to. That they'd all had something go wrong in their lives: divorces, deaths, diseases, deficiencies, accidents, nutty relatives stuffed in a basement somewhere — expectations that didn't fit reality; dark, unplanned swerves of fate; falls their families had taken. Each kid with their own personal Black Lagoon that skateboarding somehow rendered less terrifying.

Will and Jonah were by far the best skateboarders in Thunder Bay, which wasn't saying much, but it was something. Though Will could see the true reverence the others reserved for Jonah. The way their jaws loosened as they looked at him sidelong. The way they sat down when he arrived, embarrassed they didn't move with anything close to his exactness and grace. While Will's style was jerky — he did strange things with his right hand, an involuntary bird claw with the fingers — Jonah was ever more elegant, languid, full of feline poise, all lithe power and confidence. He sizzled down Thunder Bay's rough streets like water poured over hot rocks, skating with a complete, evident joy — a free person, open to the air, unleashed upon the world.

Will often dreamed of what a skateboarder Marcus would've been if he'd stuck with it. His low center of gravity, his quick reflexes, his pure abandon and clever, resourceful mind. He would've been incredible, maybe even better than Jonah, like a comet streaking across the city. Will's one hope was that there were skateboards wherever that lakeboat had brought him, and some other fearless, lost children for him to ride them with.

When summer was over, Jonah and Will sent their footage away to be developed, and to their astonishment most of the reels came back usable. After a tutorial from his mother, Will threw himself into editing, using her old dusty machine that spliced and taped the clips together. Will began with the skateboarding footage, cutting the usable clips in which they actually landed their tricks into one pile, and placed their more gruesome falls into another, including the one where Will hit the ground so hard both his shoes flew off and Jonah's near castration on a handrail a month earlier. The rest of the footage he put in a box in Toronto.

Since it only added up to a few minutes, he cut other clips he'd shot (he'd got the idea from his mother's films, which he'd finally watched and found unnerving and occasionally beautiful, even though nothing happened): interactions with people on the streets of downtown, clips of buses and seagulls and bright-yellow fire hydrants, shots of Angela grinning in her hospital bed and decrepit old Pool 6 guarding the lake. He even put in a flash of Charlie's hardened face — the only time he'd ever allowed Will to film him. When it still didn't feel substantial enough, Will cut up films he used to watch when he was Inside, including the scene of the Creature swimming inches beneath the unaware woman in the Black Lagoon, and distributed these randomly throughout. For the last scene, right after Jonah rolled away from the handrail he'd miraculously slid, a feat so impossible and precarious it still seemed like special effects, Will inserted the shot where the front of a barn nearly fell on Buster Keaton, his tiny body narrowly passing through the open window, unharmed, cyclones swirling around his unconcerned face.

'I love all the other stuff you put in there,' Jonah said when he saw it. 'Makes it more arty.'

'You don't think it's too weird?' Will replied. 'Like it should just be skateboarding and that's it?'

'No,' Jonah said, 'it's a masterpiece,' and Will gave him a shot in the shoulder.

For his thirteenth birthday, Will asked his mother to watch it. He dragged the card table into Cairo and set up the old projector on it.

'This is going to be radical,' she said, winking when she came in and sat down with a mug of black tea.

'Please don't say *radical* ever again,' said Will.

'I was quite radical when I was young,' she said, with a mock scowl and a fist raised straight in the air, fingers forward, thumb tucked inside.

'I'm going to have an aneurysm,' Will said, as he attached the take-up reel to the projector and started winding it manually, so it wouldn't break the fragile, hand-edited strip.

'What's this feature entitled?' said Titus, from

the doorway in his fur-trimmed parka, though it was late summer.

'It's called: *If I Fall, If I Die*,' said Will.

'Doesn't leave much to the imagination,' said his mother.

'Jonah thought of it,' Will said. 'It's because we put our worst falls in there, too, along with all the tricks we ride away from.'

'But why put the falls in?' his mother said. 'I thought movies like these were made to convince people that you're an expert. To get *sponsored*? Right?' Whenever his mother talked about skateboarding, it made his neck shrink like a salted slug. It remained the only Outside thing he hoped she'd never understand.

'Because falling is a part of it,' Will said. 'We don't want to lie and make it look like we don't fall. Because we do. All the time.'

Will flicked on the lamp and sharpened the focus.

'I believe this is going to be a spritely rollerboarding presentation,' said Titus, sitting down with a bowl of some viscous black soup he'd made steaming in his lap.

Then Will went and killed the lights. From across Cairo, Will watched them sitting together on the couch, two heads silhouetted, his mother and his uncle, the last surviving Cardiels, their little clutch of busted souls, almost enough to call a family.

'But promise you won't cover your eyes,' Will said, his hand on the projector. 'Remember when you said you'd watch *The Creature from the Black Lagoon* on my birthday?' Will said, trying to maintain a joking tone. 'We all know how that turned out.'

The air turned tense. His mother sat staring at the projector's white light, where a hair was magnified to garter snake size on the wall. She was about to say something, then held it, and then let it go. 'I can cover my eyes if I want to, Will,' she said. Even in the dark, he saw the Black Lagoon's ripple in her jaw, though only a twinge.

'Not for this movie,' Will said. 'With my movie, I make the rules.'

She took a deep breath in the careful way that seemed as if she normally breathed some other substance, but this one would do. 'All right, Will,' she said.

Then she reached up and propped her eyelids open with her fingers, exposing a lace of red vein surrounding the green marble cores of her eyes.

'You can start it now,' she said. 'I'm ready.'

As he watched the specters of his film flicker over their similarly constructed faces — his mother steeling herself against the bracing vision of her only beloved son crashing down staircases and hurtling unprotected through the sharp and dangerous world as Titus's eyes went wild with some delight not necessarily attributable to what befell the screen — Will considered how, more than anything else, the Outside had taught him that there wasn't much difference between loving someone and being afraid of them. Loving a person meant needing them to stay: alive, around. But the shadow that love can't help but cast is fear: fear they won't stay alive or around

— fear they'll be reckless, or doomed, or just walk away and not consider you ever again. With love, you're scared it will disappear. With fear, you're scared it never will. The trick, Will understood now but would never quite manage to put into practice, was getting used to both of them at the same time. It was living in between.

Acknowledgments

Immense thanks to: Bill Clegg; Zachary Wagman, Sarah Bedingfield, Molly Stern, and everyone at Hogarth and Crown; Anita Chong, Ellen Seligman, and everyone at M&S; Laura Bonner, Chris Clemans, Jason Arthur, Scott Pound, David Peerla, Amy Jones, Neil McCartney, Alexander MacLeod, Alexander Schultz, Jane Warren, Francis Geffard, Jackie Bowers, Arnie Bell, Shayne Ehman, Jean Marshall, Christian Chapman, Socorro Woodman, Rick McCrank, Dylan Doubt, Benji Wagner, and Eric Swisher; the Ontario Arts Council, particularly the Northern Arts granting program; the Canada Council for the Arts; everyone at the Thunder Bay Art Gallery; Lakehead University, including its Northern Studies Resource Centre; and David Christie and Jason Christie.

And to Cedar, August, and Lake, who make me brave enough.

And to Linda Christie, who taught me to love the Inside, and who lives Inside me still.

We do hope that you have enjoyed reading this large print book.

Did you know that all of our titles are available for purchase?

We publish a wide range of high quality large print books including:
Romances, Mysteries, Classics
General Fiction
Non Fiction and Westerns

Special interest titles available in large print are:
The Little Oxford Dictionary
Music Book
Song Book
Hymn Book
Service Book

Also available from us courtesy of Oxford University Press:
Young Readers' Dictionary
(large print edition)
Young Readers' Thesaurus
(large print edition)

For further information or a free brochure, please contact us at:
Ulverscroft Large Print Books Ltd.,
The Green, Bradgate Road, Anstey,
Leicester, LE7 7FU, England.
Tel: (00 44) 0116 236 4325
Fax: (00 44) 0116 234 0205

Other titles published by Ulverscroft:

GATES OF PARADISE

Virginia Andrews

The car crash that kills Heaven and Logan leaves Annie Casteel Stonewall orphaned and crippled. Whisked off to Farthinggale Manor by the possessive Tony Tatterton, Annie pines for her lost family, but especially for Luke, her half-brother — friend of her childhood, her fantasy prince, her loving confidante. Without the warm glow of his love, Annie is lost in the shadows of despair. And when she discovers Troy's cottage hidden in Farthing-gale's woods, the mystery of her past deepens. But even as she yearns to see Luke again, her hopes and dreams are darkened by the sinister Casteel spell . . . treacherous, powerful and evil!